keep it real

keep it real

by bill bryan

5/21/07

BLEAK HOUSE BOOKS
MADISON | WISCONSIN

Published by Bleak House Books
a division of Big Earth Publishing
923 Williamson St.
Madison, WI 53703
www.bleakhousebooks.com

This is a work of fiction. Any similarities to people or places, living or dead, is purely coincidental.

ISBN 13 (trade paper): 978-1-932557-31-2

First Trade Paper Edition

Cover photograph by Roxy Erickson www.roxyerickson.com
Cover model: Jordan Paris www.jordanparis.com
Cover design by Peter Streicher

Library of Congress Cataloging-in-Publication Data has been applied for.

Printed in the United States of America

11 10 09 08 07 1 2 3 4 5 6 7 8 9 10

For Jennifer, Will, Teddy,
Georgie, & Harry

ACKNOWLEDGEMENTS

I would like to express my deep gratitude to those people who gave me the inside dope on Reality TV, but unfortunately they are all terrified of being sued and screwed if I mention their names.

Few tasks are more thankless than helping a writer improve his work, so my hat is off to those brave and/or foolish friends who tried: Robert Ward, Katie Arnoldi, Dan Cohen, Kevin Boylan, Herb Lurie, Judy Hilsinger, Mike French, Jeffrey Goldman, and my incomparable wife Jennifer, who remains sharp as a tack despite not having slept in three and a half years.

I was very fortunate to find the perfect agent and ideal editor in one person, Al Zuckerman of Writers House.

It's hard to imagine a better experience with a publisher than the one I've had with Bleak House Books. Dave Oskin, Alison Janssen, Krystal Gabert, Joe Thornton, and especially the great Ben Leroy have spoiled me for life.

Finally, there is one person (besides me) without whom *Keep It Real* would never have been written. David Hartwell has been my best friend for the past thirty-five years (with a little time off now and then for bad behavior), and but for the benefit of his wisdom, encouragement, and stupendous sense of humor, I would likely be dead, or an attorney.

BB

chapter one

THE SIGHT OF Ms. Gutierrez naked is all bad, but the thing that really jumps right out at me is her humongous bush. Ms. Gutierrez either doesn't know or doesn't care that the modern ideal of feminine beauty requires a close-cropped pubic hairstyle, and she has therefore let nature run its unruly course. In fact, her bush is so big it's really more of a hedge, so I entertain myself by imagining a crew of landscapers mowing it down and finding several generations worth of lost baseballs and a partially decomposed cat.

Moving on to the rest of Ms. Gutierrez, I observe that once upon a time she may have had big tits, but they have long since become big teats. (Tits stick out, teats hang down, 45° is the line of demarcation. Questions?) Her stomach and buttocks have joined the Great Southern Migration, leaving behind plenty of cellulite signposts to be followed by subsequent expeditions. The overall effect of seeing Ms. Gutierrez fully exposed is to make me feel sorry for her in much the same way I feel sorry for a celebrity when he or she gets caught up in some humiliating scandal, which is to say 1 percent sympathetic and 99 percent gleefully superior.

And that is precisely the point. Mentally undressing authority figures is a trick I developed years ago as a method of short-circuiting my more destructive rebellious tendencies, and silly as this might seem, it works. Whereas I was once compelled to ask a steroid-swollen motorcycle cop if giving me a ticket made him feel better about his tiny little testicles, if I were placed in the same situation today I could make *myself* feel better simply by visualizing his tiny little testicles. This subtle adjustment has significantly improved my quality of life.

I don't mean to suggest that I have completely kicked the habit of being an asshole. On the contrary, I can incite others to violence faster than ever, and my late mother would be proud to know that scarcely a week goes by when my obnoxiousness fails to get me mistaken for an attorney. But I have learned to pick my battles, and since I have decided not to tangle with Ms. Gutierrez, it is a big help right now to picture the angry rash that her inner thighs must give each other every hot summer day.

"We only have fifteen minutes left," Ms. Gutierrez is saying. "I'm afraid we have to stay inside."

"No, Daddy!" Hallie whines and tugs on my arm. "I have to show you my Barbie car!" At seven years of age and forty-nine pounds, Hallie is still too little to drag me anywhere unless I want to be dragged, which I always do. At the moment, however, we are both at the mercy of Ms. Gutierrez.

"We don't have enough time, sweetie," I say. "Linda has to go home." It has taken many months, but I have finally mastered the ridiculous protocols of this ridiculous situation. I am to address and refer to Ms. Gutierrez as "Linda" whenever Hallie is in earshot, but strictly as "Ms. Gutierrez" at all other times. Even though I get it right, I can't help but reflect for the umpteenth time on the reasoning behind this and all the other unfair rules, and my resulting surge of hostility can only be suppressed by picturing Ms. G. as the last-place finisher in a topless sack race.

"Why can't Linda go home and you stay, Daddy?" Here we go again. My daughter is asking me a perfectly reasonable question to which I would dearly love to respond with an honest and complete answer, except that to do so would require me to speak ill of her miserable cunt of a mother (for which I could probably forgive myself), and thereby defy a very specific court order (for which experience has taught me the hard way there will be no forgiveness).

"You know why, Hallie. I have to give Linda a ride." This is technically true—Linda, excuse me, Ms. Gutierrez, and I always arrive here together in my decrepit Subaru. But Ms. Gutierrez's minivan is parked just up the street, and presumably even her two piano legs could carry her that far. So I'm essentially being forced to lie to my daughter, which may not exactly be Ms. Gutierrez's fault, but for which I would nevertheless shoot her a withering glare if it weren't for the fact that in my mind's eye, she has a thick layer of moss growing under each teat.

"Why can't she take a limo?" Hallie wants to know.

"Because limos cost a lot of money, and not everybody can afford them." Out of the corner of my eye I see Ms. Gutierrez frown. She is apparently insulted at the implication that a person of her august station—Social Worker III, County of Los Angeles—would be unable to travel the city via limousine.

"Okay, then a town car," Hallie says. "We can use my charge number." The nonchalant way that my seven-year-old suggests this compromise leaves me at a temporary loss. It must have a similar effect on Ms. Gutierrez, because she looks at her watch and discovers that it's not quite as late as it was five minutes ago.

"I guess you might be able to go and see Hallie's new toy."

"Yay!" Hallie immediately starts dragging me toward the door.

"But only for a few minutes!" Ms. Gutierrez calls after us. She sounds so momentarily powerless that I take pity and allow her to don a bathrobe, albeit one that is ugly and several sizes too small.

My daughter lives in a mansion, just a few doors down from the one the Beverly Hillbillies used to call home. Of course, mansion styles have changed since the heyday of Jed and all his kin. In fact, styles change so rapidly in these parts that my ex-wife and her current husband keep a leading interior designer and his team on permanent retainer, with the explicit contractual understanding that their work will never be "done." Designing a major player's pad is like painting the Golden Gate Bridge—you get to the end and you immediately start designing all over again. As Hallie leads me through the entry hall, I note that the decor has begun a shift away from a Nordic motif and toward Asian. I hope this doesn't mean that Anika, the hot weekend nanny I swear I'm making some headway with, will be replaced by some inscrutably unscrewable Lucy Liu-type.

"Where's your Barbie car?" I ask Hallie as we cross the vast rear patio and head for the vast rear lawn.

"On the tennis court. Sydney came over yesterday with her Barbie car and we played Barbie tennis."

We wind our way down the path to the tennis court, which is covered with fresh, black skid marks and racket dings, and within the week will no doubt be resurfaced or replaced by a top-of-the-line zendo. The Barbie car is really a Barbie jeep, a pink, plastic, miniature replica of what Barbie might have driven to the front in World War II.

"Watch how fast I can drive!" Hallie says as she climbs aboard. She clutches the steering wheel in the classic, straight-arm race car driver style, stomps her little foot onto the accelerator, and moves not one inch.

"What's wrong with it?" Hallie demands as she slams the pedal to the metal over and over again.

"Careful sweetie, you might break it."

"It's already broke, dummy."

"Excuse me, the name is Daddy, not dummy. And I think all that's wrong with your Barbie car is that somebody forgot to plug it in."

"It doesn't have to get plugged in," she says, out of patience yet again with the depth and breadth of my ignorance. "It has batteries."

"Well these kinds of batteries need to get plugged in at night," I say, but Hallie isn't listening.

"Richard will know how to fix it."

I'm not going to lie—this hurts. Any time that a man's precious little girl puts more faith in her stepfather than in her real dad, particularly when said stepfather stole said real dad's wife, plus the best part of his life's work, and is in this and all other respects the shit-sucking embodiment of evil, it's gonna hurt. And my certainty that Richard Slatkin doesn't know how to "fix" a dead Barbie car—in fact has no better understanding of how a Barbie car works than Hallie does—only makes matters worse. If I can't even get credit for the modest virtues I *do* have, what's the goddamned point of anything?

"I guess we could play regular boring tennis." Hallie blessedly interrupts my soliloquy of self-pity before it can really get going. (Trust me, that was nothing.)

"Sure. You know how much Daddy loves anything that's really boring." Hallie eye rolls, but gets out of the Barbie car and allows me to push it to the side of the court.

"We only have one ball left," she informs me as she hands me a racket. "Sydney hit all the other ones over the fence."

"That's okay. We'll just have to play extra boring."

I have no doubt that the reckless Sydney is solely to blame for knocking all of yesterday's balls over the fence, but Hallie manages to do the same with today's on her first swing. It sails completely over a stand of tall ficus trees and out of view. Hallie drops her racket and then herself onto the ground in a cross-legged, chin-jammed-into-hands pout.

"Great," she says. "What are we supposed to do now?"

"What do you want to do, sweetie?"

"Play tennis!"

Although Hallie's tone leaves a lot to be desired, I decide to give her credit for not actually vocalizing the word "dummy" this time.

"Then I'll go get the ball," I say, and I trot toward the nearest gate.

"You'll never find it," Hallie calls after me. "Richard can't even."

Fortunately I am already off the court by the time I hear this, and am therefore able to mutter, "Richard can't even swallow my load," without having to worry if such a statement is true, relevant, or appropriate as a response to a seven-year-old.

I'm hoping that as soon as I get past the row of trees, I'll discover an open meadow covered with dozens of brand-new tennis balls and Anika sunbathing in the buff. Instead I discover the top of a retaining wall, and below it a hillside covered with ivy that's been growing unchecked for almost as long as Ms. Gutierrez's snatch. The chances of finding a tennis ball, or for that matter a beach ball, in this stuff are zippo, and I'm about to elect myself to another term as Loser Parent of the Year when a speck of color catches my eye. It's a good forty feet away at the bottom of the hill, but it is unmistakably the hide of a bright yellow-green tennis ball.

"Come on, Daddy." Hallie's world-weary voice comes through the trees. "I told you you wouldn't find it."

"Oh, yeah?" I shout back. "How much you want to bet?" At this moment there is neither a Labrador nor any other kind of retriever that could be more intent than yours truly on fetching that tennis ball. The slope is too steep to walk and I briefly consider hurtling down it Inspector Clouseau-style, but the thought of requiring rescue by Richard is enough to rule that out. Instead I dash along the top of the retaining wall, toward a saddle in the hillside that should allow me to reach the bottom in one piece. The wall is longer than the court itself, and when I reach the end, I stop to catch my breath before attempting a long but survivable leap into the ivy below.

"C'mon, bitch. Get down an' suck it." The words aren't spoken loudly, but I hear them as distinctly as if whoever said them was standing right next to me.

"What's the matta, ya already suck too much dick today?" This is clearly not the voice of Richard Slatkin or any other candy-assed Caucasian. It is a male African American of indeterminate age, who seems to be demanding fellatio al fresco in the middle of the most expensive neighborhood in the known universe. But where, exactly? I can see the yard of the nearest house from where I'm standing, and it's too far for sound to carry from there to here so clearly. Besides, I happen to know that former First Lady Nancy Reagan lives there, and I doubt that she's dating again so soon.

"What are you saying, Boney?" This is a second voice, female, and maybe a little less street than the first one, but definitely not Mrs. Reagan. I realize that this conversation must be taking place right on the other side of the trees, less than ten feet from me and definitely on Richard and Sara's property. Since my daughter lives here too, this gives me a semi-legitimate reason to spy, which of course I would do whether I had such a reason or not. I am, after all, a professional observer.

I crouch low and creep as silently as I can in the direction of the voices.

"I'm sayin' you don't wanna suck my dick, they gotta be a reason. 'Nif I catch you wit it, I gonna put a cap in both a you muthafuckas."

"Honey, you want some sugar, all you gotta do is ask a little nicer."

"Don' be tellin me what I gotta do, bitch." His voice is getting louder, which gives me the opportunity to ease into the thick clump of trees without being heard.

"Hush, now," she says. "You want Richard and them to hear you talking like that?"

"I don' give a fuck what dey hear. Muthafuckas all be livin offa my muthafuckin' talent."

The first thing my eyes locate through the leaves is a blaze of bright red, which turns out to be the sleeve of a cotton sweatsuit. I edge closer until I can make out the guy wearing it. He's medium-black and handsome according to the current urban aesthetic, which does not mean that he resembles Hugh Grant. His hair is gathered into tight cornrows and he has a wispy little moustache and goatee. He's definitely smaller than me, maybe 5'10", 160, but I'd still cross to the other side of a busy superhighway to avoid him. You are of course free to take this as evidence that I'm a racist, but I submit that if an individual goes to great lengths to adopt a menacing persona, the rest of us shouldn't be faulted if we feel a little menaced. All we're really saying is, "Well done!"

"Baby, I don't know what's up your butt today . . ." The girl's tone doesn't sound especially confrontational to me, but I am evidently alone in this regard because Sweatsuit slaps her so quick and so hard that she flies sideways and crumples to the ground.

"Ain't nothin' an' nobody never be up my butt. Ya got that, muthafuckin' ho?" Just in case she doesn't, he pins her head against the concrete with his shoe and gives it a good shake. This is the first good look I've gotten at her, and even though she is presumably not at her best—curled into a defensive ball with a LeBron James edition Nike resting on her cheekbone—it's clear that she is a Big League Babe. Picturing this one naked would be both very pleasurable and very easy, since she's about seven eighths of the way there already. Only a crop-top, nicely though not excessively filled out, and a short, tight skirt interrupt an expanse of perfectly shaped and toned flesh. And I hope I don't owe Ricky Martin a royalty for saying so, but her skin really is the color mocha. Her hair is long and straight and probably costs a fortune to keep that way, and unless you're the one paying, who cares? Sweatsuit removes his foot from her face, but she stays where she is, whimpering.

"You ain't hurt, bitch," he says. "But you gonna be, you keep givin' it up to every nigga in the NBA."

She's afraid to speak but shakes her head.

"Don' be lyin'!" He rears back like he's going to kick her, and it suddenly occurs to me that I may have some moral responsibility here. Should I make a little noise, so he knows there might be witnesses nearby, or should I come bursting out of the bushes ready to throw down? Either way, what's my cover story for why I just happen to be hanging out in the middle of a hedge? And what authority do I have to do or say anything? From the bits of conversation that I've heard, it sounds like Sweatsuit and his companion are invited guests here in Richardland, while I have been admitted on a much more restricted visa. What if the end result of my effort to do the right thing is that I get even less time with Hallie than under the current outrageously unjust arrangement?

Fortunately I don't have to answer any of these thorny questions, because Sweatsuit snorts contemptuously, slides his hands into his pockets, and strolls away like nothing just happened.

"Don' think I won' fuck you up, ya hear?" These are his parting endearments, spoken matter-of-factly and without stopping or looking back.

The girl waits several moments to make sure he's really gone, then pushes herself up to sitting, clutches her knees, and buries her face between them. This is not a position that affords much modesty while one is wearing a short skirt, unless one is alone—or incorrectly assumes one is. Although I've never considered myself a Peeping Tom, and the fact that she's now sobbing makes me feel extra creepy about the whole thing, the plain truth is that you'd need a crowbar to pry my eyes off her panties. They are snow white and translucent, leaving the bare minimum to the imagination and no doubt necessitating a standing appointment at the bikini waxer. I feel myself being physically drawn forward, like an asteroid entering the earth's gravitational field, and I am only seconds away from a fiery, self-destructive plunge through the atmosphere when one of my forgotten senses breaks through.

"Daaad-deeee!" Hallie is somewhere behind me, yelling at the top of her little lungs. Her voice startles both me and the subject of my attention, and the latter quickly stands. There's a perfunctory wiping of the eyes and sweeping of the dirt off her skirt, and then she's gone, disappearing around the corner in the same direction as Sweatsuit.

In my haste to get out of the trees, I stab myself in the side with one ficus branch and nearly lose an ear to another. When I step out into the open, I see that Hallie is standing on top of the retaining wall, scanning the hillside below.

"Where are you?" she demands.

"I'm right here, sweetie! Be careful!" My adrenaline carries me to her in a flash, and I steer her away from the precipice.

"What took you so long?"

"I was trying to get the tennis ball."

"So, where is it?"

"Well…," I start to say, then realize that I am standing on something firm and round, buried deep in the ivy. I bend down to pick it up. "Right here."

This small miracle buys us less than five minutes of boring tennis, because I know better than to incur the wrath of Ms. Gutierrez. Hallie sulks all the way back up to the house, and turns her head away when I try to kiss her good-bye. This is not unusual—she doesn't understand that it's not my choice to see so little of her, and every time I try to tell her, Ms. Gutierrez cuts me off with a stern shake of her head. The court has decreed that for me to express any dissatisfaction with the visitation schedule or procedures in front of Hallie is verboten, because she might interpret such sentiments as criticism of her mother. This is another rule that is both unnecessary and insulting, because I have long since lost interest in criticizing Sara, and because there's no one assigned to prevent the faithless, conniving slut from criticizing *me*.

But I have to take what I'm given, which right now is the opportunity to plant a quick peck on the top of Hallie's head. Her hair smells like green apples, because that's the kind of shampoo she likes. I keep little bottles of it everywhere—in my desk at work, my glove compartment, my nightstand—and when I get to feeling too sad or pissed or pointless, I pull one out and take a sniff. It's not exactly how I pictured my love life at age thirty-nine, but it gets me by.

Ms. Gutierrez and I have almost reached the front door when her cell phone starts playing "I Just Called to Say I Love

You," and she quickly fishes it out of her purse.

"Hola, que paso?" she answers, then covers her free ear and furrows her brow as she tries to hear whoever's on the other end. "*Otra vez*, Papi, you're breaking up!"

All efforts by Ms. G. to improve her connection prove unsuccessful, and she's forced to ask a passing housekeeper if she can use a land line. The two señoritas head for the kitchen, leaving me to loiter in the foyer. I glance at a mirror on the wall, and am disappointed to discover that the front half of my hair is still missing. You'd think I would have gotten used to it by now, since most of my transformation from Ringo Starr to Kenneth Starr occurred years ago. Or, since I seem to be incapable of making the necessary internal adjustments, that I would have invested in a transplant, or a toupee, or at least a fucking hat. But you would be wrong—my pride and my vanity are locked in perfect stalemate, thus preventing me from either accepting the ravages of time or doing anything about them.

The sound of approaching footsteps on the hardwood floors makes me turn and receive a more pleasant surprise. It's the stunningly beautiful girl I just saw getting slapped around behind the pool house, and this time she's looking right at me and smiling. I smile back, but bigger.

"Excuse me, is that the restroom?" she asks, indicating a door I'm inadvertently blocking.

"Uh, yeah," I reply. "But someone's already in there." The lie is out of my mouth before I have time to consider how lame I'll look when it's discovered.

"Okay," the girl says, turning to go back the way she came.

"Are you a friend of Richard and Sara's?" I ask in an attempt to slow her down.

"My boyfriend is."

"I see." Long, awkward silence. "Beautiful day, isn't it?"

"Uh-huh." I sense that my witty repartee has so far failed to captivate her, so I rashly elect to play the only card I've got.

"I saw what happened out by the pool," I blurt, and all at once I have her full, wide-eyed attention. "If you need a ride anywhere, or just someone to talk to, my name is Ted."

The girl stares at me for a moment with a mixture of fear and confusion, then evidently concludes that I'm harmless.

"That's nice of you, Ted," she says softly. "But it was my fault."

"Not the way I saw it."

"Yeah well, you don't know the whole story."

"Whatever you did, it's no excuse for anybody to hit you, or talk to you that way." The reminder is clearly upsetting to her, as she has to blink back a few tears.

"You sure about that?" she asks.

"Positive," I say. "And believe me, if anyone ever wanted to beat the living shit out of a woman, you're looking at him."

She lets out a little laugh. "You use that kinda sweet talk on all the ladies?"

I hear Ms. Gutierrez thundering back toward us, thanking the housekeeper for the use of the phone.

"Look, I have to leave," I tell the girl. "Are you sure you don't want a ride?"

"Yeah," she says. "But thanks." She steps forward like she's going to shake my hand, but gives me a quick little kiss instead, right on the lips. Then she's gone and I experience about two seconds of pure, light-headed bliss before the real world enters and snarls, "Let's go."

As requested in writing by Sara's attorney, I have kindly parked my vehicle at the far end of the driveway. (I'd rather cut out my tongue than call it the motor court.) Ms. Gutierrez and I make our way past several cars that presumably belong to guests—a red Ferrari, a silver Rolls, and something black that looks like a high-end Mercedes but is devoid of any insignias or other identifying marks. This has recently become a popular automotive aesthetic in L.A.—if you have to ask what it is, you can't afford it.

In the prime spot directly in front of the main entrance is another black anony-mobile, that I believe to be a Lincoln Navigator. The windows are all too heavily tinted to see through, but the driver's is rolled down. A huge, extra-dark dude who can only be a bodyguard or a bad dream sits behind the wheel, staring balefully at us from behind his shades. I smile and nod but he doesn't move a muscle. What an asshole. Just because I'm a shabbily-dressed, middle-aged white man, walking with a hideous beast of a woman toward my battered shitbox of a car, doesn't mean I deserve to be dissed.

Does it?

chapter two

I'M AN INVESTIGATIVE reporter, or at least I used to be and will be again someday soon, so my nature is always to want to know more. After I drop Ms. Gutierrez at her minivan and wind my way down to the flatlands where us regular folk eke out our wretched existences, I consider stopping by a newsstand. Since Hallie's stepfather Richard is one of the most powerful entertainment attorneys in town, and therefore never has anyone unimportant (other than me) over to his home, I assume that Sweatsuit is a musician and/or thespian of some current celebrity. By leafing through the pages of *Vibe* and similar publications, I would probably be able to find out who he is. Maybe I'd even come across a shot of the girl in one of the men's magazines, revealing what little of her I haven't already seen. But to what end (other than the obvious, which is none of your damned business)? I'm not so desperate to be back in print that I would sell a story to the tabloids, and nobody else would care. What I saw through the leaves was interesting to be sure, but not newsworthy in any legitimate sense. Digging into it any further would therefore just be one form or another of jerking off, and as usual I'm way behind at work. So I head straight to the office.

Trevor Bane Productions occupies the top three floors of a nondescript office building on Santa Monica Boulevard in West L.A. More than two hundred of us toil there, turning out five television shows that are currently on the air and two more that are soon to be inflicted on the populace. The accepted term for the genre that these shows occupy is "Reality," but I know a bit too much about how they are made to describe them as such. In fact, I refuse to describe them at all—whenever anyone asks what I do for a living these days, I tell them that I am an IT systems integrator. It's the perfect cover, because although I have no idea what it means, so far no one has been bored enough to ask.

My actual title is senior segment producer for *The Mogul*, a series in which twenty young eager beavers compete to see which of them will be selected by America's most famous entrepreneur to become his key lackey. *The Mogul* was the number-one-rated show in prime time for the last two years, but has recently slipped a bit and is running third behind *Trailer Park Tarts* and *My Mother the Angel*. The younger and more competitive members of the *Mogul* staff are especially upset that neither of these new hits are "Reality," because if this is the beginning of a return to traditional scripted entertainment, then most of them will be returning to their traditional employment at Starbucks. I would personally jump at the chance to whip up frothy frappuccinos in lieu of my present duties, but I'm told it doesn't pay as well, and I barely make enough to cover my monthly expenses and child support as it is. (You read that correctly. I pay child support to a woman who spends more on flowers in a week than I am worth, even if I sold off all my internal organs and got top dollar for them, which I'm quite sure I wouldn't.)

I arrive at my cubicle, but before I can slump into my chair I see that a sheet of paper has been taped to my computer monitor. In handwritten, no-nonsense block letters it reads:

TED -
PLEASE SEE ME AT ONCE.
TREVOR

I wish I could claim otherwise, but my initial reaction is unbridled terror. However much I might abhor the man and everything he represents, Trevor Bane is my current meal ticket, and I have never received such an ominous message from him. I wonder how long it's been waiting there for me—it is now almost 3:30 on Sunday afternoon, and I knocked off "early" last night, around 8:15. I kept my cell phone turned off all morning so that Sara couldn't have her assistant call me and insist on changing my visit time with Hallie, which she does approximately 110 percent of the time, and because I decided everybody else could pound sand. "Everybody else," however, was certainly not meant to include Trevor Bane.

I don't even consider the elevator, and I'm up the stairs, down the hall, and outside the frosted glass doors to the inner sanctum in less than a minute from when I first laid eyes on the note. Before entering, I take a deep breath to calm myself, because Trevor can smell fear like a big game cat, and he's a lot more lethal when he pounces.

Tanya, who is as beautiful as a tropical sunset and as cold as Pluto, sits at the executive assistant's desk just outside the great man's door. I have never once found her post unoccupied, no matter the day on the calendar or the time on the clock.

"Hello, Tanya," I say.

"My name isn't Tanya, asshole."

"And my name isn't asshole, Tanya," I reply pleasantly. "Please tell Trevor I'm here."

I know good and well that the real Tanya was about eight months and five executive assistants ago, but I also know that each and every one since has been just as icy as the original, and that to be friendly to any of them is only to invite open disdain. On a more positive note, I've learned that the one thing Trevor won't tolerate is anyone wasting his precious time with complaints he considers trivial (in other words, all complaints), so I can pretty much say whatever I want to Tanya without fear of consequences. If and when she bitches about me to Trevor, she will swiftly join all of her predecessors in Tanya hell, which must look a lot like Sky Bar on a Saturday night.

She hangs up the phone and with a flick of her middle finger motions me toward the door to Trevor's inner office. I knock as I enter and find Trevor in his customary position, standing ramrod straight behind his desk, wrists clasped behind him in the style he learned during his days in the South African Special Forces. (Trevor's colorful resumé has been so widely reported in *People* and its ilk that if you don't know the details by heart, you're more out of it than Mullah Omar.) He points to his wireless headset as a way of letting me know that he's on the phone, then returns to parade rest. At least a minute goes by in complete silence. Trevor is looking at me, I don't know where else to look, and I'm about to lose my wafer-thin veneer of cool, when he finally speaks.

"Stanley, a gentleman with whom I must speak has just stepped into my office," Trevor says to his headset in his perfectly polished apartheid-enforcer accent. "I'll ring you back later this evening. Please give my love to Charmain." There can't be more than one power couple with the names Stanley and Charmain, which means that Trevor has just cut short a conversation with the president of NBC—and husband of the all-time hottest *Sports Illustrated* swimsuit model—to talk to me. My mind races, trying to think of what I could have fucked up badly enough to warrant such urgency.

"Please have a seat, Ted." Trevor takes a chair and indicates that I should sit on the extra-wide couch, where rumor has it that he conducts the lion's share of *les affaires d'amour*. You don't get to the top of the heap and stay there without some aggressive time management.

"I'm sure this comes as no surprise," he says, and that's it for the small talk. "We need to make some changes at *The Mogul*." To preserve my dignity for as long as possible, I nod sagely while conjuring up an image of Trevor being buggered by Bishop Desmond Tutu.

"Roger feels that we've lost our way, and the show no longer reflects Dominus quality."

Trevor is not known to have any detectable sense of humor, but surely he can't be serious. "Dominus quality" is a phrase used *ad nauseum* by Roger Dominus, the titular Mogul himself, to describe that elusive extra something that can only be obtained by purchasing overpriced items—luxury Wilshire corridor condos, Las Vegas vacations, embroidered golf visors, etc.—from him. Roger says "Dominus quality" so often that the network was forced to impose a limit of four such utterances per one-hour episode, and since no one, including Trevor, has the nerve to announce said limit to Roger, the task of enforcing it falls to functionaries like me. I have spent countless hours of my life editing the words "Dominus quality" out of *The Mogul*, and since Trevor pays me and my colleagues for all that wasted time, I've always assumed that he hated the expression just as much as we do. But I guess this assumption is only further evidence, as though any were needed, that I Just Don't Get It.

"I think we're all working just as hard as we did last season," I venture. "Maybe Roger is reacting more to the ratings than to the show itself."

"That may be," Trevor allows. "But in any case, he is our star as well as a brilliant businessman, and we must respect his instincts. Gwen is out and you are my choice to replace her."

No fucking way, José.

Gwen Reynolds is (or was) the co-executive producer of *The Mogul*, a position that answers only to the executive producer—Trevor. And although Trevor is extremely hands-on, he is also extremely busy overseeing his far-flung media empire. The co-executive producer therefore has a considerable amount of autonomy and personal responsibility for one of the most-watched shows on television. To say that I am unprepared for this promotion is a gross understatement. Emotions swirl—relief at not being fired, pride at being chosen over all the other senior segment producers, instant self-loathing for the above, and so on. Meanwhile, the more practical side of my brain does a quick calculation of how much more I'm likely to be paid versus how much more I'll have to deal directly with Roger Dominus and Trevor Bane, and spits out a definitive answer: not nearly enough of the former to compensate for the latter.

"That's extremely flattering," I say. "But I don't think I'm ready."

Trevor just smiles in response, ostensibly to indicate that arguing with me is beneath him so he'll just give me a moment to come around on my own.

"I mean, I really can't think of much that I'd do differently than Gwen," I hear myself blather. "And I barely get to spend any time with my daughter as it is."

"My understanding is that you have some rather unpleasant legal limitations in that area," Trevor says, catching me off guard yet again. How in the hell does he know that I'm allowed to have only an hour a week of supervised visits with Hallie? How the hell does he know that there *is* a Hallie? "Perhaps my good friend Howard Drew could be of some assistance."

Howard Drew is the best-known divorce lawyer in Los Angeles, and therefore the world. His client list reads like a veritable *Who's Fucking Over Whom*, and the mere mention of his name has sent many a stray spouse scurrying back to the barn. When dissolution is sadly inevitable (meaning when Drew's client is the one who wants out), his track record of obtaining wildly one-sided settlements is legendary. One such miracle was achieved on behalf of none other than Trevor Bane, who struck quickly at the chains of matrimony as soon as the premiere of his first prime-time Reality show—*Castaway*—won its time period. The former Mrs. Bane and her children will live comfortably ever after, but on less than one tenth of the most conservative estimate of Trevor's net worth. (I read all this in *Vanity Fair*, in a glowing profile of Howard titled "You Got Drewed.")

"Are you saying that if I agree to take Gwen's job, Howard Drew will become my attorney?" I ask. In response, I receive another one of Trevor's self-satisfied smiles. I must admit, the man is good. I could and would turn down almost any amount of money to avoid becoming co-executive producer of *The Mogul*, and not just because it will be spirit-crushing, thankless work, for which my ultimate reward will almost certainly be the same as the one just bestowed upon poor Gwen. The more important reason is that such a big and highly visible promotion will make it even harder for me to deny that this imbecilic bullshit has become What I Do, and therefore What I Am. And I want to be a Reality television producer about as much as I want to be Liza Minelli's cabana boy.

But getting a second chance with Hallie—to once again spend entire weekends with her at *my* place, far away from Sara and Richard and that horrible hag Linda (note that I've already quit calling her Ms. Gutierrez)—is something I can't turn down. And while I'm sure Howard Drew doesn't offer any written guarantees of success in court, if he can arrange it so Michael Jackson can still give a kid a bath, he ought to be able to do the same for me.

"I'm counting on you, Ted," Trevor says. "I leave for Beijing in a week, so you'll be totally in charge." This is at best half true. Trevor is indeed going to China to preside over production of *The Great Wall*, a new series in which contestants will team with Home Depot, CitiBank, and a dozen other major sponsors to overcome the various obstacles to adding an extension onto the existing Pretty Good Wall. But to say that I or any other mere mortal will be "totally in charge" in his absence is absurd. Trevor utilizes the very latest in communications technology to nitpick on every episode of every one of his shows, no matter where in the cosmos he may be. And then there's Roger Dominus, who accepts suggestions about as well as a great white shark.

"I'm deeply honored," I say. "I'll try not to let you down."

Since I've now reached the pinnacle of my unchosen profession, I guess it's time to start behaving a little more professionally. On my return trip through the outer office, I stop at Tanya's desk.

"Sorry about earlier," I tell her. "I was way out of line. Remind me of your real name."

"Fuck off and die."

"Thanks," I nod. "It kinda suits you."

chapter three

I HAVE TO share the good—or at least big—news with somebody, but who? My daughter is too young to understand, and my parents too dead, so that leaves friends. Although I have several who would likely be more impressed with my promotion, I head for the apartment of my oldest and closest confidant, Deborah Sullivan.

"That's pathetic," Deb says when I tell her. "You're such a fucking sellout."

"Thanks. I knew you'd see the bright side."

Deb lights a joint and offers it to me, but only because she knows I'll decline.

"The bright side is you can loan me five grand right now," she says. "I'm busted and so is my computer."

Casual acquaintances are often surprised when I tell them that my best friend is a woman. If I'm in the mood to startle them further, I go on to explain that Deb is no ordinary woman, but a radical feminist lesbian who considers all heterosexual intercourse to be rape. And that by this definition, I've raped her a couple hundred times. Luckily all of those assaults took place more than twenty years ago, before Deb formed her present theories of female-male relations, so she reluctantly granted me amnesty. But these days if I so much as observe that her hair looks nice, she launches into a man-hating diatribe so vicious that my balls go to war with each other over which one gets to retreat further into my abdomen. Fortunately Deb's current appearance makes it easy for me to hold back on the compliments—I've never really wanted to get jiggy with a lumberjack.

Deb and I were high school sweethearts, though I've had the earth scorched around me enough times that I no longer use that term around her. She will only acknowledge that we were friends, which we were and are. From the first day in Eleventh Grade American Lit, when I cracked a joke meant to ridicule the Fonz, but the reactions indicated that everybody except Deb and me thought that the Fonz was pretty darned cool, she has been the one who gets me the quickest and the best. I got Deb's jokes right away too, and it was only natural that we tried being a couple. Since I'd never before had a regular sex partner other than my socks, I thought that our relationship was pretty ideal. We'd laugh our asses off at all the dipshits in Fresno (our hometown) and the world at large, then we'd screw like a couple of Energizer bunnies. You can imagine my dismay, then, when I learned—early in my freshman year of college—that while one of the bunnies was having all those mind-blowing orgasms, the other little bun had none. And it was too late to attempt redress, because Deb had discovered during her first week at UCLA that female rabbits required no instruction in how to pleasure other female rabbits. They smelled a lot better too.

I didn't take the news all that well, and Deb wasn't easy to deal with while she was mastering the mores of being a dyke. We didn't see each other much over the next ten years, and when we did, she was on red alert for any indication that I still wanted to rape her (which of course I didn't if we had to put it like that, but why did we *have* to put it like that, etc.). One thing that eventually helped me understand Deb's defection to the Isle of Lesbos was realizing just how clueless I'd been as a lover. When I was in my late twenties, an understanding divorcee took me into her tutelage, and soon I believed myself to be the equal of any cunning linguist in the freshman dorm. But by then even I could see that Deb's sexual orientation wasn't really up for debate. (She was living in West Hollywood with a diminutive masseuse who called Deb "Daddy" and hissed at me like a housecat when we were introduced.) Deb accepted my apology for my teenaged ineptitude on the condition that we never speak of it again, and we haven't.

"I can't loan you five cents," I tell her. "I have to get a decent apartment so Hallie will want to spend time with me."

"You'll never be able to compete on a financial level with Mr. and Mrs. Dick. I'm afraid you're going to have to rely on your terrible personality."

"Hallie needs to have her own bedroom," I say. "It's gonna set me back at least twenty-six, twenty-eight hundred a month, plus security and all the other move-in bullshit. Call it ten grand."

"For that kind of money, I could fix my computer and finish my film," Deb says in disgust. "Wouldn't the act of contributing to something worthwhile make it easier for you to drive in every day and debase Western civilization?"

"Maybe," I reply. "But who says a documentary about the only lesbian dumb enough to get AIDS is worthwhile?" I have asked this question in various forms on many previous occasions, but it never fails to amuse me or to antagonize Deb.

"Layla isn't dumb, you insensitive shithead. She got drunk one time in her life, and that was all it took for her to be victimized by one of your kind."

"You can't get AIDS from a one-night-stand," I scoff. "Unless she got victimized in the pooper." Again, the familiarity of the exchange makes it no less enjoyable. Just as my tribulations and pretensions provide endless *schadenfreude* for Deb, hers do the same for me. And we're both pretty good about recognizing when it's time to quit joking and lend a genuinely sympathetic ear, which is blessedly not often. As I said, Deb is no ordinary woman.

"Keep your dirty money," she says as she relights her joint. "The Lord will provide."

"I had another interesting experience today, while I was up at Casa de los Cocksuckers. It's got all the classic elements of

Aristotelian drama—sex, violence, shaved beavers."

"Don't tell me you finally banged that social worker."

"Ms. Gutierrez? Please. I wouldn't fuck her with your dick." I go on to describe in detail the incident I witnessed through the trees, putting special emphasis on how hot the girl was. I decide to leave out the part about me trying to pick her up outside the bathroom a short time later.

"What do you think?" I ask Deb when I'm done with the story.

"I think you and I should have become rap stars."

Deb's pot smoking has given her the munchies, so we head out for Mexican food and margaritas, mine tragically missing the tequila. She wants me to join her afterward for an art house documentary about the plight of fundamentalist Islamic lesbians, but I beg off. Tomorrow is my first day in the new job, and I need a good night's sleep.

I get maybe an hour and a half. No matter how many times I tell myself that producing a Reality show isn't rocket science, that I'm just as capable as Gwen, that even if I totally fuck it up, getting fired would be a blessing, I get more and more agitated. By the time I'm ready to resort to sleeping pills, it's too late. I watch some satellite soft-core but it doesn't do much for me, and I refuse on principle to take Viagra to masturbate. I finally doze off, while trying yet again to figure out why anybody over the age of twelve likes *The Da Vinci Code*. I have several dreams involving Roger Dominus, including one where I'm cowering on the ground and he's threatening to kick me. I guess we won't have to fly to Vienna to analyze *that*.

Prison rules say that I'm only supposed to phone Hallie once a day, but I've discovered that between 7:30 and 7:45 in the morning, the screws are usually doing Pilates and I can sneak in an extra call. I press number one on my speed dial as I drive to the office.

“Hi Daddy,” she answers on the first ring.

“So sorry señorita, but thees ees not your daddy,” I say, doing my best sing-songy Speedy Gonzalez.

“Who is it then?” Hallie asks.

“I am Señor Juan Roberto Enrique Iglesias de Ortega y Chimichanga, at your service.”

“That’s a dumb name.”

“How dare you speak such words? I challenge you to a tickle fight, to avenge the honor of Chimichangas everywhere.”

“Daddy, can you take me shopping?”

I hesitate before answering. Naturally I want to say, “You bet I’ll take you shopping darling, just as soon as Daddy’s lawyer makes Mommy’s lawyer eat a shit sandwich.” But making even the G-rated version of such a statement would be unwise, as it might get back to Sara and Richard, and I don’t want to give them any opportunity to fortify their defenses before Howard Drew attacks.

“What ees thees chopping?” Speedy inquires. “We no have it here en Mehico.”

“I have to get ready for school now,” Hallie says, with a sad weariness that never fails to kill me. In a moment of rash desperation, I throw caution to the wind.

“Guess what, sweetie,” I say as myself. “We’re going shopping together for a whole day, just you and me.”

“You promise?” Her excitement is enough to make me temporarily forget that I have a care in the world.

“I promise. But don’t tell your mom until I talk to her about it first, okay?”

“I’ll go get her so you can tell her right now!”

“No honey, this isn’t a good time. But I will really soon, okay?

“You better,” Hallie says, in a tone that tells me I have maybe three days, tops.

Since the reality TV craze sprung up more or less overnight, and most of us assume it will end just as abruptly, the atmosphere around the production office is akin to that of a mining camp during the Gold Rush. While the grizzled, old prospector in the next edit bay may be pleasant enough coffee-break company, he or she would sooner sink his pickax into your skull than watch you claim what could turn out to be the Last Big Nugget. Laura Adler, the senior segment producer who everyone thought was next in line for promotion, was the unofficial Big Loser when Trevor picked me instead. When I enter the employee lounge mid-morning to score my eighth fix of caffeine, interrupting what is obviously a raging bitch session about me, Laura begins a shrill vocal rendition of "Hail To the Chief."

"DA DA DA-DA DA DA-DA DA-DA DA-DA DA!"

"Thank you, thank you," I say in a passable impersonation of George W. Bush. "I appreciate your appreciation."

"Hey 'Boss Man.'" The next salvo is fired by Stuart Something-Or-Other, a flamboyantly gay video editor. "Did you know that Gwen has two little kids, and her husband is also out of work?"

"That's rough," I say. "On top of that, now he has to look at Gwen all day."

"Fuck you!" Laura shouts and winds up to throw her paper cup of coffee at me, but she is restrained by another co-worker. Like I said, I haven't lost my touch.

"Allow me to clear up a couple of things," I tell the group. "One, it's completely unfair that Gwen got fired. If Roger Dominus were a decent person, he'd accept the fact that the ratings are down because the public has finally begun to lose its fascination with him and whatever that thing is on top of his head." Any reference to Roger's terrible toupee is usually good for a cheap laugh, which in this case I get from a geeky young production assistant named Myron, at least until Laura silences him with a bare-teethed snarl.

"Two," I continue, "no one could be more surprised than me that I was the one chosen as the new co-executive producer. I haven't exactly made a secret of the fact that I consider our contribution to society to be on a par with venereal warts."

"Have you shared your feelings with Trevor, smartass?"

"No, Stuart, I haven't. I was counting on you to do that for me." I'm being a little disingenuous here. Although Stuart and most of my other colleagues would rat me out for the sheer joy of doing so, we all know Trevor's policy on shit-stirring. The result is that while the working environment at *The Mogul* isn't exactly warm and fuzzy, most of the serious back stabbing occurs after business hours. Again, Trevor Bane may have single-handedly destroyed popular culture, but he's no dummy.

"My third and final point," I say. "I anticipated that many of you would be worried about Gwen and her family. For this reason I have decided that I will personally match the total dollar amount that all of you collectively are willing to contribute to an emergency relief fund on her behalf." Complete silence. I have caught them off guard and they are mine. "Knowing how selfless you all are, I have set aside one nickel for this purpose."

I've always had a quick first step, so I am out the door before Laura's coffee cup explodes against the wall beside it.

The next few days are so hectic that I keep forgetting to eat, which is good because I can't imagine when I'd find time to take a crap. I solve constant crises in the office, where six episodes of *The Mogul* are in various stages of post-production, and in the field, where the contestants are currently trying to define the Dominus quality in an out-of-favor brand of dog food. In an effort to show the staff I haven't become a management-type flaming asshole (and am still just a regular flaming asshole), I decline to move into Gwen's private office. This gives Laura, Stuart, and a few others who are still unhappy about my promotion the opportunity to glare murderously at me all day. They are particularly irate when I receive a congratulatory gift basket from Roger himself, filled with wine from the Dominus vineyard and cheese from the Dominus dairy. The card reads, "Don't make me say You're outta here!"—a reference to the famous line Roger uses at the end of each episode to dismiss one of the contestants. I find its use in the present context less than inspired, probably due to the fact that I suggested it to Trevor ten months ago when Roger needed something to put on Gwen's gift basket.

The only thing I do besides work and sleep is phone Hallie, and every time I do, she of course wants to know when I'm going to tell her mom about our upcoming shopping spree. I know that I can't allow Trevor to sneak off to China without first putting me together with Howard Drew, but the thought of confronting Trevor on any subject is about as appealing as riding a mechanical bull naked. I therefore procrastinate, but as it turns out, Trevor didn't need to be nudged.

"You heartless creep." The caller ID on my desk phone reads "SARA SLATKIN," but I'd know the tremulous, self-pitying whine of my ex-wife anywhere. "If you think you can scare me, you've got another thing coming."

"Think," I reply.

"Think about what?"

"The expression is 'You've got another *think* coming.'"

"So?" Sara cries. "You think that just because you've read more books than me, that makes you a better person?" Though we've only been on the phone a few seconds and I as yet have no idea what we're talking about, our conversation has already assumed the familiar pattern: Sara seeks to prove that I am mean, and I seek to prove that she is an idiot. Among the many problems with this debate (most notably the countless hours that have been squandered on it over the years, with neither side ever gaining an inch of ground), there is ample evidence to suggest that we have it exactly backwards. Sara, who is supposedly nice but dumb, has a lifestyle that the late Hussein brothers might have found a bit grand. And she achieved said station through the kind act of dumping me for a rich dude, and taking with her everything I cared about. I, on the other hand—the "smart but mean" one—was too heartsick to mount any sort of defense until it was much too late, and as a result I now work eighty-hour weeks for the privilege of residing cheek-by-jowl amongst a bunch of other geniuses in Culver City.

"What's got your panties in pigtails this time?" I ask.

"My lawyer got a nasty letter from your new lawyer."

"Howard Drew?"

"Yes, Howard Drew. How many new lawyers do you have?"

I suppose I should be offended by this development, inasmuch as Mr. Drew has not bothered to write or call *me*, and I have therefore not been given the opportunity to officially hire him, much less discuss legal strategies.

"Ha!" I blurt into the phone.

"You think this is funny? It's your daughter's mental well-being you're laughing at, Ted."

"Oh give me a break. All I want is a chance to have a normal relationship with Hallie."

"Normal people don't have restraining orders placed against them."

"They do if they have to deal with the likes of you."

Sara slams down the phone, which is disappointing because I wanted to find out exactly how nasty Howard's letter was, and God only knows if and when I'll hear about it from him. Nevertheless, I'm on a major high for the rest of the day. Before I head out for some fresh air mid-afternoon, I ask everybody within earshot if I can get them anything from the deli in the courtyard.

"Get me something sharp and shove it up your ass," Laura replies.

I guess the honeymoon is over.

chapter four

I EAT DINNER at my desk and don't get back to my apartment until almost eleven. Since I know I'll be moving soon, not even the sight of this wretched hovel I call home can put a dent in my ebullient mood. The smell is another matter, so I immediately open all the windows. Even though I live on the second floor, I ordinarily keep them closed because the neighborhood is sketchy and the Skipper nearly deaf. The Skipper—so dubbed by me due to his resemblance to the late Alan Hale, commanding officer of Gilligan's Island—resides directly across from me in the building next door, which is close enough that I can (and have) hit it with a loogie. Aside from his almost-famous appearance, the Skipper's main distinguishing characteristic is his commitment to possessing and enjoying the very latest in consumer electronics. His shoebox of a living room sports, among other marvels, a fifty-inch plasma TV, theatrical surround-sound, and a High-Definition TiVo. From my perspective the final item is particularly unfortunate, because even though the Skipper keeps the volume cranked at all times, he still has trouble hearing. He therefore makes liberal use of the TiVo's ability to replay the same ten seconds of *Everybody Loves Raymond* over and over, until the Skipper finally processes the punch line and guffaws.

"Live from Los Angeles, this is Action News, your number one source for everything you need to know." I thought that was kindergarten. While I get undressed, I glance out my bedroom window at the Skipper's TV, which is too big even from here. But I have to admit, the picture is pretty awesome.

"Good evening, I'm Gloria Rojas," and in Hi-Def, you can easily make out my nipples.

"And I'm Jonathan Steele. Police are asking for your help tonight in locating a fashion model who disappeared after telling friends she was going to meet a photographer."

I can't tell you when I last cleaned my bathroom, for the simple and excellent reason that I have never cleaned it. I therefore take a deep breath, cover my nose and mouth, and then dart in there, hoping to retrieve a toothbrush and toothpaste before succumbing to the deadly vapors. I hear the anchorman continue:

"Twenty-two-year-old Patrice Williams, shown here on the cover of last month's *Booty* magazine, was last seen three days ago when she left her Sherman Oaks condominium." This is enough to draw me back to the window, but by the time I get there, the picture on the Skipper's TV is of a haggard old broad who would be more likely to grace the cover of *Batty* than *Booty*.

"She lives right across the hall from me," says the woman, who is identified by a graphic as "PHYLLIS COHEN/Worried Neighbor." "She's so beautiful, I hope nothing bad happened to her." I agree, Mrs. Cohen. It's tragic when bad things happen to beautiful people.

"Ms. Williams's car, a 2005 BMW convertible, was found in a parking structure at The Grove, in Hollywood." The image of the worried neighbor is replaced by one of a spiffy, ice-blue roadster, cordoned off by yellow police tape. Because this model, the 645ci, was featured in a segment of *The Mogul*, I know that it costs more than my annual, post-raise salary—further confirmation that *Booty* pays.

"If you have any information about the whereabouts of Patrice Williams, please call the LAPD Valley Bureau Hotline at the number on your screen." I need someplace to spit out my toothpaste and I don't dare to risk another foray into the Superfund site, so I head for the kitchen. At the bedroom door, though, something makes me turn back for one more look at the TV. And what I see there makes me shoot my Crest right onto the carpet.

"Rewind it!" I leap forward and pound on the inside of my window as I shout at the Skipper, who is in his customary reclining command post halfway between his TV and me. "I know that girl!"

"Who cares?!"

"Shut the fuck up!"

These responses come from other, unseen neighbors. The Skipper remains oblivious to us all, and I realize that further yelling will be pointless. The nearest heavy object is one of the shoes I've just taken off, and I don't hesitate. I shove my window screen out of its frame and let it fall to the ground below, then hurl my size twelve tassel loafer at the glass behind the Skipper's head. My aim is so bad it's perfect, as the shoe flies right through the adjacent open window and hits the wall alongside the giant TV, causing a row of DVDs to crash to the floor. The Skipper startles, then pauses the TiVo, struggles to his feet, and turns to face me.

"What the heck was that?" he says.

"I'm sorry to bother you!" I boom, taking no chances with the Skipper's auditory issues. "Can you rewind to the last story?" I'm about to explain why this is important enough to warrant such extreme measures on my part, but I don't have to—the Skipper is evidently pleased for any opportunity to show off his technological prowess.

"You bet I can," he says, and with the thumbs of a master he sends the picture flying back toward the top of the newscast.

"Pause it on the magazine cover," I ask. The Skipper complies, and a moment later there she is, frozen in fifty inches of doubt-destroying High Definition. Right before she disappeared, Patrice Williams got beaten and threatened behind my ex-wife's house. And then she kissed me.

"Amazing what they'll let on the boob tube these days, huh?" The Skipper shakes his head at the *Booty* cover, which features the missing model lying on her back on an unmade bed, gazing straight up into the camera with an expression that says, "Come hither and fuck me." But I guess I'll have to wait in line for that, because her exquisite breasts are already covered by the hands of two different, faceless gentlemen, one on either side of her, each of them cut off at the elbow by the edge of the photo. One of these lucky bastards happens to be White, and the other Black.

"Guess they didn't learn their lesson with that whole Janice Jackson business," he continues.

"Hey you assholes, some of us have to work in the morning!" yells a female voice.

"I'm sorry," I call out to the neighbors as a group, then "Thanks very much, Skipper." I call him this without thinking, but the Skipper is apparently aware of his celebrity look-alike status, as he replies with a hearty salute.

"Anytime, little buddy."

I shut the window and immediately phone Deb.

"I can't talk," is how she answers.

"It's important."

"I'm busy. With company."

"I don't care if you're going down on the Olsen twins. I need to see you."

"Oh, for Christ's sake," Deb sighs. "Why are you such a drama queen?"

"Meet me at Swingers. I'm leaving right now."

"Can I at least floss first?"

I have twice as far to travel and I make a stop along the way, but I still beat her there. Swingers is a twenty-four-hour diner in Santa Monica, favored by edgy, creative people during the day and by those who have sailed right over the edge at night. I chose it because it's close to Deb's apartment and we often meet there for breakfast, but now I'm regretting the choice because some truly repulsive punk rock is bleating from the jukebox, and I'm the only customer with a hair color found in nature.

I take the most isolated booth available and begin poring over the half-dozen magazines I just picked up at the newsstand. The current *Booty* isn't the one with Patrice on the cover, but a reproduction of that photo is reprinted among the letters to the editor. Even in this smaller image, I am positive that Patrice is the girl I met at Sara and Richard's house, and the fact that something may have happened to her is more upsetting than I would care to admit. Several of the letters offer fervent appreciations of her appearance on last month's cover, and the editor's response promises that faithful readers will be seeing a lot more of Patrice in future issues. It also reminds everyone to keep an eye out for her booty in the soon-to-be-released action-comedy *Cover Me, Bitch!* starring Dave Chappelle and Rick Moranis.

As I hoped, I'm only a few pages into *Vibe* when I come across Sweatsuit. He's dressed differently and is in a much better mood than when I saw him—in the magazine photo, he's at a nightclub partying with the skeletal remains of Hugh Hefner, and by the looks of it, one or the other of them has just gotten off a hilarious *bon mot*. But it's definitely the same dude. The caption identifies him simply as "Boney."

"Okay, here I am." Deb startles me as she drops into the other side of the booth. "Two hours worth of deep-tissue massage down the fucking drain."

"That's the guy I saw at Sara's house," I announce, shoving the *Vibe* at her and pointing to the photo of Boney. "And that's the girl." I show her the letters page of *Booty*.

"You made me give up multiple orgasms for *this*?"

"She's missing. It was the lead story on the eleven o'clock news."

"No shit?" Deb takes a closer look at the photo in *Booty*. "How do you know it's the same person?"

"I saw that picture blown way up. Trust me, it's her."

"What did they say on the news?"

"She disappeared the day after I saw her. She was supposedly on her way to meet a photographer."

"That's not good," Deb says. "Every model who disappears on her way to meet a photographer turns up a short time later as a torso."

"I've noticed that myself."

"Have you called the cops yet?"

"That's what I need to talk to you about," I say. "I want to do the right thing, but not if it fucks me up with Hallie."

"Why would it?"

"Because I don't know how to tell anybody what I saw without admitting that I was spying. And if this guy Boney is one of Richard's clients, he'll come after me like a pit bull on PCP."

"I thought you had your own pit bull these days."

"Howard Drew? The man won't even acknowledge my existence. The last thing I want to do is make his job any harder."

"So don't," Deb shrugs. "Call in an anonymous tip."

"That's what I was thinking. I'll just tell them what I saw, but I won't use my real name or give them the exact address where it happened."

"Seems like the obvious solution," she says. "So obvious that I'm kinda wondering why I had to come down here to the Star Wars Bar and Grill to point it out."

"I don't know," I reply, stalling in the vain hope that Deb will say what I'm thinking for me. "I guess there's a part of me that doesn't want to just let it go."

"Meaning?"

"Stories like this don't just land in a guy's lap every day. When am I ever going to have a better chance to get back in the game?"

"You're thinking about selling this to a magazine?"

"Nah, probably not," I answer too quickly. "Unless, you know, it turns out to be something. I'd have to do a lot of digging around first."

"I'm confused," Deb says. "A minute ago, you were afraid to get involved. Now you want your name in lights."

"What can I tell you? I'm a complex individual."

Our waitress, an ill-tempered Amazon wearing black fishnet stockings and a ten-carat Rhinestone nose ring, interrupts to take our order. In the silence that follows, Deb studies the two photographs again.

"I'm going to say something that's going to piss you off," she announces.

"What else is new?"

"I don't think the reason you're afraid to call the cops has anything to do with Hallie."

"Of course it does," I insist. "What if this chick Patrice turns up in Fiji, blowing Ben Affleck? You think Judge Steinbitch is going to look favorably on the fact that I was creeping around in the bushes eavesdropping, while I was supposed to be interacting appropriately with my daughter?" I am referring to Los Angeles County Superior Court Judge Stephanie Steinberg, who presided over my divorce and related matters, and who has shown blatant bias against me ever since I drove Richard's Hummer through a small portion of his beach house and into the Pacific Ocean. (More about that later, maybe.)

"That would be a perfectly credible line of reasoning if you were a pussy," Deb says. "As we both know, however, you are a prick. And pricks don't think like pussies, even when they should."

"So what am I 'really' afraid of?" I ask, just to be difficult.

"You're afraid that if you tell the cops what you saw, it'll leak and then you'll no longer have an advantage over all the other news pricks who are out there poking around for a big story."

"Well even if that's true, I can't just keep it to myself. What if 'Boney' here did off her, and I'm the only one who has any evidence?"

"You have a clear moral obligation to come forward and you ultimately will, because you're just a prick, not an asshole," she says. "But you also feel like you're getting the shaft—again. And one thing that might ease the pain is if I, a person who knows of all the countless injustices you've already suffered, am able to realize what a selfless thing you're about to do."

"Why do I get to have the most unsupportive best friend in the history of the world? You could have made Mother Teresa feel like she was out for herself."

"She was. Fucking twat."

We spend another twenty minutes debating how much information I must, as a good citizen, share with the police versus how much I'm entitled to hoard for personal enrichment and glory. Deb points out that if I don't give them the address where I saw Patrice and Boney, they won't know to question Richard, Sara, and everyone else who was at their house that day. I counter that unless Boney beat Patrice up over brunch, none of them will be able to add much to my account anyway. The only salient facts are that he accused her of cheating on him, hit her, and threatened to harm her. Deb ultimately agrees that if I impart this much, I've done my duty and can then pursue the story on my own with a clear conscience. She asks how, as a practical matter, I'm going to do that with my tongue stuck in Roger Dominus's rectum, but then sees that I'm not in the mood for any more of her skepticism and lets it drop.

Even the homeless have gone cellular, so it's harder than ever to find a working pay phone. I finally get dial tone in a phone booth/urinal alongside a Shell station on Lincoln Boulevard and punch in the number for the police tip line, but while it rings I have a sudden image of a subterranean command center, with rows of crisply efficient operatives bathed in the glow of their computer screens, ready to trace my call instantly and sic Keifer Sutherland on me. Rationally, I realize that any such concerns are pure paranoia—California's fiscal woes make it more likely that my call will be received by a Reagan-era answering machine and played back weeks later by someone who makes Sergeant Schultz look like a workaholic. Nevertheless, I choose certain safety over potential sorrow, slamming the receiver into its cradle before anyone answers.

I decide to place my anonymous call from the Tom Bradley International terminal at LAX, since I figure it must be populated at all hours and pay phone use won't stand out there as such an anachronism. In the latter assumption I am mistaken. Citizens of all nations and socioeconomic strata pace about the terminal, shouting into cell phones and headsets in their native tongues. A man with a nice enough turban but no shoes is using one of the pay phones as a desk in order to scribble down the information he is receiving over his Nokia. When I approach and pick up the receiver three partitions away, he looks at me in alarm, says what I interpret as "Hold on Mahatma, some freak wants to use the pay phone," and scurries off.

I am now thoroughly convinced that I'm being ridiculous, so much so that I'm startled when a real live human picks up the phone on the other end.

"Valley Detectives, DeRosa." A female human, at that.

"Yes," I say. "I have some information about Patrice Williams. The missing model?"

"I'm the officer assigned to that case. What is your name, sir?" The question makes me realize that I have completely forgotten my plan to disguise my voice.

"Mah name?" I reply with an accent that is meant to be subtly Southern, but comes out as a full Foghorn Leghorn.

"If you'd rather not say, that's fine," she says.

"Why thank you." I decide to give in fully to my inexplicable impulse to channel a giant animated rooster. "Under the circumstances, ah do believe that ah will avail myself of your kind offer to remain in-cog-neato." I think I hear Detective DeRosa stifle a laugh before she continues.

"All right, sir. What information do you have about Patrice Williams?"

"This past Sunday, yours truly saw Miss Williams gettin' beat on and berated in a most uncivilized fashion. The perpetrator was a musician who goes by the name of Boney. He's a… colored fella."

"We know about her relationship with Raymond Bonaparte." Raymond fucking *Bonaparte*? I'm going to war with a descendant of Napoleon? "Where were you when you witnessed this incident, sir?"

"Ah deeply regret that discretion prevents me from divulging that precise location," Foghorn says. "But ah can assure you that it was quite brutal, and if anything has happened to that poor girl, then ah strongly suspect that Boney is your man."

"Okay," she says. "Is he by any chance a friend or business associate of yours?"

"He most certainly is not." My paranoia suddenly returns and I scan the terminal for cops. There are several in sight, but none of them seem to be looking in my direction. But then again, they wouldn't, would they?

"Ma'am, ah really must run along now."

"I understand, but if you could just…"

"Ah have said all that ah am prepared to say. Ta-ta."

"If you think of anything else, call me. Detective DeRosa," she manages to get out before I hang up and stride away briskly. The turban guy, believing I'm coming after him, panics and seeks asylum from the counterman at Quizno's.

chapter five

NOT NEARLY enough hours later, I drag my ass to the studio in Burbank where we tape the *Mogul* conference room scenes. The climax of each episode is when Roger points at one unlucky contestant and delivers the world's only trademarked termination notice: "You're outta here!" When the show premiered three years ago, the expression became an immediate sensation, and soon you couldn't turn on a TV or radio without being subjected to the spectacle of Roger Dominus showing the door to an inferior cheeseburger or long distance plan.

I find Roger in the makeup chair inside his private dressing room suite, which at the moment is as tense as NASA during a shuttle reentry. Several of Roger's underlings (not the stooges who advise him on the show—those two colossal talents now have their own agents, hence their own dressing rooms) are dealing with assorted crises via their wireless devices, while the makeup woman brushes lightly at Roger's cheekbones and the hair guy tries to appear busy without actually touching any of Roger's "hair." Only The Mogul himself is relaxed and content, directing his benevolent gaze toward the sole individual who is worthy of it—the one in the mirror.

"Good morning, Roger," I say to announce myself.

"Hey, big guy." He flashes the famous smirk at me and winks. "How's it feel to be the head honcho?"

"It hasn't really sunk in yet." Perhaps it will when you learn my name.

"Don't worry, you're a natural born killer," he says. "And trust me, I know one when I see him." A cloud of murderous envy darkens the face of Roger's chief assistant, and I can't help but stand a little taller. Such is the power of a genuine star—no matter how insincere and cheesy you might know him to be, the tiniest shard of his attention is enough to give your spine a raging hard-on.

"Have you decided who you're going to fire today?" I ask Roger. If necessary, all of the people present in the dressing room can later be called as witnesses to the fact that I have come to ask and not tell Roger who to let go. I'm here merely to help him arrive at his own decision, which I happen to know will be to fire a competent but unexciting mortgage broker named Barry.

"I'm 99 percent there," Roger says. The hair and makeup people could no doubt play these well-worn parts themselves by now. "But I'd like to hear your thoughts before I make up my mind."

"Well, we have some concerns about Jason," I say. Anyone legitimately searching for a business executive would indeed have concerns about Jason, a young man from Texas who looks great in a Brioni suit but cannot add. We must take other factors into account, though, namely that the Dominus Group needs another vice-president about as much as I need a Pap smear, and that Jason is presently involved in an important, multi-episode story line. Several weeks ago, our night-vision lenses captured him engaging in some heavy petting with Stacey, a girl-next-door type from Des Moines. We then contrived to get Jason alone on the Dominus yacht in Newport Beach with LaFonda, our reigning urban villainess. We outfitted every stateroom with hidden cameras but needn't have bothered—LaFonda's knees were on the deck before the vessel cleared the dock. The video evidence—with tasteful pixilation of the tender bits, of course—won't be revealed to Stacey and the rest of the world for two more episodes, so Jason's place in the corporate structure is secure at least until then.

"Yeah, but I think the kid might surprise us," Roger says. He doesn't know Jason from J. Lo, but the routine calls for him to reject the first name I bring up, then agree with the second.

"Okay. The other person we're not sure about is Barry."

"That's exactly who I was thinking of," he replies. "Nice girl, but she lacks that extra something." Nice *girl*? Shit, he must have thought I said "Carrie," a foxy pharmaceutical rep who was dismissed toward the end of last season.

"Uh, actually, I meant *Barry*," I stammer. "He doesn't have that extra something either." My eyes dart around the room to see whether anyone is paying attention.

"That's what I just said," Roger snaps, piercing me with The Look. If receiving Roger's nod of approval is the equivalent of mainlining Cialis, then getting The Look is the equivalent of chemical castration. Although he employs it frequently as a management tool (as well as for more personal reasons, such as insufficient foam on his cappuccino), you will never see The Look on any episode of *The Mogul*. Trevor decided from the get-go that America would see Roger Dominus as "tough but fair" rather than "successful but sociopathic" (those may not have been his actual words, but you get the idea), and my colleagues and I are therefore obliged to edit out all traces of The Look.

"Right," I respond, as soon as I can remember how to make sounds. "Sounds like we're on the same page, then."

"Why don't you write up some of your ideas," Roger says, giving The Look a brief safety inspection in the mirror before re-holstering it. "I'll decide if I want to incorporate them into what I have."

"Will do." Actually, already did. The "ideas" Roger refers to are to be found in the script I wrote days ago for the conference room scene, which we are about to shoot. It is a quite comprehensive document, containing everything from the questions Roger will use to grill the contestants about the amenities at the Dominus time-share resort in Acapulco, right down to the big payoff: "Barry, you're outta here!" It won't become official, however, until Roger incorporates these random musings into his own script, which bears an uncanny resemblance to an empty file folder.

The beheading of Barry goes smoothly—way too smoothly, in fact, because no matter how many times I call "Cut!" and take him aside, I cannot persuade the condemned man to look the least bit distraught. I'm tempted to tell Barry that his pig-headed insistence on maintaining professional poise is why he's getting the axe, but such disclosures are strictly against policy. Ultimately, I'm forced to resort to a technique we call "enhanced reality." Between takes, while the hair stylist makes sure that the taxidermy atop Roger's head hasn't sprung to life, I stroll over and stand beside him. I have already made sure that the cameras continue to roll.

"Barry, is that a spot on your tie?" I ask. Across the table, Barry looks down and searches in vain for signs of a stain.

"I don't see one," he says.

"Okay, just checking." I wait until he is done re-smoothing his tie, then I let loose with a sudden fake sneeze so loud that the hair guy dives for cover. Barry looks up, startled for just a moment, and that's all I need. When you see these two snippets on TV, their order will be reversed: After Roger says, "You're outta here," the previously stoic Barry will look shocked. We will then cut back to Roger as he stands to leave the room, and finally to the shot of the defeated Barry hanging his head low. I hope that this little peek behind the curtain doesn't spoil anyone's experience of watching *The Mogul*, but I doubt that it will because my target audience for this story is people who can read.

The next challenge awaiting the surviving contestants involves promoting a Celine Dion concert at the Dominus Coliseum, an entertainment venue in Las Vegas that is connected by monorail to both the Dominus Bali Hai, a Polynesian-themed hotel/casino, and the Dominus Stratford-on-the-Strip, which presumably caters to people who enjoy slot machines and Shakespeare. In the first season of *The Mogul*, Trevor tried to tape all the episodes in real time, meaning that if a conference room scene was shot on a Wednesday night, the next cluster fuck began bright and early Thursday morning. This relentless schedule took such a toll on cast and crew alike, however, that Trevor was forced to relax it, and we now have the luxury of a full day off after each "You're outta here," plus an extra day of rest after every fourth episode. The sacking of Barry ushers in one of these extended holidays, and though I am already exhausted, I resolve to use every bit of it to work on what I have decided is my Real Job.

Unlike Channel 6 *Action News*, the *Los Angeles Times* finds nuclear proliferation and similarly dreary topics to be of greater import than the disappearance of a *Booty* cover girl. Patrice Williams doesn't even make the front of the California section, and the brief article about her on page B3 is illustrated with what appears to be a high school yearbook photo. The *Times* should thank God and Rupert Murdoch that it doesn't have to compete with the latter's *New York Post*, which would no doubt splash the sexiest available street-legal shot of Patrice across its entire front page, under a thought-provoking headline such as "SNATCHED?"

I learn from the stodgy coverage in the *Times* that Patrice is a native of Diamond Bar, one of the many places in Southern California that exist for me only in radio traffic updates. She is the youngest of five siblings, and not the first to become newsworthy. Antoine Lincoln, a half brother, enjoyed a brief career in the Canadian Football League before a knee injury forced him into early retirement at San Quentin. Patrice graduated from high school and attended L.A. City College while working as a waitress and movie extra, appearing in such instant classics as *House Party 9* and *Nigga Please!* According to Mystique Smith, a half sister, Patrice's big break as a model came when she was chosen to be one of the three scantily-clad elves gracing the cover of the smash hit rappin' Christmas CD, *Ho Ho Ho*. She has reportedly dated several professional athletes and entertainers, but no mention is made of one Raymond Bonaparte.

There is plenty of information about Boney available on the Internet, although much of it is conflicting. There is disagreement as to his birthplace—it's either Compton or West Covina; the true identity of his maternal great-grandfather—a Zulu tribal chieftan or Frank Sinatra; and Boney's criminal record, which may or may not include an arrest for murder. I note that his most fervent fans are the ones who insist that Boney did indeed cap a fellow performer by the name of Nasty P. outside a South Central titty bar. Boney's detractors, sort of a gangsta rap counterpart to Swift Boat Veterans for Truth, insist that the whole incident never occurred. Although there are many references to Boney's romantic liaisons (including a May-September fling with actress Winona Ryder, the public portion of which began with a surprise arm-in-arm arrival at the *Vibe* hip-hop awards, and ended three weeks later with his-and-her fat lips), the name of Patrice Williams is nowhere to be found.

Most of the top Google search results lead to PR mentions for Boney's upcoming release, *Wuh Duh Fuh U Lookin At?* iTunes offers a free sample of the title track and I start to play it at my desk, but this attracts the unwanted attention of my co-workers, and in any case, the probative value is doubtful when the only lyric I can make out is "Yo!" Boney's musical bio is also written in an unfamiliar idiom, but I am able to piece together some basic career facts. He is a relative old-timer of twenty-six, although he only seems to have arrived on the national rap scene in the last couple of years. *Wuh Duh Fuh?* will be his third full-length CD, and while his debut effort—*Up Da Butt*—was a *success d'estime*, the eagerly anticipated sophomore outing *Way Up Da Butt* was apparently derivative and proved to be a commercial disappointment. Boney clearly needs a hit.

I get the phone number of his record company from information, then find an empty editing room so I can make a call in privacy.

"Muthafuckin' Music," a receptionist answers. 411 had it listed under "MF Music," but that's apparently because Verizon is a reactionary, racist organization.

"Yo baby," I say, having boned up on my street dialect by tuning my car radio to a five-hundred-pound African American DJ called, appropriately enough, Big Boy. "Hook me up wit yo peeps in PR."

"Ight nigga, but I sho ain't yo baby." I take this as a small but important validation. After a couple more rings, another female voice answers.

"Muthafuckin' PR. Ramona speakin'."

"'Sup, sistah. I gots to get wit whoever be in charge of givin' out da face time wit my main man Boney."

"Whoever be you?" Ramona asks, with a good deal more suspicion than I feel is warranted.

"I's Jamaal Jihad from R an' K Magazine. We wants to put my boy Bone on da muthafuckin' cover."

"I ain't never heard of no R an' K Magazine."

"It stand for Rapin' an' Killin'. You gots to check it 'fore you wreck it."

"Maybe I will an' maybe I won't," Ramona says. "But you ain't gettin' no sit down with Boney nohow."

"Now see here, bitch . . ."

"Who you callin' a bitch, bitch?" From Ramona's end of the line, a loud bang is followed by silence. It appears that Jamaal Jihad has had one of the briefest careers in the history of music journalism.

Trevor Bane Productions has an entire department called "Research," which would more properly be called "Rip-Off." Each of Trevor's many shows is a kissing cousin of something that came before it, and the task of the Research Department is to identify those ideas worth stealing before some less worthy producer does so. Every satellite feed in the world is connected to a bank of souped-up TiVos on the top floor of the building, where six multi-lingual staffers sift through them day and night, searching for Trevor's next brainstorm. It's a high-pressure, high-stakes enterprise: Trevor rewarded the researcher who saw the seeds of *The Mogul* in a micro-budget Serbian series with the keys to a brand-new Mazda. But when Smoot-Hawley Productions, Trevor's principal competition, beat him to the punch with an Americanized version of *Pimp My Burro*, the entire department got the sack.

I stay friendly with the folks in Research because it's the only place in this vast TV production complex where you can actually watch TV. Sometimes when I'm pulling an all-nighter editing and I hit the wall, the only way to clear my head is to grab a Diet Pepsi and take in a few minutes of Cambodian women's wrestling. Earlier in the day, I asked a researcher buddy of mine named Bob—or maybe it's Bill—to record the local news on as many channels as possible. Now I head up there to see if there's anything new on the Patrice story.

There is. Sort of.

"I'm Jennifer Chu reporting live from Venice, where another young model has come forward to tell a terrifying tale of what happened when she went to meet a so-called photographer." The shot widens to include a tall, blond girl who apparently did not list "credibility" among the requirements when selecting her breast implants. "Standing beside me is Brandy Meadows, who has appeared in numerous popular magazines, including *Hog Rider* and *Easy Pickins*. Please tell us what happened to you, Brandy."

"Well I saw this ad in the newspaper?" Brandy says in a thick Southern accent. "The guy seemed pretty nice and everything? So I went to meet him at his studio? Only it turned out to be a van?"

"Go on," says Jennifer Chu, putting a sympathetic hand on Brandy's arm. I decide that this particular broadcast is unlikely to yield concrete information as to the fate of Patrice Williams, so I select another.

"Then what happened?" A reporter on Channel 3 is asking a pretty African American girl.

"I axe him where his equipment was, and he pull out his johnson." All across the television dial, great minds have evidently thought alike on the subject of how to present the Patrice story as breaking news, even though absolutely nothing has happened. I scour every channel, but learn nothing useful except that *Maxim* photographers typically don't use disposable cameras.

I'm on my way out the door when Bill-Bob manages to coax one more newscast out of his hard drive. The Channel 12 *Evening Report* tries to distinguish itself from its rivals by taking a more thoughtful approach to local news, and as a consequence attracts approximately as many viewers as a low-rated cable show, such as the Home & Garden Network's late-night entry, *Watching Paint Dry*. Despite its snooty pretensions, Channel 12 can't bring itself to ignore the Patrice story altogether, but has instead buried it just before the second set of commercials. Apparently every model in Southern California who was ever accosted by a fraudulent photographer and lived to tell about it is now under exclusive contract to one of the higher-profile news operations, so the hapless Channel 12 reporter has resorted to covering a crime story by interviewing the police.

"I'm live outside the LAPD station in Van Nuys, where I'm joined by Detective Sargeant Susan DeRosa." Standing beside the reporter is Detective DeRosa, a brunette who appears to be in her mid thirties. She's no Patrice Williams, or even a Brandy Meadows, but she is a lot more attractive than I imagined while I was talking to her on the phone. She looks appropriately serious yet not severe as she listens to the reporter's lead-in.

"Detective, are there any new developments in the investigation into the mysterious disappearance of Patrice Williams?"

"No." The detective appears to be completely at ease with the brevity of her answer, which is more than can be said for the reporter.

"Well . . . can you elaborate?" he asks.

"Not really," says Detective DeRosa. The flustered reporter presses his earpiece to his head, the better to hear the invective no doubt being hurled at him through it by his producer.

"I knew I liked her," I say, breaking into a huge grin.

"Who?" Bill-Bob is multi-tasking, helping me while he also searches for an entertaining concept that may or may not be lurking beneath the surface of a documentary about the Hutus and Tutsis. "Is there a show in it?"

"Nah," I tell him on my way out. "No way to turn it into Reality."

I don't have time to drive back to LAX, so I settle for the pay phone outside a 7-11 on Santa Monica. Three middle-schoolers with fancy skateboards and negligent parents loiter a few feet away, creating a surprising variety of sentences using only the words "fuck" and "dude." I deposit my coins and dial, but this time a male voice answers.

"Valley Detectives, O'Neill." I have already decided to stick with my established vocal disguise, but it feels even more ridiculous doing it for the benefit of some crusty Irishman.

"Yessuh, ah was wondering if ah might have a word with Detective DeRosa," Foghorn says at an uncharacteristically subdued volume.

"You'll have to speak up," says the old copper. Oh, fine.

"Ah say ah say, Detective DeRosa, *s'il vous plait*!" My sudden Kentucky-fried outburst causes the teenagers to interrupt their discourse and stare at me.

"Fuck, dude," says their spokesman.

"She's out in the field," the cop tells me. "But she left instructions that if a Mr. Leghorn calls, we're supposed to give him her cell phone number." Detective DeRosa is not only attractive and amusing, she's also well-versed in classic cartoon characters. I think I'm in love.

"Suh, ah am indeed Mr. Leghorn," I say, and in return he

gives me the number. Before I dial it, I decide to purchase a bit of privacy.

"Hey fellas," I say to the skaters in my normal voice. "Here's ten bucks. You can have this one now, and another one in a few minutes if you go away while I make another phone call."

"Dude, there's fuckin' three of us."

"Dude," I reply, "what difference does it make if you hang out on this fuckin' curb or that one?" They just stare back at me. "All right, ten each." The punks grab the first installment out of my hand and skate away.

"Detective DeRosa," she answers.

"Ah say ah say, little darling. It is yours truly."

"Oh, hello. Or should I say 'Cock-a-doodle-do'?"

"Ah regret that factors beyond my control have forced me to adopt this most undignified demeanor." I drop into Foghorn's most seductive tones. "Perhaps one day we can meet under more agreeable conditions."

"Am I being hit on by poultry?"

"Certainly not, madam. Or is it . . . mademoiselle?"

"It's detective. What can I do for you?"

"Firstly, may ah extend my compliments as to the extremely entertaining manner in which you bushwhacked that television news hound."

"Thanks. My captain didn't think it was so funny."

"Then your captain quite obviously has a stick up his patootie, and please tell him ah said so."

"I'm gonna let you handle that one, Foghorn," says Detective DeRosa. "Anything else on your mind?"

"Well as a matter of fact, ah was a-wonderin if you were able to learn anything further about the matter of our mutual concern."

"Actually, it works the other way," she says. "Since I'm the police officer, you're supposed to give me information."

"And indeed ah did, to the utmost of my ability. Ah am simply curious if you were able to uncover any additional details about the scandalous scene ah witnessed."

“Sorry, but it’s against policy to discuss an active investigation with anyone outside the department.”

“No need to apologize, little lady. Yours truly completely comprendos.”

“I will tell you one thing, though,” says the detective. “If we can’t get anything more specific about Raymond Bonaparte, then it looks like that’s a dead end.”

“Ah see. Ah sincerely wish that I could be of greater service.” I do hate disappointing her, and I guess she can tell.

“Hey, don’t beat yourself up,” she says. “You’re only one rooster.”

chapter six

I HAVE GIVEN up on the concept of unassisted sleep, so as soon as I arrive home I head straight for the Tylenol PMs. They invariably leave me with a morning mush-brain that is impervious to coffee, which I nevertheless guzzle by the gallon in a desperate attempt to clear my head, which forces me to repeat the whole poisonous cycle the next night, and the next. As stupid and self-destructive as this is, I periodically allow myself to become over-the-counter-Elvis for the simple reason that I cannot bear to look at the clock on my nightstand and see anything with a "3" in front of it.

"3:47," it says when I open my eyes, but the big red numbers are meaningless. I not only can't remember where I am, I can't remember what I am. All I know is that there is a loud, braying noise coming from somewhere near the numbers, so I instinctively reach for it. Now I have the hard little noisemaker in my grasp, and I see that it bears a message on its own backlit display: "Call from Trevor." This penetrates my cerebral cortex in a way that mere caffeine cannot, so I quickly press the green button.

"Ted Collins," I say, doing my best to sound as though I'm in the middle of a million things.

"Hullo, Ted." It is indeed the King of Reality, his imperial presence undiluted by the vast distance between us. "I hope I didn't wake you."

"No no, I was just planning my day."

"I fear it's about to become considerably more difficult," Trevor says. "I've just seen the numbers."

"The numbers?" As a relative newcomer to the field, and a heavily drugged one at that, I momentarily forget that just as civilized people worship but one God, television people worship but one set of digits.

"We tied with FBC in the overnights, and we lost the time period in men eighteen to thirty-four. We may come up a bit in the nationals, but not enough to prevent Roger from having a major meltdown." I'm not totally clear on the ratings mumbo-jumbo, but I'm willing to take Trevor's word as to its likely impact on Roger. And I'm 100 percent certain that I don't want to be anywhere near a Dominus-quality meltdown.

"Unfortunately," Trevor continues, "it's all going to land on you."

"Me?" I can't help but ask.

"Perhaps it doesn't seem fair." You could say that, considering that I have about as much influence over how many people watched last week's episode of *The Mogul* as I do over solar flares. "But it goes with the territory," Trevor says. "Ordinarily I'd be on the next plane out in order to manage the situation on the ground, but I regret that won't be possible."

"No need to worry, I'm sure we'll be fine."

"Don't be an ass," Trevor snaps. "I give you a 10 percent chance of surviving the day." If this is his idea of an inspirational pre-battle speech, it's no wonder that Nelson Mandela ran his ass off the continent.

"What do you want me to do?"

"You must beat him to the punch by coming up with something bold," he says.

"I'm not sure I know what you mean," I say. (How about "I quit"?)

"Ted, I have only a few moments, so allow me to speak frankly. You are one of those exasperating chaps who walk around thinking you're smarter than everyone else, despite overwhelming evidence to the contrary. If I were to describe your type for casting purposes, I would call you the perpetually underachieving snob."

"Okay," I hear myself say, although the only healthy response would be, "LA-LA-LA-LA-LA-LA!"

"You now have a once-in-a-lifetime opportunity to put your so-called brilliance to the test," Trevor continues. "I am about to have a dinner meeting with the third-ranking government official in China. I shall therefore be obliged to drink Scotch and consort with underage prostitutes for the next eight hours. If I show disrespect by allowing myself to be called away to the telephone, I will be jeopardizing a $30 million-dollar profit. Do I make myself clear?"

"I think so."

"Good," says Trevor. "This is your main chance, and if you fail without giving it your all, you won't ever be given another."

The line goes dead, and for several moments I would be perfectly happy to do the same. For me, living in a world ruled by the Trevor Banes and Roger Domini requires a certain detachment, perhaps even a bit of denial. I'm not saying it never occurs to me that their *modus operandi*—flitting around the world by private jet, carrying on love affairs with a series of beautiful and famous women, implicitly inviting the rest of mankind to suck ass—might be preferable to sucking said ass. But on the whole, I manage to maintain my self-esteem by telling myself that I live by an entirely different set of values. I'm just temporarily drawing a blank as to what those are.

Going back to sleep is obviously out of the question unless I finish off the Costco-size bottle of Tylenol PMs, and my self-pity, like the rest of me, doesn't run that deep. I instead yield to the extremely rare impulse to clean my living quarters, beginning with the ghastly bathroom. When both it and the kitchen are ship-shape, I decide that the vacuum Deb gave me two crappy addresses ago is ready for its maiden voyage. I am impressed with the path it cuts through the flotsam on my living room floor; the people in the apartment below me less so.

After I've had a shower in my spotless bathroom and enough Columbian Supremo to revive the situation-comedy, I drive to the office. Of course I have no clue as to how to save *The Mogul*, but I have at least the beginnings of a plan to save myself. I figure I still have a small window of opportunity to parlay my status as co-executive producer into more time with Hallie, but if I don't jump through that window quickly, Roger will almost certainly slam it on my dick. And although dawn is just breaking across Southern California, I know there is at least one person who will already be hard at work.

"Top of the day, Tanya," I say as I come through the doors to Trevor's office suite.

"Jesus!" she shrieks, and despite my dour mood I am pleased to see that she is sufficiently startled that she actually bothers to hide the *Star* she is reading.

"Are you sure you should be working on your dissertation during office hours?" I ask.

"What do you want?" she sneers.

"Howard Drew's home address."

"No way."

"Way, Tanya. I just got off the phone with Trevor, and he told me to get it from you."

"He did not."

"Call him and ask him," I suggest. "Although he did mention that he'll be tied up for a few hours, and anyone who interrupts him without an excellent reason will thereafter be unable to get a job blowing baboons on The Animal Channel." I can tell from the subtle tightening around Tanya's collagen-enhanced lips that at least part of this jives with what Trevor has told her himself.

"Come on," I prod her. "If anyone asks, I'll swear I got it from one of the other Tanyas." She considers her options for another moment, then scowls and begins entering a password on her computer keyboard.

"Don't look!" she screeches, and I dutifully turn my back until I hear her scribble something and then tear a sheet off a notepad.

"Thanks," I say, taking the paper from her and confirming that it does indeed have an address written on it. "Maybe I can find some way to make it up to you—drinks, dinner?" I say this not because I have any real interest in or chance at nailing Tanya, but because I know she's feeling a little violated, and it's only fair to give her a chance to regain her equilibrium.

"In your dreams, loser."

Now how can anyone say I'm not a thoughtful guy?

Howard Drew lives on North Cliffwood Drive in Brentwood, a stone's throw from the old O.J. Simpson spread on Rockingham. It's both a lovely neighborhood to call home and an excellent one for a divorce lawyer to meet potential clients while out walking the dog, since the only reason most of the residents *have* dogs is to give them an excuse to go outside and phone their mistresses. Many of the driveways are gated, but the circular one in front of Drew Castle is not, so I am able to pull my car right up to the front door. My watch says 7:12, an unconscionable hour to be dropping by uninvited, but propriety is a luxury I can no longer afford.

I ring the bell, wait ten seconds, and am about to ring again when a voice comes booming through the intercom speaker.

"What is it?" It's definitely an Alpha male, and one who is currently breathing quite heavily. Christ, I've interrupted the poor man while he's trying to capitalize on his wake-up woody.

"I'm sorry to bother you, Mr. Drew," I say, damning the torpedos. "It's Ted Collins."

"Who?"

"Ted Collins. Your new client? Referred by Trevor Bane?"

"Okay, Ted fucking Collins," he says. "What are you doing

. . . ah, shit. Jody, go let this guy in. I'll talk to him while we finish up."

I have about half a minute to stand there and contemplate just how I'm going to accomplish the very serious business at hand while watching Howard Drew's ass impersonate an oil derrick. But when the door is opened by a guy who looks like a *Mogul* contestant, and he's wearing a tank-top that says "PERSONAL TRAINER," I put two and two together and breathe a sigh of relief.

The gym is in the pool house, and is equipped with everything except hot chicks at which to gawk. Howard Drew is no doubt above such longings of the common man, or at least more keenly aware of their cost. As I am shown in by Jody the trainer, the divorce lawyer to the stars is pushing an elliptical cross-training machine to the very limits of its capabilities.

"Whoa, ease up," Jody says, looking at a heart-rate readout and numerous other vital signs being fed wirelessly to a laptop computer. "You're at 175."

Howard pays no attention to Jody, and pumps the machine even harder while aiming his beet-red countenance directly at me.

"I don't see clients at my fucking house," he wheezes.

"Yes, I'm very—" I say before he cuts me off.

"Or without a fucking . . ." gasp . . . "appointment."

"I realize it's—"

"Or at seven o'clock in the . . ." He's now really struggling for air, and it seems cruel not to help him.

"Fucking morning?" I suggest. Howard jams the heel of his hand into the machine's emergency stop button. Jody the trainer jumps to his side and hands him a towel as he dismounts.

"Hey stud, we need to cool you down after a sprint like that," Jody says.

"Fuck off," Howard rasps. He mops his face once then throws the towel back at Jody. "Go tell Marta to have my smoothie ready in five minutes."

"Okay, but you at least have to keep moving," Jody says. In

response, Howard stands as still as a stop sign and stares at the trainer until he leaves. I leap quickly into the void.

"Mr. Drew, I know how lucky I am that you agreed to take my case," I say. "And I know how far out of line it is to show up at your house like this."

"So far, so obvious."

"Unfortunately, I had no choice. There are some new developments that could have a major impact on my case."

"What kind of developments?"

"Before I get into that, I wonder if you could bring me up to date on what's happened so far." I can see how close he is to attacking me with a dumbbell, so I try to sound as pitiful as possible. "Please, sir. I really need to know."

"I'd have to look at the file," he sighs, disgusted with both me and with himself for giving any ground. "Off the top of my head, I think I sent 'em a letter telling 'em we want full physical and legal custody of your son . . ."

"Daughter."

"Whatever. I also let 'em know we'd be filing an order to show cause why that cocksucker Slatkin's income shouldn't be used to calculate how much child support you get."

"You mean Richard would have to pay *me*?" I ask, unable to conceal my giddiness at the concept. "Is that legal?"

"It is if I say so, pal."

"So how did Sara's lawyer respond?"

"Same way any competent professional would," he shrugs. "Told us to fuck ourselves. The only thing they agreed to was getting rid of the supervised visitation and going back to the custody order you had before you went bat shit and drove through their ski lodge."

"It was their beach house," I say.

"I got a lot of nut-ball clients," he shrugs.

"They really put that in writing?" I ask. "No more supervised visitation?"

"Sure. Unlike some people, they know better than to insult

me. But they won't even think about getting serious on our other demands until we're closer to the hearing date."

I take a moment and a deep breath. I know what I've come to do, and everything is now perfectly positioned for me to do it. But… but nothing, you pathetic pussy.

"As soon as I leave here, I will be faxing a letter to your office," I inform the mighty Mr. Drew. "In it, I will be instructing you to contact opposing counsel immediately and accept the offer that is on the table, without qualification." Although he says nothing, Howard's various reactions are each strong enough to register plainly across his face. First there is confusion, as though he must have misunderstood me, followed by fury, since he's pretty damned sure he hasn't, and finally concern over the possibility that in addition to being crazy, I might also be armed.

"Don't worry," I tell him. "I'll show myself out." I turn and head back the way I came, but Howard rushes to head me off alongside the pool.

"Just a minute," he says, stopping me with two stiff fingers to the sternum. "Who the fuck do you think you are?"

"As of this moment, I am your client," I respond. "And according to the rules of the California State Bar, you cannot terminate your representation simply because I have instructed you to accept a settlement proposal."

"You've got a lot of nerve lecturing me about the State Bar. Guess who's the immediate past fucking president?"

"You are. Which is why I'm sure you're familiar with the rules."

"Okay, smart guy," he says. "Let's say you're right. Why not just be a normal little prick and call me at the office to discuss your case?"

"Mr. Drew, I don't mean to be rude, but I've got a big day ahead of me, and I really don't have time to go into all the details." I try to step around him, but he jumps sideways to block my path.

“Gimme at least the short version, or you’re going in the pool. Nothing in the Bar rules against that.” It is clear that he means his threat seriously, and less than clear that my younger but long-neglected physique could prevent him from following through on it.

“Okay,” I say, then launch into a rapid-fire explanation. “If I tried to reach you at the office, I’d never get through. I’d be told you were in court, or in depositions, or in New York, although I’m guessing you rarely travel east of the 405. When you finally called back a week later, you’d make sure it was at a time when I’d be least likely to answer the phone. You guys must have highly-paid researchers on staff to calculate when a client is most likely to be tied up in a meeting, or taking a crap. But let’s say I anticipate all that and I always keep a phone right on top of the toilet paper. I ask you where we are in the case, you grudgingly tell me, and I say I want to accept the current offer. You chuckle condescendingly and tell me maybe I should read a few of the books and magazines that have been written about you, then decide whether I’m better off calling the shots myself or letting you do it for me. And of course the correct answer would be the latter, except for the fact that I’m about to get blamed for *The Mogul* going down in flames, and therefore you’ll never call me back at all. My ex-wife will view the fact that I am no longer represented by Attila the Attorney as a sign of weakness, and will move in for the kill. Since I will have no job and thus no money with which to fight her, she will succeed, and any future play dates I’m lucky enough to have with my daughter will be conducted through barbed wire. So all in all, this seems like as good a time as any to settle.” While I catch my breath, Howard considers what he’s heard.

“There are several flaws in your brilliant strategy,” he ultimately intones.

“I’m sure there are. That’s why nobody pays me five hundred bucks an hour.”

“Six-fifty,” he corrects me. “And a fucking bargain.” I bow, conceding the point. "But if this is what you really want to do, I suppose I can accommodate you."

"Thank you, sir."

"Knock off the 'sir' shit, fuckface. I'll have one of my people draw up a letter to opposing counsel, accepting their offer. I'll also have them prepare a letter from you, addressed to me, terminating my representation effective immediately and releasing me from any and all malpractice claims. We'll execute the two documents concurrently."

"Sounds reasonable," I say. "Now if you'll excuse me, I really must get going." I step around him and am almost to the door when he speaks.

"So what's the big crisis with Trevor's show?"

"The ratings are down."

"How do you know they're gonna blame you?" Just hearing his own question spoken aloud makes him realize how stupid it is, and he waves me off before I am obliged to answer. I turn once again to leave, and in the process collide head-on with a uniformed maid who is carrying a foamy, pink drink on a tray.

"Ayy!" the maid yells, as the liquid sloshes onto her uniform and the glass flies off the tray. I make an effort to grab it in mid-air, but wind up with only a handful of pink froth. The glass shatters on the walkway.

"Sorry," I say, licking my fingers. "That's pretty good, what's in it?"

"Get the fuck outta my house!" Howard Drew suggests, and I see no point in further debate.

chapter seven

I CALL DEB and ask her to meet me for breakfast at Swinger's. She gets a kick out of hearing how I handled Howard Drew, although she fears that I may be a little out of my league.

"When your boss finds about this, he's gonna screw you so bad you're gonna have to start wearing diapers."

"So long as I get rid of Ms. Gutierrez, I don't care if I have to start wearing tampons."

"When are you gonna talk to Dominus?" Deb asks.

"I don't know," I say, scrolling through the missed calls on my cell phone. "He's called me seven times in the last hour, but I haven't picked up."

"Good strategy. He seems like the kind of guy who will eventually take a hint."

"I'm hoping that if I piss him off enough, he'll fire me right away and I can get to work full time on the Patrice story."

"I hate to sound like your mommy, but maybe you should think twice about that," she says. "You're getting paid a lot of money, you've got health insurance. Theoretically, all that could translate to getting laid."

"I don't care. The only reason I took the job was so Howard Drew would represent me. I've already gotten everything I need out of the arrogant bastard, so it's time to move on to the kind of work I should be doing."

"Number one, you're saying that at least partly because even at your advanced age you'd rather quit than get canned, which as your friend I must tell you is truly pathetic. And number two, you don't even know if there really *is* a story. The bimbo could have taken a powder, or maybe it's just some publicity bullshit."

"The point isn't whether it turns out that there's a story," I say. "The point is I need to find out if there's a story, because that's who I am."

"You aren't going to break into the chorus of "My Way," are you? Because in case you didn't notice, I'm eating."

My cell phone rings. I glance at the caller ID, then show Deb that once again it's Roger calling.

"Just get it over with," she says. "If you really don't care about being fired, you can tell him whatever you want."

"Fine. I'll tell him I'm working on a terrific new *Mogul* episode about a homicidal homeboy."

I press the Send button, but before I can get the phone to my ear, Deb snatches it away and hangs up on Roger.

"That's it!" she says.

"What's what?"

"The solution to all your problems. Do an episode about Boney."

"Are you out of your carpet-munching mind?" I give Deb the most dismissive look and wave I can muster, but it has no discernible effect. I sigh, annoyed at being forced to take this shit seriously. "It's a dumb-ass Reality show, not *60 Minutes*."

"Aren't all the stories about selling something?" she demands.

"Yeah, pretty much."

"And didn't you say Boney has a new CD to sell?"

"Roger Dominus can't sell gangsta rap."

"Why not?"

"Because he's about as fly as the Mormon Tabernacle Choir."

"Maybe that's why the ratings are down."

"You want me to tell him that the solution is to start shucking and jiving?"

"I thought you didn't care what you tell him."

"With all due respect, I'm not sure your experience in the world of Sapphic film festivals translates to mainstream media." Deb's only response is to grin broadly at me.

"What's so fucking funny?" I demand.

"Whenever you know you've lost an argument, you reach for the dyke jokes."

I refuse to give Deb the satisfaction of telling her I'll think about her scheme. But as I drive back to the office, I can't think about anything else. The fact is that even if I had all the free time and money in the world, I have no solid plan for how to proceed with my Patrice/Boney investigation. Reporters usually write about crime investigations only after they're over, for the simple reason that cops have so many tools that we don't, i.e. handcuffs, hot lights, and the nearly universal human reluctance to becoming the cellblock bitch. Convincing a perpetrator or an accomplice to talk without the use of such leverage is very difficult, not to mention dangerous. And I already know that getting to Boney is going to be especially challenging, due to his status as an up-and-coming celebrity, and mine as an impoverished honky. So I have to admit, the notion of gaining access to his world via *The Mogul* is diabolically clever.

It's also not completely crazy. Trevor's genius, much as it pains me to call it that, was to realize that prime-time entertainment and advertising could be blended into a single seamless entity. *The Mogul* is a show about people trying to sell things, which happen to be the same things that the show's advertisers are trying to sell, so just try using your TiVo to fast-forward through all the commercial content in *that*. Trevor's instructions to me this morning were come up with something bold that would placate Roger. Devoting an hour of network prime time to a recording artist from Muthafuckin' Music would certainly meet the first requirement, so all I really have to worry about is the second. And since I still have several hours while

Trevor and his Chinese hosts are busy tag-teaming teenagers, the field is mine.

Another thing working in my favor is our opponent in the ratings battle. The main reason that *The Mogul* has begun to slip (other than the fact that it sucks) is that Fox recently moved a hot, new sketch-comedy hour called *The Louie Joe Show* into our time period. Louie Joe is a gangly African American comic who specializes in the portrayal of male characters who are lazy, thieving, and drug-addled, and female characters who, in addition to the above qualities, are also hoes. It's not the sort of material that's likely to meet with the approval of the NAACP or Oprah, but it meets with the approval of enough ordinary folk that it just beat the once-mighty *Mogul*. The numbers for *Louie Joe* have been steadily building since the beginning of the season, and there has already been lots of discussion about how to counter the threat next year. But the current panic affords me the opportunity to suggest an immediate, radical solution—a heavily promoted episode targeted squarely at Louie Joe's core audience. I instinctively sense that the hyper-competitive Roger Dominus will respond to the idea of taking the fight right to "that skinny little spear chucker" (his term, not mine).

There are also financial and logistical considerations. The entire season of *Mogul* episodes are carefully planned and scheduled well before production begins on the first one, and changing a show mid-stream is almost unthinkable. To begin with, most of the segments are built around a single sponsored product, and if Trevor has already collected that money and sold the corresponding commercial time, he can't very well just tell a major advertiser, "Never mind." Again though, there is an opening I just might be able to wriggle through: approximately one quarter of the episodes, including the one we are about to shoot, have no overall outside sponsor, but are instead hour-long ads for various corners of the Dominus empire. This week, the contestants are supposed to do battle over the promotion of a Celine Dion concert at one of Roger's Las Vegas venues. The promotional value is no doubt enormous, but if Roger can be convinced that there is equal or greater value in going after the "urban" TV audience, he just might be willing to make the switch. And who's to say that Boney's bling-bearing peeps wouldn't drop just as much cash at the Dominus hotels and casinos as Celine Dion's aging, fixed-income fans? The Boney crowd will certainly be around for many more years, with the exception of the relative few who get prematurely capped.

I'm actually starting to look forward to selling the idea to Roger, but then I remember another equally important task—selling it to Boney, or his handlers. This ought to be a cinch, since the prospect of flogging a new CD to the 40 million people who watch *The Mogul* should cause any marketing professional to soil himself with glee. On the other hand, the idea could strike them as coming out of left field, and there may be some concern that Boney will lose some street cred if he subs in for Celine Dion. But if you think about it, our show is really the perfect vehicle for a rap star. Is there any better word to describe Mr. P. Diddy than "Mogul"?

A bigger challenge than persuading Boney's people may be simply getting them on the phone. You'd think that being the producer of one of the top shows on TV would open pretty much any door, and it will—eventually. But there's so much brazen bullshit in the entertainment business that people are understandably wary of strangers. The official bios of some of the biggest names around—David Geffen, Brian Grazer, Steven Spielberg—feature shameless stories of fraud and impersonation used to advance their early careers. My experience is that these days, no one in a position of power ever accepts a call from someone they don't know, and they don't return it until they've run a thorough background check. Since I don't have that kind of time, I need to short-circuit the process, and unfortunately I can only think of one way.

First I decide to face the music, or at least the first couple of bars. I turn my phone back on and hit Send.

"Do you have a death wish?" It's not Roger answering his own phone, of course, but rather his Chief Flunky.

"Please tell Roger I'm sorry I wasn't able to speak to him earlier," I say.

"Oh, no no no. You're going to do that yourself."

"I'll be happy to, but not just yet."

"Don't even think about hanging up on me again," he hisses, but he sounds a lot more scared than scary.

"I'll be at my desk in about an hour, and I'd love to chat with Roger then if he's available," I say, then hit End. I make no claim to clairvoyance, but my hunch is that right now, someone is receiving a very special edition of The Look.

The receptionist at the Century City law firm of Epstein, Barrington & Slatkin, LLP (known universally within the business as Epstein Barr), must be very good at what she does, because she has her own set of bodyguards. Two hulks with dark suits and curly wires coming out of their ears stand on either side of the lobby, watching me as I approach the desk.

"Ted Collins to see Richard Slatkin," I announce, and one of the security slabs immediately strides forward. I called Richard on my way over here to beg for a bit of his time, and although he agreed to see me, he is evidently taking no chances with my intentions. I suppose I can't blame him, in light of the tragic events of November 22nd, aka the day I took his Hummer for a swim.

"I'll show you to Mr. Slatkin's office," the slab says.

"Great," I say. "Did you just happen to be headed that way?" My escort doesn't acknowledge the question, and he makes sure that I walk half a step ahead of him as we navigate the hallways. The walls are lined with proof of Epstein Barr's global hegemony in the field of entertainment law—movie posters, gold records, and dozens of photographs of the most beautiful and talented people in the world, locked in loving embrace with their geeky attorneys.

Richard slouches behind his desk, which could comfortably seat twelve for dinner, but has nothing on it at the moment except a telephone and the heels of his Gucci loafers. He raises his eyes from *The Wall Street Journal* as I enter, but doesn't move any additional muscles.

"Ted," he says.

"Richard." I force a smile and it must look passably non-psychotic, because he gives a slight nod to the security guy. The latter takes a seat just outside the open door, and I slide into a chair facing Richard.

"To what do I owe the pleasure?" he asks.

"I need some of your professional expertise."

"Really?" He cocks an eyebrow. "That may present a conflict with another client. Besides, I heard you have very capable new counsel." Regardless of Sara's reaction to the letter from Howard Drew, I knew it would at least buy me a little respect from her husband. It's no doubt why he agreed to my urgent and unprecedented request for a meeting.

"This has nothing to do with Sara or Hallie," I tell him. "It's an entertainment matter."

"I very much doubt I can help."

"Can you at least listen for a few minutes?" He responds with a patronizing smile and hand gesture, so I continue. "I don't know if you heard, but I just got bumped up to Co-E.P. of *The Mogul*."

"No, but congratulations." The first part of that sentence is a bald-faced lie, since my promotion made the front page of both *Variety* and *The Hollywood Reporter*, and Richard hasn't missed an issue of either since he was seven. The second part is merely insincere, which somehow makes it extra satisfying to hear.

"Thanks, it's a hell of a big job. Especially with Trevor gone to China."

"Yes, our people in Beijing were able to open a few doors for him. As a courtesy, of course." This is code for the fact that although the tight-fisted Trevor refuses to give a percentage of his profits to Epstein Barr or any other law firm, he is such a big fucking deal that they're willing to work for him for free just so they can drop his name.

"I hear it's going well," I say. "But between the time difference and Trevor being so busy, I'm pretty much on my own here." Richard's eyes widen ever so slightly, which I take as evidence that so far my plan is working. In the cheesy melodrama that Richard, Sara, and I have been acting out over the last half-dozen years, my role has been that of the Putz. Now I intend to play into that by making Richard think that he has a fresh opportunity to scam me.

"I'm sure you're up to the challenge," he says, then ever so casually swings his feet down off the desk.

"We'll see. Right now I've got a big one." I tell him about the ratings being down, which of course he already knows. Then I start to employ a little creative license.

"Roger Dominus is totally freaked out," I say. "He wants to go after Louie Joe's audience."

"How does he propose to do that? Grow an Afro?" Richard chuckles at his own joke, and I silently promise myself never to make another crack about Roger's hair.

"He wants to scrap an episode we're supposed to shoot with Celine Dion and do one with some rap star instead."

"Which rap star?"

"He doesn't even know," I whine. "He expects me to find one who wants to be on *The Mogul*."

"I see." Richard's wheels are now turning so fast I expect to see smoke rising off his scalp. "So what's your plan, Ted?"

"Well obviously, I need to talk him out of it. I was hoping you could give me some legal arguments." Richard does his best two-second impression of A Guy Who's Thinking.

"I'm afraid nothing comes to mind."

"What about the commitment to Celine Dion?"

"Our office happens to represent Celine. She has a multi-year deal with the Dominus hotels, and promotion is completely at his discretion."

"That sucks," I say, shaking my head. "I don't know what I'm going to do."

"Why don't you try doing your job, which is to give Roger what he wants."

"You mean actually produce an episode with some rapper?"

"Why not?" Richard proceeds to rattle off many of the same arguments that I plan to use on Roger, which is simultaneously both validating and nauseating.

"I hear what you're saying," I tell him after he's delivered an impressive off-the-cuff oration that touches on network programming philosophy, shifting demographics, and the cultural legacy of Ol' Dirty Bastard. "But we need to start shooting in a couple of days. Who could I get on that kind of notice?"

This is the moment of truth. God only knows how many rappers are on Richard's client list, or how many more he's currently trying to steal. It's suddenly clear to me that a featured spot on *The Mogul* is way too big a plum to bestow on a garden-variety gangsta like Boney, and my whole scheme is about to go down in flames.

"How about Boney?" he says.

"Who?"

"Boney. Have you ever heard *Up Da Butt*?"

"Not in a musical context."

"You ought to try listening to something besides classic rock," Richard sniffs. "Boney is a major artist, and he's got a killer new CD coming out."

"Is he a client of yours?"

"As a matter of fact, he is. Although I wouldn't recommend him if I didn't happen to know he'd be perfect for your show." I wonder if there's some special school where they teach you how to shovel it like that.

"Is Boney available?"

"I'd have to check," he says. "But first I'd need a firm commitment from you." I offer Richard my own rendition of The Thinker, then slowly nod.

"He sounds perfect."

Convincing Roger of this dubious proposition is much easier than it should be. Since his office is also in Century City—it's not hard to find, just look for a fifty-story phallus with the word "DOMINUS" plastered on all four sides—I swing by there right after I leave Richard. I offer Roger only the briefest of apologies for being incommunicado, then launch right into my pitch. I don't know if it's because he's already worn himself out by emasculating his assistants (the one I spoke to earlier is nowhere to be seen), or if it's because he's so desperate to hang onto his ratings supremacy, or if—heaven forbid—my plan actually makes some sense, but he buys into it with nary a negative comment. He doesn't even raise the issue of how much MF Music will be paying for the huge plug, which at the moment is nothing since I didn't bring it up with Richard.

Nevertheless, I'm now feeling so cocky that I decide to press my luck. I drive back to my own office and wait half an hour, during which time I'm reasonably confident that Richard will have crowed to Boney and his managers about his big coup. I then call him up and tell him it ain't happening.

"I see," Richard says, sounding not nearly as panicked as I'd hoped. It's too late for me to turn back, though.

"When I told Roger it was a freebie, he hit the roof," I tell him.

"Why did you say that?"

"Well, I don't know. You didn't bring up money, and I didn't think it was my place to ask, since you're doing me such a big favor in the first place."

"This isn't personal, Ted. It's business."

"Uh-huh." It's also a good thing Richard can't see me, because I've broken into a huge, shit-eating grin and I have to cradle the phone on my shoulder so that I can flip him off with both hands.

"The record company has an ample promotion budget, and I'm sure that something can be arranged," he says.

"Really? Wow, that'd be awesome." I tell him that the standard fare for being featured on *The Mogul* is \$3 million bucks, which again he already knows, but that in light of the unusual circumstances, I could probably get the deal done for a measly mil. In consideration of such a generous discount, we would only ask that Boney agree to perform half a dozen concerts free of charge, at dates and locations to be determined by us. We would also need complete and immediate access to Boney's home and schedule, since we have so much work to do in such a short time. Richard doesn't see how any of that should be a problem. I hang up and involuntarily leap into the air, pumping my fist.

"YEEEE FUCKING HA!!" Everyone stops what they're doing and stares at me. Laura Adler doesn't know why I'm so psyched, but apparently she doesn't need to. She stands, places the one personal effect on her desk—a framed photo of a scrawny kitty-cat—into her purse, and quietly heads for the elevator.

"Keep in touch!" I call after her.

chapter eight

OVER THE NEXT several hours, I work like Martha Stewart on Mountain Dew. My goal is to make enough progress on the switch from Celine to Boney that when Trevor checks in, it'll already be a done deal. The production crew takes the news pretty well. Due to the Battan Death March nature of the work, most of the surviving field producers and technical personnel are twenty-somethings, and their iPods are a lot more likely to be loaded with West Coast rap than French Canadian schmaltz. The same is generally true of the cast, although everyone assumes that the change somehow favors the two remaining black contestants, and the others ratchet up their fear and loathing accordingly.

I catch a break when Trevor calls Roger before he calls me. So by the time we talk, the fact that I have somehow succeeded in appeasing our eight-hundred-pound gorilla, perhaps combined with the fatigue brought on by trying to keep up with China's Minister of Muff Diving, has taken the fight right out of Trevor. He asks me a few good questions, for which I pull from my ass a few so-so answers, and that's pretty much that. Before he hangs up, he even congratulates me on squeezing so many free concerts out of Boney, and muses as to whether we can incorporate them into a new series for MTV. His use of the word "we" gives me another one of those conflicted reactions, when I can't decide whether I should go buy a new BMW or shoot myself.

I've gotten so good at pretending to be a producer that I temporarily forget the whole point of this exercise, which is to spy on Boney. *The Mogul* is going to spend two full days at his crib, which is good, but the flacks from Muthafuckin' Records will be stuck to me like Krazy Glue, which is bad. I need another set of eyes and ears, and there's no one on our staff I can trust. So I call Deb.

"We're doing the Boney episode," I tell her. "I want to hire you as a camera operator."

"Camera operator? It's my idea, I should be the goddamned director."

"In the first place it's a Reality show, so there is no goddamned director. In the second place, I need you to be inconspicuous so you can do some snooping around."

"I don't know," she says. "I'm pretty busy with my own project."

"Can you please not break my balls for once? Just help me out for a few days, then you can get back to the sad tale of the unluckiest little lesbo."

"How much does it pay?"

"A lot more than sitting around your apartment, wearing out another vibrator. And I might even throw in a couple of bucks out of my own pocket, in recognition of your creative input."

"You can get me a new Betacam or you can bite me," she says. I don't have time to haggle, so I agree to Deb's onerous terms and we arrange to meet later to discuss strategy.

A few minutes later, I get a call from Howard Drew's assistant, advising me that the two documents are ready to sign. I tell her I'll come by their office before the end of the day, but after we get off the phone I begin to reconsider. The reason I insisted on accepting the custody deal that was on the table was because I was sure I was going to get fired, possibly as soon as today. Now, however, by selling my superiors on a preposterous plan designed strictly to further my own selfish interests, I have greatly improved my professional standing. It'll be four to six weeks before anyone sees even a rough cut of the Boney episode, and my position should therefore be secure for at least that long. Why not see how it goes before I settle with Sara, or sever my ties with Howard? After all, he and I have developed quite an effective working relationship.

"What the fuck do you want, you little weasel?" are Howard's first words upon answering my call.

"I just wanted to apologize again for this morning," I say.

"That sure means a lot."

"I also wanted to tell you that I changed my mind about the deal, so we need to send a different letter."

"You can tell that to your new lawyer, dickhead."

"Actually, I've decided not to make a change in representation at this time."

"Oh, you have?" I can hear the smile creep into his voice, as he gathers some of his very best Private Reserve profanities with which to say that the decision really isn't up to me.

"Yeah, I just got off the phone with Trevor, and it looks like he and I are going to be partners on a new show for MTV. I guess I was just being paranoid earlier." Howard is quiet for a few moments, and I assume it's because he's contemplating human nature. Specifically he's thinking about Trevor, his hundreds of millions of dollars, and his matrimonial future. Although Trevor is on record all over the place that he doesn't plan to remarry, Howard knows that the chances of this are slim and none. Everyone—even Hef, for God's sake—lets his guard down again sooner or later. And the only thing as certain as Trevor's second marriage is Trevor's second divorce. Although Howard hardly needs the work, it would be a shame to let some other attorney steal such a prize.

"Is that right?" he says, the wind having completely deserted his sails.

"Yeah. Maybe I'll even be able to pay my legal bills." Howard responds with the obligatory laugh, which makes my victory so complete that I feel bad for him. What good is it to reach the top of your profession and live like a king if you can't even kick the shit out of a complete nobody?

It is a well-established law of nature that success in competitive endeavors makes men horny. In fact, it makes whole countries horny—every year, the nation that cheers its team to victory in the World Cup finals sees a major spike in its birth rate nine months later, while the losers experience an even more dramatic decline. (This is the sort of statistic that lends credence to Deb's theory that a lot of intercourse should really be classified as rape. It's hard to believe that all those face-painted soccer hooligans are asking nicely.) The reason I'm thinking about this phenomenon right now, when there is so much to be done and I can't afford to be taking any mental side trips, is that a number of employees at Trevor Bane Productions suddenly look extremely fuckable. Take Jessica Levine, one of the field producers—I'd like to take her right there on her desk, even though I've worked with her for almost a year and the thought has never previously crossed my mind. Or how about Tiffany Huge-Tits, whose equally huge ass no longer seems like such a barrier to entry? This thought balloon must be quite easy to read, because while I'm staring across the room at the bulbous Tiffany, Myron, the production assistant, comes by and nudges me with his elbow.

"The bigger the cushion, the better the pushin', right boss?" Myron gives me a big conspiratorial grin. I think it's time to get a little fresh air.

But alas, they're everywhere. Did that chick at the Coffee Bean always have such a great rack? And how old are those giggly girls in the plaid skirts? I'll bet they'd like to be on TV. Wait, there's a hot *and* legal blonde walking on the opposite side of the street. If I ditch my latte and run, can I intercept her at the crosswalk? Yes I can, although up close it turns out she's pushing sixty. At least she smiles back at me as she passes, so I turn to check her out from behind. Pretty saggy, but there's something to be said for experience, right?

Perhaps because I realize that I'm about to commit a terrible crime, I call the police.

"Detective DeRosa speaking."

"Ah say ah say," I say.

"Well, hello. Where've you been, you big cock?"

"Just one step ahead a that darned dog. How goes the investigation?"

"I'm afraid we don't have anything new," she says. "What about you?"

"As a matter of fact I do have somethin', little darlin'." I pause to make sure that none of the patrons of the laundromat where I've come to use the payphone are within earshot. "Yours truly has concocted a most cunning ruse to sniff around the home of Mr. Raymond Bonaparte."

"Really? How?"

"Once again, ah regret that certain details must remain strictly hush-hush. For now, that is. One day, ah promise to reveal all."

"Fair enough. What have you turned up?"

"Nothin' yet. Mah first foray into the Bone yard is gonna be tomorrow mornin'."

"I see."

"Ah was thinkin' that perhaps ah could be of some service, if you have anythin' in particular ah should be on the lookout for."

"I guess we could start with Patrice Williams."

"Heh-heh, lemme write that one down."

"Actually Foghorn, if I tell you what to look for and you find it, the courts will probably consider that an illegal search and seizure. If you discover something on your own and bring it to me, now that's a different story."

"Ah get the picture, little darlin'."

"Will you call me afterwards?"

"Ah most certainly will." I pause, trying to work up my nerve.

"Are you still there?" Detective DeRosa finally asks.

"Yes'm. I was just, uh… lookin' for the right words."

"For?"

"For expressin' mah interest in you as, how should ah put it . . ."

"A hen?"

"Yes ma'am."

"Well, that's very flattering. But I don't really see where it can go."

"Does that mean that you are presently involved with another suitor?"

"No, I'm not." My heart soars. "But I'm also not hard up enough to have phone sex with a cartoon character."

"Ah say ah say, I certainly wasn't suggestin'—"

"Relax, I'm just messing with you," she says, cutting me off. "You seem like a fun guy, and I could stand to have a few laughs. But you're a potential witness in one of my cases, and that means I can't have a personal relationship with you."

"Ah see."

"Unless you're willing to wait until it's all over—the investigation, the trial, the appeals."

"No offense, little darlin', but you might not be what we call a spring chicken by then."

"You may not be either, Foghorn."

"Animated individuals don't age," I tell her. "Especially since they figured out how to draw Viagra."

On my way back to the office, the clock on my dashboard reads 2:50 PM, which happens to be my least favorite time of day. That's when Hallie gets out of school and stands on the sidewalk with her classmates as the carpool line creeps past. About one day in ten Sara's car will be in that line, and when she sees it Hallie's face lights up as if it were Santa's sleigh. The rest of the time, the nanny is sent to fetch her. I know this because I used to park down the street and watch, until one of the neighbors ratted me out to the school principal, who told

Sara, who told her lawyer, who told Judge Steinbitch. So now I try to do something to distract myself every day at 2:50, but it never works. I have some internal mechanism that's as accurate as an atomic clock, and five days a week it forces me to picture Hallie's sad little expression when she spots the nanny's car.

Our VP in charge of physical production is Jack Herrera, an ex-military man who is incapable of speaking in anything softer than a full shout. Trevor only deals with him during production meetings, and the unwritten rule is that Trevor sits at one end of the longest conference table in the building, and Jack at the other. At such a distance Jack's dB level is tolerable, but the staffers in between them are subjected to varying degrees of sonic assault every time he opens his mouth. For this reason, people begin showing up for production meetings as much as half an hour early, in order to secure one of the coveted seats near the safe end of the table. This accomplishes two things for clever Trevor: he's never kept waiting; and even if he's late himself, he can easily determine who was on time.

Jack's initial response to my request that he hire Deb as an extra camera operator is a flat and deafening "NO!" I have come to his office prepared for such resistance, however. I reach under my coat and produce one of the small electric megaphones that our field producers use to coordinate crowd scenes.

"I really wish you'd reconsider," I say to Jack via the megaphone. Since he is less than four feet away from me, and his office is barely big enough to accommodate his desk and chair, the effect is quite impressive.

"What the hell do you think you're doing?" Jack booms back at me, rising to his feet.

"Beg your pardon?" I say, trying to sound as deferential as a person can while speaking through a bullhorn inside a closet.

"How'd you like me to shove that thing where the sun don't shine?"

"No thanks," I thunder pleasantly. "But I sure would appreciate it if you'd hire Deborah Sullivan." Behind me through the open door, I can hear various staffers figuring out what's going on and cracking up.

"You think just because Trevor's in China, you can start throwing your weight around?" It's clear that Jack wants to charge out from behind his desk, but is being held back by a well-founded fear of bursting an eardrum.

"No Jack, and I sure hope I'm not coming off that way." The megaphone has a volume control, which I crank up to the max before continuing. "I respect you too much as a colleague and a friend."

Jack eventually relents on the subject of Deb, but also lets me know that at his earliest convenience he intends to run me through with a bayonet.

chapter nine

SINCE I INTEND to put most of my focus on searching for clues as to the fate of Patrice Williams, I need a second-in-command who actually gives a shit about the show. I select Jessica Levine, because she has both lots of experience as a field producer and a perfectly shaped hiney. The rest of her is nothing to write a sonnet about, although she does get style points for having a hip but obviously expensive wardrobe. The first meeting at Boney's is for planning and location scouting purposes only. I ask Jessica to drive, so that we can arrive at Chez Boney in her high-end Lexus rather than my inexcusable Subaru. On the way there, I fish for details about her personal life, and learn that because she is so busy, she only dates men who are financially secure, have no ex-wives or children, and are willing to postpone sex until after marriage. Yet in spite of these rigorous requirements and a face that's only slightly above average, she seems to be busy every night. Is this fair? I mean, if I advertised for girls who are attractive, easily aroused, and about to be deported, how many dates do you think *I'd* get?

Boney's crib is in North Hollywood, a section of L.A. that doesn't appear on many maps of the stars' homes. I can see the appeal of the area, though: big, flat lots for less than half the price of equivalent Westside real estate; proximity to Hollywood, downtown, and all the other places where the action is (the more established celebs, and me if I had the money, prefer Brentwood and Pacific Palisades, the places where the action isn't); and greater diversity. You might ask how I can aspire to live in one of the lily-white enclaves of the mega-rich, yet list diversity as a plus. I would respond by saying that race is a very complex issue in America, and someday I plan to research and write a serious book on the subject. I just pray to God I get to do it behind some big gates in Malibu.

Boney's long driveway is gated at the street. Jessica pulls up to the intercom box and is about to push the Call button when the sky suddenly goes dark on my side of the car. The Shaq-size bodyguard I saw in the SUV at Richard and Sara's house has somehow appeared beside us, and he taps a giant gold ring against my window. I thought I might be running into him at some point, so I have done everything within reason—submitting to a $14 scalping last night at Supercuts, donning a sport coat and shades—to change my look. But he's caught me off guard, so I'm momentarily paralyzed and Jessica has to roll down my window for me.

"'N I help you?" the big fella asks in a manner that suggests that assistance may not be his true calling.

"Yes, we're from *The Mogul*," I squeak. "We're here to see Boney."

"Yo name?"

"Ted Collins." He stares at me for a few seconds, then bends down to check out Jessica.

"I'm Jessica Levine," she says, no longer sounding quite so coolly confident herself.

"Falla me," he says. The gate opens and the bodyguard begins trudging slowly up the driveway.

"Are we supposed to follow him in the car or on foot?" Jessica asks.

"You got me," I say. "Why don't you give him a friendly little toot on the horn and ask?" Jessica gives me a thanks-a-lot look, then eases up on the brakes and we begin creeping along behind our guide. After about a hundred feet, the driveway widens into a motor court that dwarfs any other I've seen. Of the half-dozen vehicles parked in it, Jessica's Lexus is easily the least valuable and most understated. There's a sunshine-yellow Mercedes convertible with a matching satellite dish mounted on the trunk lid; a Range Rover that has been lowered to within a few inches of the ground; a cigarette boat on a trailer, both of which bear the name "GETTIN BONED."

The bodyguard points us toward the far edge of the area, and Jessica parks next to an all-black Bentley. A guy who looks like he could be the bodyguard's big brother sits at the wheel of the Bentley, and he gives us the obligatory dead-eyed glare as we get out of the car. At the front door, our guide passes us off to a smoking-hot female assistant. I wish I could tell you what everybody's name is, but no one seems willing to share such secrets, even when Jessica and I stick out our hands and introduce ourselves. The first one of our hosts to volunteer any personal information is also the first who doesn't need to.

"Lovey Mack," he says, stepping forward to greet us as we enter the living room. "You must be Mr. Collins."

"Please call me Ted." Better yet, please call me a cab, because I can already see that this was a really bad idea. For while there may be some question as to the legitimacy of Boney's rap sheet, Lovey Mack's credentials as a violent felon are absolutely impeccable. The well-manicured hand that is presently shaking mine has been found guilty of choking the life out of one man, administering severe beatings to several others, and is alleged (but not proven) to have fired the gun that killed rap star Biggie Smalls. I don't see how he could ever get his fingers around a trigger, though, because each one of them is roughly the size of a salami and bears a ring that could double as a hood ornament.

"You got it, Ted," he says. "And who might this lovely young lady be?" He flashes a toothy smile at Jessica, who looks as though she's going to wet herself.

"This is Jessica Levine, one of our best producers."

"Pleasure to meet you, Jess'ca," Lovey says, then takes her

trembling hand and kisses it. Despite being about a hundred pounds overweight and smelling like the perfume department at Neiman Marcus, Lovey Mack sees himself as simply irresistible.

I suppose I should have prepared Jessica—and myself—for a possible encounter with Mr. Lovey Mack. He is after all the founder of Muthafuckin' Music, and therefore the undisputed God-muthafucka of West Coast rap. In my online research, I learned that Lovey personally discovered Boney, produced his first album, and appeared as a performer on many of the tracks, including the enigmatic ballad "Lovey Gonna F U Up". On the other hand, nobody said anything about him being involved with the *Mogul* shoot, and it is common knowledge that a judge ordered Lovey to divest himself of his interest in MF Music several years ago. But the main reason it didn't occur to me that he might be here is that he is supposed to be in prison.

"Boney, are you gonna be polite and greet your guests?" It's only when Lovey says this that I notice the small figure sitting behind him.

"Hey y'all," he says softly, without getting up. It is indeed Boney, but he is so far removed from his swaggering public persona, and the thuggish one I saw with my own eyes, that I wouldn't have recognized him if I wasn't standing inside his house. He is slumped on a couch in the darkest corner of the room, and is stark naked but for a pair of black thong underwear and mirrored shades. I introduce myself and Boney mumbles something incomprehensible in response, then takes a long pull from the bottle of Courvoisier he's holding between his knees.

"Don't worry, he'll be all right as soon as the cameras start rolling," Lovey says, before dropping into a more confidential tone. "The boy's having some woman troubles. I bet you know how that is, don'tcha Ted?"

"Absolutely," I say. Sometimes you just want to kill 'em.

"What do you want to do first, sit down and talk or take the tour?" Lovey asks.

"Maybe the tour," I say, and look at Jessica. She nods, which is good because I was starting to worry she'd gone catatonic on me.

"Right on," Lovey says. "Bone, you gonna show these folks around, or you want me to?"

"I do it," Boney says, lurching to his feet. "'S my muthafuckin' house." His first few steps are a little unsteady, but by the time he moves past us he's gotten the hang of it. "C'mon y'all," he orders.

We follow Boney into the grand entry hall. I find it a bit awkward to walk behind a man who's wearing nothing but a narrow ribbon that disappears between his butt cheeks, and I sense that Jessica is having the same issue because she suddenly seems very interested in everything on the walls, including the paint.

"This here's the Damn Nigga room," Boney slurs. "We call it that 'cause every time somebody come in the front door, first thing they say is 'Damn, nigga!'" On the assumption we are supposed to find this funny, I laugh. But Boney shoots me a hard look in response.

"You say that when you come in?" he demands.

"Uh, no," I say, stalling while I try to read him. "I was with Jessica here, so I said 'Damn, bitch!'" As every standup comic knows, there is no easier way to get a laugh than cussing to a drunk. Boney busts up and offers me his fist for a bump of solidarity.

"Damn, bitch!" he cackles. "From now on, this be the Damn Bitch room." To make it official, he demands bumps from Lovey and Jessica as well. No matter what else I get from this entire experience, it will be worth it just to have seen the uber-JAP Jessica Levine keepin' it real with a drunk rapper in a cock sock.

Boney continues to chug-a-lug Courvoisier as he shows us around the ground floor. It includes all the rooms and appointments customarily found in the homes of the rich and famous, albeit with some unconventional decorating touches. Hides of all kinds, both with and without fur, are the default choice for upholstery, area rugs, and toilet seats. I can't help but notice that there is at least one fire extinguisher mounted in every room, which I guess is a good idea if you and your guests frequently find yourselves ablaze. Jessica maintains a pretty good poker face throughout, even when Boney points out the gynecological stirrups attached to both ends of his billiards table.

"Y'all ready to check out the Boom-Boom room?" he asks as we return to the main hall.

"You mean that wasn't it?" I ask.

"*Hell* no," Boney replies, and we follow his ass crack up the big curving staircase to the second floor. His bedroom is vast, but not as vulgar as I expected based on the rest of the house. The bed is a run-of-the-mill king, and I can see no handcuffs, trapezes, or even provocatively-placed mirrors. The only sexually suggestive thing in the room hangs on the wall opposite the bed, and although I've seen it before, it startles me all the same: It's a poster-size, framed enlargement of the *Booty* magazine cover, featuring the nearly nude Patrice Williams.

Jessica notices the poster at the same time I do, and we both gawk at it.

"Isn't that the girl who's been in the news lately?" Jessica asks.

"'Fraid so," Lovey Mack says. "That's Boney's girlfriend, Patrice."

"She ain't my girl!" Boney shouts. "She ain't nothin' but a muthafuckin' ho." Boney stares menacingly at the poster. Lovey walks over and puts a brotherly arm around his shoulders.

"Ease up, dog. These folks don't need to hear you carryin' on about Patrice."

"Then get 'em the fuck out my house!" Boney pushes away from Lovey, who gives me what must be his idea of an apologetic look.

"It's okay," I say. "If my girlfriend was missing, I'd be upset too."

"Damn straight," Boney says. "'Specially if everybody be tryin' ta say you killed her."

"Ain't nobody sayin' that, now," Lovey says sharply, trying to nip the topic in the bud.

"Fuck they ain't. Police wanna know where I was every muthafuckin' minute. They got some chick-wit-a-dick detective wanna put my ass on death row. Not the record company neither, the real one." Boney glares again at Patrice. "I hope you happy, bitch!" He flings his Courvoisier bottle at the poster from five feet away yet somehow manages to miss. The bottle doesn't break, but leaves a big dent in the drywall and a brown stain on the carpet below. Boney stalks out of the room, leaving the other three of us at a momentary loss for words.

"Maybe this isn't the best time to do the episode," Jessica says, breaking the silence. Lovey Mack and I respond quickly and in almost perfect unison.

"No," we blurt, both of us really meaning, "Yes, it sure as shit is," although presumably not for the same reasons.

"We're totally committed, it's too late to change," I say by way of clarification.

"You don't have to worry about Boney, I'll set him straight," Lovey adds. Jessica looks at me like I'm crazy, then shrugs.

"You're the boss."

"Okay, let's get to work," Lovey says, motioning us toward the door. Before I follow him out, I step closer to the poster. Below the black male forearm that covers Patrice's left breast is a personal inscription: "The only hands I want touching me are yours, Baby. Love, PW."

Lovey, Jessica, and I sit around the dining room table for the next two hours, going over the *Mogul* shooting schedule. Lovey is accommodating to a fault, and Jessica soon returns to her usual efficiently annoying self. I chain-sip bottles of Fiji water in order to justify frequent bathroom breaks, but every time I get "lost" on my way back, a member of the household staff magically appears to redirect me. I thus have no opportunity to look for dead people or other clues, but I console myself with the knowledge that snooping will become much easier once our production crew arrives and starts breaking everything. We don't see any more of Boney, although an occasional distant crash and/or "Muthafucka!" confirm that he is still at large.

Lovey's phone rings repeatedly during our meeting but he only answers it once, to talk to yet another person named "Dog." This particular canine must be a major player, because Lovey promises him floor seats for tonight's Laker game plus a super-stretch to get him there. He then hangs up and apologizes for this interruption by his pain-in-the-ass parole officer. Lovey summons the entire entourage one by one and orders them to introduce themselves, which is how we learn that Boney's bodyguard is named Delawn, and that his absurdly buxom personal assistant answers to "Peaches." Lovey makes sure everyone understands they are to cooperate with us fully, and while none of the staff overtly complains, their body language suggests that they might as well be getting marched into the hold of a slave ship.

Our business concluded for the day, we thank Lovey and tell him we'll be back in force at the crack of dawn. As we drive past the gate on our way out, I offer a jaunty wave to Delawn, who evidently feels that "cooperation" does not include much in the way of social niceties. He flips me off.

Jessica immediately begins whining about the trauma to which she has just been subjected, reminding me that she is a graduate of NYU Film School and has way too much self-respect to allow herself to be sexually harassed. I tell her no offense, but I don't think Boney was attracted to her, and that we certainly would have been able to tell if he was. Jessica doesn't find this amusing, but I calm her down by wildly overstating what a great job she did, and promising to take her with me when I leave my present post in order to produce the exciting new series Trevor and I are doing for MTV. Of course Jessica's professed interest in working for me on a show no one's heard of is pure bullshit, but her desire to position herself as my replacement on *The Mogul* is genuine. She therefore does what I'm praying she'll do, which is shut her pie hole and let me think.

"Pull over there," I abruptly command, pointing to the first gas station I see. "I gotta pee again." Jessica steers her Lexus into the station, and decides she might as well fill 'er up while I empty 'er out. I get the restroom key from the attendant, but after making sure Jessica isn't watching, I trot over to the phone booth in the far corner of the lot. By now, I know the number by heart.

"Detective DeRosa," she answers.

"Ah say ah say, little darling. Yours truly has had a most interesting day."

"Yeah? How was Boney?"

"Ah would have to describe the boy as bereft. He's runnin' around drunker than a redskin on Columbus Day."

"What else?" she says.

"Mistah Lovey Mack was also present, and ah must say ah found him to be a most agreeable fellow."

"Of course he's going to be agreeable. You're the co-executive producer of a big TV show."

"True," I say, in the second before my brain can IM me a reminder that this is information Detective DeRosa is not supposed to have. I drop the receiver and spin around to run, but there isn't much point because she is right behind me, sitting at the wheel of a Ford Explorer with a cell phone to her ear. She lowers her window and offers me what I guess is meant to be a consoling look.

"Ah say ah say," she says.

chapter ten

I AM ABLE TO convince Detective Susan DeRosa that my colleague Jessica doesn't know anything about Boney and Patrice, and we should keep it that way. I tell Jessica that "Sue" is an old friend I just ran into, and that she's offered to give me a ride back to the office so we can catch up. Even in my numb shock at what's happening, I can't help but notice that Jessica takes an instant dislike to Sue—there's nothing like the entrance of Attractive Female #2 to make Attractive Female #1 suddenly fear she might be missing something.

We get in Detective DeRosa's Explorer, and she suggests that we talk at a restaurant outside the immediate area, so as to avoid any chance encounters with Boney and his posse. I'm only too happy to agree, because you usually don't get booked and fingerprinted at a restaurant.

"You're not under arrest," she says.

"What happens if I get out of the car and walk away?"

"I'd probably arrest you."

"Then I guess we'll stick with Plan A."

"Tell me about the first time you saw Boney," she says as she pulls onto the Ventura Freeway headed west.

"Before we get to that, do you mind telling me how you figured out who I am?"

"It wasn't too hard. I'm sure you're a great TV producer, but you're a lousy spy."

"That's not true. I happen to be an extremely mediocre

producer."

"You told me you were going to meet with Boney today, so I staked out the house. I ran the license plate on your friend's car, contacted her landlord to find out where she works, then called her office and found out she was with you."

"So now everybody at work knows the cops are sniffing around?"

"Nope. I said I was Linda from Editing."

"Pretty good," I'm forced to acknowledge. "You must be tough to cheat on."

At Detective DeRosa's request, I describe in detail the altercation I witnessed between Patrice and Boney, including when and where it occurred. This requires me to reveal my supervised visitation arrangement, and to offer a brief explanation as to how a nice and gentle guy like me came to be mislabeled as a dangerous psychopath. I stress that I never hit or even threatened Sara, and that when I took Richard's car on a joyride through his house, he wasn't even home. The detective accepts (or at least doesn't challenge) my reasoning as to why I tried to remain anonymous in my dealings with her. I give her the short version of how I used the *Mogul* ratings crisis plus Richard's craven opportunism to gain access to the suspect's hideout, and an account of today's first visit.

"Seems like you're going to an awful lot of trouble just to satisfy your curiosity," she says when I'm done.

"It's a little more than that." I hesitate for a moment, then decide I have nothing to lose by letting her in on the master plan. "I'm planning to write a big story about this, maybe even a book. See, I'm really an investigative reporter."

"You mean you're not really a producer?"

"No. Well, sort of. I mean, the job is real, but it's not really who I am."

"No offense, but are you one of those guys who's never been who you really are?"

"No," I say after giving it some thought. "I was doing

pretty well until my marriage bit the dust."

"Yeah?"

"Yeah. I was working for the *New York Times*, and doing a lot of magazine stuff on the side. But I got blindsided by the divorce, and I did a little acting out in my professional life."

"Burned some bridges, did we?"

"Actually, we burned all the bridges. The tunnels, too."

"I understand," she says. "I went through a divorce myself a few years back, and it was hard not to let it affect my work."

"You shoot anybody?"

"Nobody important."

She chooses as our lunch destination a restaurant overlooking the sailboats in Marina del Rey, perhaps on the theory that there aren't many African American yachtsmen. Since it's now the middle of the afternoon, there aren't many other customers of any kind. We take a table by the window, and I get my first good head-on look at Detective DeRosa. Although her hair is brown like what's left of mine, her eyes are a dark gray-blue, which I find both intriguing and somehow soothing. Her lips are full, which I like, but not overly so, as you see so much of these days courtesy of collagen. (There are a couple of girls at the office who make Angelina Jolie look like she misplaced her dentures.) I guess the thing I like best about Detective DeRosa is that she's one of the very few good-looking women who don't become less so after you hear them talk.

"So," she says, "you don't think Boney had anything to do with Patrice's disappearance?"

"I don't know. He seemed really upset about it."

"That doesn't mean he's innocent. I hear O.J. still gets all misty when he thinks about decapitating Nicole."

"What about the photographer Patrice was supposed to meet?"

"There wasn't one."

"What do you mean?" I say, surprised.

"Before we go any further, we need to set a few ground rules."

"Such as?"

"Such as you can't share any confidential information I give you with anyone else, for as long as Patrice Williams is missing."

"What if you never find her?" I ask. Detective DeRosa frowns at the notion.

"You still have to wait six months," she says.

"Three."

"Four and a half, and not one day less." I extend my hand and we shake on the deal.

"Anything else that could get me an official police spanking?" She abruptly withdraws from the handshake.

"The only other rule is, you have to tell me everything you know as soon as you know it."

"Gee, is that all?"

"In exchange, I'll tell you everything I can, so long as it doesn't jeopardize the investigation."

"Who gets to decide that?"

"Me, of course."

"You drive a hard bargain, Detective. But I'm in." I offer her my hand again, but this time she ignores it.

"In answer to your question about the photographer," she says, "I think Patrice invented him. She didn't have anything written down on her calendar, and her modeling agency didn't book anything for her that day."

"Maybe she was trying to do some work on the side, so she didn't have to pay a commission."

"I thought about that, but everybody I talked to says it'd never happen. If anyone from the agency saw one of the pictures in a magazine or a catalog, they'd dump her and nobody else would pick her up. They make sure all the models know that."

"What if the photographer promised her the pictures would only be for his private use?"

"Anything's possible," she shrugs. "But this girl's career is pretty hot, and she's had a lot of generous boyfriends. It's hard to imagine her agreeing to pose for some random guy's beat-off album."

"Okay, let's say she made the whole thing up," I say. "The question is why."

"Presumably as a cover for what she was really doing."

"Or who she was really doing."

"Yeah. You saw for yourself that Boney has some jealousy issues. We know from the phone records that ever since he and Patrice first started seeing each other, either he or one of his homeys calls her every half hour, day and night."

"Saying she was on a shoot would be a good excuse to shut her phone off for a while."

"That's what I'm thinking, Foghorn."

"So Patrice tells everyone she's got a gig, and instead she drives to The Grove. Then what?"

"Depends on what she has in mind. She could be meeting somebody for lunch, but that'd be pretty risky, considering that every asshole in the free world is walking around there." The Grove is a wildly popular outdoor mall in Hollywood, where all the leading national "lifestyle" retailers and upscale restaurant chains are clustered around a megaplex movie theater.

"You mean you don't like to hang out at The Grove?" I say.

"I'd rather hang out in hell."

"Will you marry me?"

"Let's try to stick to the subject. Say you're Boney and you think Patrice is messing around on you. What would you do if she tells you she has a photo shoot?"

"I guess I'd try to find out if she really does."

"Like maybe by having another female call the modeling agency, claiming to be Patrice, saying she just wants to confirm the time and location?"

"Did somebody do that?"

"From Boney's house, two hours before Patrice left her

apartment. Whoever it was talked to an assistant, who told her there must be a mistake because there wasn't anything on the schedule." I'm impressed, and I'm not afraid to say so.

"Wow. You're some kind of dick."

"The words every girl longs to hear."

"So do you think Boney followed her?" I ask.

"I think he had somebody else do it for him. The security video at The Grove shows that Patrice's BMW arrived at the garage at 1:17 PM. Around 1:30, a large African American male was seen hurrying down the sidewalk on 3rd Street. He ran into another pedestrian and almost knocked him down."

"Is that on the surveillance tape too?"

"Unfortunately, no," she says. "But the big guy must have made quite an impression, because three different witnesses were able to pick him out of a photo lineup." She takes a photo from her shirt pocket and hands it to me. "Delawn Purvis, Boney's bodyguard."

"Holy shit," I say, looking at a mug shot of an extra-sullen Delawn. "They really killed her."

"Maybe," she says.

"What do you think this dude was doing there, shopping for placemats at Pottery Barn?"

"Let's assume he was following Patrice. She could have been meeting somebody in the garage and leaving in that person's car, but if so why was Delawn on foot?"

"Because her final destination was within walking distance," I say after a moment of consideration. "There's all kinds of motels and apartments around there, and if anybody spots her car at The Grove, she can just say she was shopping."

"Not bad," Detective DeRosa nods. "Maybe you have a little dick in you too."

"I'm going to ignore that," I say. "Have you showed her picture to all the property managers and desk clerks in the area?"

"Yeah," she says. "Nobody recognizes her, but maybe that's because her date took care of the arrangements."

"So what do you do next?"

"Keep digging. Try to find out who Patrice was seeing on the side. Mostly keep tabs on Boney and Delawn."

"Why not arrest them, or at least search the house and the cars?"

"My captain doesn't think we have enough to get a warrant, and he's probably right."

"I guess that's where I fit in," I say. "I'm your eyes and ears inside the Bone yard."

"It's not my first choice of how to conduct an investigation," she says. "No offense."

"None taken. Although I would like to point out that I'm a pretty resourceful guy and a trained observer."

"Yeah? What color is the leather on my car seats, brown or black?"

"Brown."

"Black. And they're cloth."

"You got me," I acknowledge. "Now, what color is that thing between your teeth?" She reflexively blushes and covers her mouth with her napkin, while using a fingernail to search for a food particle that isn't there. "And I got you, babe," I say. She throws the napkin in my face. Progress.

By the time Detective DeRosa delivers me back to the office, I'm seriously late for what is known officially as the Contingency Planning meeting, and unofficially as FWC—our double-top-secret code for Fucking With the Contestants. This is the vitally important session when all of us *Mogul* producers put our heads together and decide what fiendish obstacles we're going to throw at the cast during the upcoming episode. As an example, had we gone ahead as planned with the Celine Dion concert, we were prepared to pay a hefty bribe to a Las Vegas dry cleaner to temporarily "lose" the gown Celine had planned to wear on stage. To further complicate matters, the claim ticket would supposedly be in a file folder that had been entrusted to one of the contestants, and which one of our field producers would have swiped from said contestant at an opportune, off-camera moment. The requirements for a successful FWC are to create a grave crisis ("Celine refuses to go on without that gown!"), and to make sure it results in plenty of finger-pointing among the cast members ("Maybe you wouldn't have lost the file if you weren't so busy flashing your [BLEEP] at Mr. Dominus!") I used to ask myself which was more amazing, the fact that the audience falls for such obviously contrived horse-shit week after week, or the fact that a mix-up at the dry cleaners has become the stuff of modern drama. But that was back before I became the Shiznit.

I take my place at the head of the conference table and ask Jessica to summarize what has been discussed so far. The most intriguing idea comes from Mfume Salaam, the first African American, first Harvard graduate, and first former contestant to ascend to the upper echelons of Trevor Banes Productions. He was clearly the strongest competitor during the first season of *The Mogul*, and Trevor kept him in the game right to the very end. But just as America isn't quite ready for a president named Hillary, it isn't quite ready for a mogul named Mfume. So the first big winner was the long-since forgotten Dave, but either because Trevor felt guilty (which I highly doubt) or because he knows a bargain when he sees one, he offered Mfume a job as a field producer on *Castaway*. Mfume graciously turned it down, but after a German bank bought out the Wall Street firm where he was working and fired Mfume's entire department, he called Trevor to see if the opportunity was still available. It was, and the smart money says that if Trevor ever anoints a successor, it will likely be Mfume. That would certainly be an admirable and ironic completion of the circle for Trevor, who once upon a time fled South Africa to avoid being fitted for a flaming tire.

Mfume's pitch for an FWC is to reap maximum advantage from our guest star—Boney—by arranging an encounter with those people most likely to be offended by him. The overall story calls for the two contestant teams to devise and execute marketing campaigns for Boney's upcoming album, *Wuh Duh Fuh U Lookin At?* Since the teams will have minimal budgets and even less time, their efforts will necessarily be of the grass-roots variety, i.e. hawking the CD on the street, or convincing a DJ in a local club to play it, which will cause the hottest cast members to strip spontaneously to their skivvies on the dance floor. (Since we're pointing out ironies, please note that while the premise of the episode is that these small-scale promotions are the key to success in the current fractured media landscape, the only reason anyone would actually bother with such lemonade stand-style efforts is to tape them for the benefits of the millions who never go anywhere or do anything, except watch TV and buy things they see there.)

Mfume proposes that as soon as we know which shopping mall or other public place the contestants have chosen for their direct-sales approach, we fax in anonymous tips to the local chapters of all the conservative "decency in media" groups, advising them of the exact time and place that the next abomination will be taking place. I point out that some of these groups may not have heard of Boney, but Mfume is way ahead of me, having transcribed all of the lyrics on *Wuh Duh Fuh* and attaching copies of same to generic (as in sender unidentified) fax cover sheets. I can't help but chuckle as I imagine someone at the neo-Fascist Focus on the American Family reading the words of "Don't Cry, My Brother," which begins:

> *Don't cry, my brother, just 'cause I block your shot so bad I bust your muthafuckin' nose.*
> *Don't cry, just 'cause I get with your old lady and now she be havin my lil' muthafucka.*
> *Don't cry, my brother, or I be bustin' a cap right in your eyeball.*

Although Jessica and a majority of the other producers

object strenuously, insisting that *The Mogul* is not the proper forum for such highly charged cultural collisions, I give Mfume the thumbs up. Who knows, maybe we'll actually make an interesting show. At the very least, we'll give Rush Limbaugh another reason to jiggle his gelatinous jowls.

Just to be safe, I also approve several standard-issue FWCs, such as setting off the fire alarm during the big dance scene at the nightclub, which should provide the double benefit of forcing our contestants to improvise a new promotional plan, and forcing several of the more shapely ones out onto Hollywood Boulevard in their underwear. (I make a note that if at all possible, I should be present for the shooting of this scene.) I also consider but reject a suggestion to tell one of the contestants on camera that her mother might have breast cancer, not because it isn't true (it's more of an exaggeration than an outright lie, since her mother does indeed have a routine mammogram scheduled, and why have a mammogram unless you might have breast cancer?); or because it isn't nice (the contestants have all signed releases explicitly authorizing us to be "cruel, manipulative, deceitful, and/or hateful" in our pursuit of reality); but because it isn't original—a few weeks back, we told one of the other contestants that his father might have to part with one of his balls. Let it never be said that Ted Collins compromises when it comes to Art.

chapter eleven

THE DAY FLIES by so quickly that I almost forget to call Hallie before she goes to bed, something I haven't done since the last time I was in jail. She's pretty short with me on the phone, giving one-word answers to my questions about her day, and refusing even to acknowledge my impression of Madonna trying to sing "Like a Virgin" after she's gone senile. It's pretty clear that Hallie thinks I'm full of caca about our promised shopping trip, and why shouldn't she? So far, the net result of my big promotion, which I only accepted in the hope that it would lead to more time with Hallie, has been to give me less. I still believe it can work out the way I planned, but if it keeps up like this I'll eventually have to acknowledge that I'm kidding myself and give the whole thing up. And give it up I will, because a life without Hallie would be no life at all.

I bring a long and exhausting day to a close by meeting Deb for a near-beer. I tell her all about Boney, Lovey, and getting busted by Detective DeRosa. I don't want to give Deb any indication of my romantic interest in the detective, because she tends to view all of my potential mates with distrust. This is either because I tend to make poor choices (and I will concede that there is some evidence to that effect), or because Deb still has a vestigial, irrational sense that I belong to her. I'm no evolutionary sociologist, but if I were, this would make a fascinating research thesis—the bedrock of female sexuality is not the desire to fornicate, nor even to procreate. It is the desire for a good cat fight.

In my fatigue, however, I let my guard down and one time refer to Detective DeRosa as "Susan." That's all it takes.

"Susan?" Deb pounces. "Who the fuck is that?"

"Detective DeRosa."

"Did she tell you to call her Little Susie?"

"I don't remember," I lie. "Why?"

"Because this is an extremely dangerous situation, and you shouldn't trust a cop whose primary concern is wiggling her ass at you."

"Trust me, she's not wiggling her ass."

"That's what you said about Sara, remember? Just before you accidentally fucked her and ruined your life." Although this assertion is both unkind and uncalled for, there is a small kernel of truth in it. When I first met Sara, our relationship was theoretically professional. She was working as a development executive ("D Girl" in the common parlance) for a TV movie producer, and therefore her job was to scour the newspapers and magazines for potentially entertaining human misery. She contacted me after reading a story I wrote for *Harper's* about a ten-year-old boy named Pablo who hitchhiked by himself from Honduras to L.A. in an unsuccessful effort to find his mother. Sara and I had a lunch meeting, and although I found her to be attractive and fun, I also found her to be as dumb as dirt. I might have been more inclined to overlook her intellectual shortcomings and ask her out, but at the time I was dating Hannah, a photographer who was good company, good (enough) in bed, and had the unprecedented distinction of meeting with Deb's grudging approval. (In fact, the only serious spat Deb and I have had in the last two decades occurred after I broke up with Hannah. Deb swiftly seduced her, then informed me that she had cleared up some silly misconceptions Hannah had about the location of her G-spot. But I digress.)

Deb insisted that Sara's true interest was in me, not my story. Deb didn't believe that any of the networks would be willing to make a movie about a pre-pubescent Latino, and as usual, she was blunt about it.

"Who's going to play little Pablo, Freddie Prinze Jr.?"

I kept hoping for the big Hollywood score, though, and so I continued to accept Sara's invitations for lunches and drinks, even after it became clear that she hadn't even finished reading my *Harper's* piece. In my defense, I can only say that my mom was still alive back then, and she loved TV movies (although she sure didn't give a shit about Pablo). When Sara asked me to come to a dinner party at her place, I went alone, on the rationale that this was the correct business decision, and that even if Sara's intentions were not honorable, mine were. The two elements I failed to factor in were: (a) alcohol; and (b) testosterone. When you put those two together and stir, good intentions don't stand a chance. I thus discovered that Sara was way more than good enough in bed, and after allowing my relationship with Hannah to run its course (which it did by approximately 11:25 the next morning), I entered into the most physically passionate period of my life.

Sara and I made love around the clock, pausing only for work, food, and bladder infections. Deb warned me about the possibility of pregnancy, but Sara was supposedly on the pill and I frankly didn't even care. I don't know if I accept the romantic conceit that there is a single perfect person out there for me, but I have come to believe that there is a single perfect vagina. And at the time, I lacked the emotional maturity to separate the two. So when Sara broke down one night and told me she'd missed her period, I started crying too and said I hoped she would have my baby. After it was confirmed that my wish was going to come true, I took the traditional step of asking her father for her hand in marriage. I was only a little disconcerted when he burst out laughing before bestowing his blessing, and he explained his odd behavior by claiming to have thought of a great joke he'd heard earlier in the day about Monica Lewinsky. Sara and I had a perfect wedding, a perfect daughter, and might have had a perfect marriage had we not belatedly discovered that we couldn't stand each other.

But that's all ancient history, and I refuse to let Deb keep raking me over the coals about it.

"Detective DeRosa is just doing her job, and so am I," I say.

"Sure, whatever," Deb replies. "But just before you get off, I want you to think about engaging in a bitter custody battle with a woman who's packing heat."

I get home just in time to catch the late news, courtesy of my neighbor, the Skipper. Since there has been nothing new for days regarding the disappearance of Patrice Williams, Channel 6 has nearly run out of breathless bulletins to issue on the subject. Neither the print nor broadcast media have even discovered that she was dating Boney, which should be pitifully easy for any enterprising reporter to do. I guess they haven't because the kind of journalist who works at the *Times* considers him- or herself to be above missing bimbo stories, and the kind of journalist who works at a local TV station is a moron. (I'm bending over backwards here not to generalize.) Tonight, *Action News* can do no better than to tell us that Patrice's whereabouts remain unknown, and to use her occupation as a segue into a hard-hitting exposé about some *Maxim* models cavorting on a beach in Brazil. I may not have a printable story yet, but the competition isn't exactly breathing down my neck.

Perhaps this is why I am able to bag five drug-free hours of shuteye, a feat I'd like to see Rip Van Winkle or even George W. Bush pull off under my current circumstances. I rush through the shower, shave, and clothing selection procedures (the latter of which consists of determining which shirt looks most misleadingly clean), and I'm on the road ahead of morning rush hour. In twenty-first century Los Angeles, this unfortunately does not mean that I am able to fly along at whatever speed suits my fancy, passing only the occasional milk truck. It means that although every lane of every freeway is choked with vehicles, and has been around the clock since around 1986, as a reward for rising in the middle of the night I will be granted an amount of airspace approximately 10 percent larger than my car. And if I am as nimble as Jackie Chan and as lucky as David Schwimmer, I just might be able to ride that little pocket all the way to my exit without ever being forced to come to a dead stop.

This is more or less what happens on my trip to North Hollywood, although I do have a few stressful moments when the driver of a school bus uses her horn and high beams to indicate that at 68 mph, I am slowing her down. I change lanes as quickly as I can, and although I'm not all that shocked when every single student on the right side of the bus flips me off as they pass, it is a little troubling to see a pint-size lad with braces brandishing a handgun.

If you didn't know better, you might conclude from the number of production vehicles parked on Boney's street that we had chosen this unlikely location to recreate the siege of Troy. Another of Trevor's innovations that everybody in the Reality game now takes for granted was to assign a separate field producer/camera team to each and every contestant, plus several more to capture the bigger picture. The reasoning is that since our stars are essentially amateur improv actors being thrust into inherently dull situations, not every word out of their mouths is likely to be scintillating. So when one of the contestants *does* say something worthwhile, whether by sheer serendipity or (most often) by repeating verbatim a suggestion from a desperate field producer, you damn well better have a camera there to record it. The downside of this overwhelming-force approach to production is that it results in thousands of hours of video that some unfortunate souls must watch and "log." In layman's terms, logging is the tricky task of ingesting enough stimulants that you'll be awake when someone utters something intelligible, but not so much that you'll be too jittery to write it down.

The Mogul is out in such force this morning that if I were just any fuckwad, I would be obliged to park two full blocks from Boney's house. Since I am the co-executive fuckwad, however, I am entitled to a space in the driveway. The only problem is that the overweight, off-duty LAPD officer who we are paying to control access to this highly coveted real estate clearly doesn't believe that anybody important would be driving a dinged-up Subaru.

"You have a business card, my friend?" he asks. I am tempted to put my friend in his fat fucking place, but I curb the impulse by imagining him trying and failing to look at his penis without a mirror. I fish a card from my wallet and hand it to him.

"I don't see where it says 'Executive Producer'," he announces. "You'll have to park this thing on the street." The blood rushes to my face and my fingers to the door handle. Officer Stubby-Chubby and I are almost certainly headed for mutually assured destruction, when a familiar voice catches us both unawares.

"Is that my man Ted Collins?" Lovey Mack booms as he approaches, having abandoned his Bentley and driver in the middle of the street. Although Lovey is a notorious criminal and his very presence here arguably constitutes a violation of his parole, the officer comes to attention as though he were the supreme commander of Allied Forces.

"Good morning, Mr. Mack," the cop says.

"You ask me, it's still nighttime," Lovey says. The cop laughs and shakes Lovey's hand, in the course of which a piece of folded US currency passes from the latter to the former. It's so smooth and routine that I feel like I'm watching Fred Astaire grease the maitre d' at "21."

"I almost didn't recognize you," Lovey says, turning to me. "Where's the homeless dude you jacked that car from supposed to sleep tonight?" I chuckle at my own expense and shake Lovey's hand, but alas I come away with no gratuity. I do receive the cop's grudging permission to park in the driveway, however, and after I do so, Lovey and I walk toward the house together.

"Boney oughta be in lots better shape today," Lovey says. "I had the doc give him something to help him sleep."

"I guess he's pretty worried about his girlfriend, huh?"

"Yeah," he says, shaking his head. "I keep telling him 'Relax, the ho's gonna show.'"

"How can you be sure something bad hasn't happened to her?" I ask.

"You mean something bad like a bullet?"

"Okay," I nod as though this hadn't previously occurred to me. "Something like that."

"As you mighta heard, I know somethin' about the bullet business," Lovey says. "People almost always get shot for a good reason."

"So maybe somebody had a good reason."

"The only person with a good reason to kill that girl is Boney," he says. "And he didn't do it." I'm not about to press my luck further by asking him how he knows this, but I don't have to. "The dumbass really loves that nasty lil' slut."

"I see," I tell him. But the truth is, I'm more confused than ever. Has Boney somehow managed to fool Lovey, despite the latter's experience and savvy in all matters of the heart and of homicide? Or is Lovey actually in the know about what happened to Patrice, and simply trying to protect Boney by throwing me and everyone else off the scent? Or is it possible that in this instance, Lovey is being both wise and honest, meaning that Patrice is alive and well, and I am chasing a non-story?

As excellent as all of these questions are, they'll have to wait. I have not one but two very full agendas for the day, the first of which is to produce a prime-time TV show, and the second of which is to snoop around for sufficient evidence to send the guest star to prison, or worse. Yes, I have considered the possibility that if Boney and Delawn are guilty of murder and duly convicted, they could receive the death penalty. And while I'm theoretically opposed to capital punishment, I don't foresee any moral crisis should that come to pass—it takes so many years for the state of California to get around to gassing anybody, I'll be too old to remember that I had anything to do with it.

Detective DeRosa has given me an ambitious set of goals, with the top priority being to pinpoint exactly where Delawn lives. Police surveillance has indicated that the massive bodyguard rarely leaves the property, so he must have his own room either somewhere in the main house or above the six-car garage. If I locate Delawn's quarters and I have enough time, I am to slip on a pair of rubber gloves and search for torn and/or blood-stained garments, shoes, etc. I'm under strict orders not to remove anything, though, because this would almost certainly lead to future legal challenges by the defense, and in any case the big lesson of the O.J. murder trial is that local juries are not overly impressed by science. (Actually, it's unfair to single out the good citizens of Los Angeles in this regard—a solid majority of Americans believe that while Darwin's *Origin of Species* and everything that followed in its path are baseless speculation, the Bible is objective reportage. By comparison, this makes the Simpson jurors look like Nobel laureates.) Detective DeRosa's plan is to gather enough details about the crime so that when she confronts Delawn with them, he will confess and rat out Boney. This sounds workable, but I would definitely prefer to be among the observers in the dark little room on the other side of the two-way mirror, rather than one of those assigned to break Delawn.

Our production personnel are milling about in the motor court, drinking coffee and ogling Boney's fleet. Lovey and I go our separate ways, with him continuing into the house and me trying to look like I'm in charge. I spot Deb among the troops, but I make only the briefest of eye contact, not wanting to call any extra attention to her. We have already divvied up the spying duties, with me looking for Delawn's digs while Deb seeks to gather whatever human intelligence she can by kickin' it with Boney's staff. Meanwhile, the show must go on, but I see no reason why Jessica, Mfume, and the other field producers shouldn't be able to handle it without any input from me.

"We've got a big problem," a frazzled Jessica says as soon as I approach.

"Which is?"

"Boney's bodyguard—that Delawn guy, you know who I'm talking about?"

"I think so," I say. "Tall, dark, and handsome?"

"He comes out here a few minutes ago and wants to know what kind of car Roger Dominus will be arriving in. I tell him a charcoal-gray Maybach. He goes inside for a minute, then comes back and says he can't."

"Delawn seems like a fair-minded fellow. I'm sure he had a perfectly reasonable explanation."

"Apparently Boney just got a charcoal-gray Maybach, and he says it has to be parked right in front of the door when Roger arrives," Jessica says. "Either Boney or Delawn must be getting paid by the car people."

"So why don't we just ask Roger's people to use one of his other limos?"

"I just got off the phone with them, and Roger says he's either coming in the Maybach or he's not coming at all."

"Sounds like a case of dueling kickbacks," I observe.

"Exactly," she whines, on the verge of hysteria. "What are you going to do about it?"

The first thing I do is silently congratulate myself for not sleeping with Jessica. Then I get an idea. I catch the eye of Myron, the PA, and wave him over.

"What's up, boss?" he says, trotting to my side.

"I want you to go out back and measure the lawn," I tell him.

"The whole thing? It's really big."

"I need something a little more precise than that, Myron."

"Okay, boss." Myron dashes away. I take out my cell phone and speed-dial HQ.

"What are you doing?" Jessica asks. "This isn't *Jerry Springer*; we can't park a car on the lawn." I shush her so I can concentrate on my call.

"Trevor Bane's office."

"Tanya, this is Ted Collins. I need you to connect me with Trevor in China right away."

"Eat shit," she says prior to putting me on hold, but I nevertheless have a strong hunch I'll get through. Sure enough, not twenty seconds later, Trevor's voice comes across the line loud and clear.

"What's the trouble, Ted?"

"Nothing major," I say. "But we could use a little help from your friends in Washington." I briefly summarize the double-Maybach dilemma, and my proposed solution, which is to have Roger arrive not in any make of car but rather in his Bell Jet Ranger helicopter. In addition to the statement that such an entrance makes about the penile magnitude of the passenger, Roger relishes any opportunity to reinforce his brand. And while he is too tasteful to have "DOMINUS" painted across the side of his automobiles, he has no similar compunctions about his aircraft. Roger is forever coming up with thin pretexts as to why we should use his prominently labeled planes or choppers in *Mogul* episodes, and he would no doubt take the latter to the market to pick up a quart of milk were it not for the pesky FAA regulations as to where you can land one. It is these same rules which stand in the way of my present plan to turn Boney's backyard into a temporary helipad.

"That shouldn't be a problem," Trevor says. "Give me thirty minutes to make some calls, then have the pilot check with air traffic control." The reason Trevor can be so confident of his ability to secure the cooperation of Homeland Security et al. is because he served as one of the executive producers of the last presidential inauguration. This doesn't mean that he was in charge of the event, of course—he had very little creative input, no authority, and was obliged to pay $500,000 for the privilege of being politely ignored. But when he needs little favors, like having a US Navy carrier battle group shoo the paparazzi away from his *Castaway* locations, or permission to land a helicopter in a quiet residential district, it's a nice credit to have on his resumé.

"Are you having any other difficulties?" Trevor asks me.

"No, it's all coming together," I tell him. "Any problems over there?" I expect Trevor to dismiss the question as another example of my impertinence, but he doesn't.

"It's a bloody nightmare," he sighs, the first time I've ever heard him sound fatigued. "We've got hundreds of protestors showing up every place we try to shoot. They claim we're out to destroy the dignity of China."

"That's ridiculous. Why would we care about that?"

"Trust me, Ted. There's no reasoning with the little yellow bastards."

"Well, there's always the Tiananmen Square solution," I say. Trevor doesn't immediately reply, and I suddenly remember that he is severely irony-deficient. His silence suggests that he is seriously considering rolling in the tanks.

"I didn't really mean—" I hasten to clarify, but he cuts me off.

"I must ring off now," he says. "Good luck today." The line goes dead and a chill runs some quick laps up and down my spine. Trevor wouldn't really . . . he *couldn't* really . . . Christ, I better play it safe and stay away from CNN.

chapter twelve

OUR ASSISTANT DIRECTORS clear the motor court and Delawn brings the victorious Maybach over from the garage. Once it has been positioned in such a way that you can't reach the front door to the house without climbing over it, we are ready to shoot our first scene—the five remaining contestants arriving by van. Since they supposedly don't yet know who lives here or what their next assignment will be, their instructions are to look mildly puzzled as they step out and survey the surroundings. Greenhorns have a tendency to overact, however, and on the first take they all go as wide-eyed as Dorothy when she wakes up in Oz. This is the sort of workaday challenge that Jessica excels at addressing, and by the time she's finished reaming the contestants through her bullhorn, their phony-baloney wonderment has been replaced by some very credible gun-shyness.

I learn that Trevor has prevailed as promised with the aviation authorities, and so we move our cameras to the rear lawn to capture the landing of Roger's whirlybird. Mfume has another brainstorm, which he runs past me and I enthusiastically endorse. We radio to Roger's pilot to circle for a few minutes while we hustle our three female contestants off to the wardrobe trailer. Once they have returned and everyone is in position on the edge of the lawn, we summon Roger from the sky, and because all of the women are now wearing short, summer-weight dresses, they have a heck of a time maintaining their modesty in the helicopter's hurricane-force rotor wash. LaFonda, our resident skank, is particularly unsuccessful in this regard, allowing her dress to fly up completely over her head. This exposes a fetching bra-and-panty set that just happens to be on the cover of the current Victoria's Secret catalog. It's a pretty racy moment by *Mogul* standards, and one which the Trevor and the network may not want to spend much political capital defending to the FCC. Unless, of course, Victoria wants to cough up some serious scratch.

Rotor wash and Roger's hair don't mix, so we all wait while the engine is shut off and the blades slowly come to a complete stop. The Mogul then emerges, looking as natty as ever in a navy Zegna suit. This is one of two uniforms Roger wears, the other consisting of golf shirts and slacks from the Dominus Collection. We had a brief debate at our production meeting as to whether this visit to Boney's crib called for business or casual wear, and opted for the former on the grounds of racial sensitivity—when Roger is dressed for the links, he tends to treat everyone around him like a caddy. As the cameras roll, Roger strides across the lawn to where the contestants are lined up and gives a very professional delivery of the portion of the script he's been able to memorize.

"Good morning," he says. The rest of Roger's speech, like all of his others, comes in the form of a call-and-response with Sandy, our script supervisor, who stands just off camera.

"How are you feeling?" Sandy says.

"How are you feeling?" Roger asks the contestants.

"Great, Mr. Dominus," they reply.

"Are you ready for something a little different?" Sandy says.

"Are you ready for something a little different?" Roger repeats.

"Sure," say the contestants.

"Good," says Sandy.

"Good," says Roger, and so on. At the beginning of each season this system takes some getting used to, and one of the nervous contestants inevitably answers a question before Roger has had a chance to ask it. But it only takes a single application of The Look to ensure that doesn't happen again, and by this point in the game we have the opposite problem—if Roger says something that Sandy didn't say first, no one is sure if it really counts.

Using this three-words-and-a-cloud-of-dust approach, it takes Roger the better part of an hour to explain today's mission. For dramatic purposes, we have decided to withhold the identity of our guest star until he makes his entrance, and so Roger refers to him only as "a major hip-hop artist whose happening sound we've all been groovin' to for a long time." We give Roger half a dozen tries to get this line just right, and each time I feel badly for the contestants, since they are the only people present who can't clamp their hands over their mouths to keep from howling.

I soon grow tired from the effort of stifling my own laughter, and duck into the house. I find Lovey and Boney sitting at the kitchen table, drinking Dr. Peppers and watching the shoot unfold through the window.

"You tellin' me this shit's the biggest thing on TV?" Boney says when he sees me. Despite this rather cool reception, I am relieved to see that he is both fully clothed and ostensibly sober.

"It moves a lot faster after we edit it," I tell him.

"Thanks," Boney says. "That be the kind of information that us stupid niggas need."

"I didn't mean to—"

"He knows you didn't," Lovey interjects. "Boney's just playin', right?"

"Yeah," Boney agrees, albeit in a tone that doesn't seem particularly playful.

Lovey requests that I review the day's schedule, and I make my best effort to do so concisely. Perhaps not concisely enough, though, as I am less than halfway through it when Boney dons a pair of earphones and fires up his iPod. I pretend not to notice and continue for Lovey's benefit, but this begins to seem a bit silly after Lovey steps into the next room to answer a call on his cell phone. I eventually stop talking to myself and look at Boney, who is nodding to the beat and gazing balefully at the goings-on outside the window. I try and fail to get his attention by waving at him, and only then resort to touching his forearm. He spins and flashes me a look the likes of which I've seen only once before, when the very same individual directed it at a cowering Patrice Williams. He yanks the earphones from his head.

"You want somethin'?" he snaps. Saying "Never mind" doesn't seem like an sensible option and I can't think of any others, except to stick with my original bad idea.

"I just wanted to say that this must be a tough time for you," I say. "If you ever need to take a break or anything, just let me know." While Boney doesn't jump up and give me a hug, the ferocity fades from his expression.

"I 'preciate that," he says. Since I'm still alive, and I don't know how much time I'll ever get alone with him, I take a calculated risk and forge ahead.

"You still haven't heard from her?" I ask.

"Maybe I ain't never gonna hear from her."

"Why do you say that?"

"Gotta prepare myself for whatever the Good Lord has in store."

"Yeah," I nod. "He works in strange ways."

"You got a girl?" Boney asks.

"Not right now. I had a wife till not too long ago."

"Least I ain't that stupid," he says.

"You've never thought about getting married?"

"'Course I have. Any bitch worth bangin' know how to make you think about it." I laugh, and Boney not only joins in, he offers me his fist for a bump. Lovey returns to the room and is pleased to find us bonding.

"Say, how'd you like to be the new president of Muthafuckin' Music?" Lovey asks me. "None of the rest of us been able to knock a smile outta that nigga."

Jessica sends a PA to tell me that we are ready to shoot Boney's on-camera introduction. At his insistence (as relayed earlier through Delawn), this will take place at the front door of the house, even though doing so will require us once again to reposition the entire crew. I can hear Roger in the background, complaining as vociferously about this as he does about everything else that causes him the slightest delay, so I hustle out to the back lawn to give him a co-executive hand job. After telling him how great he was in the last scene, I mention our gambit with the rotor wash and the summer dresses, pointing out that the last-minute costume change will require us to re-shoot the van arrival at the front door anyway. Roger loses interest in the production details as soon as I mention LaFonda's near-nakedness, and demands to review the videotape right away in the privacy of the production truck. Since he is presently married to his fourth perfect ten, I find his zeal to get a peek at an 8.5 in her undies a bit surprising. But I guess that's the attitude that makes Roger and America itself great—there is simply no such thing as "enough" democracy, or prosperity, or pussy.

During the troop movements, I manage to get a moment alone with Deb while we stand in line for the Porta-Potty.

"You got anything?" I ask, looking around to make sure no one is watching us.

"I think Delawn's room is above the garage," Deb says. "He keeps going up and down the stairs around back."

"Good work. I'll check it out."

"You learn anything from Boney?"

"Yeah. All attractive women are cunts."

"I could've told you that."

At our meeting yesterday, Lovey Mack said that he knows Roger Dominus. The fact that Roger says he's never heard of him doesn't necessarily mean that either one is lying. One of the first things I learned upon arriving in L.A. almost twenty years ago is that the definition of "knowing" another person is highly subjective and open to individual interpretation. For instance, it is perfectly okay to claim that you know Brad Pitt if you once shared an elevator with him, so long as there were fewer than three other passengers and Brad said "Hey" in your general direction. On the other hand, it is equally permissible—and often advisable—to show no signs of recognition when you bump into one of your first couple of wives. I assume that Lovey met Roger at one of the hundreds of parties and VIP cluster-fucks they have each attended over the years, and that while it was a significant moment for Lovey, Roger filed it away under the general heading of "There goes the neighborhood."

But we've all recently expanded our horizons, and when at last I bring Roger into the house, he and Lovey greet each other like a couple of old Tri-Delts at the thirtieth annual toga party.

"Lovey, where the hell have you been hiding?" Roger says.

"Roger, my man. You're looking good," Lovey replies as they shake hands and slap each other on the back. "I'd like you to meet a very talented and hard-working young man. Say hello to Boney."

"It's a pleasure," Roger says. "I've heard a lot about you."

"Yeah, I heard a lot about you too," Boney says. Lovey laughs like this is the funniest thing anyone has ever said, and we all join in. By now the ritual fist-bumping is becoming second nature to me, although it may be worth noting that on this occasion it is initiated by Roger. When we're done toasting each other with our knuckles, Lovey is the first to notice that half a dozen members of Boney's staff have suddenly materialized around us and are gawking openly at Roger.

"What do y'all think you're doing?" Lovey says.

"Yeah, ain't you niggas heard it ain't polite to stare?" Boney adds. The onlookers quickly begin to scatter, but Roger comes to their rescue.

"Hold on now, they're just kidding," Roger says, beckoning everyone toward him. "I'm Roger Dominus." The lovely Peaches is the first to take Roger's outstretched hand, and as I watch him greet each beaming face in turn, I marvel yet again at the power of celebrity. Not twenty-four hours ago these very same people gave me the cold shoulder, and I automatically forgave them because hundreds of years ago, some Americans behaved poorly toward some Africans. But on the present-day plantation, I am just as much a slave as any of them, and after the frosty reception I received, it's both surprising and a little hurtful to see them showering such adoration on the Big Massah himself. Of course, this sort of resentment is probably childish. If it bothers me so much, I should simply make more African American friends, and let them see that I am a regular human being, just like them. Or maybe I should get on TV.

It's time to "reveal" Boney to the contestants. Lovey first asks me to remind all of the camera crews that they are not to aim their lenses in his direction, and I oblige. Deb already has her own instructions to shoot some surreptitious footage of Lovey, and slip the tape into her pocket when no one is looking. Detective DeRosa thinks it could prove useful to have video evidence that despite a judge's order, Lovey is still clearly in control of MF Music. I feel a little pang of guilt, because so far Lovey has been pretty darned lovable. Then I remind myself that I'm only seeing what he wants me to see, and that even Pol Pot could no doubt be fun around the water cooler.

Somebody calls "Action!" Boney opens the front door and greets Roger in much the same old-friends fashion that Lovey demonstrated so convincingly a few minutes ago. We have suggested to the contestants that appropriate reactions upon seeing Boney might be surprise and then excitement, but as usual they need a little help expressing these subtle shadings for the camera.

"Hey! Look surprised!" Jessica screeches through her bullhorn. "Now look excited!"

Although Roger's introduction of Boney to the contestants is arguably the most important sequence of the day, it is also the best opportunity I'm likely to have to slip away unnoticed. Delawn, along with the rest of Boney and Lovey's combined entourages, stands just behind our cameras, watching the magic unfold. I know from experience, however, that it won't take them long to discover that the only reasons to watch a Reality show being made are: (a) you're getting paid to do so, and you really need the money; or (b) you're terminally ill, and you want every remaining minute to seem like an hour.

Delawn stands between me and the garage, and if I try to walk past him, either he or one of his co-workers is likely to notice. But if I take a stroll in the opposite direction, toward the Porta-Pottys, and then duck behind them into the garden, I should be able to circle all the way around the house and reach the garage without being seen. I wait for the right moment, and it arrives when Roger tries to tell the contestants that "Boney's red-hot," but it comes out, "Boner's ed-hot." The spectators roar with laughter—as everybody in showbiz knows, bloopers are guaranteed crowd-pleasers, as are dick jokes. The Holy Grail of having both occur simultaneously can often be enough to earn one a place in television history.

In this case, it gives me a chance to make my move. I walk as briskly as I can without arousing the suspicion of anyone who might happen to see me. Fortunately Roger has learned that even though self-deprecation may not be in his nature, the best way to handle a blooper is to act as though he finds it just as hilarious as everyone else. I make it all the way around the huge house and he still has the audience busting up by repeating variations on the theme.

"I forgot, I'm not supposed to talk about boners in prime-time," he says. The ensuing convulsions allow me to pass unseen through the one stretch where I can't avoid being out in the open, and I safely reach the shelter of the garage. I quickly climb the exterior staircase that Deb saw Delawn using, and am relieved to find the door at the top of it unlocked.

Inside, I find myself at one end of a long corridor that runs the length of the building. There are at least six doors facing onto the corridor, all of them closed. This daunting sight is almost enough to make me bail, but instead I take a deep breath and knock on the first one, armed with nothing but a flimsy cover story about looking for the bathroom. Getting no answer, I slowly open the door and step through. I appear to be in the dimly lit storeroom of a Sportmart—racks and racks of athletic wear, the tags still on them, occupy the middle, while boxes of shoes, basketballs, and other gear are stacked high along both walls. While there is definitely a felonious feel to the place, there don't appear to any dead bodies. There is also no bed or other sign of habitation, so I move on to Door #2. It opens onto another storage space, this one filled with hubcap "spinners" and other automotive accessories, also still in their original packaging.

On a hunch, I skip the next few doors and go to the one all the way at the end of the corridor. I also skip knocking, and instead just walk right in. Now we're talking. Not only is there a king-size bed, there's also a twin bed shoved at right angles against the foot of the king, so as to make an extra-long sleeping surface for an extra-long hombre. Other than that, the only other piece of furniture is a table, on top of which sits a thirty-five-inch TV with built-in DVD player. Delawn's cinematic taste (if indeed this is his room) is well-defined, as all four titles in his library are installments of a series titled *Black Pegs/White Hoes*.

There's a small adjacent bathroom that I scan quickly, noting that the current issue of *Booty* is on the back of the toilet. I'm mostly interested in the closet, which turns out to be both smaller and neater than I hoped. Two black suits, a couple of shirts, and the requisite sweats are the only hanging items, and there isn't much more on the shelf above. The most promising feature is a half-full laundry basket on the floor, and I'm about to delve into it when I remember my crash course in police procedure. I locate the rubber gloves provided by Detective DeRosa, but getting them on is another matter. I don't know if it is because they are too small, or I'm too nervous, but after an absurd amount of pulling and tugging the first one is still only halfway down my right hand when I feel my phone vibrate in my pants pocket. The right pocket, of course.

"Shit," I say, trying to grab it. I'm incapable of gripping with all five of my fingers temporarily straitjacketed, and I'm unwilling to give up the hard-won headway I've made with the glove. So although it takes me a while, I somehow manage to get my left hand into my right pocket, pull out my phone, and see that it's Deb calling. I flip it open.

"I'm inside Delawn's room," I say.

"That's too bad," she replies, "'cause in about ten seconds, so's Delawn."

chapter thirteen

At the same instant, I hear the door at the other end of the hallway swing open. Pure animal instinct tells me to run for my life, but reason replies that I would be putting myself on a collision course with a much larger and more ferocious beast. The only other escape route is through the window, and even if I was willing to jump, there isn't time to deal with the mini-blinds and screen. Judging by the sound of the approaching footsteps, there isn't time for much of anything. So I dart as quickly and as quietly as I can into the bathroom, and lie down in the tub. As I hear the outer door open, I coax the opaque shower curtain a little further closed. As long as Delawn doesn't come in the bathroom, there's a chance he won't discover I'm here.

He comes directly into the bathroom. As his gargantuan upper body brushes up against the shower curtain, I resort to the final solution of someone desperate to become invisible—I close my eyes. This has the effect of accentuating all of the sounds inside the small room, so it's practically deafening when Delawn unzips his pants. I hear his belt buckle crash to the floor and the toilet seat groan as he lowers his weight onto it, then suddenly everything else is obliterated by a violent explosion. My eyes shoot open, expecting to confront the smoking barrel of a gun, but instead a slightly smaller discharge helps me identify the source of both blasts as Delawn's anus. Confirmation comes first in the form of a big ker-plop, followed soon thereafter by a tsunami of stench.

The effort required not to gag makes me even more conscious of the sound of my breathing. If Delawn settles in for a long sit-down, the room will eventually grow quiet and it will become almost impossible for him not to hear me breathing. The back of the tub is no more than three feet from the front of the toilet, meaning that but for the shower curtain, Delawn would be looking down at the top of my head. He provides a temporary reprieve by flushing Torpedo One down the tubes, but to my tremendous chagrin the next sound I hear is that of him flipping through a magazine. Even in my terrorized state, the irony of having my career as a sleuth begin and end courtesy of *Booty* is not lost on me.

But Delawn has another surprise in store. As the toilet finishes refilling, I hear him fumble for something in his pants, and then a series of tones as he dials a number on a cell phone. This causes me to remember for the first time in… what, sixty seconds? that I still have my own phone in my hand, and that I never ended my call with Deb. Without moving anything but my eyeballs, I'm able to see that according to the LED display, we are still connected. The good news is that if this is true and Delawn does attack me, Deb may be able to testify as to what she heard. The bad news is that if she makes even the slightest sound on her end, Delawn will immediately become aware of my presence.

A female voice answers Delawn's call, but I can't make out what she says.

"'Sup, baby," Delawn rumbles. "It's Long Dong Silver." Now there's a golden oldie. I would have thought that Delawn was too young to have paid attention to the confirmation hearings for Justice Clarence Thomas. Maybe they teach it in the schools during African American History month.

"Hold on, I's puttin' you on speaker," he says. I hear another beep and then the sound of the phone being placed on the edge of the tub, practically right on top of my skull. I can even feel the shower curtain billow and brush up against my hair, no doubt because every one that I have left is standing on end.

"You hearin' me?" Delawn asks.

"Yeah, ah kin hear you," she says. And ah kin definitely hear you too, madam, because you're practically shouting in my ear. "You wanna use the Visa or the MasterCard?" she asks. Her Daisy Duke dialect is one that is generally associated with the deep South, but in point of fact can be heard in trailer parks nationwide.

"Don' matter, it's all good," Delawn says.

"All raht, ah'll put in on the Visa. You wanna hold while ah get the authority-zation?"

"Fuck no, bitch. I's at work."

"All raht Long Dong, don' get yer titties all twisted," she says. "What chew wanna talk about?"

"Where be yo husband?"

"Same place he always is," she says with a bored sigh. "Down at the prison."

"What he be doin' there?"

"Whatever it is them guards do all day. Beatin' on niggers, ah 'spose."

"Beatin' on niggas," Delawn repeats ominously. "Ever think 'bout what some a them niggas might do if they bust out?"

"Well, we do live jes' up the holler," Daisy muses. "Ah sure hope if they bust out, they don' come this way." I suck my entire lower lip between my teeth and bite it hard enough to leave scars.

"Oh they be comin'," Delawn says. "They be comin', and they be pissed." Now begins the unmistakable sound of sexual solitaire—yet another reason to be deeply grateful for the presence of the shower curtain.

"Uh-oh," she says. "Ah kin't even call nobody, on account a we didn't pay the bill an' they done shut off our phone." I suppress the impulse to ask how it is that she can then be speaking to us. Such unwanted intrusions of logic are why I was never able to make it as a Hollywood screenwriter—I have virtually no ability to suspend my disbelief. As I'm thinking about this, Delawn receives an unwanted intrusion of his own.

"You have an incoming call," an automated voice announces over the speaker.

"Muthafucka," he says. "Don' go nowheres, ya hear?"

"All raht." I hear a tone as Delawn pushes a button on the phone.

"What?" he barks.

"Don' you be sayin' 'What' to me, boy," says another female voice, one that clearly takes no guff from jailbirds or anyone else.

"Sorry Mama, but I's kinda busy right now," Delawn says.

"Well I be mighty busy too," Mama says. "Busy tryin' to figure out why somebody wants to give my no-good, high school dropout of a son a hundred thousand dollars."

"Come on, Mama, you promise not to be bustin' me no more 'bout that."

"No I did not, Delawn Pentecostal Purvis. I mos' certainly did not." Delawn sighs heavily.

"I gotta put you on hold a minute, Mama." He presses the button to return to his first call. "Yo baby, I gotta get you back."

"All raht," Daisy says. "Ah oughta be home from Wal-Mart in a couple arrs."

"Don' you be goin' to no muthafuckin' Wal-Mart!" Delawn orders. "Jus' stay right there on the muthafuckin' phone!"

"Okey-dokey, Smokey. It's yer nickel." Delawn switches to the other line again.

"Mama, I can't be talkin' about this now. I come see you on Sunday, 'ight?"

"You want your poor ol' mama to go from now till Sunday without sleepin' a wink?"

"No ma'am, I jus'—"

"Go take a look at youself in the mirror, if you can find one big enough, and axe youself how bad it musta hurt when a lil' ol' girl like me had to bring all that into this world."

"You know I love you, Mama," Delawn whines. "Why else I be tellin' 'em to put a hundred grand a my money in yo bank account?"

"Prob'ly so's the police can't find it."

"Come on, now."

"No, you come on, Delawn. Ain't I told ya, ya can't hide nothin' from the Man upstairs? If you be carryin' somethin' heavy on your soul when your time come—and considerin' the kinda folks you run with, your time could be comin' any minute—you gonna spend eternity in a fryin' pan called Hell. So I want you to tell me right now, what terrible thing did you have to do to get all that money?"

"I didn't do nothin', Mama," Delawn says, starting to choke up. "I swear it on a stack a Bibles."

"Mm-mm-mm," Mama sighs, having apparently exhausted her bag of tricks. "What am I gonna do with you, boy?"

"Everythin' be all right," he says. "I see you on Sunday."

"I 'spose you will, if we both live that long." She hangs up, and after Delawn clears his throat twice, he presses the button on his phone once again.

"You still there, baby?" he asks.

"Yeah, ah'm still here," Daisy says peevishly. "But them horny niggers from the prison already came and left."

Ten minutes later I'm alone with Deb inside one of the *Mogul* equipment vans. My concerns about anyone seeing us together have been overridden by my need to high-five over my good fortune.

"How much could you make out?" I ask her.

"Every word," Deb says. "It was like a fiber optics ad."

"I was afraid you'd say something and he'd hear you."

"I'm not an idiot, you idiot. I put my phone on mute. And I borrowed somebody's bullhorn so I could call in the cavalry if things turned ugly."

"I wish I'd had some way of knowing all that. You see this here?" I say, pointing to my Adam's apple. "It's actually one of my balls."

"So what are you gonna do now?"

"Call Detective DeRosa and tell her to break out the

champagne, because this guy is going down. All we have to do is throw Mama in the cooler and Delawn will sing like he's trying to get on *American Idol*."

"Oh now it's 'we,' is it? Which one are you, Cagney or Lacey?"

I try to sound a lot cooler and more professional when I reach Detective DeRosa, but my giddy jubilation somehow seeps through. She tells me not to get too excited, which really pisses me off because I'm the one who just risked death (whether by violence or by asphyxiation) to get the goods on Delawn, and because when it comes to sexual role-playing, I'm no good at being the hysterical one. (Not too long ago, I conducted an experiment to see if I could modify my mating habits. The idea was to go as far in the opposite direction from Sara as possible, so I allowed myself be set up on a date with Willa, a high-powered, no-nonsense commercial realtor. I adapted well enough to having her be the one to call me, to her picking up the dinner tab, and even to her monopolizing the conversation with tales of how she exploited the soft underbellies of all the weaker capitalists. But we hadn't been making out in her Corvette for more than a minute when, apropos of nothing, Willa asked me if I was into anal. And before I could even think of an appropriate answer, she told me not to worry, she'd be gentle.)

Detective DeRosa must be able to detect that I'm annoyed, as she hastens to make things right.

"Don't get me wrong, this could be a huge break in the case," she says. "It's just that I've had so many great leads turn into dead ends that now I force myself not to get my hopes up."

"Got it," I tell her, having decided to sulk.

"The main thing I want to say is that you did an awesome job, Foghorn."

"Nah, I didn't do much of anything."

"Of course you did. I guarantee, there's no way I could have pulled it off."

"Sure you could," I say. "You're a woman and you used to be married. You must know how to just lie there."

It seems like an entire day has passed, so I can't understand how Roger, Boney, and the crew can still be working on the scene at the front entrance. Then I remember that: (a) it's actually only been about twenty-five minutes; and (b) in that amount of time, you're more likely to see detectable movement from a glacier than from a Reality show. The audience has vanished completely, and I learn from Jessica that this is because she ordered all non-essential personnel off the set. Apparently every time Roger started to utter the word "Boney," several members of the peanut gallery kept cracking up, long past the point where either the speaker or the subject found it the least bit amusing. This must be when Delawn felt his fateful urge to purge.

Speaking of Delawn, I spot him around the side of the house, chatting up a chunky blonde wardrobe assistant. Part of me feels like I should take the lass aside and let her know what kind of dude she's dealing with, but I'm not quite sure how I would put it. Besides, all I can say for sure about Delawn is that he has some very specific turn-ons, and there's no law against that. If I was to be totally honest, I'd have to admit that I'm kind of disappointed to have missed hearing about the rest of the prison break myself.

Jessica eventually decides that we have enough footage of our star at this location to make the whole mess some unfortunate editor's problem. Within minutes Roger is waving from the window of his helicopter to Boney's employees, who applaud and cheer the lift-off as though it's part of a magic act. We then turn to the rest of our shooting schedule, beginning with a scene in Boney's home recording studio where he plays a few tracks from *Wuh Duh Fuh* for the benefit of the contestants. As the first drum beats thunder through the room, the shameless LaFonda dances over to Boney and starts to grind against his leg. She no doubt regrets this when Boney's response is to place a McDonald's sack over her head. The other contestants are not the sort of people who listen to a lot of hardcore rap, and we get some interesting reaction shots when they hear the chorus of the title track:

Wuh duh fuh u lookin' at, white boy?
U better not even be lookin' at me.
Wuh duh fuh u lookin' at, white boy?
U never seen a nigga takin' a pee?

But despite these colorful departures from the standard *Mogul* aesthetic, we're still engaged in the same basic enterprise of producing a high-end infomercial. Soon the contestants have split up into two groups—the "Dominators" use Boney's study as their conference room, while the team calling itself "Roger That" remains in the recording studio. Lovey has helpfully provided stacks of marketing materials used by MF Music to promote previous releases, and I am happy to see that our contestants have no scruples whatsoever about recycling the better ideas and presenting them as their own. Soon it becomes just another day at the office, and I'm even starting to feel a little drowsy when a surprise phone call snaps me back to full combat readiness.

"Hi, it's me," she says.

"Me who?" I ask, though even without Caller ID, I'd know damned good and well.

"Sara," she replies. I consider saying, "Sara who?" but instead I just leave her hanging. "I need to talk to you, Ted."

"This isn't really a good time. I'm working."

"It's important," she says. "It's about Hallie."

"Did something happen to her?" I've already taken several automatic steps in the direction of my car.

"No, she's fine. This has more to do with the future."

"What about it?"

"I can't have this conversation over the phone. Can you meet me somewhere?" The unprecedented nature of the question leaves me temporarily unable to answer. I have not been alone with my former wife for so much as five minutes since the day she informed me—over the phone—that she was leaving me for Richard.

"Like where?" I finally ask.

"Any place you want," she says. "How about the Bel-Air?"

chapter fourteen

I LIKE A LOT of things about being a man. I like the male sense of honor, and appetite for adventure. I like the straightforward way that men communicate and compete. I even like the stupid and self-destructive aspects of maleness, particularly when they generate colorful catastrophes that you can entertain your buddies with later. The only thing I don't like about being a man is having a penis.

You probably think I'm exaggerating to make a point, but I assure you that I am not. Because right now, on my way to the Hotel Bel-Air and weaving in and out of traffic like a carjacker on crystal meth, I feel so ashamed of what I'm doing and yet so powerless to stop myself that all I can do is pray I'll lose control and crash into a bridge abutment. I wish to stress that what I am experiencing is not a simple case of "thinking with your dick," like when you're giving the babysitter a ride home and it dawns on you that being eighteen is really a completely arbitrary definition of adulthood. To be sure, the consequences of that sort of reasoning can be unpleasant. But even if they take away all that a man holds dear, including his liberty, he can still lie there in his bunk at night and have a chuckle about the whole thing with his cellie.

If I ever again sleep with Sara, however, I will take the secret with me to my grave. I mean, who would I tell? Following our divorce, Deb put up with my anguished pining far longer than anybody else, but even she ultimately announced that if I continued to express any desire for Sara in her presence, she would take a sledgehammer to my scrotum. The people who cared about me felt the need to adopt such harsh stances not only because enough is enough, but because the unique circumstances of the situation made my continuing attraction to my ex-wife incomprehensibly pitiful (in Deb's typically unsparing description, "like a Jew trying to tunnel into Auschwitz.") But I don't even know why I'm thinking about sex—the only reason Sara and I are meeting in the bar of the Bel-Air is because it's close to her house, and it's a quiet, comfortable place to talk. On the other hand, it *is* a hotel…

STOP THIS NOW! A surge of self-loathing shoots all the way from my head to my foot, which stomps down on the brake pedal. A loud screech of tires behind me is followed by blaring horns and screaming motorists, but fortunately no crumpling metal or shattering glass. I pull to the side of the road and try to compose myself. Why is what I'm doing such a big deal? Former spouses who share children talk to each other all the time—as the saying goes, once you have kids, there's no such thing as divorce. Another piece of folk wisdom holds that sooner or later, almost everybody bumps uglies with the ex.

But Sara and I aren't everybody. I've already described how we met and got married, only to discover that our mutual interests didn't extend much beyond humping. And after Hallie was born, they didn't extend even that far. In despair I turned to the all-but-forgotten teachings of my Catholic faith, which tells frustrated young fathers to sublimate. For those of you who didn't grow up in the One and True Church, sublimation is the act of turning inappropriate sexual energy into something more righteous and useful, such as work. If you want to practice, every time you start thinking about the neighbor lady's ass, go out and chop some firewood. When the pile becomes taller than your house, it's time to move.

Fortunately I loved my job, and I happily took on every extra assignment I could get. I was already respected as a facile writer who could reliably bang out a quick story, but now I became known as someone who could handle the heavy lifting as well. Editors started giving me the assignments that other reporters avoided because they required a lot more research, interviews, and fact-checking to produce the same amount of finished product. That's how I became an investigative journalist, the role in which I had my biggest triumph—followed swiftly by my most humiliating defeat.

Four years ago, yours truly was awarded the highest honor in journalism—the Pulitzer Prize. It was for a series of articles in the *New York Times* about how untreated sewage had been dumped into the ocean and made a group of surfers down in Huntington Beach deathly ill. If I failed to mention earlier that I have a Pulie, it's because while a reporter who constantly reminds people of his past glories is merely annoying, a Reality TV producer who does so is certifiably pathetic. I can also honestly say that I don't remember receiving the prize—on the day of the ceremony, I got so drunk that I passed out backstage and wet my pants.

To explain how I happened to choose such an inopportune occasion to get shit-faced, I'll have to rewind another year or so. Sara had been diagnosed with post-partum depression and began taking Paxil. We had been warned by her doctor that loss of libido was a possible side effect, but considering that I was already getting less love than Theodore Kaczynski, this seemed like the very definition of a moot point. In any case, I was willing to support anything that might make Sara smile again. At the very least, I was hoping that the right medication might lessen her tendency to emphasize points in our frequent arguments by hurling heavy objects at my head. (I managed to dodge most of those, but the recent retreat of my hairline exposed a scar from the time Sara caught me off-guard with the business end of a spatula.)

In addition to psychopharmacology, I also tried more traditional means of placating my beloved. We hired enough nannies and housekeepers to empty out several Mexican villages. My job allowed me to work from home, and whenever I needed a break from the writing, I took Hallie and we went for a walk, or played peek-a-boo or chase-the-baby. Sara rarely joined in or even watched any of these domestic scenes, choosing instead to leave for lunch at around 10:30 every day and return no earlier than 4:00. She described this as her "work," and the claim was not completely without merit, inasmuch as that's mostly what development executives do—have expensive meals with other development executives. The only significant difference between Sara's job before Hallie was born and afterward is that during the former, she got a paycheck, and I didn't have to spring for all those fancy lunches.

Although our single-income status didn't particularly bother me, it bothered Sara a lot. She often became despondent over the fact that no one took her seriously any more, and the one time I tried to lighten things up by joking that no one ever had, I spent the next week sleeping on the futon in Hallie's room. Since neither Paxil nor any of the subsequent meds made a dent in Sara's depression, she resorted to the final solution for many of the mentally unhinged residents of Los Angeles—she became a movie producer. Along with Leslie Mulholland, another young woman whose limitless potential had been snuffed out by a thoughtless infant, Sara formed MNM Productions, which officially stood for Mommy 'n' Me (but which I privately referred to as "Me 'n' Me").

Sara and Leslie rented an office in Santa Monica, hired a buff young male assistant, and began scouring the landscape for film properties. Since they had no track record, no credibility, and very little money (we were pretty well tapped out, and Leslie's husband refused to contribute any of his vast inherited wealth unless it was on a strict *pari passu* basis, which is Latin for "I ain't carrying your broke ass"), the world did not exactly beat a path to their door. The established agents wouldn't even have coffee with them, and Sara and Leslie concluded it could only be because they had been cruelly and prematurely deprived of their hotness. They therefore acquired one new personal trainer, two new wardrobes, and four new tits, yet still they couldn't lay their hands on a story anyone wanted to make into a movie. Then one day Sara learned that such a rare and precious commodity was sitting right under her nose, or at least it would have been if she ever allowed her nose to stray anywhere in the general vicinity of her husband.

The Huntington Beach toxic surf story had all the elements of a great movie—a true, gripping tale of political corruption; a heroic, heartbreaking saga of a mother's fight to save her son and exposé the people whose greed had nearly killed him; and hundreds of hot bods in bathing suits. On the morning that the series started running in the *Times*, I received the first of several big-money offers for the rights from the major studios, who saw in it a rare combination of Oscar-caliber gravitas and woody-caliber prurience. Since the heroine (the young surfer's hippie-chick mom) was in her thirties but looked even younger, every star from Lindsey Lohan to Demi Moore was pitched to me as "perfect" for the role. But I turned them all down, and against the unanimous advice of my agents, friends, and colleagues, I eventually sold the rights to MNM Productions for the princely sum of one dollar.

The question I've asked myself about a billion times since is "Why?" To be sure, Sara applied a lot of pressure, employing both the carrot—her suddenly resurgent interest in the ol' sucky-fucky—and the stick—the forty-eight hours of stony silence that followed every occasion in which she asked me about the movie rights and I wouldn't give her a straight answer. It was clear that if I wanted to save the marriage, I had little choice but to capitulate. But how badly did I really want to save the marriage? Aside from my realization that Sara and I were about as good for each other as Courtney Love and a pharmacist, I also had little respect for her as a mother. And I knew that I would forever resent the way she held my hog hostage to her career ambitions. So although for Hallie's sake I didn't "want" a divorce, I recognized that it was probably inevitable. Which brings us back to the question of why I would hand over the most valuable thing I was ever likely to own to someone I would soon be looking at in life's rear view mirror.

The only logical answer is Guilt. I hate to pick on the Catholics—God knows they have their hands full, what with the competition for followers from the newer and even sillier Christian denominations, and the lawsuits brought by all the former altar boys who claim to have been cornholed by the clergy—but I have an unhealthy propensity toward Guilt, and it had to come from somewhere. Regardless of its origins, I sure wish Guilt would go back there and leave me alone. It's not the same thing as conscience—your conscience has the important ethical function of helping you make the right decisions today, while Guilt can only make you feel shitty about whatever you thought was right yesterday, you selfish prick. In addition to permanently stooped shoulders, Guilt also leads to a lot of even worse choices, all made in the vain hope of trying to get the moral toothpaste back in the tube.

That's as good an explanation as I can come up with for why I signed over the rights to a story worth millions for a buck. Even though Sara and I jointly made the mistake that was our marriage, I felt that my status as "the smart one" (our dumb/mean dynamic had already been well established during dozens of 3:00 AM arguments) somehow meant that I was more at fault. And since I would eventually be the one to leave her (for no matter how stupid she was, surely *she* would never leave *me*), giving Sara such a valuable present ahead of time would be like drawing a "Get Out of Jail Free" card. In Catholic economics, relief from such a major load of Guilt is worth more than every anal fissure in the Archdiocese of Boston.

My agent tried his best to look out for me in the deal negotiations, but the poor bastard got zero support from his battle-weary client. Even without such a disadvantage, my guy would have been no match for his adversary—the infamous showbiz shark Richard Slatkin, who had recently become MNM's legal counsel and official henchman. I later learned that this was no coincidence—Richard heard through the grapevine that two female nobodies somehow had the inside track on getting the rights to the highly coveted Huntington Beach story, and he called to invite them to lunch at Danilo's. Sara and Leslie of course accepted, and then drove themselves and everyone around them crazy trying to locate such a restaurant without calling Richard back and admitting they'd never heard of it. Shortly before the scheduled lunch, they were about to give up and make the embarrassing call when Richard's assistant phoned to say that a town car was on its way to pick them up. It whisked them to Santa Monica airport, where they joined Richard aboard the Gulfstream V that got them to Danilo's in the idyllic Northern California wine country town of St. Helena in plenty of time for their reservation.

The girls were no doubt too giddy from their taste of the good life—and a lot of Pinot Noir—to ask themselves why Richard would roll out such a thick, red carpet to attract the likes of them as clients. I might have raised the question myself, but I never got the chance because Sara didn't mention her little plane ride when she got home that night, or for that matter ever. I learned about it a year later from a private detective to whom I paid an obscene sum to unearth information that served the sole purpose of making me feel like an even bigger chump. California's divorce laws are no-fault, meaning you can have video of your spouse enjoying a gang-bang with the Hell's Angels and it's not going to do you a bit of good—unless of course you're into that sort of thing.

But even if I'd figured out that Richard was really after my story, I still couldn't have guessed why. Only recently did I get the full low-down, in a phone call from a former associate at Richard's firm who was going through the twelve steps of AA and had reached the one where he had to make "amends" to everyone he'd ever screwed personally or professionally. I thus learned that, unlikely as it sounds, two of the key roles in the breakup of my marriage were played (unwittingly) by Academy Award© winners Jim Carrey and Hillary Swank. Carrey had been Richard's biggest client for years, until he was lured away by Paul Rosenbloom, another all-powerful entertainment lawyer. Richard considered this not only unfair but downright immoral, and vowed not to rest until he'd received justice by stealing Rosenbloom's number-one client, Ms. Swank. The latter was rumored to be interested in playing the ailing surfer's mom, and would no doubt have been wonderful in the part. But Hillary Swank proved to be much more faithful to her attorney than my wife was to me, and Richard therefore made sure that the role went instead to former Bond girl Denise Richards. This casting choice was the single biggest factor that turned the movie (*Terrible Tide*, aka *Catch a Wave and You're Sittin' On Top of a Turd*) into a straight-to-video piece of shit bigger than the entire Pacific Ocean. On the other hand, it did provide Denise Richards's then-husband Charlie Sheen with a few months of blessed peace, in exchange for which he was more than happy to fire his attorney Paul Rosenbloom and replace him with Richard Slatkin.

I've gone into all this sordid detail because some of the things I did over the years that followed were frankly not too pretty either. You don't go from the top of the heap to the bottom of the barrel without leaving a fair amount of wreckage in your wake. And if you're in a custody battle with an ex-spouse who has unlimited resources, it's guaranteed that each and every piece of said wreckage can and will be used against you in a court of law. So although I have no personal recollection of many of my transgressions, they are all disgustingly well documented and it would thus be pointless for me to deny or minimize them. Instead I will summarize a few illustrative events below[1], for those of you with nothing better to do than to rehash painful moments from someone else's past. I respectfully request that you consider my actions in context—if you suffered a series of blows like the ones I did, you might have a couple of off days yourself. Asshole.

[1] In addition to the aforementioned incident involving Richard's Hummer, I did substantial damage on other occasions to his Ferrari (baseball bat) and to Sara's Beemer (interior bonfire). Most of my anger was misdirected, however, especially at my undeserving colleagues—I am told that I called my editor at the *New York Times* "the kind of Hebe who makes us all wish for a good pogrom," and a short time later, my new boss at the *Los Angeles Times* "a big smelly cunt." As employment became harder to come by, drinking and coke-snorting opportunities became easier. I was busted once for DUI, and once for doing a line off the counter at Denny's (by the uniformed patrolman sitting three stools down). I never finished writing my book about Huntington Beach, and was eventually sued by the publisher to recover the long-gone advance. The lapses I regret most, though, are the ones that cost me long-term friendships: my college roommate never forgave me for inadvertently urinating on his grandmother, who had the misfortune to be convalescing in a guest room that I somehow confused with the WC. A fellow journalist whose company I long enjoyed severed our relations after a lively debate over US policy in the Middle East ended with me kneeing him in the 'nads. I even did my best to ruin my friendship with Deb: borrowing money and never paying it back; failing to show up for dates we made; making endless crude jokes about her carpet-munching lifestyle. One night I got thrown out of a bar somewhere downtown and found myself with no dollars and just enough sense not to drive. I called Deb, who despite having the flu dragged herself out of bed and came to get me. By way of gratitude, I resumed my drunken lesbo-baiting, cracking myself up by telling her that the best cure for any illness was a hot beef injection. Having finally had enough, Deb pulled over onto the shoulder of the Santa Monica Freeway and said if I got naked, she'd fuck me right then and there. Mostly to see what would happen, I did as instructed. She shoved me out the door and drove off with my clothes, yelling, "Consider yourself fucked!"

It didn't matter one iota that I had been planning to leave Sara anyway—as anyone past puberty knows, when it comes to dumping, it is far better to give than to receive. My scheme to preemptively assuage my guilt by giving Sara her big break as a producer could not have backfired any worse—it set in motion a chain of events that left me with a bottomless, uncontrollable rage that could easily have killed me, or some poor bastard who cut me off in traffic. I gave her a goldmine and then *she* left *me*? For a fucking *lawyer*? And what the hell was in it for him? Richard was able to seduce Sara easily enough while she and I were still together (I wouldn't be surprised if they had a mile-high threesome with that other round-heeled ho Leslie on their way back from their first lunch date), and once they signed his retainer agreement, what was the point of continuing to pursue her, or of divorcing his first wife and actually *marrying* her, for godsakes? I've never had the occasion to ask Richard this question and I doubt I ever will, so I can only assume that although he and I may disagree on most subjects, we concur as to which are the three most important factors to consider when making any major life decision—your dick, your dick, and your dick.

chapter fifteen

The parking valets at the Hotel Bel-Air are trained to walk around every car and note any pre-existing scrapes and door-dings on the back of the claim ticket before handing it to the customer. In the case of my battle-scarred Subaru, this is a lengthy and humiliating process that I try without success to waive. The excessively diligent valet has finished recording the damage only to the driver's side and a small portion of the front bumper when Sara pulls up in a brand-new Porsche Cayenne.

"Hey," she says with a wistful smile as she gets out of her car and comes toward me.

"Hey," I cleverly reply. I am prepared for a handshake or even a peck on the cheek, but not for the full-body hug that Sara gives me.

"It's good to see you," she murmurs into my ear. Such a sultry greeting from a sexy and well-heeled woman instantly elevates my status in the eyes of the parking attendants, and I receive my claim check without further delay. Sara and I walk over the covered footbridge and down the lush garden path toward the bar. She says something about not having been here since Angelina and Billy Bob's third wedding, but it's mostly just white noise because I'm still reeling from the sudden change in her attitude, not to mention her appearance. On the rare instances when we meet face-to-face, usually at the office of Hallie's shrink for "family therapy" (which of course only began after we were no longer a family), Sara comes dressed either in baggy sweats or one of her dark wool church lady get-ups. Today she's wearing a brightly embroidered silk vest with no shirt beneath it—a look that offers a strong testimonial as to the effectiveness of plastic surgery and Pilates—and a pair of jeans that probably cost $500 and are worth twice that for the perfect way in which they package her pooper. I follow the latter to a dark corner of the bar, where we sit on a couch that isn't quite big enough to share with someone you loathe.

"I need a drink," Sara announces, and tells the waitress to bring a bottle of Chardonnay.

"Iced tea for me," I tell her.

"Oh come on," Sara says. "A glass of wine isn't going to kill you."

"No, but it might encourage me to kill you. And there's too many witnesses."

Sara laughs, but then looks a little unnerved when I don't.

"What's on your mind?" I ask.

"First of all, I want to apologize about the other day," she says. I must look as clueless as I am, because she tries to jog my memory. "On the phone? Remember, I hung up on you."

"Isn't that how we always end our calls?"

"I was just a little freaked out by that letter from your lawyer. Richard convinced me that it was really bad."

"Not really, unless you're you."

"After I calmed down, I was able to understand where you're coming from," Sara says. "I'm not going to fight you."

"On which part?" I ask, a bit more eagerly than I should.

"Any of it," she says, and it's all I can do to keep from leaping up and performing a Terrell Owens touchdown dance.

"Are you sure you've read the whole letter?" I ask instead. "It's almost two pages."

"I've got it right here," she says, taking a folded-up document from her purse. "Do you want me to sign it?"

"I think we should probably let the lawyers handle the paperwork," I say, both because I was born with a strong psychological need to appear insouciant, and because I know that Sara's signature wouldn't mean shit anyway. There is no such thing as a "final" child custody arrangement—if the judge issues a ruling on Monday, either side can file a petition to modify it on Tuesday, and keep doing so over and over until the child turns eighteen and tells everybody to fuck off. Of course, if Sara is truly ready to play fair and isn't going to change her mind, then we can stop going to court altogether. But I can't believe this is really going to happen—our history has left me with some trust issues that are unlikely to be resolved without years of therapy, or the more expedient murder-suicide.

"Okay," Sara says. "I'll tell Richard I want it done tomorrow." She raises her wine glass for another clink against mine. It's all just too much.

"Sara, I don't mean to be cynical, but what is it exactly that you want from me? Because no matter what it is, all you have to do is ask and you can be sure that if I possibly can, I will say no."

"I deserve that," she says. "But I don't think you can say no to this, Ted. I want you to promise that no matter what happens, you'll think about Hallie and put her needs first."

"What the hell is that supposed to mean?" I ask, partly confused but mostly insulted. "I always put Hallie first."

"You have in the past," she says. "I'm talking about the future."

"Is there some particular reason why you think I might be inclined to change and become more like, say, you?"

"Nice," Sara says. "There are two reasons things could change. One is that you finally seem to be getting your act together. Richard says you're like the hottest guy in TV."

"Yeah, it's just Ryan Seacrest, then me," I say.

"Don't slam yourself. I'm really proud of you." She leans over to put her hand on my knee, and I would probably have enough self-respect to swat it away were it not for the unobstructed view that I am now being afforded of her magnificent breasts. Help me, Mr. Wizard.

"The other big change that's happening is in my life," Sara says as she returns to her own end of the couch. "Things might not be so easy for me for a while."

"What do you mean?" I ask.

"Richard and I are having problems," she says. I have been predicting the demise of Sara and Richard's relationship since the day I first learned of it, yet I am still completely blindsided.

"You're kidding," is all I can muster. Sara shakes her head and suddenly her eyes are full of tears. My arms open instinctively to comfort a crying woman, but then my brain shoots them a sharp, "Not *this* fucking woman." I end up frozen in a position that must look like Pavarotti holding a high note. Sara turns her head away to wipe her eyes, allowing me to stage a semi-graceful retreat.

"I don't expect you to have any sympathy," she says, then clears the lump from her throat before continuing. "When everything was going good for me, I wasn't very nice to you."

"Why weren't you?"

"I guess 'cause I'm a bitch. And I was scared. Don't ask me what of."

"I wasn't going to," I say, as frostily as I know how.

"Please, Ted." She leans forward to touch me again, but this time I'm ready for her and I keep my eyes above her neckline. "All I'm asking is that before you take your revenge, try to think of how it will affect Hallie." The tears start to well again. "I'm asking you to be better than me."

"Fair enough," I say after a long pause. She throws her arms around me.

"Thank you," she sobs into my shoulder. "Thank you."

Sara wants me to stay while she has another glass of wine, and I'm tempted for all the obvious and bad reasons. But I also need to check in with Deb and Detective DeRosa, and perhaps to pay a bit of attention to my job. Sara pays the check (another first!) and we make our way back to the parking lot. Her Cayenne waits right by the entrance, and I walk her to it while one of the attendants runs off to Reseda or wherever they took my car. She turns to me and I'm prepared for another hug, but definitely not for what she lays on me instead.

"Do you think we could ever be together again?" she says.

"Excuse me?"

"I don't know if it's really over between me and Richard, and I'm sure you're seeing somebody. But just hypothetically, if someday we were both single."

"And insane?"

"Okay, never mind," she says, and now I get the cheek-peck. "Thanks for coming here and talking to me."

As I watch Sara drive away, I think of a million other things I might have said, half of them variations on "You've got a lot of nerve, bitch" and the rest on "Let's get a room." The overall effect of such internal confusion is to make me mad as hell by the time the valet arrives with my Subaru. I point at the badly dented and rusting passenger side.

"Hey man, look what you did to my car!"

The Bel-Air is nestled in a canyon that is difficult to reach, both for Lookie-Lous and cellular signals. But as soon as I drive down into the flats, my phone starts ringing and I see that it's Deb calling.

"What up, Caucasian?" I say.

"Where the hell are you?" Deb sounds agitated. "I've been calling every two minutes."

"I was in a dead spot. Did something happen?"

"Not really. Unless you count me solving your whole fucking mystery as 'something'."

"Care to elaborate?"

"Not over the phone," Deb says. "Meet me by the falafel place in the farmer's market."

"When?"

"I don't know, dipshit, how about a week from Wednesday?"

"Okay, relax. I'm on my way."

"You better have Angie Dickinson meet us there too." This is undoubtedly a reference to Ms. Dickinson's long-running role as *Policewoman*, and thus to Detective Susan DeRosa. Deb and I have not yet discussed when (if ever) I might introduce her to Susan, and there are several potential negatives I need to consider first.

"I don't know if I can reach her," I say in an effort to stall.

"You're the worst liar in the world," Deb says. "It's a wonder you've ever gotten laid."

She hangs up on me and I start to call her back, but after all these years I know that it's easier to win an argument with an ayatollah than with Deb when she's got the bit in her teeth. So instead I call Detective DeRosa and ask her to come to the farmer's market right away.

I have her meet me next to Jimbo's Jambalaya stand, which is on the other end of the market from Fozzi's Falafels, and this gives us a chance to sit and talk alone for a few minutes before I introduce her to Deb. As soon as I reveal that I have let someone else know about our secret working arrangement, the detective's features darken and for a moment I fear I'm about to get pistol-whipped. I quickly explain that Deb is my best friend of more than twenty years, and totally trustworthy. For some reason I feel it is also pertinent to mention that while we were once "an item," Deb is now a doctrinaire bull-dyke, and our relationship therefore strictly platonic. Unlike most people, Susan has no visible reaction to this part of my personal history, and maintains her stern expression while I go on to tell her about Deb's phone call, and eventually run out of things to babble nervously about.

"So this friend of yours is here now?" she asks.

"I imagine so."

"Then let's go talk to her." She stands and I do the same.

"I'm sorry I didn't . . ." I begin, but she has already turned her back on me and walked away.

Deb is indeed waiting for us by the falafels. I make the introductions and the three of us sit at a round table.

"Mr. Collins tells me you may have some information about the disappearance of Patrice Williams," Susan says. *Mr. Collins*? It appears we've lost a little ground.

"I think I do," Deb says.

"Before you tell me what it is, I need to make a few things clear. Although Mr. Collins reported an incident he allegedly witnessed involving Patrice Williams and Raymond Bonaparte, and Mr. Collins mentioned that he planned to investigate further in his role as a freelance journalist, I gave him absolutely no encouragement to do so. I instead advised him that his best course of action was to allow us trained police officers to do our jobs. Is that consistent with what Mr. Collins told you?"

Deb casts a bewildered glance in my direction, and I give her a tiny nod.

"Uh, yeah," Deb says. "I guess that sums it up pretty well."

"So you never believed that either you or Mr. Collins were acting in cooperation with the police?" I furtively shake my head, but it's unnecessary because Deb now gets the idea.

"No," she says. "In fact, I hate the friggin' pigs."

"Glad to hear it," Susan says. "So what information do you have?"

By way of answering, Deb reaches into the grimy fanny pack she carries in lieu of a purse, takes out a 4x6 snapshot, and places it on the table. Susan picks it up first and studies it, then hands it to me without comment. The photo is of two people—Boney and a much bigger, bearded black dude I don't recognize. They're both wearing the *de rigueur* rapper uniform of sweats, shades, and knit caps. The big guy has Boney in a friendly headlock.

"Are we supposed to know who this is?" I ask.

"Not necessarily," Deb replies. "Although you have seen him before." Perplexed, I start to reexamine the photo, but Susan abruptly snatches it out of my hand and stares at it again herself.

"It's her, isn't it?" Susan says.

"Not bad, Detective," Deb says with an admiring nod.

"Who's her?" I ask, trying to get another look at the photo over Susan's shoulder. "Her who?"

"I considered the possibility of a disguise, but not this much of a disguise," Susan tells Deb, both of them ignoring me. "When was this taken?"

"Last Halloween. The fat suit and the elevator shoes are from a commercial Patrice worked on."

"Wait," I say. "That big scary-looking mofo is Patrice Williams?"

"Yep," Deb says. Susan lets me take the photo from her and I look closely at it. Although I suppose it could be Patrice hiding under all that hair and clothing, it could just as easily be Osama bin Laden, or Oprah.

"How do you know it's her?" I ask Deb.

"I saw all the shots of her getting into the costume. Peaches keeps 'em in a scrapbook in her bedroom at Boney's place."

"How did you manage to sneak in there?"

"I didn't," Deb says. "Peaches invited me."

"How did you get her to…" I start to ask, but Deb silences me by making a "V" with two of her fingers, placing them over her lips, and flicking her tongue back and forth between them. I raise my hand to stop her. "'Nuff said."

"No, there's more," Deb says. "Up until the night before Patrice disappeared, the costume was stored in one of those rooms above Boney's garage. When she came to get it, she told Peaches she needed it for a photo shoot the next day. She also told her not to say anything to Boney."

"Why would Peaches be more loyal to Patrice than to the guy she works for?" I ask.

"Let me guess," Susan says, then she and Deb reprise the fingers-and-tongue act in perfect unison.

"Okay, I'm going to have to remind you both that this is a family restaurant."

"Awesome job," Susan tells Deb as she stands and reclaims the snapshot from me. "Now I've gotta go do mine."

"Good luck," Deb says. They shake hands and Susan starts to leave.

"Hold on a minute," I say.

"Can't," Susan replies without slowing, so I have no choice but to get up and give chase.

"I'll call you later," I tell Deb.

"You know where I'll be," Deb says, bringing her fingers back to her lips.

I catch up with Susan in the parking lot. She's striding purposefully in the direction of The Grove, which is directly adjacent to the farmer's market.

"Where are you going?" I ask her.

"I'm not at liberty to say."

"Come on, we have a deal."

"We *had* a deal. You broke it."

"I might have bent it a little. And aren't you glad I did?"

"No," she says, stopping dead in her tracks and wheeling around to glower at me. "Just because you stumbled on some potentially useful information doesn't excuse the despicable thing you did to get it."

"Despicable? Isn't that a little harsh? It's not like I smeared menstrual blood on a Muslim."

"I don't like having my trust betrayed."

"Me neither," I say. "In fact, there's something I've been meaning to bring up with you on that subject."

"Yeah, like what?"

"Like when somebody calls the confidential police tip line, he doesn't expect to have some eager beaver with a badge sneak up behind him and go 'Boo!'"

"I'm trying to find a possible victim of violent crime."

"So am I. And don't waste your breath telling me how you're just a humble public servant and you don't care about publicity, or promotions, or having the biggest dick in the precinct. Figuratively speaking."

"You think being a reporter is more noble than being a cop?" she asks, with the word "reporter" given the inflection normally reserved for "pedophile."

"I think that's a fascinating debate topic for another day," I say. "In the meantime, we have work to do." She glares at me a moment longer, then wordlessly resumes walking. I keep pace by her side.

"Are we going to review the security tapes?" I ask.

"No," she says. "*I'm* going to review the security tapes, and you're going to stand there like a fucking statue."

We present ourselves at the Grove security office, where Susan seems to be a familiar presence. She introduces me simply as "Ted Collins," and I do my best to remain statuesque while she has one of the rent-a-cops cue up the composite surveillance video to a point just after the arrival of Patrice's BMW. It only takes a few minutes to find the first image of Patrice in her bad dude costume, getting on the escalator in the parking garage. From there she enters the main "town square" part of the mall, where her bogus bulk makes her easy to spot as she walks among the other pedestrians. She goes into and out of the Apple store and Crate & Barrel, then buys a movie ticket and enters the lobby of the multiplex.

"Show me the emergency exits," Susan says.

The security guy obliges, and when we see Patrice slip out the back door of the theater and walk south toward 3rd Street, the hair on the back of my neck jumps to attention.

Susan makes one more attempt to ditch me, but this time it's pretty half-hearted because her focus is on orchestrating another door-to-door search, concentrating on the streets south of The Grove and looking for a missing person of an altogether different description. I stand by patiently, listening while she has an unsatisfying phone conversation with her supervisor.

"Captain, I respectfully disagree," Susan says. "The sooner we act on this information, the more likely—" She holds the phone away from her ear while the captain barks something at her. "No sir, I am not privy to your other manpower issues." A shorter burst of barking. "Yes sir, I will certainly do my best until such time. Thank you, sir." She hangs up and makes like she's going to hurl her phone, but doesn't.

"I beg your pardon, mademoiselle," I say á la Pepe LePew. "Eez zere some way zat I may be of service?"

Susan uses a color copier at a Kinko's on Beverly to enlarge and reproduce the snapshot of Patrice in costume. She makes me wait in the car, because the prospect of anyone finding out that she let a reporter ride shotgun on her investigation is making her as nervous as a cat at a Vietnamese cookout. I try to put her at ease by reminding her that it's really the other way around—Deb and I were in possession of the photo first, and I probably would have already used it to find Patrice if I didn't have to deal with some dim-witted detective slowing me down. This doesn't quite have the calming effect I was aiming for, but at least it gets her to stop worrying and resumé snarling.

We divide the search area and split up, agreeing to keep in frequent phone contact. Impersonating a law enforcement officer is a felony and I've promised Susan I won't do it, so I wait until she's out of earshot before I knock on the first apartment manager's door and say, "Police!" On my fourth try, I hit paydirt.

"Yah, I know that big schvartze," says Mrs. Lipowitz, a little old lady with a hump that would make Igor envious. "He's vun uf my tenants."

chapter sixteen

I SUMMON SUSAN and she's there in a flash. Mrs. Lipowitz's spine may be showing its age, but her mind remains as sharp as her breath, which up close is a real knee-buckler. She has laid eyes on her tenant, "Mr. Johnson," exactly twice—once just over a year ago when she first rented him a one-bedroom apartment, and then not again until last Monday, which happens to be day that Patrice Williams disappeared. In between, Mrs. Lipowitz has observed various people coming and going from the apartment, including a pretty girl and several other big schvartzes, but never Mr. Johnson. He always pays his rent on time and by mail, in the form of a Western Union money order. Mrs. Lipowitz wishes that all of her tenants would pay in this fashion—there's nothing worse than some chatty sheygitz dropping off a check in the middle of *Judge Judy*.

Mrs. Lipowitz leads us to #217 and knocks on the door.

"Hello in der, Meesta Johnson!" she hollers. She waits a few seconds, knocks again, then takes out her passkey.

"Would you mind letting me do that?" Susan asks her.

"Vutever you say," the landlady replies, surrendering the key. "Ve don't vant no trouble from ze Gestapo." Mrs. Lipowitz titters at her own joke and shuffles off toward her apartment. Susan pulls rubber gloves over her hands and paper booties over her shoes, then makes me do the same. She then startles me by producing a snub-nosed .38 revolver from somewhere under her armpit.

"Whoa," I say. "Maybe you'd better let me hang onto that." Susan doesn't acknowledge the suggestion. She releases the safety, then lowers the gun to her side and with her other hand carefully inserts the key in the door lock. Before she turns it, she has one more twinge of trepidation.

"I really shouldn't be letting you do this," she says.

"That's what all the nice girls say." Susan looks like she might kneecap me, but opens the door instead. The curtains are closed tight, but enough light leaks through for us to see that no one is present in the main room, dead or alive.

"Hello!" Susan calls out. "Police officer!" Getting no reply, she shuts the door behind us and takes a quick glance into the kitchen—also unoccupied—then advances toward the hallway leading to the rest of the apartment. I follow her, noting that the living room, though furnished, doesn't look lived in. There are no newspapers, magazines, or any other type of clutter, and the framed art posters on the wall are generic crap from Bed, Bath & Beyond. The place seems more like a model home, or maybe a porn set, than someone's residence.

The same holds true for the boudoir—queen-size bed, nightstand, and chair, all perfectly neat and characterless. The closet contains no clothes, only a few empty hangers.

"Shit," Susan says, and re-holsters her weapon. I am equally disappointed, but our spirits perk up a moment later. Susan uses the end of a pen to ease open the drawer of the nightstand, and inside is a veritable supermarket of sin: one baggie of pot; one stoner's pipe resting in an ashtray; one pocket mirror with razor blade, short straw, and coke residue on top of it; one box of ultra-thin condoms; and one economy-size tube of KY Jelly, half gone.

"Yikes," I say. "No wonder she doesn't have a lot of time to read." Susan gently slides the drawer closed, then drops down to the floor and shines a mini flashlight under the bed. Again using her pen, she fishes out a sheer white thong that gives me an instant sense memory of Patrice huddled on the ground behind the pool house. Susan dangles the panties in front of her nose and takes a sniff of the crotch.

"Now if I did that, you'd probably call me a perv," I say.

"I'm trying to get an idea of how long it's been there," Susan replies, unamused.

"And?"

"Not too long." I cock an eyebrow but decide it's best that I don't offer to confirm her finding. Susan drops the thong into a plastic evidence bag and seals it.

"Aren't you going to look under the covers?" I ask. She shakes her head.

"I'm gonna leave the bed just like it is for the lab guys." I follow as she takes a quick look in the bathroom—nothing there except a roll of toilet paper and two towels—and the linen closet, totally empty. We return to the living room and Susan notices something we both missed in the dim light on our first time through: on the floor alongside the couch is a copy of the *Booty* issue with Patrice on the cover. Susan carefully picks it up by its edges. The magazine is almost the same size as her evidence bags, and Susan struggles to slip it into one without smudging any possible fingerprints. This is why she isn't looking when I casually open the fridge and find that it is chock-full of Patrice Williams.

"Ahhh!" I shout, jumping back and smashing my head against the kitchen cabinets. "Fuck!" Susan knocks me aside and catches the door to the refrigerator just before it swings shut. She reopens it all the way and squats down to take a look inside. After a few seconds, I regain enough of my composure to lean forward and peer over her shoulder. All of the shelves and drawers have been removed, leaving just enough space to store one medium-size, Grade-A corpse. Patrice is in an upside-down jackknife position, with the back of her head resting on the floor of the fridge and her posterior pressing against its ceiling. She is naked but for her bra and panties, and a congealed stream of what first looks like barbecue sauce—but is of course dried blood—runs down both sides of her neck and spreads out across the bottom of the fridge. It's not until the puddle starts to ooze out onto the kitchen floor that the odor hits me, which proves that in times of high stress your senses can play funny tricks on you. A second ago I didn't notice any smell at all, and now it's like I'm downwind from a slaughterhouse.

"Jesus!" I gasp, pulling my shirt over my mouth and nose.

"Don't you puke in here," Susan snaps, a split second before I realize that's precisely what I'm about to do. "Outside!" She grabs me by my collar and belt and bum-rushes me to the front door. The first surge of reverse peristalsis hits the moment I reach the hallway, but I manage to turn it back. Just in time to catch the one that will not be denied, Susan yanks my shirt off over my head and holds it over my mouth. The crime scene thus remains uncompromised, but now I truly don't have a thing to wear.

When it comes to high-profile murders and the media, history has proven that yellow plastic police tape is no match for an army of creative and highly motivated sleaze-bags. LAPD policy is therefore to stay as far below the radar as possible until after the CSI team has wrapped up its field work. Susan and her superiors conduct all of their sensitive communications by cell phone, eschewing the radio frequencies that are closely monitored for any mention of violence involving famous and/or white people. Mrs. Lipowitz is also kept in the dark, because apparently not even a cloistered nun can resist the temptation to get her mug on *Access Hollywood*. I don't even bother trying to convince Susan to let me hang around, because in spite of what I said earlier, I know she's gone way out on a limb for me already and I don't want to get her in any trouble. Besides, it's now cold and dark outside, and I'm topless.

Fortunately my car is only a block away, and there is a wide range of athletic attire strewn about the trunk. I choose a Santa Clara University Broncos jersey that I believe I last wore while playing pickup basketball several months ago, and which could only be considered "clean" when compared to a shirt full of vomit. As I drive towards home, I call Jessica Levine to see how the rest of the shoot went at Boney's—okay—and to check what time we start in the morning—we don't, schmuck, it's our day off. (How could I have forgotten, even momentarily, a godsend of such colossal proportions?) It's clear from Jessica's tone that she doesn't feel I'm paying enough attention to my job, but I couldn't care less. I hang up and realize that my initial shock at the discovery of the body has given way to something that feels a lot worse, and before I know it there are hot tears streaming down my face.

Even though I'm alone—and there is no solitude in the world more absolute than the solitude inside one's automobile while driving around L.A.—I feel terribly embarrassed. I'm not so Stone Age that I think men shouldn't cry, but why am I having such a strong emotional reaction to the death of Patrice Williams? It's not like we were friends—it would be something of a stretch to say that we even really met. We had a brief, anonymous encounter, which she would have quickly forgotten if someone hadn't murdered her first. Have I been harboring some pathetic fantasy that I would see her again one day and that we would, as the kids say, hook up? Or did Patrice and I make some tiny human connection that I'm now mourning the loss of? Maybe it's neither—maybe I'm just a big pussy who's never found a dead chick in a fridge.

By the time I get home, I realize that I am as exhausted as a transvestite at a televangelist convention. It takes a superhuman effort to get my car into a parking space and my ass into bed, and I don't even care that the Skipper's surround sound is blaring an episode of *Desperate Housewives* that he's tortured me with at least once before. I fall asleep instantly and don't stir till sunup, when I awaken wearing all of my clothes and one of my shoes. If I have any dreams involving dead girls and major appliances, I can happily report that I don't remember them.

Refreshed and ready for action, there are a lot of tasks I should attend to on both the Patrice story and the *Mogul* episode. But there is something much more important that I've been neglecting, and so at 8:00 AM exactly, I call Sara and tell her I'm coming to pick Hallie up and take her for the day. Although nothing has yet changed legally and I will therefore be violating a court order by having an unsupervised visit, my recent experiences have made taking such a risk seem pretty tame. (It's hard to be scared of a slap on the wrist from Judge Steinbitch after you've survived Delawn taking a dump at point-blank range.) Sara not only doesn't argue with me, she says that Hallie will be thrilled. It's nice to see what a positive impact dread and despair can have on someone's personality.

The apartment is still relatively clean from my recent janitorial spree, so at least I can bring Hallie here without grossing her out. I do not, however, own a single book, toy, or anything else likely to amuse a child who lives in a Palestinian refugee camp, much less one who lives in Bel-Air and owns a six hundred square foot doll house. A strong internal voice says that just by thinking this way, I'm becoming everything I hate. Then an even stronger one says, "I'm going to Disneyland!"

But when I mention this plan to Hallie, it doesn't have quite the thrilling effect I'd hoped for.

"I hate Disneyland," she says. I couldn't agree more, but the sudden collapse of my fail-safe strategy leaves me up Paternity Creek without a paddle.

"Come on, what's wrong with it?" I ask.

"It's cheesy," Hallie says. "But not like Gouda or Jarlsberg. More like that nasty stuff they squirt on nachos." Who could argue with an analysis as trenchant as that?

"Okay, so we won't go there." Fortunately she doesn't ask where we'll go instead, which gives me time to think as we drive away from Richard and Sara's house. Unfortunately, all of the attractions that come to my racing mind either suffer from the *fromage* factor (Knott's Berry Farm, Magic Mountain, Universal Studios), or else don't seem age-appropriate for Hallie (the Getty Museum, the jazz festival at the Hollywood Bowl, the strip clubs by LAX). Then I realize that they call such things "diversions" for a reason, and that all I really want is to hang out with my daughter and do nothing more adventurous than watch *Animal Planet*. I also know that children actually crave boundaries, and whenever a parent projects calm, loving resolve, a child will quickly and happily accept whatever limits she is given. So I abandon all of my fancy schemes and check us into the Beverly Hills Hotel.

The so-called "Pink Palace" has undergone a complete renovation since the last time I stayed here in the late 1980s. They've also renovated the prices, and I would be obliged to use the available limit on two or three of my overtaxed personal credit cards to cover a single night's stay. To save everyone such embarrassment, I instead plunk down the Trevor Banes Productions card that I have agreed in writing never to use for any purpose not directly related to *The Mogul*. Maybe I'll invite Boney and his posse over to play shuffleboard.

Hallie is suitably impressed with our suite. Although she has stayed in many of the finest hotels of the world, the list does not include any in her hometown. The sheer decadence of my spur-of-the-moment decision has her running from room to room and squealing with excitement, which as I recall is exactly how her mother behaved the first time I brought her to a place like this. Watching Hallie, I have the same reaction that I had back then watching Sara: satisfaction with the short-term results, concerns about the long-term costs. I'm in a *carpe diem* kind of mood, though, so we immediately order a $70 room service breakfast (worth every penny) and pay $14.95 to catch *Agent Cody Banks 2* on pay-per-view (grand larceny).

Those costs are nothing next to what the boutique off the lobby wants for a couple of mid-range swimsuits, but since they graciously allow us to charge everything to our room, I get Hallie the two bikinis she's having a hard time deciding between, the suit that she thinks makes me look "less old," and some *au courant* European cover-ups for us both. We then proceed to have a great time at the famous pool, where for almost a century the biggest stars in the world have come to display their wares. There are no faces I recognize among the sunbathers today, but there are plenty of undiscovered pieces of talent to whom I would happily offer my own face as a chaise lounge. I mostly keep my attention on my date, however, and the only other person I talk to is the father of a girl about Hallie's age. While our daughters race each other underwater, we make small talk that inevitably leads to "What do you do?" I try to sound modest while telling him that I am the producer of *The Mogul*, and he does the same while telling me that he is the Sultan of Brunei.

After a couple of hours in the water, Hallie is tired and wants to go back to our room. She's barely touched her $18 chicken fingers when her eyelids start to hang heavy, and she lets me carry her to the bedroom and tuck her in for a nap. You can't really know how much happiness such a small, everyday thing can bring until you've had it, lost it, and found it again. I stretch out on the couch in the living room, and since I have nothing to read, I decide to do a little channel surfing. To my surprise, it turns out that somewhere along the line, TV has become darned good. There's a fascinating documentary about a nuclear submarine on The Learning Channel, but during the commercial I flip around and get caught up in some gripping golf coverage. When that's over (after a sudden death playoff, no less), I switch to a show that follows a real-life couple around while they search for a home to buy. Ordinarily I find the process of looking at houses even for my own potential purchase to be about as appealing as a colonoscopy. But in my present state of contentment, I feel no resistance or resentments toward anything—even a Reality show.

I must have drifted off, because when I'm awakened by my ringing cell phone, two gay guys on the telly are trash talking each other about their respective choices of window treatments. They each have a compelling argument, and I consider letting the call go to voice mail so I can see who ultimately bitch-slaps whom. But when I see it's Susan calling, I pick up right away.

"How's it going?" I say.

"It's going," Susan replies, sounding as bone-weary as I was last night. "They took the body out around four this morning, so I don't think anybody even noticed."

"Do they know how she died?"

"Yeah. Somebody with a lot of arm strength grabbed her from behind and practically cut her head off with a big knife."

"There's only two people who could do a thing like that," I say. "And I'm pretty sure one of 'em was playing golf in Florida."

"Where are you right now?" she asks.

"Shacked up at the Beverly Hills Hotel with a hot young babe."

"I see," Susan says, nonplussed by this news.

"My seven-year-old daughter," I explain. "This is the first time I've been alone with her in a year, so I decided to splurge."

"Got it," she says, then goes on to tell me that in order to get a warrant to search the bank records of Delawn's mother, she must present a judge with an affidavit from me that describes the telephone conversation I overheard. Susan has already prepared the document and needs to get my signature on it as soon as possible, so I ask her to bring it by the hotel.

Hallie gets up from her nap and immediately wants to head back to the pool. My main man the Sultan and his entourage have apparently called it a day, but there are plenty of new playmates in the water for Hallie. With the help of several translators, she explains the finer points of Sharks & Minnows to them, and a spirited game begins. When Susan calls to tell me she is in the lobby, I ask her to come find me at the pool. I quickly put on, then just as quickly take off, my new cover-up, remembering that "European" is generally interchangeable with "faggy."

Despite the fact that Susan looks as tired as she sounded on the phone, it gives me an unexpected thrill to see her emerge from the hotel building and walk toward me. I consider standing and greeting her with a hug, but then think better of it and it's a damned good thing I do. When I glance over toward the pool to check on Hallie, I see that she is being neither a shark nor a minnow, but rather a suspicious little spy-fish, staring balefully at Susan. I smile and wave at Hallie, but she doesn't reciprocate. Oh, well. Maybe I'll get to have a girlfriend when I'm eighty.

Susan perches uncomfortably on the edge of a chaise lounge while I read the affidavit.

"This looks fine," I say after I'm done.

"Then sign it and I'm on my way." Susan hands me a pen and I add my signature at the bottom of the last page, but hesitate before I give it back to her because I realize that this may be my last chance for a while to squeeze information out of her.

"What else did they turn up at the apartment?" I ask.

"Not much," she says. "Somebody gave it a good scrub-down after the murder."

"So you have no physical evidence?"

"I wouldn't say that," Susan says. "The lab found a semen stain on the underwear that was under the bed. And there was fresh seminal fluid inside the victim's vagina."

"So she had sex right before she was killed?"

"Not necessarily. It may have been deposited post-mortem."

"Jesus," I say. I restage the killing of Patrice Williams in my head, adding in the new information that Delawn is possibly a necrophiliac. The whole scene is so gruesomely vivid that I am temporarily transported away from the Beverly Hills Hotel, and I don't hear or see the person who approaches and stands right in front of me until Susan pokes me in the arm to bring me back to the present.

"I said excuse me, is that chair taken?" the pretty, smiling woman says, pointing to the vacant chaise lounge on the other side of me. Except it's not a pretty, smiling woman at all. It's my wife.

chapter seventeen

I MEAN MY *ex*-wife.

"Hi," Sara says. "Hallie called and invited me to go swimming with you guys." Sara turns to Susan, who has already stood up and retreated several steps. "I hope I didn't interrupt anything," Sara says.

"Uh, no," I say, struggling to my feet. "This is Susan. Susan, Sara." The two women exchange awkward "his and handshakes. I can't help but notice that while Susan is certainly attractive, you'd never say that while she was standing next to Sara. And to supplement all her natural gifts, Sara keeps an army of designers, stylists, cosmeticians, and physicians busy keeping everything just right. One glance at her is enough to make my wallet ache.

"If you could just go ahead and sign that contract, I'll be out of your hair," Susan says to me. I have completely forgotten about the affidavit and pen that I still have in my hand.

"Oh, right, sure," I say, adding for Sara's benefit, "Work stuff." I scribble my signature where required, fold the paper, and hand it to Susan, and only then notice that Sara is now staring hard at her.

"Mommy!" Hallie shrieks. She abandons her new pals and comes running across the pool deck at Sara, wrapping her arms around her mother's waist. But Sara doesn't even acknowledge Hallie, and her gaze doesn't waver from Susan.

"Do I know you from somewhere?" Sara asks.

"I don't think so," Susan replies, sliding the affidavit into a file folder and making to leave.

"Are you in the business?" Sara continues, ignoring her daughter's desperate desire for attention.

"No, not really. I'm sorry, I have to run," Susan says, then to me, "Thanks." She turns and walks off, Sara tracking her all the way around the pool.

"Mommy, where's your bathing suit?" Hallie demands.

"In my bag," Sara says absently. "Ted, who was that woman?"

"Just one of our vendors from the show," I say. "They make a big deal about having signed contracts for everything."

"She looks so familiar," Sara says, as Susan disappears into the main building. I shrug as nonchalantly as possible.

"Come on, I'll show you where the bathroom is," Hallie says, using every bit of her strength to drag Sara away by the arm. I sit and try to figure out what the hell just happened. When did Hallie call Sara? It had to be while she was in the bedroom and I was dozing on the couch. And why? I guess because children want their mommies and daddies to be together, period. It's not necessary that the parties be attractive, decent, and obviously meant for one another, á la *The Parent Trap*. You and the former missus can both be obese, bitter, and doing hard time for mutual assault—as soon as you get paroled, the kids will conspire to have you show up at the same Sizzler on your anniversary.

Most importantly, what are the potential repercussions of Sara running into Susan? I can only describe them as numerous and dire. Since Sara presumably met Patrice on at least one occasion—the same day I saw her—she would naturally take an interest in the media frenzy concerning the model's disappearance. Therefore she has no doubt seen Susan on the news, and if and when she realizes this and tells Richard, he might figure out that I'm using *The Mogul* to try and nail Boney. Even if he doesn't, my connection to Susan will mean an abrupt end to our shoot, which will leave us with an expensive but worthless partial episode. It will also probably lead to some seriously vindictive legal action, and somehow I don't think Trevor will feel obligated to cover my lawyer's fees. Perhaps worst of all, it will mean that I will have no further opportunities to snoop, and thus no further usefulness to Susan.

Hallie and Sara emerge from the changing room, and I recognize Sara's bikini as the same $600 number in the lobby boutique's window display. Sara's body is as well-proportioned and nearly as firm as the mannequin's, and I note that both the men and women around the pool take a good, long gander at her as she and Hallie come toward me. Maybe as a small consolation my buddy and fellow ass bandit the Sultan of Brunei will return, see me with Sara, and give me the thumbs up.

Hallie insists that all three of us get in the pool, and soon we find ourselves drafted into the still-raging war of the fishes. One quality not generally associated with sharks is ambivalence, which is why I make a make a very poor one when Sara is the last remaining minnow and it is therefore my job to swim over and "eat" her.

"Get her, Daddy!" Hallie screams as I allow Sara to cross the pool for the third time in a casual backstroke, unmolested. "You have to get Mommy!" Of course I can't be upset with Hallie—she doesn't know anything about the ugliness that went on between Sara and me, and she never will. I made an absolute promise to myself years ago never to play that card, no matter what Sara does or how mad it makes me. The down side of protecting Hallie from the truth, however, is that she is left with only the meaningless clichés that grownups employ to "explain" divorce to kids: "Mommy and Daddy still love each other, we just can't live together anymore." "Why not?" "Because we like to do different things." "What kinds of different things?" "Well, at night Daddy likes to read, and Mommy likes to get butt-fucked by Richard." Without this last piece of information or something equally problematic, it's almost impossible to get a kid to drop the subject. So I reluctantly swim over and tag Sara on the foot, and I'm relieved to see that my fingers don't immediately rot and fall off.

We get out of the water and Hallie wants to order up some more chow. As Sara peruses the poolside menu, I wonder how I will keep from strangling her if she tries to stick me for a $17 salad. Perhaps she reads my mind, because all she asks for is a $4.75 iced tea. After Hallie places her own order she runs off to the potty, and I avail myself of the opportunity to ask Sara a question that has been gnawing at me for the past half hour.

"What the fuck are you doing here?"

"I told you, Hallie called and invited me."

"Yeah? She also invited me to go with you and Richard on safari last year, but you may have noticed that I didn't pop up from behind a wildebeest."

"I was afraid if I asked, you'd say no."

"That's a great defense," I say. "Maybe you can license it to Kobe."

"I'm sorry, Ted. I just wanted our daughter to see that her parents could still be friends."

"Especially since you're getting ready to turn her whole world upside down again, right?"

"That's got nothing to do with it," Sara says, then after a strained silence adds, "I guess I should go." But before she can make a move, Hallie comes running back from the bathroom and jumps on her lap.

"I've got a great idea," Hallie announces. "Tonight Mommy can sleep with me in the bed, and Daddy can sleep on the couch."

"Oh I can't spend the night, sweetie," Sara says.

"Why not?"

"Just because." They go back and forth like this a few more times before Hallie gives up and falls into one of her pouts. I'm so pissed at Sara for ruining our perfect day that I can't speak either, so we turn into a pretty quiet group. Finally Sara breaks the silence.

"I just remembered where I've seen that Susan woman," she says. My heart sinks the tiny remaining distance to the ground. Sara continues, "The b-i-t-c-h almost backed into me a couple of months ago at the Beverly Center."

"Really?" I say. Sara's memory board has evidently short-circuited again, and I have never been more glad to be reminded that she is an idiot.

"Then she got all bent out of shape because I honked my horn," Sara says. "We both got out of our cars and I swear, I was this close to slapping her."

"I didn't like her either," Hallie says emphatically.

"Well I doubt I'll ever see that b-i-t-c-h again," I say. "But if I do, I'll tell her to drive more carefully."

Sara leaves shortly thereafter, and I manage to coax Hallie out of her funk by getting her a mani-pedi at the hotel spa, which according to the sign out front is "by" someone or something called La Prairie. If you think it should cost less than the full listed rate of $135 to paint the teensy-weensy nails of a seven-year-old, I'm afraid that you and La Prairie just don't see eye to eye. I am aware that by showering all of these obscene indulgences on Hallie, I'm both teaching her an unhealthy lesson and setting an unsustainable precedent, but I don't care. After the last few miserable years, seeing my little girl smile is worth any amount of Trevor's money.

I have to be at work early tomorrow, so I take Hallie back to Sara and Richard's just before her nine o'clock bedtime. She fights me on it at first, but I'm eventually able to convince her that soon she'll have her own room at my new place, where she can stay for as long as she wants. After I drop her off, my plan is to head back to the Beverly Hills Hotel—after all, the suite is paid for until tomorrow, and by any standard it's an improvement over the execrable address where I normally hang my hat. But my internal autopilot takes me toward my apartment, and by the time I realize the mistake, I've traveled far enough that I say to hell with it and keep going. Who knows, maybe I miss the Skipper.

I call Susan and discover that she is feeling a little b-i-t-c-h-y.

"You suck," she says in lieu of "Hello."

"I didn't know she was coming," I whine in my own defense.

"Well you should have. Have you gotten the nasty, threatening phone call from her husband yet?"

"No, and I'm not going to. Sara has you mixed up with some woman she got into a cat-fight with over a parking space."

"She could still figure it out later."

"Later it's not going to matter."

There's no point in debating it, but we do anyway for a few minutes. Although I wish that Susan weren't all pissed off at me (again), I at least find her style of argument to be logical and, for the most part, fair. Listening to her build her case that I am an untrustworthy douche bag, I have a strong sense of déjà vu. Maybe I'm being reminded of the good old days with Deb, when it was possible to have a spirited Socratic exchange followed by some equally spirited screwing. This is *not* the same thing, by the way, as a "passionate love/hate relationship." I experienced a lifetime's worth of that in my six years with Sara, and while I won't deny that the fightin' 'n' fuckin' combo has its initial charms, it simply doesn't hold up under a long-term cost-benefit analysis. Think of it as a game of musical chairs, with the chairs representing the sex and the music your wretched existence all the moments of the day when you're not getting laid. The analogue for the inevitable deterioration of the love/hate relationship is the gradual removal of the chairs, and the more they take away, the more craven you become about trying to leap on one at any cost. And of course when the music stops for good, only one player gets to sit. The other gets to go beat off for a couple of years.

I ultimately offer Susan an apology, and she responds with one of her own, acknowledging that her mood is mostly due to exhaustion and nervousness about tomorrow. Since all the evidence has now been collected from the murder scene, and every neighbor who might have seen or heard anything has been interviewed (the latter effort having unfortunately yielded nothing beyond what the landlady already told us), it is now time to reveal the fate of Patrice Williams to the world.

This will happen in the following manner: At precisely twelve noon, Susan will ring the doorbell of Patrice's mother out in Diamond Bar and deliver the terrible news. At the same time, Boney will be performing and then signing autographs at Universal City Walk, with the entire *Mogul* crew on hand to record the event. I will personally make sure that at least one camera—Deb's—is focused on Boney at all times. The assumption is that shortly after Patrice's family is informed of her death, one of them will call Boney and we will be able to capture his reaction—not only what he says, but also his body language—on tape. While this strategy probably won't yield any evidentiary slam-dunks, i.e. Boney covering the mouthpiece of his phone and high-fiving with Delawn, Susan nevertheless believes that we shouldn't miss such a rare and valuable opportunity to document the defendant-to-be's behavior when he hears the "news." Later in the day, a press conference will be held at Parker Center, where the chief of police himself will announce Patrice's death and vow to bring the killer or killers to justice.

As the lead detective on the case, Susan would ordinarily appear right alongside the chief. But in light of Sara's untimely appearance at the Beverly Hills Hotel, Susan has decided to avoid the glare of the TV cameras until the *Mogul* shoot is over and I no longer have access to Boney. I promise to make it up to her by giving her the full hero treatment in the print version of the story, and to fight to the death against any attempt to have Denise Richards play her in the movie.

Roger Dominus will not be on hand for today's shoot—once he's given the contestants their assignments for the episode, they won't see him again until he makes his entrance to the dreaded conference room. My colleague Jessica Levine concedes that she may have fudged this point a bit when seeking permission to film at City Walk from the young VP of Special Events at Universal. Jessica may also have stretched the truth when she described the music that Boney will be performing on the outdoor stage as "Old School R&B." If any higher-ups from corporate HQ happen to visit City Walk while Boney is serenading shoppers with selections from *Wuh Duh Fuh*, it is quite possible that the poor VP will lose his job. On the other hand, he's already scored himself a date with the always-in-demand Jessica Levine.

I get to the location at 11:00 AM, half an hour before Boney and his entourage are scheduled to arrive. Our crew and the "Dominators" are all in place and there isn't much to do except wait, so I use my cell phone to tell Deb to bail on the dreary production meeting and meet me at the Starbucks on the other end of the mall. Once there and seated in a quiet corner we go over the plan, and Deb assures me that whatever Boney does when he gets the phone call about Patrice will be captured in its entirety by her camera. She then asks why Susan has opted to be way out in Diamond Bar instead of right here where the action is, and I explain about the unfortunate incident yesterday at the Beverly Hills Hotel with Sara.

"You ASSHOLE!" Deb shouts, banging her coffee down on the table and scaring the crap out of me and everybody else in the place.

"Take it easy," I murmur. "It wasn't my fault."

"Bull fucking shit," Deb says. A pimply teenaged barista comes out from behind the pastry case and approaches us.

"Excuse me, ma'am," the barista says. "I'm going to have to ask you to watch your language or lower your voice."

"Whatever, dickweed," Deb growls at the kid. He retreats and Deb turns back to me. "You're going to let her do it again."

"Do what again?"

"What do you think, moron? Fuck up your big story."

"Sara is not going to fuck up my story."

"What makes you so sure?"

"In the first place, she didn't even recognize Susan. And the game's just about over anyway."

"What's that supposed to mean?"

"The cops are going to take Delawn and his mama in for questioning tonight," I tell her. "Delawn's gonna freak and call Boney, Boney's gonna freak and call a lawyer, and the lawyer's gonna freak at the thought of TV cameras pointed at anybody except him. So we're history after today anyway, and Sara can't fuck anything up."

"You've been saying that for eight years," Deb replies. "And every time you turn out to be as wrong as kiddie beauty pageants."

"Okay," I say, getting annoyed. "Tell me how she's going to ruin the story."

"I don't know how. But I guaran-fuckin-tee you she'll find a way."

I leave Deb and stroll back toward the stage area, and along the way I get a call from the yet-again frazzled Jessica.

"We're going to be late," she bleats. Jessica is currently with the "Roger That" team a short distance away at Boney's house. The plan for this morning was to tape Boney doing a bunch of call-in guest spots (which were supposedly booked by the contestants—yeah, right) on local radio stations. At the last minute, however, Lovey Mack informed us that Boney would instead be laying down a new rap track in his home recording studio with an up-and-coming MF artist known as Lil' Killa. I resent Lovey's blatant attempt to use *The Mogul* to plug another one of his acts while I'm trying to use it to revive my career and destroy his livelihood, and I tried to thwart Lovey by claiming that the network's censor won't allow anyone whose stage name is a felony to appear on prime time. But Lovey wouldn't budge, and apparently the session is going slowly due to Lil' Killa's speech impediment.

"The kid can't say three words in a row without stuttering," Jessica says, referring to Lil' Killa. "I think he's retarded or something."

"Did you tell Lovey that we have to stick to the schedule?" I ask.

"He won't listen," Jessica wails. "At this rate, we could be here for another hour."

I tell Jessica not to panic, then I hang up, check my watch, and proceed to panic. If Boney gets the call from Patrice's family before he reaches City Walk, our whole plan goes up in smoke. Fortunately I have no trouble reaching Susan, who is parked down the street from Patrice's mother's house. She tells me not to worry, she'll just stand by until I give her the go-ahead. She also shares a juicy piece of news, hot off the presses. The police search of Delawn's mother's bank records (which my affidavit made possible) has confirmed that $100,000 was indeed deposited to her account during the past week. $50,000 came in the form of cash brought into the Wells Fargo North Hollywood branch, and a search of Boney's bank records shows that exact amount being withdrawn, also in cash, on the same day. The other $50,000 was wired from a bank in the Cayman Islands, where secrecy laws and Byzantine corporate structures make it virtually impossible to learn the identity of the sender. I'm about to ask Susan what she makes of this when I'm rudely interrupted by a fat, middle-aged male tourist who invades my personal space.

"'Scuse me, can you tell me what all a these cameras are here for?" I frown at Fatty and point to the cell phone I'm holding to my head, but this doesn't deter him in the slightest. "Those fellas said you were the man in charge." He points to a cluster of crew members, who whenever they're approached on location by curious civilians love nothing more than to deflect the dipshits onto the producer.

"We're shooting a TV show," I say, then turn my back on him.

“You are?” he says, once again stepping in front of me. “Is it one I might’ve seen?”

“Sounds like you’ve got work to do,” Susan says to me over the phone. “Call me when he gets there.” She hangs up and I’m left with no one to talk to besides His Rudeness.

“I don’t know, sir,” I tell him. “Do you watch a lot of television?”

“A fair amount, I guess.”

“Really? How do you find time with all your triathlon training?”

A few minutes past noon I get another call from Jessica. The interminable recording session with Lil’ Killa is finally over, and Boney and company are on their way. I tell everybody to look alive, and as soon as I see the familiar Maybach enter the parking lot, I call Susan and let her know that the moment of truth has arrived. Delawn glides the Maybach to a stop alongside the red carpet that has been provided by our kind hosts at Universal, and he comes around to open the rear door. This kind of star treatment is guaranteed to draw a crowd, and many of the hundred or so gawkers who have gathered behind the velvet ropes begin applauding the moment Boney steps out, though I can tell by the looks on their faces that most of them have absolutely no clue as to who he is.

The logical way to address this lack of familiarity would be to have Boney perform first and sign autographs second, but I’m concerned that as soon as he starts rapping about his rod, the welcome mat will be yanked out from under us *tout de suite*. So we do it the other way around and direct Boney to his seat behind the table that is stacked with copies of *Wuh Duh Fuh*. It is now the responsibility of our contestants to whip up some wild enthusiasm in the passersby, or at least find a few of them willing to accept a free CD. This proves to be easier said than done, however, as the weekday crowd at City Walk is made up mostly of visitors from the Midwest who were assured that they wouldn't run into anybody who looks like Boney as long as they didn't take the wrong exit off the freeway. The Dominators nonetheless give it the old college try.

"Check it out, they're giving away free stuff over there," I hear LaFonda tell a blonde mother-daughter duo in matching Terminator t-shirts.

"What kinda free stuff?" the mom asks suspiciously.

"It's a brand new CD by Boney," LaFonda says. "And let me tell you ladies, it is the bomb." Team Terminator must believe that an actual explosion is therefore imminent, because they scurry off in the opposite direction. Undaunted, LaFonda moves on to her next target, who happens to be the tubby, ill-mannered tourist who pestered me a little while ago.

"How you doin' today?" La Fonda asks him, then continues without waiting for an answer. "I bet you'd be doin' a lot better if you had a free CD."

"Well sure, but how do I get me one?" he asks.

"You just come right over here," LaFonda says, taking the man's hand and leading him over to Boney's autograph table. The camera crew assigned to LaFonda keeps pace alongside them and I follow, curious to see how Boney will relate to this particular segment of his fan base.

"What's your name?" LaFonda asks the fat man.

"Vernon," he says.

"Vernon, I'd like you to meet Boney."

"'Sup, V-dog," Boney mumbles while making a few felt-tipped squiggles on one of the CD cases. He holds it out to Vernon, but rather than take it from him, Vernon suddenly reaches into his pants pocket.

"Muthafuck!" Boney cries as he dives under the table.

chapter eighteen

Delawn, who stands a few feet away keeping a close eye on the proceedings, jumps forward and grabs Vernon's wrist just as it comes out of his pocket.

"I got the gat!" Delawn shouts, but what he wrests from Vernon's fingers is not a handgun but a harmless, folded-up piece of paper.

"Take your hands off of me or I'll have you arrested," Vernon orders, with an authority he didn't previously display. He snatches the paper back from the confused Delawn and then addresses Boney, who is just poking his head out from under the other side of the table.

"No sir, I will not accept your filth and depravity," Vernon announces loudly.

"What are you, some kinda racist?" LaFonda says, after first making sure she's still on camera. "I bet you've never even heard any of Boney's music."

"I don't have to," Vernon tells her, then unfolds his piece of paper and begins reading aloud. "I sit with your bitch in my crib. Getting my tip licked while the Lakers is on." With a shudder I realize that the words must be Boney's and the speaker must be a member of one of the media watchdog groups I authorized Mfume to anonymously tip off about Boney's public appearance. In all the excitement of the last few days—Sara's shenanigans, me finding a dead body, and nearly becoming one myself—I managed to forget all about this upcoming episode of Fucking With the Contestants. And of course no one has reminded me, because no one is supposed to—due to the extremely sensitive nature of FWCs, Trevor forbids us from ever discussing them outside of the conference room (which is regularly swept for listening devices). I find Mfume's face among the crowd behind our cameras, and he grins and gives me the thumbs-up.

"Somebody get this fat old bitch outta my face, 'fore I knock him out," Boney says.

"Are you threatening me with physical violence?" Vernon says.

"You see any other fat old bitches in my face?" Boney says. What the hell was I thinking? One thing I clearly *wasn't* thinking was that the assault of the bluenoses would collide head-on with our efforts to capture Boney on tape as he hears the news about Patrice. I glance over at Deb and see that at least she's holding up her end, keeping her camera steadily focused on Boney.

"Stop trying to destroy our children!" This battle cry comes not from Vernon but from a female voice somewhere behind him. I turn and see that the new demonstrator is a woman in her thirties who I wouldn't mind doing, but I'm guessing I won't get the chance because she's just unfolded a sign that reads "GOD HATES HOLLYWOOD." Nearby, several other clean-cut bystanders lock hands and launch into a hymn.

"Deep in my heart, I do believe," they sing. "We shall overcome, some day, some day."

"Man, I do not need this shit," Boney says. "Let's go, D." Delawn starts to clear a path for Boney's exit, but I rush to intercept them.

"We can't leave yet," I tell Boney.

"Maybe *you* can't, muthafucka."

"Give me five minutes to clear these people out of here," I tell him. "If we don't shoot this scene today, there's no way we can finish the episode in time to air it." Boney doesn't answer, but at least he stops trying to walk through me.

"Where the fuck is Lovey?" he asks Delawn.

"He say he have a meetin'."

"Meetin' my ass. That nigga be pissin' me off big time."

"Just five minutes," I repeat to Boney, and back away before he can refuse. As soon as I'm out of earshot, I press Redial on my phone. After a couple of rings, Susan picks up.

"DeRo—"

"Don't tell them yet!" I blurt out, but before Susan can reply I hear the sounds of hysterical grief coming from her end of the line. "Shit," is all I can say.

"Is there a problem?" Susan asks.

"Never mind, I'll handle it," I tell her, and return the phone to my pocket. I check again on Deb, whose camera continues to stick like glue to Boney. I then hurry over to where Jessica, Mfume, and our other producers are standing.

"I'll be curious to see how you edit this," Jessica snipes, her arms crossed in the classic "I told you so" pose, just in case I forgot that she was staunchly opposed to this FWC. I ignore her and turn to Mfume.

"We've got to shut this protest down," I tell him.

"What for?" Mfume says, understandably irked that I want to kill his brainchild. "It's just starting to get good."

"Boney's going to bail, and we can't afford that," I say.

"All right," Mfume sighs. "Where's the guy from City Walk?" Jessica points to a frightened-looking little rabbit standing a few feet away in what has to be his father's suit. He's jabbering urgently into a walkie-talkie. "What's his name?" Mfume asks.

"Brandon Fein…" she says, but Mfume is already gone.

"Brandon, I'm Mfume Salaam" he says, striding over and pumping Brandon's quivering hand. "Looks like we have a little problem here."

"Yes, I'm afraid we're going to have to cancel the event immediately," Brandon says.

"Let's not overreact," Mfume says. "We just need to round

up all these white supremacists and anti-Semites and run 'em out of here."

"Sorry, but that would be against company policy," he says, then takes a confused look at the protestors. "How do you know they're anti-Semitic?"

"Let's stay focused, Brandon," Mfume says. "We have to shoot this scene, and you gave us permission to do it here."

"But the agreement specifically gives us the right to rescind at any time, in our sole and absolute discretion," Brandon burbles, and just in case we don't believe him, he produces the document from his jacket pocket and points urgently at the relevant passage.

"Have you ever seen *The Mogul*?" Mfume asks Brandon.

"I watch it every week. But—"

"Have you ever wondered how we take a bunch of completely interchangeable camera whores and turn them into distinct characters? You know, like the nice guy, the sneaky guy, the slut?"

"I'm not sure what this has to do with—"

"It's called editing, Brandon," Mfume continues. "Through the miracle of editing, we can make anybody look like a hero or a villain. For example, you can be the courageous young executive who stood up for the First Amendment. Or, if you prefer, you can be one of the Nazis."

"That's… outrageous!" Brandon sputters, his face turning purple. "I'm Jewish!"

"Me too," Mfume says. "That's why we have to stick together." He gives Brandon's shoulders a squeeze of solidarity, then leaves the poor bastard to consider his various unsavory options.

"That was awesome," I tell Mfume when he rejoins our group.

"You gotta love Reality," he replies.

Over by the autograph table, things are getting a little out of hand. The attractive protestor I noticed before has grabbed a copy of *Wuh Duh Fuh* and is trying to ignite it with a fireplace lighter.

"This flame represents the Hell that awaits all sinners!" she says.

"That CD represent fourteen dollars, bitch," Boney says, trying to snatch it back from her without getting burned. I rush over and speak privately in his ear.

"Security is on their way," I tell him. Boney starts to snarl something back at me, but whatever it is gets obliterated by a loud BANG! right next to my head. Boney and I both instinctively duck at the noise and consequently knock each other to the ground, just as two more explosions go off in rapid succession. The next thing I hear is a cacophony of screaming and shouting.

"He's got a gun!"

"Jesus save us!"

"Muthafucka!"

Feet fly in every direction, and I get kicked several times in the stampede. By the time I'm able to struggle back to standing, Boney has done the same and is wildly waving around an automatic pistol. There are no obvious targets to shoot at, however, as almost everybody has either run or hit the deck and stayed there. The only person standing his or her ground, in fact, is Deb. Her mission was to keep Boney in her viewfinder, and that's exactly what she's doing.

"Damn, dog, where you hit?" I can barely hear Boney talking to me through the loud ringing in my ears. I look at my clothes, but see no blood or other signs of injury.

"I don't think I am," I say, but then realize that Boney isn't talking to me at all. He's looking down at Delawn, who remains sprawled on the ground.

"I dunno," Delawn wheezes. "Here?" He touches the middle of his massive chest, and his fingers come away dripping blood.

"Shit," Boney says. "I gonna get them muthafuckas." He sprints off toward the parking structure. I see Deb start to follow him, then stop and look at me. After taking another glance at Delawn and thinking for a moment, I beckon her toward me. Then I kneel at Delawn's side and begin talking softly to him.

"Hey, Delawn," I say. "Where does it hurt?"

"You a doctor?" he moans.

"No, but I once took a lifesaving class so I could be a counselor at camp. And based on that, I'd say you're in deep shit."

"Get a muthafuckin' doctor."

"The ambulance is on its way." This must be true, as I can hear multiple sirens approaching. I make sure Deb has her camera trained on Delawn before I continue. "But if you don't make it, your mama wouldn't want you to die with anything heavy on your conscience."

"How you know my mama?" Delawn says, trying to grab at me but stopped cold by the agony that any movement clearly causes him.

"Just relax," I tell him. "I know all kinds of things. Like I know you killed Patrice Williams." Delawn's eyes, which a second ago were tiny slits, now open wide and stare into mine with a combination of shock and fury. "All you have to do to ease your soul is tell me who paid you to do it."

"Fuckin' liar," Delawn rasps. His voice is now so weak that Deb must move her camera and its attached microphone to within a few feet of his face.

"You know I'm not lying, Delawn," I say. "You told somebody to deposit a hundred thousand dollars in your mama's bank account." Dim as they now are, his eyes again register surprise that I possess such information. "Just tell me who," I coax him.

"Liar," Delawn whispers once more, then clams up in order to devote all of his energy to the task of staying alive for ten additional seconds.

LAPD shuts down City Walk and commandeers a Mexican-themed restaurant called Mucho Macho to serve as a temporary field headquarters. Once inside, the first thing I do is phone Hallie's school and tell them to let her know that her daddy is all right and will call her later. Some snippy assistant principal informs me that according to the instructions on file, communications with Hallie can only come from her mother or stepfather. I tell the woman that in that case, I would like to leave a message for the assistant principal instead: eat shit. I then phone Sara and ask her to get word to Hallie, and hang up before she can ask me too many questions. Let her get the details the same way she keeps up with all other current events, by reading *Us Weekly*.

The contestants and all production personnel from *The Mogul*, plus any other witnesses who didn't have enough sense to escape while they could, have been herded into Mucho Macho and are being interviewed one at a time by a team of detectives. The former protestors, nine in total, are sequestered in the semi-private "Sombrero Room" in order to avoid any further clashes between them and our crew. In the immediate aftermath of the shooting, an African American sound engineer shouted an accusation that Vernon, the leader of the protestors, tried to kill Boney. City Walk security guards tackled Vernon and apparently broke several of his ribs, but found no weapons. The protestors retaliated by claiming that the assailant was not a man at all, but an avenging angel who would be returning soon to deal severely with all remaining sinners. This in turn led to a Red State/Blue State screaming match that touched on fundamentalism, freedom, and the frequently asked but never satisfactorily answered question of whether Sponge Bob Square Pants is gay.

On the side of the restaurant where I'm sitting, some people remain convinced that the Christian crusaders are responsible for the bloodbath. But several others claim to have seen a young black man in a hooded sweatshirt running away just after the shots were fired, and a still-hysterical Jessica Levine insists that it was Boney himself who shot Delawn. I know this is nonsense because Boney and I were practically slow-dancing at the time the bullets flew, and he couldn't possibly have pulled his gun until afterward. Jessica's mind is playing tricks on her, but of course it's no use trying to convince the fool woman of that. All I get for my well-intended efforts is a diatribe about how the whole thing is really *my* fault, which she claims already to have communicated via her Blackberry to Trevor. And Boney isn't around to dispute Jessica's charge—the last anyone saw of him is when he ran off toward the parking garage.

The most likely way to shed some sober light on what happened would be to review the footage from the seven *Mogul* cameras that were rolling at the time of the shooting. But we can't do that because the first LAPD lieutenant to arrive on the scene seized all of our tapes, including Deb's, as evidence. It is thus only a matter of time before the cops see Delawn's final close-up and single me out as a guy with some 'splainin' to do. In anticipation of this, I called Susan and gave her the short version of what happened, and she is presently on her way here from Diamond Bar. I'd rather not make any official statements until Susan and I have a chance to get our stories straight, so I spend most of my time hiding out in the excessively disinfected "Caballeros" restroom. That's where I am, perched on the throne with my pants down in case anyone peeks under the partition, when I receive a call from an ecstatic Trevor Bane.

"Congratulations, Ted," he says. "You have vastly exceeded my expectations, which I must confess were rather limited."

"Uh, thanks," is all I can think of to say.

"I'm looking at a helicopter shot on Fox News right now. It appears they're getting ready to remove the body."

"Sounds like you folks over there in China know more than I do."

"I take it you can't get a decent camera angle from where you are," Trevor says.

"Not really," I reply, inasmuch as I'm looking at a toilet paper dispenser and a magic marker drawing of a hirsute pudenda.

"Not to worry, we'll use the network's footage."

"Are you saying you actually plan to go ahead with the episode?" I ask, incredulous. The response is the first honest-to-goodness belly laugh I've ever heard from Trevor.

"That's a good one," he says. "It's taken a while, but I think I've finally caught on to your sense of humor."

"Great. I'll try to keep the zingers coming."

"No time for fun and games now, I'm afraid. I have a million calls to make."

"Okay, I guess I'll just wait to hear from you. Unless you want me to have somebody else killed."

"That won't be necessary," Trevor says, back to his usual all-business mode. "But please tell Jessica Levine that she's fired."

I abandon my hideout and find that crew and protestors alike have gathered around the TV in the cocktail lounge. There's a lot of jostling and standing on tippy-toes in an effort to get a better view of the screen, in spite of the fact that the event being televised is happening live right outside the restaurant's front window. Through it Deb and I watch alone as two slightly-built coroner's deputies struggle to slide Delawn's enormous corpse onto a gurney.

"Siddown, there's nothing to see," a police sergeant barks at the TV viewers, but since this is clearly nonsense, no one feels obliged to obey. The timing of the distraction is fortuitous, because just then Susan enters Mucho Macho with a grim-faced older cop. She indicates with a nod that Deb and I should follow them toward the rear, and we're able to do so without attracting any unwanted attention. The four of us enter the vast stainless-steel kitchen, where the cooks and busboys are easing their boredom with the help of a number of items that appear to have been liberated from the bar.

"Please vacate this room immediately," the older cop says to the kitchen staff, but nobody budges until he adds *"Vamos, viene la migra!"* Within seconds, we have the place to ourselves. Susan introduces the senior flatfoot as her boss, Captain Cardenas.

"Detective DeRosa tells me you've both been very helpful to her investigation," says Captain Cardenas.

"We're just trying to do the right thing," I say.

"I bet," the captain says. I take an instant dislike to the man —there's nothing worse than a smartass. "I've got some serious problems with the way the detective has conducted her investigation, but that can wait," he continues. "Tell us about this video you took of the victim before he died."

"He didn't admit to anything," I say. "He just kept calling me a liar."

"Did you get the shooting on camera?" he asks Deb.

"I don't know," Deb says. "Your people didn't let us look at the footage."

"Go tell Murphy to bring the videotape and something to watch it on," Cardenas orders Susan.

"Yes sir," Susan says, and exits through the swinging door.

"Captain, while we have a moment, I'd like to make something clear," I say.

"What's that?"

"Detective DeRosa never told us any details about the police investigation, and we didn't tell her in advance about any of the things we did. So she really didn't do anything wrong."

Captain Cardenas narrows his eyes and assesses me for a few moments before responding.

"Thank you for that very helpful input, Mr. Collins. Now can I give you some?"

"Okay," I say.

"Nearly every one of the fine officers under my command has been trying to get in DeRosa's pants for years, and it ain't happening." In a more confidential tone he adds, "I think she's a dyke."

To keep from busting up, Deb must fake a sudden coughing attack. Since I find nothing funny about the captain's inappropriate and obviously ill-informed comments, I shoot Deb a dirty look, which only amuses her even more. Susan returns, followed by another cop pushing our video playback cart. While he looks for an electrical outlet, Susan notices that Deb is doubled over and gasping for breath.

"Are you okay?" Susan asks her. Deb nods but cannot manage speech. "Looks like something must've gone down the wrong way," Susan says. Deb now has no choice but to run for the door, and I can hear her shrieking with laughter all the way to the bathroom. Susan gives me a puzzled look which I answer with a dour shrug.

We begin viewing the raw footage from the seven cameras, and right away it's clear that most of it is going to be as useless as a self-help book. Each of our videographers is supposed to cover a single contestant, and they know that the penalty for straying from their assignment is to be summarily canned. (I'm all for artistic freedom, but if we didn't enforce this rule we'd forever find ourselves with seven different angles of the hottest chick.) Unfortunately, by the time the shit went down at City Walk all of the contestants had figured out that the only safe way to play today's game was from the sidelines. Even LaFonda, after her initial confrontation with Vernon, quickly retreated into a t-shirt shop, and at the moment the shots rang out was trying to convince the shop's owner that "Wuh Duh Fuh" means something hilarious in Japanese. It's hard to blame any of the contestants for their caution—on the one hand they know that the whole point of *The Mogul* is to make whatever product we're pushing that week look good; on the other, it must be hard for them to see how in the current political climate a broadcast network can possibly side with a guy who likes to sing about the virtues of sodomy.

Thank God for Deb, or at least for the tape from her camera. Deb herself I can do without right now, because ever since she returned from the bathroom, she's been sneaking the serpent-tongue at me every chance she gets. There's no faulting her camera work though, as Boney never leaves the frame or goes out of focus for more than a second. Watching the moments leading up to the shooting is a lot scarier than it was to live through them, because this time I know how it turns out. There's Boney, berating the female protestor and grabbing at the CD she's trying to set on fire. Half of Delawn can be seen on the right edge of the picture. Next I make my entrance, putting an arm around Boney and whispering something in his ear. Because I've approached Boney from the same side as Delawn, I crowd him out of view. As Boney turns to deliver his surly reply, another partial figure appears directly behind me—someone about my height, maybe a little taller, but that's as detailed as the description is going to get because all the tape shows is the back of a dark sweatshirt, and a hood that's pulled up over its wearer's head.

At the first explosion, the camera lens jerks and momentarily loses its subject, but recovers in time to follow Boney and me as we topple over together. The other two shots are heard and the screaming begins, and then while he's still on the ground Boney reaches into his the back of his waistband and pulls out his gun. Susan informs us that it is a Glock 9mm, the choice of discriminating gangstas the world over. Boney stands and looks all around for somebody to blast, then notices Delawn at his feet. Susan stops the tape and begins rewinding it.

"Shit," Deb says. "I missed everything."

"I wouldn't say that," Susan says. She pauses the picture just before the first shot went off, then advances it frame by frame until the image suddenly blurs. The disruption was caused by Deb's instinctive flinch when she heard the bang—she ducked, as anyone would. This caused the camera on her shoulder to momentarily tilt downward, and by freezing on one of the resulting images, Susan is able to give us a fuzzy but nevertheless chilling view of the killer's shoe. It's a distinctive black-and-yellow high-top, the kind of $150 affair that according to the commercials will allow anybody to dunk a basketball backwards.

"I do some of my best work when I'm peeing my pants," Deb says.

"That's not all we can learn from this tape," Susan says. She reverses it a few dozen frames and freezes it again where the killer first enters the picture. "What this tells me is that it was supposed to look like an accident, but it wasn't."

"Huh?" I contribute.

"When a bodyguard is standing next to the person he's supposed to be protecting and he gets shot, what does everybody say?" Susan asks.

"He did his job, which is to take the bullet," says Captain Cardenas.

"Whoever planned this wants everyone to think that, but the shooter wasn't after Boney," Susan says, touching each of the frozen figures on the monitor screen with a pen to make her point. "If he was, you would have been the one in the way." For emphasis, she makes a pistol with her thumb and forefinger and shoots me.

"He must have had two orders," the captain says. "Take out the bodyguard, and make sure you don't hit this Boney guy." We all stare at the monitor and consider the implications.

"Well, it makes sense," I eventually say. "Delawn was the only person who could testify against Boney. So now he's in the clear."

"Boney must have paid somebody to kill Delawn," Deb says. "Maybe you can get him for that."

"Don't bet the ranch on it," says the captain. "When these guys start smoking each other, anyone who knows anything about it gets amnesia." I want to challenge Cardenas on his defeatist attitude, but deep down I know that he has a point. The murders of Biggie Smalls and Tupac Shakur, though each occurred on a public street and were witnessed by dozens of people, remain officially unsolved years later. And in yet another rap star killing, Snoop Dog was arrested and put on trial but was acquitted due to the unreliable nature of the witnesses, perhaps coupled with the jury's inability to understand why the life of one unabashed sociopath was worth any more or less than the life of another.

"So I guess that's it then," I say. When nobody bothers to disagree, I feel a sudden and powerful need to be anywhere but here.

chapter nineteen

When you need to think, sometimes it's good to get behind the wheel of a car and just drive. Four-thirty on a weekday afternoon in L.A. is not one of those times. Fifteen minutes into my big road trip I haven't even made it to the top of the on-ramp, and the only thought in my head is how much I want to pulverize the puke in the GMC Yukon who keeps cutting me off. So when I finally get on the freeway, I take the first exit off of it and pull over in front of the nearest establishment, a dive bar which is naturally called the Palace. Inside, I take a seat at the bar among the other courtiers and order myself a Diet Coke.

Here's the problem in a nutshell: I've never stopped seeing myself as a "real journalist," meaning someone who seeks, finds, and reports the truth, regardless of the consequences. I justify my contribution to the pointless pack of lies known as Reality TV on the grounds that it's the only job I can get right now, or at least the only one that offers me a prayer of getting my daughter back. And oddly enough, that prayer has now been answered—in spite of my cynical attitude and self-serving schemes, I am a big success. All I have to do is ride this perfect wave of dumb luck right into a new house, a new car, maybe even a new wife—if Hallie approves, of course. If she doesn't, I'll do the selfless single-dad thing and bang a busload of twenty-somethings whenever she's at her mom's.

So why am I eyeing the row of bottles behind the bar, and

seriously considering trading in my Diet Coke for a Diet Martini? Does it matter that much to me if Boney gets away with killing Patrice and Delawn? It's not as if I really knew either one of them, nor as if they didn't freely choose the violent world in which they lived and died. It's entirely possible that the only person I'm feeling sorry for here is me. I'm being forced to abandon one or the other of the two loves of my life, and as Sophie could tell you, that kind of choice really blows. I don't mean to suggest that I face a difficult decision right at the moment—no one would publish any story I write that connects Boney to either death, because without some solid evidence, he'd sue for libel and win. The only sane course now is to go along with whatever vulgar extravaganza Trevor cooks up, and leverage it into the biggest raise I can get. The hard choice I'm having my nose rubbed in is one I made almost two years ago. Allow me to explain:

You'd think there would be one newspaper editor somewhere in this vast country willing to take a chance on hiring a Pulitzer Prize winner, no matter how far he'd fallen since his salad days. And you'd be right—there was exactly one, Bud Turley of the *Benton County News*, in Bentonville, Arkansas. After I bottomed out then cleaned up for good, I realized that I would probably have to start my comeback somewhere other than New York or L.A. I weighed the merits of towns that were small but quaint and relatively close, like Santa Barbara, against those that were farther away but also bigger and more interesting journalistically, like San Francisco and even Miami. What the newspapers in each of these disparate locales had in common, however, was that as soon as their Human Resources people spoke to their counterparts at any of my former employers, they immediately called in the Haz-Mat team to remove my resumé from their desks. I widened my search parameters to include all the appealing towns from coast to coast, but soon realized that if I wanted to remain a journalist, livability was something I would have to live without. Eventually I queried every rag in every hell-hole in the English-speaking world, and the only job offer I received was from the brave and/or foolish Mr. Turley. He told me he "got a kick" out of hearing how I mooned the mayor of L.A. at a press conference, and as long as I'd gotten that sort of thing out of my system, I could be either the Woodward or the Bernstein of Bentonville, take my danged pick.

Despite Bud Turley's kindness and the many hidden charms of Northwest Arkansas (did you know that more than thirty million chickens are slaughtered there every day?), it's a long way from the Pacific Ocean, and I feared that if I moved there for even a few years, I might lose Hallie for good. But the alternative was continued unemployment, and Deb and I were both growing tired of my tenancy on her couch. On the very day that I accepted my fate and prepared to retrace in reverse the historic trail of the Beverly Hillbillies, I received a call from out of the blue that solved one problem even as it created another. Tom O'Brien, a guy I'd worked with at the L.A. bureau of the *New York Times* before he got fired for fucking too many interns (the unofficial limit is two; Tom rang up eleven, an impressive number under any circumstances and positively heroic when you consider that his wife also worked at the bureau), tracked me down and told me about an opening for a field producer on a Reality show called *My Best Friend's Girl*. (Please tell me you don't require an explanation of the premise.) I had no experience in TV as a producer and precious little even as a viewer, but the job was Tom's to give and mine to take. At the time it was an easy call—I could get my own place to live and not have to surrender any of the precious hours I was allowed with Hallie. And naturally I would continue to look for newspaper jobs closer to home, and do freelance magazine assignments on the side.

But as I quickly learned, there *is* no "side." I kept thinking that because the shows I was working on were so mindless (*My Best Friend's Girl* quickly bit the dust, but Tom brought me along on his next two gigs, *Take My Ex-Wife—Please!* and *Black Eye For the Queer Guy*), I should be able to complete my work on them in my sleep, and have no trouble finding time for the more important stuff. But as the folks who eviscerate all those chickens down in Arkansas surely know, just because a job ain't rocket science doesn't mean it won't take a little something out of you. The formula for making these shows is to hire a dozen or so reasonably (but not excessively) intelligent producers, run 'em 'til their wheels fall off, then hire some more. There is no overtime, no weekend, and most of all, no whining. I've always told myself that my indentured servitude is only temporary and that I'll find a way to get back into journalism, but when I'm honest I have to admit that it would take some sort of miracle. That's what the last few weeks have been, starting from the moment I first saw Boney arguing with Patrice and ending when Delawn left this mortal coil, taking his secrets with him. Call it miracle interruptus, or just one long professional prick tease. Either way, the effect is to make it clear that when I picked Hallie over journalism, it was probably for keeps. And even though I know I made the right choice, it doesn't make the loss of my other true love hurt any less.

The final insult to Patrice Williams is that the news of her death ranks a distant second to that of her presumed killer. By the time I return to the office, the local evening newscasts are in full roar and the City Walk shooting dominates all of them, for the simple reason that according to the rules of television, Fear tops everything, even Sex. The ideal lead story is whichever gruesome tragedy causes the most viewers to say, "Holy crap, that coulda been me!" The choice of Delawn's killing over Patrice's as the more newsworthy event is therefore a no-brainer, since millions of Southern Californians have visited City Walk, while only a few hundred thousand believe themselves to be smoking hot babes. Besides, since Delawn had the presence of mind to get himself capped outdoors, the helicopter shots of his murder scene are a lot more informative than those of Mrs. Lipowitz's saggy roof. Even the press conference that had been scheduled to announce the discovery of Patrice's body is hijacked by a barrage of questions directed at the chief of police about today's shooting. Yes, City Walk is still a safe place to take one's family. No, there aren't any suspects in custody at the present time. And no, the chief would not care to comment on the allegation by Rep. Maxine Waters (D-South Central) that the LAPD's failure to prevent rappers from killing each other is due to institutional racism.

A major worry expressed by each of the news anchors is for the safety of Roger Dominus. Since at the time of the shooting Roger was three thousand miles away, playing golf with the president of Panama on the latter's private course, this concern eventually begins to seem overdone.

There's also a lot of fretting as to the fate of the contestants, due to the fact they were caught right in the middle of their fifteen minutes of fame. Although LAPD makes it clear that no one besides Delawn Purvis was killed or injured, the complete unavailability of the contestants for interviews has fueled rampant speculation as to the reason for such uncharacteristic silence. Channel 6's live on-scene correspondent floats the most intriguing theory, which is that one or more of the cast members were in fact mowed down and that a frantic nationwide search is presently underway for look-alikes to carry on in their stead.

Although I enjoy a crackpot conspiracy theory as much as the next guy, the actual cause of their disappearance is more prosaic: While we were all stuck inside Mucho Macho waiting to be interviewed by the cops, Trevor's in-house lawyer personally delivered a letter to each member of the cast and crew, reminding us of our contractual commitments not to discuss anything about the show with outside parties. While this does not preclude answering questions from a police officer acting in his or her official capacity, it most certainly and specifically does preclude talking to reporters or anyone else looking to make a buck. Turning real life into real money is what Trevor does, and he's not about to let any other shit-heel cut in on his action.

After Roger and the contestants, the most eagerly sought eyewitness is me. Word has apparently leaked out that not only am I the producer in charge of *The Mogul* in Trevor's absence, but that I was standing directly between Boney and Delawn at the time of the shooting. Every media outlet in the country therefore wants a piece of me, and there are over a hundred messages waiting on my desk from various reporters and editors. Several of those marked "personal" are from people I indeed used to count as friends, but who stopped returning my calls years ago. These are the only ones I phone back, as I enjoy telling them how truly sorry I am to be both unable and unwilling to provide them with doodily squat.

In the middle of these petty pleasures I get a surprise visit from one of the Tanyas, who informs me that I am to present myself at the network's Hollywood headquarters at 3:30 AM to prepare for a live appearance on *Good Day USA*. (The reason for the absurd hour is because the national morning shows all originate in New York. Every West Coast guest complains about the inhuman sacrifice, but of course no one ever turns down an invitation. The next time you see California Gov. Arnold Schwarzenegger on *Today*, remember this and take pity on the man. For in spite of the fact that his face is instantly recognizable in every mansion and mud hut the world over, Arnold is still such a publicity slut that he's willing to pop up and start primping in the middle of the night whenever Meredith Vieira crooks her finger.)

It makes sense that Trevor has chosen to give the first news exclusive to *Good Day*—it's on the same network as *The Mogul*, which provides great opportunities for cross-promotion (another part of the swell trend of turning everything into a commercial). It also makes sense that I am the spokesman Trevor has designated to represent the show—although everyone would obviously prefer Roger, there's no practical way for him to describe the City Walk tragedy without addressing the inconvenient fact that he wasn't there.

I made the rounds of the morning shows during the Huntington Beach days, and while I'd like to say that the circumstances of my return to the national spotlight diminish its appeal, I have to admit they really don't. As that great visionary Jerry Springer realized years ago, there is no shame in anything, including impregnating your Grandma, if it buys you a few minutes on national TV. I call Hallie to tell her to watch me on *Good Day* in the morning, but she doesn't sound all that impressed, perhaps because Governor Arnold drops by her house regularly to have brunch and hit on her mom. I get better reactions from the adult males in my address book, because they all know that while the trickle-down theory of economics may have been discredited, the trickle-down properties of star-fucking are proven scientific facts.

Here's how it works: If you go to a dinner party and mention that your best friend (in such situations, every acquaintance is automatically upgraded to best friend) is the guy who narrowly escaped death during the Media Event of the Week, you will be granted the floor for long enough that if you possess even the tiniest shard of charisma, you should be able to parlay it into somebody's panties. And even if you're one of the unlucky other dudes at the dinner, and your plans to pork the best-looking chick are thus cruelly dashed, all you have to do is speed to the nearest bar and retell the tale with yourself in the role of the best friend. (The success of these later initiatives hinges in part on one's ability to remember one's best friend's name.) I'm not a mathematician, but I would estimate that due to the sensational nature of the City Walk story and my central role in it, my appearance on *Good Day USA* should result in at least a four-tier pyramid of pussy.

I'm about to go home and toss around sleeplessly for a few hours when Susan calls. She wants to know if I'm planning to come clean with Trevor about the genesis of the Boney episode, and I tell her I don't think so. Susan concurs with my reasoning — since there's currently no way for me to write about it, why inform the admiral that as soon as he left the bridge, I intentionally steered his flagship onto the rocks? Sure, *The Mogul* caught a break when Delawn unexpectedly ate lead, but I can hardly take credit for that. If Trevor ever learns the true story behind how our cameras happened to be on hand for the blessed event, I'll last about as long as one of Britney's husbands.

With that in mind, Susan's concern has to do with my futile attempt to extract a confession from the dying Delawn. Trevor will eventually see that the tape of that exchange—his lawyer has already filed an *ex parte* motion to compel LAPD to return all of the seized evidence forthwith, which in layman's terms means right fucking now—and it will be difficult if not impossible for me to explain the things I said to Delawn without revealing the whole dastardly scheme. Susan has already taken the liberty of consulting with Deb about the matter, and together they have decided on the Rosemary Woods solution, so named after the White House secretary who "accidentally" erased eighteen and a half minutes of audiotape that might have proven President Richard Nixon was directly involved in the Watergate break-in. (In its initial use, the Woods method was quite effective and might even have saved Nixon's presidency, had other tapes not revealed that virtually everything the terrible bastard ever said or did was impeachable.)

Susan and Deb's proposal is simple—before returning the tape in question to Trevor Banes Productions, they will "spot-erase" the audio, starting at the point when the first gunshot is heard. The video will remain intact, but since the camera never sees more than the back of my head, not even a lip-reader will have any way of knowing what I said to Delawn. There will be several plausible explanations for how the sound might have been lost, and no way for Trevor to retrieve it whether he buys any of said explanations or not. I thank Susan for thinking about me and endorse the plan, wishing only that I could also spot-erase large portions of the recent past from my brain.

"There's something else I want to talk to you about," Susan says. "What are you doing right now?"

"Going home," I tell her. "I have to be in Hollywood at three-thirty in the morning to go on *Good Day USA*."

"Well big shot, you're gonna spend half your time driving back and forth. My place is in Hancock Park, why don't you crash here for a few hours?" The suggestion catches me completely off-guard, but I do my best to stay cool and not show it.

"You live in Hanpock Hark?"

She gives me the address and I tell her I'll be there as soon as I take care of a few things. Although I don't elaborate, these things consist primarily of sprinting to my car and driving like a lunatic straight to her apartment. Except it's not an apartment at all, it's a house; a small but very nice one on a great block lined with some of the oldest, most stately homes in L.A. I'm convinced that either I've made a navigational error or else Susan is seriously on the take, because this looks more like the kind of place that a successful young lawyer or maybe two gay screenwriters might hang their berets. The street and the house number are both exactly what I wrote down, though, so I walk up to the front door and ring the bell.

"It's open," Susan calls from inside. I let myself in and notice right away that the interior is equally well-appointed. "Is that you?" she says from somewhere toward the back of the house.

"No, I couldn't make it. I hear you have a great house though."

Susan enters, towel-drying her hair. She's wearing sweat pants and a man's long sleeve dress shirt, which I confess is not exactly the way I was picturing her on the way over. Nevertheless, the small amount of bare skin—still pink from the shower—visible below Susan's sweats gives me a little tingle. For God's sake, when did I become a foot fetishist?

"Thanks," she says. "Lots of people make lame cracks about how I must be on the take."

"Idiots."

"I bought it right after the Rodney King riots in '92. They looted a few stores around here, and all the yuppies bailed. I paid less than half of what the previous owners did."

"Very shrewd, detective."

"Yeah, now all the cops who live out in Canyon Country or one of those other armpits think I'm a frigging genius. At the time, they said I was gonna get gangbanged every night by the Crips."

I follow Susan to the kitchen and sit at the breakfast table while she makes us tea. Even though her outfit didn't come out of a lingerie catalog, it's a definite turn-on just to be alone with her like this. I flash back to a scene from my early twenties, the first time a girl with her own place and no roommates invited me over. I remember being breathless with anticipation about what was going to happen, at least for the ten seconds between when I arrived and when she grabbed my pecker. Susan moves at a more measured pace.

"Milk or sugar?" she asks as she pours our tea.

"I take my chamomile the same way Bogey did," I tell her. "Straight up."

She brings the two cups to the table and sits facing me.

"So what did you want to talk to me about?" I ask.

"A couple things," she says. "First of all, have you been wondering why Boney changed his mind and decided to have Delawn killed?"

"Maybe a little," I shrug.

"Well, what do you think?"

"You're the dick," I never get tired of saying. "You tell me."

"There are several possibilities. One is that Delawn got greedy and tried to shake Boney down for more money to keep his mouth shut. Another is that Boney never changed his mind at all. He paid Delawn up front to kill Patrice, and he always planned to have him hit afterward."

"Those sound like reasonable theories," I say. "You have any others?"

"Just the one you're obsessing over."

"I'm not sure what you mean."

"You're going to make *me* say it?" she groans. I don't respond, so Susan sighs and continues. "The other possibility is that your ex-wife remembered who I was and let her husband know you were up to something. He told Boney, who got nervous and figured he'd better not take any chances with Delawn."

After a pause I say, "Something along those lines might have occurred to me." The truth is that I have vigorously suppressed any and all thoughts about Sara playing such a role, strictly to preserve my own precarious sanity.

"I figured it would sooner or later, but I don't think that's what happened," Susan says. "You should just put it out of your mind."

"Okay, done," I say. "And while we're at it, there are a couple of other silly fears I'd like to put to rest."

"Such as?"

"Occasionally I make mistakes. Someday I'm going to die. A few men may have larger penises."

"I'm afraid I can't help you with those," says Susan. "But even if Richard Slatkin did figure out what we were doing, there's no way he'd tell Boney."

"Why not?"

"Smart lawyers don't take dumb chances. Richard knows that if he tips Boney off and as a result somebody gets wasted, he's an accessory to murder. Why take that kind of risk for one client? He's got hundreds of 'em, and more beating down his door every day."

"If you really believe that, why were you so upset when Sara surprised us at the pool?"

"Because I thought it might mess up our case when we put Boney on trial. The defense would raise all kinds of crap about you and me getting together to frame him so we could get rich and hang out at fancy hotels. Trust me, that's how they'd play it."

"I guess we'll never know for sure what happened."

"Welcome to my life. Every investigation, even the ones where we put somebody away, ends with a bunch of loose ends. I used to let it keep me up at night; now I don't."

"What's your secret?"

"Belief in a higher power," she says. "Vodka."

"Unfortunately, I was excommunicated from that faith."

"You should see the look on your face whenever you talk about your daughter. You can't get that kind of joy out of drinking or singing hymns."

"It's nice of you to notice," I say, embarrassed by the sudden tightness in my throat.

"That's why you've gotta let this stuff with her mother go. You have to deal with the woman at least until Hallie turns eighteen, so if you keep thinking she wrecked your big story, you're gonna be walking around pissed off for another ten years." I consider explaining to Susan why I no longer remember any other way to walk, but I don't have the heart to rehash the whole Huntington Beach saga just now.

"I get your point," I tell her. "I'll do my best."

"Good. Now the other thing I want to clear up is sort of embarrassing."

"To you or me?" I ask. Susan answers by pointing at herself. "I guess I can handle that," I say. "Go ahead."

"Your friend Deb told me what Captain Cardenas said when I was out of the room."

"You mean about you being a . . ." I complete the sentence with a little fingers-and-tongue action.

"Yeah, that."

"Forget about it. I already did."

"I'm trying," Susan says. "Being a female cop and single, it's not like I don't hear that shit every day. But usually it doesn't bug me this much."

"What are you trying to say?" I ask. Susan looks me straight in the eye.

"I'm not into girls. And I thought maybe you oughta know that."

Here it is, the moment I've been waiting for. I've always been the kind of guy who needs either an obvious invitation or a belly full of booze before I can pounce, and since I no longer drink that means I spend most nights pouncing on myself. But now Susan DeRosa, who I'm attracted to on every level (including several I didn't even know I had) has just flashed me an unmistakable green light. I'm thrilled, I'm flattered, and I wish I'd worn a bigger pair of pants. Yet for some unknown reason, I can't bring myself to reach across the table and touch her, or even to open my mouth and speak. Every second that passes makes the one that comes after it seem longer, and soon the awkwardness becomes unbearable.

"You have to get some sleep," Susan says, standing abruptly. "Let me show you the guest room."

chapter twenty

SUSAN PROVIDES ME with an alarm clock, which is helpful because it gives me something to stare at for the next three and a half hours. After calling myself a homo for about the hundredth time, I try to engage in some slightly more sophisticated self-analysis. The best theory I can develop to explain my Mr. Freeze act in the kitchen is that although I need the ladies to make the first move, I no longer trust them when they do. This is the logical result of my long and painful relationship with Sara, who taught me that when a woman does the choosing, she's getting something she wants, but there's a good chance that all the man is getting is laid.

But Susan is not Sara. She's a straightforward, self-reliant woman who has done a lot better for herself than I have. The evidence of that is all around, from the dark walnut hardwood floors below me to the fancy crown molding above. If I were in my own bed, I'd be looking at a yellowed, cottage cheese ceiling and listening to the Skipper cough up lung cookies. Susan clearly doesn't need me to take care of her—if anything, it's the other way around. So what the hell am I afraid of? She's right down the hall, probably lying there awake just like I am. All I have to do is knock on her door, say something clever like "How do I know you're not a dyke?" and our glands will pick up the conversation from there. But as anyone who's ever stood at the top of a high-dive for too long can tell you, at a certain point jumping becomes physically impossible.

Before saying good night, Susan insisted that I could take a shower without waking her, and at 2:15 AM I decide to take her up on it because I feel like a zombie and smell like a goat. Since I have no clean clothes to put on afterward, bathing is only a partial solution to these problems. But TV is an audio/visual medium, so there's really no practical reason why the guests can't reek.

At the side entrance to the network news facility on Sunset, a security guard checks my ID against his list, then hands me off to Maya, a cute, young production assistant who says she'll take me to Makeup.

"Gee, do you really think I need it?" I ask her. Maya gives me the wary sort of look generally directed at street crazies, which I suppose is only fair since I smell like one. I follow her through a maze of corridors to the brightly-lit makeup department. As I enter, I am mildly surprised to find another customer already being fussed over at such an early hour, and positively dumbstruck when I see who it is.

"Hullo, Ted," he says.

"Trevor?" is all I can muster.

"Sorry to chase you out of bed in the wee hours, but I wanted to speak to you in person so I can be sure to get all the details right," Trevor says. "And in the event that my plane was delayed, you might have been asked to go on in my place."

He peppers me with a million questions about the City Walk affair, and I answer them about as well as a person choking on his own bile can. Luckily I don't have to worry about my body language, because Trevor keeps his attention focused squarely on his own reflection in the mirror. This allows him to experiment with various facial expressions he might need to employ on camera, and to give himself a refresher course in how to wink. A few minutes before show time, Maya escorts us down to the studio, where Trevor is seated on the set and I on a stool just off camera. He continues to ask me for clarification of various data points until the stage manager gives him the one-minute warning. Trevor then advises me that he would find it easier to concentrate on his performance without the distraction of my personal aroma.

Naturally I want to go straight to my car and burn rubber, but that might seem rude unless I had a good excuse and I just can't think of any that would be credible at four o'clock in the morning. So I sit with Tanya in the green room and watch as Trevor is interviewed by Jane Buckley, the *Good Day* host in New York. Even in my sullen frame of mind, I have to concede that Trevor's military training serves him well—he recounts the story concisely, with just the right amount of understated drama, and accurately describes how close I was to the gun when it went off. Any notoriety I might achieve from Trevor's telling is undercut, however, by the fact that he identifies me only as "one of my men." The question of where General Bane was positioned during the engagement (on higher ground atop the Great Wall of China) never comes up.

From my perspective, the only fresh development in the City Walk shooting is that it now has a sponsor. Jane Buckley shows why she's worth every bit of her $7 million annual salary by keeping a straight face while she reads the following off the teleprompter:

"Trevor, you're a decorated combat veteran. Is there anything that people can do to protect themselves from this kind of senseless bloodshed?"

"Yes, there is, Jane," replies Trevor. "In these difficult times, when we must cope not only with random violence but also with the constant threat of terrorism, we can no longer rely solely on the police. We all need to take responsibility for our own safety and that of our loved ones."

"You mean we have to start carrying guns?" Jane asks. "Because that's going to be a problem with some of my little evening purses." Someone must have tipped Trevor off that Jane was going to make a funny, because he chuckles.

"Don't worry Jane, you don't need to trade in your handbag," he says, then drops the patronizing smile. "In all seriousness, if everyone on the street carried conventional firearms, we might actually be at greater risk." No shit, Rambo. "But fortunately there are some wonderful new products that can safely and inexpensively provide us with a good deal of personal security. I happen to have one of them in my pocket right now."

"Well come on, don't hold out on us," Jane says. Trevor reaches into the breast pocket of his sport coat and produces a wooden cylinder about the size of a Cuban cigar.

"This is a brand-new device called The Shocker," he says. "It's basically a miniaturized version of the stun guns used by law enforcement officers to temporarily render suspects harmless by administering a powerful but non-lethal electrical shock."

"Haven't stun guns been around for a while?"

"Yes, but the previous models licensed for personal use, such as this one," Trevor says, holding up a stubbier object, "all required direct contact with the subject's body. The Shocker can be used from up to twenty feet away."

"Wow," Jane says. "Can you show us how it works?"

"I'm afraid I don't have a volunteer with me at the moment. But I promise you'll see The Shocker and several other revolutionary self-defense tools in action on *The Mogul* next week."

Next *week*? Trevor must have left the better part of his brain in Beijing, because there is no way we can possibly shoot, edit, and deliver a new episode in eight days. The normal production cycle is twelve weeks, and even at that leisurely pace it exacts a toll on the troops akin to that of trench warfare.

"You can bet I'll be watching," Jane assures us. "Trevor Bane, thank you for—"

"Excuse me, Jane," Trevor interrupts, looking off camera. "I've just been handed something that might interest you." He holds up a little black cocktail purse that was apparently just lying around the studio, then opens it and slips The Shocker neatly inside.

"Oh my gosh, it fits!" Jane says.

"Yes, and still plenty of room for your cosmetics." Trevor grins into the camera and winks.

I congratulate Trevor on his (blow) job well done and ask him if he'll be coming into the office later. He says no, he'll be coming in right now, and it's clear he expects me to do the same. Anticipating my request to stop by my apartment for a clean shirt, Trevor tells me I can instead have one from the extensive closet he maintains at work. I am even welcome to use his private shower, so long as it's not for more than the time he customarily allots for a thorough scrub down—ninety seconds. Then he and Tanya step into the back of his waiting limo, and before the driver can even get the door closed, Trevor is dialing a number with one hand and unzipping his fly with the other.

It's not quite 5:00 AM when we arrive, but the call to arms has already been heard and heeded throughout the Southland. Not only is the entire *Mogul* production team on hand, but dozens of staffers from other Trevor Bane shows have also been pressed into emergency service. There can be no doubt that this combined army is the most formidable ever assembled for the purposes of producing a single, shitty Reality show. It fills the largest open space in the building, and Trevor must stand on a desk in the middle of the room to address everyone.

"No one has ever before attempted what we're about to," he orates. "We have a chance, my friends, to make television history." Trevor continues in this grandiloquent vein for several minutes, which gives me a chance to scan the faces of my co-workers as they listen. Though some are still sleepy and one or two seem to have attitude problems (two or three counting me), the vast majority of them are clearly eating this shit up. I'm tempted to leap onto the desk beside Trevor and belt out a lusty "Sieg!" because I guarantee I'd be answered with more than one "Heil!"

But as I'm sure you've guessed, I do no such thing. With

Trevor's return to his familiar place at the helm, my boldness has returned to its familiar place under a rock. We break up into various smaller squadrons, with my assignment being to generate a rough cut of the first two acts. In TV, an "act" is defined as the period between one set of commercials and another, so my team of producers and editors will have to turn the footage we've already shot—hundreds of hours of raw dreck—into fourteen minutes of coherent, highly polished dreck. Normally this would take no less than three weeks, but Trevor is only giving us until this time tomorrow. To help motivate the staff, he has announced a number of prizes that will be awarded to those who come closest to killing themselves without letting it slow them down. I recognize each of the awards—a Las Vegas getaway, a cell phone with unlimited free night and weekend minutes, several cases of Coors Light—as promotional considerations that cost Trevor absolutely nothing, yet from the applause he receives you'd think he'd just endowed an orphanage. Once again I am moved to wonder, "Is it just me?"

Shortly before 7:00 AM, I slip away from my desk to call Hallie and let her know that Daddy won't be on TV after all. (*Good Day* airs on a three-hour tape delay on the left coast, so Trevor's little infomercial is about to begin anew on our local network affiliate.) Sara answers the phone and to my chagrin, she is in great spirits.

"Hi!" Sara says. "Your show is all over the news."

"I'm aware of that. Can I speak to Hallie?"

"Sure, hang on." She puts me on hold then comes back. "She's on her way."

"Thanks."

"Hey Ted, you know that stuff I told you about at the Bel-Air? Just forget it, all right? I was having a bad day." Although I promised Susan I would try not to, I can't help but make certain dark inferences. Sara has swiftly repaired her marital rift, perhaps by providing something of value to Richard. At around the same time, Boney has decided that his safest course of action is to have Delawn killed. And the only known link between these simultaneous sharp turns is a knucklehead known as me. "Are you still there?" she says.

"Yeah. And I'm fucking thrilled about it."

Hallie is very sweet, telling me that *Good Day USA* sucks anyway and Jane Buckley has fake boobs. I don't have time to get into how my seven-year-old might know such a thing, because I must get back to work and I also want to call Susan.

"Looks like you got benched," Susan says. In the background, I can hear Trevor's crisp account of the City Walk affair blaring from her TV.

"To tell you the truth, it was kind of a relief," I say.

"Really?"

"No."

"Sorry," she says. "Will you be at your office in about three hours?"

"Probably. Why?"

"I have to come by there to deliver the tapes. Maybe I can buy you a cup of coffee."

"I guess, if I can break free."

"You know, you're weird. Normal guys don't start acting cold and distant until after I sleep with them."

I know I should call Susan back and tell her I'm sorry to be acting like such a loser. But, unfortunately, it ain't acting. The huge number of editing decisions that have to be made and the impossibly short time I have to make them are actually blessings, because they force me to forget about everything other than the tasks at hand. I allow no interruptions over the next few hours except a call from my old friend Tom O'Brien, and I only take that because Tom told the receptionist that it was absolutely urgent. It turns out that in an effort to get maximum value from my appearance on *Good Day USA*, last night Tom phoned a number of hot prospects and told them to be sure and watch his best buddy Ted in the morning. He even issued invitations to a big cocktail party this coming weekend, with me as the guest of honor and him as the only other straight male. Now the whole thing is down the shitter and Tom's going to look like an unprincipled sleaze unless I figure out some way to get my ass on a nationally televised news show.

Tanya uses the public address system to order all producers to report immediately to the large conference room. By the time I talk Tom down off the ledge and refill my coffee, Trevor is already seated at his end of the table and is clearly impatient to get started. Worse, every other chair is taken but for one at the opposite end next to that other lovable ex-solider, Jack Herrera. Just looking at the man makes my ears ache, and I consider asking one of the lesser toadies clustered around Trevor to give up his or her seat. After all, I am the co-executive producer and the person single-handedly responsible for this opportunity we all have to make bad television history, so why should I have to suffer? But who do I bump—Mfume, who I like and respect? How about Noah, who I don't like but feel sorry for, because being gay, bald, and flabby is such an unfortunate package? No, but how about—

"Ted, would you mind sitting down," Trevor says. I cross the room and take my place beside Jack, whose sneer says he couldn't be any happier if he were back at Guantanamo Bay, torturing towelheads. Trevor begins describing the revised shooting schedule, which will turn the episode that had been conceived as a sales pitch for a music CD into one for a personal stun gun. The new plan is classic Trevor—simple, straightforward, shameless. First, the City Walk sequence will be "enhanced" with additional footage to be shot on a sound stage. Using a "green screen" effect (like the one used to superimpose wacky TV weathermen over their dull maps), the new shots will be combined with the old to make it appear that all were recorded at the same time. Although the official line is that we are only doing this to make up for certain gaps in the camera coverage, *The Mogul* is not bound by any Stone Age standards of journalistic ethics. In other words, if I magically disappear and

Trevor shows up in my place, that would be what's called an enhancement.

Next, the contestants will scurry for the safety of two Chrysler minivans, each piloted by a professional driver who will put them through some fancy evasive maneuvers on their way out of the parking lot. (Another location must be found to stand in for the original, because our boy Brandon has already been "reassigned," and his unimaginative replacement couldn't be made to see the value of promoting City Walk as an exciting place where visitors might see somebody get executed.) Trevor solicits opinions as to whether it would constitute an excessive departure from Reality to have the lead minivan smash through the gate arm at the exit. I feel it would and am about to say so when Jack booms, "Goddamned great idea!" and I become temporarily disoriented.

The minivans will then speed toward the Bat Cave, aka Dominus Plaza. When they arrive, private security agents will meet them and verify the identity of each contestant with a retina scanning device, presumably to ensure that the evildoers who killed Delawn haven't also sent a doppelganger to assassinate The Mogul. Mfume asks if we'll need to see close-ups of the equipment and Trevor says no. This means that the manufacturer of the retina scanner is paying only a modest sum—probably around $200,000—and for that kind of chicken feed you certainly can't expect to get your logo showcased on primetime TV. You can however, get a nice little puff piece on the official *Mogul* Web site, so that anyone who watches the episode and wonders where to get himself one of them nifty eyeball dealies can easily find out. The same holds true for every single product you see on *The Mogul*, and even some that you don't, such as Roger's preferred brands of cologne, toothpaste, and undershorts.

Trevor is about to divulge the next beat in this spellbinding saga when Tanya enters and whispers something to him.

"That won't be possible," Trevor says crisply and returns to his notes, but Tanya reluctantly murmurs to him again. In response Trevor grimaces first at her, then at me. "Ted, come along," he says, then stands and exits. I hurry to catch up with him as he marches down the hall.

"What's up?" I ask.

"The police are here to return our tapes, and for some unfathomable reason they insist on delivering them to you and me personally."

We arrive at the reception area. Even though she warned me she was coming, it still takes me a moment to recognize the uniformed officer with the businesslike expression as the babe I should have boffed last night.

"I'm Trevor Bane," he says, shaking her hand.

"Detective Susan DeRosa, LAPD."

"I believe you've met Ted Collins."

"Yes, hello again."

"Detective."

"These must be our tapes," Trevor says, indicating the cardboard box on the counter beside Susan. "Thank you for bringing them." Trevor reaches for the box, but Susan's hand gets there first. Their eyes lock on each other's, and for a split second it appears I'm about to witness a rare incidence of Trevor losing his shit.

"If you could spare a few minutes, there's something I'd like to discuss with both of you in private," Susan says.

"I'm afraid this isn't a good time," Trevor says. "But if you will telephone my assistant . . ." He tries to pull the box away mid-sentence, but Susan refuses to loosen her grip. Seeing anyone defy Trevor is great; seeing Susan do so fills me with pride that's completely out of proportion to the current scope of our relationship. Another brief stare-off ensues, but Trevor quickly calculates that irrespective of his legal rights and titanic testicles, his time and energy will be best conserved through compromise.

"Please follow me," Trevor says. He leads us to the nearest empty office, closes the door behind us, and then crosses his arms across his chest.

"I'm sure that Mr. Collins has told you that he spoke to the victim just before he died," Susan says.

"Yes," Trevor replies. In my recap of yesterday's events, I told Trevor that I knelt beside the wounded Delawn and spoke to him briefly. Since I knew that Susan and Deb were erasing the audio, I was free to make up any dialog for myself that I wanted. Out of sheer perversity, I told Trevor that in my capacity as a minister of the Universal Life Church, I gave Delawn the Last Rites. (The part about being a minister is absolutely true—when Deb and I were in high school, we lied about our ages and mailed in $5 each to become ordained members of the Universal Life clergy. We did this not out of any youthful religious calling, but because we were hoping to use our priestly ID cards to buy beer.) Luckily Trevor wasn't particularly interested in the Last Rites, because if he'd asked me to repeat them the best I could manage would be something along the lines of "Later, dude."

"One of your cameramen got a very clear picture of that moment," Susan says. "But apparently there was some malfunction with the sound."

"I'll have my technical people take a look at it," Trevor says, still clearly wondering what this bullshit is all about.

"My commanding officers and I have a concern about the public seeing that tape. We feel it could place Mr. Collins's life in jeopardy." This gets everyone's attention, especially Mr. Collins.

"I'm not sure I follow you," I say.

"We're investigating various possible motives for the shooting," Susan says. "If the victim was targeted because he had some damaging information against someone, and that person sees that he said something to you before he died, then the people who killed him might fear that you now have that information."

"Pardon me, but that is utter rubbish," Trevor says. "The man who was killed obviously wasn't the target. He was the bodyguard, and I must say a damned good one."

“It’s our policy to consider every alternative,” Susan says.

“As a taxpayer, I certainly appreciate your diligence,” Trevor says. “But I can assure you that Ted is far too valuable an employee for me to place him at risk.”

“On behalf of the police department, I’m very glad to hear that,” Susan says. “And I’m sure your insurance company will be too.” She stares Trevor down one more time and then hands him the box of tapes. Trevor immediately turns on his heel and exits without another word. I regard Susan in silent awe for several moments.

“I just have two things to say,” I tell her. “One is that you’re my all-time biggest hero. The other is that if you ever give me a look like the one you just gave Trevor, I won’t be able to get another boner for as long as I live.”

chapter twenty-one

EVEN WITH THE reinforcements who have been added, the breakneck pace of the production schedule requires a lot of multi-tasking. Since I have already given my editing teams enough work to keep them busy for several hours, Trevor asks me to serve as his lieutenant on the afternoon shoot at Dominus Plaza. As with all such requests there is no practical way to decline, but I nonetheless try hard to think of one. It's not just that I don't want to spend extra time around Trevor right now (though God knows I'd rather endure a bad case of crabs). The guy I really can't bear the thought of seeing is the one who's *really* getting away with murder. The new script calls for our cameras to lose track of Boney in the panicked flight from City Walk, and for one of the contestants to insist that she saw him get shot. Later, in the safe confines of Dominus Plaza, Boney's dramatic reappearance will unleash a flood of tears, hugs, and heart-warming music, the latter available on CD or by Internet download for only $1.99.

In the over-the-top opulence of the Dominus Plaza lobby, I introduce Boney and Lovey Mack to Trevor. Boney seems a bit subdued, perhaps because he's wearing dark glasses and has smoked so much weed that he smells like Bob Marley's favorite hat. Seeing Trevor and Lovey side by side is a reminder that for all the gains of the civil rights movement, we're still a long way from true equality. Because aren't these two guys essentially the same person? Each sprung up from out of nowhere, and using nothing but his own insight, cunning, and balls turned the entertainment business upside down. Yet only one of them has received the proper recognition for his accomplishments—a prison record. Trevor and I extend brief, bogus condolences about Delawn, but no mention is made of Patrice. None of the news reports ever connected her to Boney, and I guess they never will.

Roger is waiting for us in his penthouse office.

"Hallelujah," he says when he sees Trevor. "Hand over your passport, you're no longer allowed to travel."

"I gather things have been rather lively in my absence," Trevor says as they shake hands.

"That's one word for it," Roger replies. "Say what you want about Celine Dion, people don't shoot at her."

"I promise you have my full attention until we wrap," Trevor tells Roger. "So let's take these lemons Ted has given us and make some lemonade."

Once the cameras are in position and rolling, we bring in the contestants and they breathlessly describe what happened at City Walk. Their natural tendency to ham it up comes in handy for once, since seeing a man shot to death should be at least somewhat upsetting, even if he isn't famous. All Roger has to do is sit behind his desk and nod indulgently as though he were Ward Cleaver hearing about what sort of mischief Wally and the Beave have gotten themselves into this time.

When Boney makes his "surprise" entrance, the bullshit really busts loose. Amy, our Mormon contestant, is so relieved to learn that Boney has survived she drops to her knees while hugging him. Trevor likes the visual but doesn't want to offend the sensibilities of the network's Salt Lake City affiliate, so he quietly asks LaTanya to perform the maneuver during the second take. Amy is understandably miffed at this blatant theft of her intellectual property, and until Trevor manages to mollify her, she and LaTanya trade elbows like a couple of power forwards battling for position in the paint.

Once all the poignancy has been strip-mined from the situation, it's time to get down to business. The fiction concocted to explain the convenient presence of a big box of stun guns is that the Dominus Plaza Security department was preparing to add them to its arsenal. But as I learned on the drive over here, The Shocker didn't even officially exist twenty-four hours ago. It was an experimental and highly secret device developed by a Chinese government/industry consortium. Trevor learned of its existence several days earlier when his pal the Minister of Culture sent some personal representatives armed with Shockers over to deal with the demonstrators who were mucking up Trevor's Great Wall shoot. Their first target was the protest leader, a defiant young woman who had been garnering lots of sympathetic attention because of how cute she looked in a mini-skirt—at least until The Shocker abruptly caused her to lose control of her bowels. Trevor sensed right away he was onto something, and when he heard about the City Walk incident, he knew what it was. He made a quick deal with the Chinese, tossed a case of Shockers in the back seat of his Gulfstream, and made a beeline for home.

As Roger distributes Shockers to Boney and each of the contestants, he sternly reminds everyone that they are not toys. And to prove it, we're going to zap a few folks just to see what happens. The "volunteers" who will be on the receiving end of 900,000 harmless volts are three extras who are each being paid $150 for their services as human lightning rods. In addition to our customary release form, which states that Trevor Bane Productions owns everything but is responsible for nothing, the extras have also signed a hastily-prepared addendum that reads: "I know that being shocked with a stun gun might seriously injure or kill me and I don't care." If I were Trevor's attorney, I would have skipped the legalese and gone with something less open to interpretation, i.e. "I am a worthless piece of shit."

Although The Shocker could (and no doubt will) prove useful in a variety of situations, particularly family quarrels, its biggest selling point is its portability. This fits perfectly with the public's ever-increasing—and completely erroneous—perception that we are most at risk when we leave home. To make this point we need to stage our demonstration of The Shocker outside, and due to our time constraints the service alley leading to the Dominus Plaza loading dock will have to stand in for the mean streets of America. Trevor sends me and a production assistant down ahead of time to give the sparkling-clean space some urban grit, which we do with the help of a dumpster full of trash, a graffiti artist, and some cans of washable spray paint. Although Roger approved this set decoration and has been assured it will in no way be connected with the Dominus name, he nevertheless scowls darkly when he sees it. I hope he doesn't look closely enough to see that I have authorized the graffiti artist to insert "The Mogul sucks ass" among the hieroglyphics.

Our rainbow coalition of pretend bad guys includes Claudell, a large African American; Chuey, a heavily-tatooed Hispanic; and Steve, a swarthy Middle-Easterner. They are all extremely polite and grateful for their big break, as I suppose anyone would be if he were about to be lit up like a Christmas tree in prime time. When we're ready to roll, the cheerful Claudell is the first subject to step forward. The scenario calls for Boney and the contestants to look on as Roger strolls down the alley, wearing his usual trench coat and self-satisfied smile. He will then hear something and turn around to find Claudell sneaking up behind him with a knife. Roger will calmly reach into his pocket for his Shocker, take aim, and fire. We rehearse the scene once, miming the final step, and Claudell naturally overdoes his reaction, dancing around like Wile E. Coyote does when he's getting such a nasty shock you can see his skeleton right through his skin. Then we do it for real and the effect is much more dramatic.

When Roger presses the firing button on The Shocker, a tiny dart flies out of its tip and hooks on Claudell's shirt. The dart remains attached to The Shocker by a wire, and although it's almost too thin to see, it carries enough electricity to make the strapping Claudell drop his knife and crumple like a puppet that's had its strings severed. He writhes on the ground for several seconds making horrible, inhuman sounds, and after he stops it's readily apparent that his loss of muscle control was complete, even if he's not wearing a mini-skirt. Several of the contestants rush to make sure Claudell is alive (he is, thankfully) and to help him to his feet. For a moment he seems to have no idea where he is or why he has a load in his drawers, but then he notices the dart hooked to his shirt and follows the wire to The Shocker, which remains in the hand of the smiling Roger.

"You okay, big guy?" Roger smirks. Claudell's response is to go bug-eyed with fright and try to bolt in the opposite direction. His legs are so rubbery that he falls flat on his face, but he immediately scrambles up and resumes his escape.

"For heaven's sake," Trevor says to me. "Go tell that chap that if we don't establish he's all right we can't use any footage of him at all."

"Okay," I reply, but by this time Claudell is already thirty yards away and still picking up speed.

"Oh never mind, you'll never catch the bloody kaffir," Trevor says in disgust. "Where are the others?"

Anticipating this question, Chuey and Steve have already begun to back away quietly, and given another few seconds might have made a clean getaway.

"You two," Trevor snaps, beckoning the terrified extras to his side. "We must show that you haven't been injured, do you understand? Take as much time as you need to compose yourselves, we can edit all that out later."

"That dude shit himself," Chuey says.

"Yes, and if he'd stuck around I would have bought him a nice new pair of trousers," Trevor replies. "Now he'll get nothing."

"'Scuse me sir, but I don't think I want to do this," Steve mumbles.

"Me neither," Chuey chimes in.

Trevor employs every carrot and stick he can think of, but Chuey's fears and Steve's build on each other and become so great that when Trevor takes a Shocker out of his pocket to show them how small it is, they assume he's going to use it on them and they take flight.

"Disgraceful," Trevor says, watching them scamper away. "I guarantee you this would never happen in a serious country like China."

"I'll call Casting and have them round up some more riff-raff," I say.

"There isn't time, Ted," he says. "I'm afraid we're going to have to shock you."

"*Me*?"

"Here," Trevor says, handing me his Shocker and taking several steps back. "You do it to me first, so you can see there's absolutely nothing for an intelligent person to be afraid of." He spreads his arms wide to give me a bigger target.

"Uh, question," I say. "If you're willing to get zapped, why don't we just have Roger zap you on camera and call it a day?"

"Because my face is recognizable all over the world," Trevor says. "It would be a distraction." Trevor has substantially overstated his global celebrity, but I can't dispute the fact that he's had his puss in *People* more often (around twenty times) than me (never).

"Wouldn't one of the PA's be more credible as bad guys?" I ask.

"They're both women."

Trevor graciously gives me a minute to deliberate. I began the day expecting to appear on national television as an Important Producer. Now I've been demoted to the role of Incontinent Thug. Of course I can just say no, and I doubt Trevor would fire me. He'd be exposing himself to a wrongful termination suit, which he would probably lose unless he could show that being electrocuted is part of my job description. (I've never read my phone book-size employment contract, so I suppose it could be.) But it suddenly dawns on me that this sort of defensive thinking is exactly what separates the Ted Collinses from the Trevor Banes, the Roger Dominuses, even the Richard Slatkins of the world. If any of them were in my shoes, he wouldn't be seeking refuge. He'd be seeking cash.

"All right, let's give it a go," I announce, and take aim at Trevor's chest with my Shocker. The abrupt disappearance of all the blood from his face tells me he didn't really expect to have his bluff called. "No, wait," I say, lowering my weapon. "Something's bugging me."

"What's that?" Trevor asks, visibly relieved.

"Well this whole episode was my idea, right? But you're the one who's going to make all the extra money off of it."

"Don't be silly, Ted. Of course I'm going to give you a substantial raise."

"That's very generous. But I was thinking it might be more appropriate if I got a little piece of the pie."

"What bloody pie?" he barks, even more agitated than he was when he thought he was about to get fried.

"The profits from selling these things," I say, referring to The Shocker in my hand. "Just like, I don't know, 10 percent?"

I'm grateful to have a self-defense tool in my hand, because Trevor's werewolf-like physical transformation suggests that I may need to use it. I wonder if he is more furious at me for my outrageous demand, or at himself for putting me in a position to make it. Because we both know that the only leverage I have is my knowledge of the shady stun gun deal, and there is absolutely no reason why he had to divulge any of its "shocking" details to me in the first place. Maybe it was jet lag, or maybe his multinational magnificence simply became too much for him to hold inside. Whatever it was that compelled Trevor to deviate from his usual discretion, it's clear from the look on his face that he now bitterly regrets it. But I guess it's clear from the look on mine, that's tough shit.

"Two percent," he says.

"Seven, unless you'd rather talk about some stock options."

"Seven it is. Now would you be so good as to do your goddamned job." He points at the set, where Roger and the cameras are waiting for some fresh meat.

"You first, remember?" I say, once again leveling my Shocker at him. Trevor stares daggers at me for a beat, then raises his hands in resignation. "Just kidding," I tell him, dropping The Shocker into my pocket. I'm sorry to report that our senses of humor no longer appear to be in sync.

Professional actors use various techniques to get ready for a big scene. Being an amateur, I prepare by locking myself in a toilet stall and pretending I'm giving birth. When I feel like I've purged everything except my essential organs, I return to the set, ready to face the music. To make myself look more felonious, I borrow a knit cap from one of the camera operators and a wife beater from another. I ask everybody how I look, and LaFonda replies that she might consider doing me.

I wish I could describe the next few minutes more fully, but being hit with that much voltage is sort of like running your brain through a blender. One second I'm skulking along behind Roger, and the next I'm staring up at foxy little Amy and wondering why she's pinching her nostrils. When my memory begins to reboot I have the irrational instinct to mimic Claudell's hasty exit, but I am proud to say that I fight it off. The cameras thus get to capture the light-hearted moment when Roger comes over to help me up and we share a laugh and a handshake, thus proving that while The Shocker will temporarily incapacitate even a cold-blooded criminal, it's also safe enough to use on your drinking buddies.

The production schedule now calls for Boney and the contestants to resumé giving away CDs on the streets of Santa Monica, secure in the knowledge that each has in his or her own pocket a sure-fire means of self-protection. This is complete horseshit, of course—Delawn was packing a .357 Magnum, and a lot of good it did him. In recognition of this, Trevor has supplemented the Shockers with enough well-trained and heavily-armed bodyguards to protect the leaders of the G8 nations. (This private army will naturally remain out of camera range.) Either Boney or I could tell Trevor that such a large extra expense is unnecessary, since everyone who's supposed to be dead already is. But apparently neither of us is so inclined.

In fact, I'm not inclined toward much of anything. The combined effects of stress, sleep deprivation, and an artificially induced seizure make me crave the comforts of home. I don't expect Trevor to grant me more than a few hours off, but he surprises me by telling me to take all the time I need. Perhaps watching me spaz out on the cement has made him feel guilty. More likely, he's so pissed about being shaken down for a slice of his big score that he's glad to get me out of his sight. Or maybe he just doesn't care for the scent of burning flesh.

Whatever it is, I'm sure not complaining. My car is back at the office so I hoof it a couple blocks over to the Century Plaza Hotel and take a cab from there to my apartment. Once there, I make the cave ready for some serious hibernation. I close all the windows and curtains, turn off all the phones, and deploy a set of foam earplugs as a last line of defense against the Skipper. Leaving nothing to chance, I also toss down four Tylenol PMs, which is double the recommended dosage but far from a personal best. In the twilight state just before I drift off, I see Roger aiming his Shocker at me. But when he presses the button, instead of an electrically charged dart it fires a stream of one hundred dollar bills. Now that's what I call turning lemons into lemonade.

I don't wake up for good until shortly after 9:00 AM, and I'm too groggy to calculate how many hours of sleep that makes—roughly a shitload. I take my time in the shower, and when I emerge I feel ready for anything Trevor can throw at me. I even have a little bounce in my step as I descend the stairs to the street and my car. When I see it's not there my first thought is that someone must have stolen it, and I begin to laugh at the concept. Then I remember how I got home and I reach for my cell phone to call another taxi. Before I can dial I must turn the thing on, and it immediately informs me that I have thirty-seven new voice mail messages. Trevor must be having a full-scale hissy-fit, but what else is new.

"Good morning, Eddie," says a female voice behind me. I know without looking that it's Ursula, a lonely old bag who lives on the ground floor and would talk to a fire hydrant if it had ears (though she'd probably get its name wrong).

"Good morning, Ursula," I say, trying as always not to be rude but also not to engage.

"I see you're having to fight the women off these days."

"Oh yeah, with a stick." I have no idea what she's talking about, but if you think I'm going to ask, you've obviously never had an Ursula for a neighbor.

"That little chippie who was here in the middle of the night sure wasn't taking no for an answer," she says. "I thought she was going to break your door down." This triggers some dim recollection buried deep in my cerebellum—did I dream that someone was pounding on my door? I turn to look at Ursula, and as I do I notice someone get out of a car parked across the street. It's a skinny black kid, and the quick glimpse I catch of him gives me another shot of déjà vu. Maybe I'm still asleep.

"You must've had other company, eh?" Ursula continues, poking me playfully on the arm. My eyes remain locked on the black kid, though. Even though he hasn't so much as glanced in my direction and is now ambling slowly away down the opposite sidewalk, something about him scares the shit out of me. Is it just the color of his skin? No, I decide as he strolls past a vacant parking space, allowing me to see him from head to toe. It's the color of his shoes.

chapter twenty-two

"URSULA, MAY I please use your phone?" I say as calmly as I can. I have already taken her by the arm and begun steering her toward the open door of her apartment, which is twenty feet away but may as well be a mile. It doesn't help that Ursula, as she has informed me many times, has two bum hips.

"I don't know, Eddie," she says, confused by my abrupt about-face. "Is it local or long distance?"

"Local," I assure her. Ursula expresses some other concerns but I don't hear them because I'm focused on a few of my own, such as the bullets that are about to pepper my back. I don't let myself turn around, though, until we're inside Ursula's door and I'm closing it behind us. The skinny black kid is nowhere in sight, and hopefully he didn't see where we went.

"What's gotten into you?" Ursula asks, nervous.

"There's a man with a gun out there."

"Oh, dear God."

"You need to call 911." I aim Ursula toward the phone on a side table, then deadbolt the door and snap the front curtains shut. Using my cell phone, I dial Susan's.

"Where the hell are you?" she answers.

"In a neighbor's apartment. I think the guy who killed Delawn is outside."

"Shit. Call 911."

"We're doing that right now." Ursula has indeed dialed, and is waiting for someone to answer.

"Dispatch, this is three Delta niner," I hear Susan say. Alert Culver City PD there's a two-seventeen in progress at 4-5-1-2-7 Jasmine. Request they respond all units Code 3."

"Copy, three Delta niner," a voice replies through Susan's radio.

"Where have you been all night?" Susan asks me.

"In my bed, sleeping."

"I came by there and practically beat the door down. Your fucking scumbag boss released the tape."

"What?"

"You and Delawn are all over the news." As I'm processing this, a noise makes me jump. It's somebody jiggling the front door knob from the other side. I manage to shush Ursula before she can scream, and then herd her toward the rear of the apartment.

"He's trying to get in," I whisper to Susan over the phone.

"Is there another way out?"

"The back door." Being on the ground floor, Ursula's unit has an exit from the kitchen to a narrow path that runs along the side of the building. "I'm using it." I shove the phone in my pocket, unlock the back door, and am about to run when I hear a loud crash behind me. Delawn's killer is trying to kick down the front door, and it sounds like he's not going to have too much trouble. Ursula grabs my arm and looks at me with unbridled terror. There are only two things I can think to do, and unfortunately the one I feel morally obligated to choose is to give Ursula a piggyback ride.

"Grab on," I tell her, hoisting her up by her thighs like I do with Hallie. Ursula doesn't seem to weigh much more than a seven-year-old, probably because I have more performance-enhancing chemicals pumping through me right now than Major League Baseball. At the rear of the building the path ends in a locked gate, so I turn the other way and sprint, or whatever the proper verb is to describe running as fast as you can with an old lady clinging to your neck. How about sprint + waddle = sprawdle.

"Look out, Eddie!" Ursula shouts, to alert me to an open kitchen window that like any other sighted animal I can see perfectly well for myself. I duck under that obstacle and hurdle a garden hose, and just like that we're at the street. I have no intention of stopping here, however, so I turn and sprawdle up the sidewalk, away from the building. We pass a mailman and two women pushing baby strollers. One of them is the type who believes in educating her infant by naming everything she sees in an identical sing-songy cadence.

"Look Nathaniel, there's a doggy, and there's a tree, and there's a man and his mommy playing horsie."

I hear a siren wail in the distance, which both gives me comfort and makes Ursula suddenly feel a lot heavier. I stop and set her down, but that proves to be premature.

"Move, muthafucka!" somebody shouts, and down the block I see the mailman dive for safety. It's the only sensible thing to do, because the kid with the distinctive high-tops and the equally distinctive handgun is headed this way. And he definitely ain't sprawdling.

There isn't time to drag Ursula onto my back again, so I scoop her up like I'm about to carry her across the threshold of the honeymoon suite. Our pursuer has us in sight and will catch up in a matter of seconds, so what would really come in handy is some shelter. Just ahead a car pulls out of the subterranean garage of another apartment building, and the automatic gate begins to close behind it. I turn and dash down the ramp, nearly tumbling ass over tea kettle in the process, and duck around the first corner inside the garage. I hear the kid's footsteps pounding down the ramp behind us, but he's a few seconds too late and the gate is now closed.

"Muthafuck!" he yells, rattling the gate loudly. It's made of vertical metal bars six inches apart, and when the kid thrusts his arm through them, Ursula and I get much too good a look at the gun in his hand. At least the sirens are getting closer, so we might have a chance.

Or not. As I place Ursula back on her feet, I hear another noise and turn to see a girl in workout clothes enter briskly through a door at the far end of the garage. She uses the remote control on her keychain to unlock the door of a Mustang and is about to climb in.

"Hey!" I shout, my voice echoing through the garage. The girl stops. "Don't drive out there!"

"Why not?" she says.

"There's a guy with a gun." She looks doubtful. I want to run to her, but I can't leave our corner without passing in front of the gate and thus becoming an easy target in an arcade game called "Cap the Old Honky."

"Whatever," the girl says. "I'm gonna be late for yoga." With that she hops in her Mustang and fires it up. I look around frantically. There are only two cars Ursula and I can hide behind, and the closest thing to a weapon is a half-empty bag of potting soil. I grab it and pull Ursula down with me between the two cars. Maybe if I wait until the kid gets close enough . . . but on second thought, why do that? When now, thanks to a revolutionary new technology . . .

I shove my hand into the pocket of my coat and pull it out, clutching the nearly-forgotten Shocker.

"What is that, Eddie?" Ursula whispers.

"It's better than nothing."

The yoga chick backs out of her parking space and roars toward the gate. I take Ursula by the shoulders to make sure I have her full attention.

"When you hear this," I say, snapping my fingers right next to her ear, "I want you to do something to distract him. Do you understand?" Ursula nods, but she's so freaked out I doubt she really does. Either way, the electric gate is now beginning to open for the Mustang, so there's no time for clarification. I scuttle around to the front of the car parked nearest the gate and flatten myself on the garage floor. Peering under the chassis, I see the kid's high-tops as he enters. He proceeds slowly and swings wide around the corner to avoid being jumped. Then he stops and I see one of his hands reach to the ground. He's bending down to look under the cars.

I snap my fingers, too softly the first time for even me to hear, then again, apparently loud enough for everyone. The kid quickly straightens and moves in my direction. To avoid a face-to-face shootout, my only option is to launch a desperation dart at his pant leg. But just as I'm about to do that, Ursula springs into action.

"Over here, jigaboo!"

The kid spins around. I feel I should apologize to him for Ursula's racial insensitivity, but I suppress the urge long enough to stand up and shoot him in the back.

When Susan arrives ten minutes later, the suspect is already cuffed and glowering at me from the back of a Culver City PD car. I give Susan a quick rundown, and she has much the same reaction as the cops who got there ahead of her—there is no fucking way a civilian can legally possess a Taser. She does manage to talk the sergeant in charge out of arresting me, however, which is nice because I'd hate to share a holding cell with the guy who just tried to gun me down. He has no ID on him and won't answer any questions, but the 1986 Buick Le Sabre he left in front of my apartment is registered to one Leonora Hill of 1283 East 70th St. in the heart of the 'hood. His weapon is a Taiwanese knockoff of a Glock, and the bullets in its clip are of the same type used to kill Delawn. If the ballistics match, then the cops will have a solid murder case against the kid, and hopefully he can be persuaded to testify against the person who hired him.

Before I can focus on Boney, though, I must give some thought to Satan's other personal assistant. By releasing the tape, was Trevor actually trying to get me killed? Probably not, because he couldn't have known that Delawn really was the intended target at City Walk, and therefore he didn't believe anyone would come after me. He let the news division have the footage simply because it was so valuable—it's not every day the folks at home get to watch a real person bleed out. Trevor no doubt received something equally juicy in return, maybe even a commitment for another series, and he didn't take seriously the notion that he was placing me in danger. On the other hand, he did assure Susan that he wouldn't put the scene on the air, and he seems to have changed his mind right after I extorted some serious scratch from him. So in the event I did get rubbed out, it would just be another in Trevor's endless series of win-wins.

Trevor's pointed ears must be burning, because my phone rings and it's him.

"Ted, are you all right?"

"Of course, Trevor, why wouldn't I be?" I say, affecting a jaunty air.

"I've just been told that you were involved in some sort of mishap."

"Oh, bollocks. It was really more of an annoyance, a spot of bother."

"Well the important thing is, you're safe," Trevor says. "I don't know if you've heard, but some incompetent swine down in editing misunderstood my instructions and sent the network news boys that clip of you talking to the bodyguard."

"You're kidding," I deadpan.

"I'm afraid not. Naturally I fired the bloody bastard." And no doubt bought him a first-class ticket to bloody Brazil.

"That'll teach him," I say. "Now if you'll excuse me, I have to go acquire a new identity."

"If you're that concerned, why don't I send over a security detail?" Trevor says. I want to tell him to shove his detail where the sun don't shine, but maybe that's not the smart move. They say keep your friends close and your enemies closer, and there's nothing to be gained by telling Trevor what I think of him, as least not yet. I'm sure that if and when I get around to it, he'll still be a puss-filled sore on a pig's asshole.

"I'm on my way over to the police station, so I should be okay for a while."

"Very well, but call me straight away if anything changes. Oh, and they want you to be on *Good Day USA* tomorrow morning."

After we hang up, I call my friend Tom O'Brien and tell him he'd better stock up on the condoms.

This time I know better than to try and reach Hallie at school. I phone Sara and am relieved when my call goes straight to voice mail. I leave a message telling her that they might be hearing about me on the news, but that I'm perfectly fine and she should tell Hallie not to worry. As I hear these words come out of my mouth, I realize they're almost exactly the same as the ones I used after the City Walk shooting—and they definitely aren't getting any more credible. This time I wasn't merely standing next to someone who got killed—I was supposed to *be* that someone, and if I hadn't gotten extremely lucky, my precious little girl would be without a father right now. This makes me more angry than sad, which I suppose is a good thing since I doubt that me bursting into tears is going to cause Boney to stop being such a meanie.

The name of the young man who ended Delawn's life and tried to do the same to mine is Lawrence Taylor Jones. "L.T.," as he is commonly known, lives part-time with his mother and two sisters at the address on East 70th St., and part-time at various local detention facilities. Counting today, he has been arrested fourteen times, for offenses ranging from vandalism to attacking his junior high woodshop teacher with a Skil saw. L.T. is also a suspect in several drive-by shootings that bear the telltale signature of his social set, the Rolling 73rd St. Crips. But no matter how many past murders are pinned on L.T., he's unlikely to receive the death penalty, because he just turned sweet sixteen.

None of this information is gleaned from the suspect himself, as he has refused to utter a word since his arrest. A computer scan of his fingerprints led to his rap sheet, and the registration on the Buick to his mother, who also has nothing to say except, "When you muthafuckas gonna gimme my muthafuckin' car back?" While Ursula and I complete our formal statements to a sergeant at Culver City Police headquarters, Susan takes one more crack at L.T. in the adjacent interview room. After a few minutes she emerges and passes the sullen youngster off to a uniformed cop.

"You owe me five bucks," the sergeant says to Susan. "I knew that kid wouldn't tell you anything."

"Actually, you owe me five," she says. "He told me to show him my cooze."

Susan and I give Ursula a ride home. To make her feel safer I offer to get Ursula a hotel room, but she'll have none of it. After so many years of chasing her audience down the sidewalk, she's understandably excited about the prospect of them coming to her. I can't really think of why anyone would want to hurt the old dear anyway, unless they were stuck with her on a long car trip. Three live trucks from local TV stations are parked in front of our building, so we let Ursula off down the block and watch to make sure she's okay. As soon as one of my other neighbors sees her and points her out to the TV crews, they descend on her as though she were a cross between Jesus and Jenna Jameson.

"One at a time, please," the radiant Ursula tells them.

With that good deed done, I suddenly realize that I'm famished. And it's no wonder—between being electrocuted and nearly murdered, I've totally forgotten to eat. Susan takes me to Junior's Deli on Westwood Boulevard, which somehow attracts a steady clientele of cops without offering a single variety of donut. While I commit aggravated assault on a pastrami sandwich, Susan stews about where to go from here. It's obvious to any half-wit that Boney is behind the deaths of both Patrice and Delawn, but the evidence against him is entirely circumstantial. If we lived in a country that wasn't so concerned about legal technicalities—let's say Saudi Arabia—Susan's job as a detective would be easy. (Of course, being a woman she wouldn't even have such a job, since the Saudis aren't so stupid as to arm the enemy. But work with me.) She would simply arrest Boney, bring him down to the station, and ask him a few questions while tightening a table vise around his testes. With forensic tools like these at their disposal, the Saudi police have a much better conviction rate than their US counterparts, and maybe that's why hip-hop has never really caught on there. The Riyadh PD would have long ago solved the murders of Tupac and Biggie, and taken all the fun out of lesser publicity stunts like spraying bullets at Lil' Kim.

But thanks to our namby-pamby Bill of Rights, Susan isn't allowed to beat, burn, or otherwise torture the truth out of Boney. It doesn't look like L.T. is going to shed much light on the situation either, and you can't really blame him. He knows from firsthand experience that Boney takes vigorous exception to tattle-tales, and it's no secret that the police do an imperfect job of protecting people. Not long ago, right here in L.A., a small-time dope dealer who wanted to lessen his jail time made a deal with the DA and squealed on his supplier. The cops busted the bigger fish and locked him up on the same cellblock as the guy who ratted him out, whom he promptly strangled. I'm guessing that wasn't what the informant thought was meant by "receiving a reduced sentence."

While Susan thinks about how to get Boney, I think about how to dissuade him from getting me. I could call him up and tell him he has nothing to fear, but how would that conversation go? "Dude, I know you're going around wasting everybody, but I can't prove it, so lighten up, okay?" The blunt truth is that I probably can't do anything to stop Boney from coming after me, and this realization is oddly liberating.

"Why don't we sting him?" I ask Susan.

"Meaning?"

"I get him on the phone, say that Delawn told me all about Patrice, and unless he pays up I'm going to the cops. When I go to collect the money, I'll wear a wire."

"Too risky," Susan says. "We don't let civilians do that kind of stuff."

"Boney's already trying to kill me, so what's the difference?"

"The way the department looks at it, if you get killed on your own time, it's unfortunate. If it happens while you're working for us, it's a fucking disaster."

"Gee, how come they don't paint that on the side of the squad cars?"

Any resentment I might be feeling about LAPD's self-serving policies is quickly banished by the arrival of a towering chocolate sundae. Susan watches as I cut it down to size.

"You really think you can pull it off?" she asks after a long silence.

"Absolutely," I say, partially stifling a belch. "Next I'm having the apple pan dowdy."

"I'm talking about Boney."

"Look at it this way," I tell her. "If you're in a situation where you need somebody who can fight, you get a fighter. If you need somebody who can negotiate, you get a negotiator. And if you need somebody who can lie, you get a Reality TV producer."

"If I can sell my captain on it—and that's a big if—you have to do everything exactly the way I tell you to."

"No problem. In case you haven't noticed, I excel at following orders."

"I mean it, Ted. I can't let you get hurt."

I have a strong urge to lean across the table and get our first kiss out of the way right here and now, but there are other cops all over the place and I don't want to embarrass Susan. So I settle for nudging her foot under the table, and when she nudges me back it's more exciting than a lot of the orgasms I've had.

"Are you going to invite me over to your house again someday?" I ask.

"Maybe," she says. "Unless Boney shoots you in the pecker."

While Susan goes off to sell the idea to her superiors, I drop by the office. As I walk through, every head turns in my direction and I make a rough estimate of how many people are glad I survived versus how many are inclined to raise bail money for L.T. Some of my co-workers are hard to read, but let's just say that based on initial impressions, I have no plans to run for office.

Trevor is of course unburdened by normal human emotions. While he showed complete disregard for my safety, it wasn't because he doesn't "like" me. It was because it was in his economic self-interest. And Trevor's luck being what it is, I did something even more useful than allowing myself to be killed – I stumbled on a way to make him more money. He's waiting for me in his office with a heartfelt apology about the whole videotape mix-up, and yet another revised shooting schedule. The key feature of the new one is a reenactment of how I escaped from L.T. and brought him to heel with the help of The Shocker. Trevor listens while I describe the actual event, then asks my thoughts about two small creative adjustments he has in mind. The first is that I shoot the actor portraying L.T. in the chest instead of the back. The second is that the role of Ursula be played by this month's *Playboy* centerfold. Inasmuch as Trevor is the undisputed master of the Reality genre, who am I to quibble?

"In light of your extra workload, I feel it's also appropriate to reconsider the division of profits," Trevor tells me. "I'm willing to grant your original request for 10 percent."

"That sounds fair," I say. Trevor's gleeful smile suggests that he didn't expect me to roll over nearly so easily. "But I need one other provision," I continue. "In writing."

"Of course."

"If I happen to die anytime soon, my daughter gets my share. And instead of 10 percent, it's 50."

Since I refuse to budge off of my demand, and insist upon having a fully executed document memorializing our agreement before I leave his office, Trevor decides to take no more chances with my personal well-being. He assigns Moshe and Chaim, two of the ex-Mossad agents who act as his drivers and bodyguards, to stay by my side 24/7. Neither of them is much of a conversationalist, but it is kind of cool to mosey down the street between a pair of Secret Service-types. Men get out of your way, and women actually check *you* out. It's no wonder Bill Clinton can't keep it in his pants.

We aren't shooting the reenactment for several days, Susan hasn't received an answer yet from the brass about our proposed sting, and I can no longer be bothered with anything as mundane as my actual job. So Moshe, Chaim, and I take Trevor's limo—which has been "hardened" and is guaranteed to withstand a direct hit from a mortar round—out for a little joyride. Our first stop is at Deb's place to pick her up, then at Sara's to get Hallie. Limos are of course nothing new to my little princess, but she's apparently never done anything fun in one, like use the Del Taco drive-thru window, or ask a group of hookers if they have any Grey Poupon. (Lest you think I'm setting a bad example by making sport of people who deserve sympathy and not ridicule, I should point out that we don't tell Hallie they're prostitutes. We tell her they're actresses.) We finish off our play date by going ice-skating, which judging by the amount of hard falls and *sotto voce* swearing is not a popular activity in Israel.

We're on our way to take Hallie home when I get a call from Susan. I don't want Moshe and Chaim to overhear our conversation, so I ask if I can phone her back. When we arrive at Sara and Richard's house, I tell the bodyguards I have to use the toilet and convince them that there are unlikely to be any Crips lurking in the Slatkins' powder room. Once I have a little privacy, I call Susan and learn that Captain Cardenas has approved the sting operation on Boney.

"How did you convince him?" I ask her.

"I implied that I was interested in you on a personal level," Susan says. "I figured my colleagues would rather explain how they let you get killed than how you managed to get busy with the station lezbo." Even though Susan's suggestion of our romance was strictly strategic, it still makes the hair on the back of my neck stand up and salute.

On my way out of the powder room, I nearly run into Richard and another man who are also on their way to the front door.

"Ted!" Richard says, startled. "What are you doing here?"

"I was dropping Hallie off and I had to use the bathroom." The man with Richard looks familiar—he's around fifty, distinguished-looking, maybe a tad too tan—but I can't place him and no one is offering any introductions.

"Next time I won't be so presumptuous," I tell Richard. "I'll pee in the koi pond."

As I walk to the waiting limo, I notice the license plate on a Mercedes two-seater parked in the motor court: BH MD. That plus the fact that Richard's guest was carrying a black bag are enough to pull him up from the recesses of my memory. He is Dr. Steven Somebody-Or-Other, and he seems to be on the news every time somebody famous ODs on OxyContin. Since Richard doesn't look ill, I must assume that Sara is the one who requires medical attention. Once again, you don't have to be Sherlock Holmes to see a possible linkage between my reversal of fortune and Sara's sudden need for a house call from Dr. Feelgood. But since this time I'm the one on the high end of the teeter-totter, I find it a lot easier to set the question aside for the time being. If it turns out, though, that Sara's blabbing to Richard about me and Susan is what caused the murder of Delawn, which in turn very nearly resulted in my own violent death, you better believe I'm bringing it up in family therapy.

chapter twenty-three

THE FIRST STEP in our fishing expedition is for me to set the hook in Boney. When we return to Trevor Banes Productions, I lock myself in an empty office (with Moshe and Chaim standing guard outside) and phone Susan. She has equipment on her end that will allow her to listen in and record the call, and also send a false caller ID to Boney.

"This is Ted Collins," I say when he answers.

"'Sup, dog?" Boney says, cool as ever. The guy tries to have me killed, then calls me his dog. I swear, these rappers are more two-faced than teenaged girls.

"I just wanted you to know that I'm still around," I tell him.

"I didn't know you was plannin' on goin' nowhere."

"That's pretty funny."

"'F you say so."

"I was hoping we could settle this thing in a more civilized way," I say.

"What thing we talkin' 'bout?" Boney asks.

"Delawn."

"That nigga say somethin' to you after he got shot?"

"As a matter of fact he did. He said you paid him to kill Patrice Williams."

"That's bullshit! My boy would never give me up."

"So you're admitting you had her killed?"

"I ain't admittin' nothin'," Boney says. "You tell this to the police?"

"Not yet."

"What you waitin' for?"

"A hundred thousand dollars. And I don't take plastic."

After calling me a cocksucking motherfucker and a motherfucking cocksucker several times each, Boney says he needs a day to round up the money. As instructed by Susan, I tell him to meet me at two o'clock the next afternoon at Lake Balboa Park in Van Nuys. I also tell him that I've given a letter in a sealed envelope to a friend, with instructions to take it straight to the police should I pass away prematurely. Boney assures me that he wouldn't waste his valuable bullets on a cocksucking cocksucker like me, and we bid each other adieu. When I hang up I notice that my hand is shaking violently, which I guess means I should either cut back on the caffeine or on the blackmailing of cold-blooded killers.

It's time to call it a day, and much as I'd like to believe Boney, a little caution is in order regarding where I spend the night. My bodyguards feel that in the case of an all-out attack my apartment would be too difficult to defend, and God knows I can't defend it on any level. We therefore check into a suite at the Sheraton by LAX, which I regret to say will never be confused with either the Beverly Hills Hotel or the Bel-Air. To be sociable, I suggest to Moshe and Chaim that we check out the pay-per-view movies, but their taste runs toward the adult and I find it difficult to enjoy *Anal Addiction IV* in the company of two male strangers. So I retire to the bedroom where I have my own TV and can watch something else. After an exhaustive review of the offerings, however, I determine that Moshe and Chaim made the best choice after all.

I don't have any Tylenol PMs, and I'm self-conscious about asking the bodyguards to get some for me. They're the type of guys who probably sleep in twenty-minute shifts with one eye open and wake up feeling perfectly refreshed. So I spend most of the night telling myself to relax, because extorting money from a gun-toting multiple murderer is really not that big a deal.

In any case, I know that Susan will do everything in her power to make sure I'm safe, and if I have to I can certainly take care of myself. After all, I'm bigger than Boney and in a fight I usually give as good as I get, although in truth the last one was during a seventh grade dodgeball game, and I'm pretty sure my adversary wasn't packing heat.

I finally drift off shortly before sunrise, just as the incoming jet traffic begins to pick up in earnest. What can be so goddamned important that all these impatient bastards need to arrive in L.A. so early in the morning? I give up around 7:00 and hit the shower, which I'm pretty sure is dispensing battery acid from the way it feels on my eyes. While sipping a deeply regrettable cup of coffee, I mentally review my to-do list, the first item on which is to lose the Jews.

First I tell Chaim that I absolutely cannot begin the day without a splash of Old Spice. He reluctantly heads for the gift shop in the lobby, muttering "Faygeleh" under his breath. As soon as Chaim is gone, the phone in our suite rings and Moshe answers it. This will be Susan, identifying herself as one of the Tanyas and telling Moshe to please hold for Mr. Bane. While Moshe is doing as he's told I return to the bedroom, then slip quietly out the door that leads directly into the hallway. I run to the fire stairs and down all eight flights, and at the ground floor I take the emergency exit to the parking lot. A sign says "ALARM WILL SOUND WHEN DOOR IS OPENED," but it doesn't and I feel gypped. Susan is waiting for me in an unmarked car, and five minutes later we're speeding north on the 405. Even under these less than ideal conditions—sleep deprived, headed for a tête-á-tête with a serial killer—just being in Susan's presence makes me feel calm and hopeful. My cell phone rings and I see that it's Trevor placing the first of what will no doubt be dozens of calls over the next few hours, none of which I will answer. I explain to Susan that I nevertheless want to leave it turned on, since the evidence of Trevor's ineffectual rage is giving me a chubby. She grabs the phone out of my hand and switches it off, thus proving that no matter how cool she is, she's still a chick.

Three hours before my scheduled rendezvous with Boney, the sting team gathers in the briefing room at LAPD Valley Division headquarters in Van Nuys. Captain Cardenas is nominally in charge, but lets Susan handle all the details. Using a map of Lake Balboa Park and a set of colored pushpins, she lays out the assigned locations and responsibilities for each of the twelve officers who are to take part in the operation. Three will be inside a special unmarked van in the parking lot, videotaping the action through a long telephoto lens. Two more will be in the trees, keeping a close eye on Boney through the scopes on their sniper rifles. The rest will be spread out through the park, using various ruses to look like civilians. Susan tells Detective Sanchez, a tough-looking young Latino, that he is to play the role of her boyfriend. The two of them will lie on a blanket and pretend to make out near the spot where I'm supposed to meet Boney. This part of the plan generates lots of wisecracks from her fellow officers, and a sharp pang of jealousy in me. I raise my hand and ask if it's a good idea, since Boney has met Susan and might recognize her. Susan promises me he won't because she'll be so far out of her normal context. I hear one of the cops in the back murmur to another, "Yeah. She'll be kissin' a dude."

The rules are pretty straightforward. If Boney brings along any members of his posse, or makes any threatening moves, or anything at all unexpected develops, I'm supposed to scream and run like a schoolgirl. (That's not exactly the way Susan puts it, but she might as well.) She also insists that I wear a bulletproof vest under my shirt. I guess it can't hurt, although it makes me look awfully puffy and the sergeant who straps it on helpfully points out that they don't do much good against head shots. I'm fitted with both a wireless radio transmitter and a miniature tape recorder, each connected to microphones that are taped to the front of my vest. We test the whole rig and everything seems to work, as evidenced by the fact that the uptight

African American detective listening in the next room is able to correctly repeat the test phrase I whisper for his benefit: "I sure do enjoy a nice firm spanking."

The videographers and snipers leave first to take up their positions around the park, followed by the other cops, in pairs. The plan is for me to drive Susan's Explorer, with her and Detective Sanchez following in the latter's Firebird. On our way out, Susan remembers a final detail she wants to go over with me and tells Sanchez to meet us in the parking lot. She leads me to an interview room, and before I know what's happening our tongues have somehow found their ways halfway down each other's throats.

"Is this standard police procedure?" I ask when we finally come up for air. Susan puts her finger to her lips and points at the spot on my chest where the microphone is attached. Since I am therefore deprived of words, my only way to communicate my sentiments about the situation is to kiss her again. As I do, it occurs to me that maybe I talk too much.

We caravan over to Lake Balboa, arriving shortly before 2:00. It's another perfect Southern California day, but everyone else must be just as bored with that concept as I am because there are only a few vehicles in the parking lot. One of them is a van with "VALLEY PLUMBING REPAIR" painted on its side, which is actually the LAPD video surveillance unit. If at all possible, I'm supposed to stand so that Boney faces the hidden camera inside the van while we talk. I wait a few minutes to allow Susan and Detective Sanchez to lay their blanket out on the grass, and I'm relieved to see they don't immediately begin dry humping.

I get out of the Explorer and head for the park bench where I'm going to wait for Boney. I think I'm feeling pretty relaxed, but maybe I'm not because a loud engine noise almost makes me dive into a trash can. Another van, this one marked with the logo of "WESTSIDE PLUMBING SUPPLY," speeds past me and lurches to a stop in a handicapped space at the end of the lot. While in theory I have nothing against physically challenged tradesmen, this one is a real pain in the ass because he's parked his rig directly in the line of sight between the police van and the bench. Captain Cardenas, who is now dressed in the standard plumber's uniform—a t-shirt that's too small and jeans that are too big—immediately gets out of the police van and knocks on the window of the new arrival.

"Yo homes, you can't park there," says Cardenas.

"Why not?" the driver of the second van says. "It's a free country, ain't it?"

I'd like to linger and see how the battle of the butt-cleavage plays itself out, but I promised Susan I wouldn't deviate from the plan. So I walk toward the designated meeting place, although behind me I can hear Captain Cardenas's voice rising along with that of the other guy. When I reach the park bench I sit and look back toward the parking lot. Cardenas has apparently decided that with Boney due to arrive any time, his options for dealing with his inconsiderate fellow plumber are limited. He jumps in the undercover police unit, backs it out of the parking space, then drives it up onto the sidewalk on the other side of the second van. It's not the most inconspicuous solution, but at least the police camera once again has a clear view of the action.

And not a moment too soon, because just then a certain charcoal-gray Maybach pulls into the lot. I guess part of me didn't believe Boney would really show, and that's the part that suddenly sees nothing all that shameful about sprinting in the opposite direction. I manage to stay put, though, and even to wave at Boney as he parks his car and gets out. He's carrying a gym bag that I assume contains a hundred thousand dollars in cash, and it occurs to me that if I'd played this whole thing a little differently, I could actually keep all that money. Given Boney's history, however, I guess I'd rather have the cops on my side. Delawn's big payday didn't seem to buy him much happiness.

"Dude, you mind giving us a little privacy?" I turn to see that Detective Sanchez, who along with Susan lies on the grass about fifty feet away from my position on the bench, is talking to the male half of another couple. The new arrivals are spreading their own blanket about halfway between me and my protectors.

"Why, you own the park or something?" the interloper responds, and something about him seems familiar. He must be another undercover cop. But then why is he getting into it with Sanchez? And why do I recognize the girl too? In a sickening flash I realize it's because she, like her companion and for that matter like me, is an employee of Trevor Banes Productions.

"Just fucking move," Sanchez snaps at the guy, a sound mixer who normally works on *Castaway*.

"Blow me," the sound guy says. Sanchez starts to stand, but Susan stops him.

"Don't sweat it, hon," she says, and pulls Sanchez close to her.

I notice that the girl, Jenny Something from Post-Production, carries a beach umbrella inside a nylon sheath. But if you look more closely you can see that it has a wire coming out one end—it's a shotgun mike, which can pick up sounds from considerable distances. They must be here to record my interaction with Boney, and that means there's also a hidden camera somewhere. I'm going to hazard a guess that it's inside the second plumbing van, the driver of which has abandoned his handicapped space and is playing chicken with an enraged Captain Cardenas in an effort to reclaim inside position.

The only good news is that Boney doesn't seem to notice. He strolls toward me with his customary insolent cool, oblivious to the fact that the latest battle in the war between the government and the media is being fought all around him. I have only a few seconds to consider the question of how Trevor found out about the sting, and the answer is who the hell cares. Although the situation certainly meets Susan's definition of "unexpected developments," I am now even more determined to stay the course and nail Boney right here and now. After all, I'm on TV.

"Here, muthafucka," Boney says, slinging his gym bag at me. I stand up and catch the bag just before it hits me in the face, which is a good thing because it turns out that a hundred grand is pretty heavy.

"Thanks," I say.

"What you oughta be catchin' is a muthafuckin' bullet."

"If I die, the cops find out all about Patrice."

"You don't know shit about Patrice," Boney hisses. "Don't even be sayin' her name, ya hear?" He's standing with his back to the parking lot, but I decide not to try repositioning him just now because over Boney's shoulder I see that Trevor's team has gained the upper hand by driving its van onto the grass.

"Then how come you're paying me all this money to keep quiet?" I ask.

"'Cause I don't trust you white muthafuckas to believe me if I say what really happened. Look what happened to my boy O.J." Boney is apparently referring to the Simpson civil trial, in which an obviously bigoted white jury interpreted the evidence differently than the sagacious panel of blacks at his criminal trial. Since Boney has played the race card, I feel I have no choice but to respond with some tactical misogyny.

"You may be black and I may be white," I tell him. "But I'll bet we have the same problems with our bitches." Boney snorts contemptuously but doesn't walk away, so I continue. "Hell, if I had a dollar for every time I wanted to kill one of mine, I wouldn't even need your money."

"He wasn't 'sposed ta kill her!" Boney shouts. Out of the corner of my eye I see Trevor's sound guy yank the headphones away from his ears and clutch his skull in pain. Boney's outburst, amplified by the shotgun mike, has apparently been a little harsh.

"What was Delawn supposed to do?" I ask Boney.

"Find out who she be fuckin' an' scare his ass off."

"So what happened?"

While Boney considers whether he wants to answer me, a loud screech of feedback comes from the direction of the sound crew. Boney and I automatically turn toward the noise, but fortunately we find both sets of ersatz lovers furiously making out on their respective blankets. Boney suddenly looks very tired and sits down on the bench. I do the same, while trying to suppress the question of whether Detective Sanchez is sporting wood.

"Patrice was cheatin' on me right from the start," Boney says, all the fight having gone out of him. "I knew it but I didn't wanna know it."

"I've been there," I tell him.

Since we're now both facing the parking lot, I can't help but be aware of what's going on with the dueling plumbers. Captain Cardenas has once again maneuvered his van past Trevor's crew and thus has an unobstructed view of Boney and me. On the downside, this game of leap-frog has brought the police van close enough to us that a toddler could hit it with a rock.

"When I can't find her and I figure it's 'cause she's with some other dude, it make me one crazy muthafucka," Boney continues. "I take anythin' I can get my hands on—crack, crystal, whatever. Smoke a lotta chronic an' drink a lotta Courvoisier too. One night a while back, I got so fucked up I told my boy D that if he ever catches her with another muthafucka I want him to kill 'em both."

"So what's the part you think people wouldn't believe?"

"I don' remember sayin' none a that," Boney declares, turning to look right at me. "An' Delawn never axe me nothin' about it till after he went and killed her." Whether on his own or with the aid of counsel, Boney has apparently crafted a diminished capacity defense to trot out if all else fails. And while it may seem weak at first blush, let's remember that an elected official once beat a double murder rap in California by claiming he was high on Hostess Twinkies.

"What did Delawn tell you about how Patrice died?"

"He followed her to that apartment, and a couple minutes

later some other big nigga shows up. D can hear 'em gettin' it on, so he busts in. Only before he can get at the muthafucka, he jump out the window. So D jus' kill my girl Patrice."

"But you didn't really want him to," I say in a tone that must convey some skepticism.

"I knew none a you cocksuckas would believe me," Boney says bitterly, and stands to leave.

"I believe you," I say, also coming to my feet. "You don't remember telling Delawn to kill her, and that's why you were so upset about it." Boney doesn't respond, but he clenches his jaw in a way that suggests he's fighting back tears. "It's also why you were so mad at Delawn you told that kid to shoot him."

With one swift motion, Boney grabs my shirt collar in one hand and pulls his Glock from his waistband with the other.

"I didn' have nothin' to do with that!" he screams, spraying spittle in my face.

"Okay, take it easy," I tell him. Susan and Sanchez are already on their feet, weapons drawn, but Boney doesn't see them.

"D was my boy, I'd never do nothin' to hurt him!" With that Boney gives me a hard shove in the chest, causing me to stumble backwards and fall to the ground.

"Police, drop your weapon!" I hear Susan shout. Boney looks around and sees heavily armed cops approaching from all directions.

"You dirty muthafucka," he says to me, raising the barrel of his gun. The resulting explosion seems to go on forever.

It is difficult to say exactly what killed Raymond "Boney" Bonaparte. In less than a second, both police snipers hit him with .30-06 rounds, one in the head and one between the shoulder blades. He also took three slugs fired from pistols and a shotgun blast from a cop who I, for one, really believed was a homeless woman pushing a shopping cart. Boney never even managed to cock his Glock. Citing department policy, Susan won't tell me if hers is one of the guns that inflicted the mortal wounds. I suspect she also has personal reasons for remaining silent, and it's just as well. If our fledgling romantic relationship goes anywhere, it's inevitable that we will have the occasional spat. And how do you win an argument about finances or frequency of sex when the other person can throw out "Oh yeah? Well how about the time I took out that guy who was about to blow your fucking head off?"

Trevor's attorney bails his people (there were eighteen of them in all) out of jail immediately, and Susan tells me it was pointless for Captain Cardenas to arrest them in the first place. Since none of the undercover cops identified themselves as such until just before the lead started to fly, the charge of interfering with a police officer will be impossible to prove. LAPD can also forget about any hope they may have of holding onto Trevor's tapes. The coroner hadn't even left the park with Boney's body before the lawyers were in court downtown, braying about the public's First Amendment right to see a man get riddled with bullets.

I make my peace with Trevor quickly and with a minimum of rancor. He cheerfully admits that he told Moshe and Chaim to monitor my phone calls, including the one I made from the office to set up the fateful encounter with Boney. Once the bodyguards learned the details of the planned sting and passed them on to Trevor, their assignment was to let me think I was sneaking away from them. And here I thought we were just three pals, enjoying a pleasant evening of hardcore porn. Trevor's justification for his actions is that my adventures grew out of my work for him on *The Mogul*, and per the terms of my employment contract he therefore owned the rights to everything that happened. Since I chose to be devious, he was forced to do the same. He is legally correct, and I can't even claim any moral superiority. While I was looking out for my interests, Trevor was looking out for his. And as usual, he was simply better at it.

Trevor is also quite reasonable about where we go from here. Although he could probably use the same passage in my employment contract to block me from writing anything about Boney, he assures me that he won't. (I thought of this potential snag way back at the beginning, but decided to forge ahead and let the chips fall where they may. For once, they didn't fall right on my balls.) Trevor says I can have all the print and movie rights to my story, as long as he gets 10 percent of the profits and I agree to cooperate fully in the production of this very special *Mogul* episode, which has been expanded to four hours over two nights. I'm also obliged to make a number of promotional appearances on various news and magazine shows, so many that my pal Tom O'Brien eventually complains that I've become overexposed and it's cutting into his action.

The public reaction to Boney's demise falls along familiar lines. Several leaders in the African American community see it as yet another case of LAPD jailing or executing people of color who dare to oppose the foreign army that occupies their neighborhoods. Lovey Mack adds fuel to the fire by hiring the late Johnnie Cochran's law firm to file suit against the LAPD, Trevor Banes Productions, the network, Roger Dominus, and a dozen people I've never heard of. I admit that I feel a little hurt not to be included in this long list of defendants, but perhaps the value of my principal asset—a 1996 Subaru—makes me an uninteresting target. In any case, Lovey and Muthafuckin' Music are sure to lose in court, but that's not the point of the exercise. The point is to generate a ton of cheap publicity and sell records. If the posthumous careers of Tupac and Biggie are any indication, Boney is set to become a much bigger star—and Lovey a much wealthier muthafucka—than either of them would have been had Boney lived.

As the guy whose civil rights were nearly violated by Boney's Glock, I find the accusations about police brutality a bit specious, and I say so in various interviews with TV and the newspapers. This makes me the hero *d'jour* on right-wing talk radio, which I find only slightly less distasteful than getting shot. But since they're all so eager to have me as a guest and won't take no for an answer, I finally agree to go on Sean Hannity's show. He asks me if I think the media are partially to blame for the violence in America.

"Absolutely, Sean," I tell him and his listeners. "Every time I accidentally come across you, or Rush, or Bill on my radio, I smash it to smithereens."

Happily, none of the fiery rhetoric from professional assholes of any stripe has much effect on the majority of the common citizens. The only mass display of emotion is outside Boney's house, where rap fans of all races come to leave flowers, stuffed animals, and a big pile of costume bling. Watching a live shot of an impromptu candlelight vigil, I'm tempted to be cynical. After all, Boney wasn't exactly John Lennon, and "Wuh Duh Fuh" isn't exactly "Imagine." But the grief on the faces of the mourners is just as real as any of those in Strawberry Fields, as is the comfort they give each other. The fact that I don't "get" Boney's music doesn't really matter. His fans get it, and it brings them together in the same way that watching *The Mogul* brings its audience together. Frankly, I envy them—I can't think of anything that would inspire me to strike the Statue of Liberty pose with a disposable lighter, and I wish I could.

With so much frenetic activity, I barely speak to Susan for several days. She then calls and invites me to her house for dinner, which leaves me both excited and a little nervous. It seems clear that The Time Has Come, and naturally I want it to be great. But will I be able to shut off all the outside noise and focus on Susan as a woman? If and when we get to the bedroom, what if I can't perform? Or, since I haven't been with a woman in almost a year, what if my performance consists of only a few notes?

I can't do much to control that, but at least I can try to make myself presentable. I've already received a fancy haircut from

Trevor's stylist, and three new outfits I've been wearing for my TV appearances. But I can't see showing up to a booty call in a business suit, so I grab Hallie and we go shopping at one of her favorite stores, Fred Segal on Melrose. Putting together the perfect casually chic ensemble is complicated by the fact that many of the employees and shoppers recognize me and want me to repeat the whole story for the umpteenth time, and also by my allergic reaction to the concept of $350 pants. Hallie and an adorable salesgirl named Georgie eventually persuade me that the Diesel jeans are killer with the $425 shirt that I absolutely must have. Since the purpose of this extravagance is to look good for Susan, I probably shouldn't be flirting with Georgie while she rings me up. But it's harmless fun and a good confidence builder, at least until my credit card gets rejected and Hallie has to put the purchase on hers.

I may have overdone my preparations, because Susan answers the door wearing sweats and a Dodgers cap. She perfunctorily thanks me for the hundred bucks worth of flowers I've brought her and turns to give me a peck on cheek, but the visor on her hat pokes me in the eye. From this inauspicious beginning we move to the kitchen, where the romantic home-cooked meal I was envisioning turns out to be two sacks from El Pollo Loco. Susan asks if I mind if she has a drink and I tell her of course not, although the half-empty bottle of Absolut on the counter suggests it may not be her first.

"Are you all right?" I ask.

"Let's sit down," she says. We take chairs on opposite sides of the kitchen table, and I brace myself for whatever reason she's about to give me as to why we can't see each other any more. But it turns out that what Susan has to tell me is even worse.

"We got the wrong guy," she says.

chapter twenty-four

"Excuse me?"

"Boney was telling you the truth."

"About what?"

"Everything."

"We already talked about this," I remind her, because indeed we did, right after Boney was killed. Susan, Captain Cardenas, and I discussed the possibility that Boney never told Delawn to kill Patrice, that the bodyguard instead acted on his own and then convinced Boney that he thought he was just following orders. Delawn's motivation presumably would have been hatred for the no-good slut who was two-timing his boss, plus a desire to demonstrate his loyalty to Boney and possibly collect a nice bonus for himself in the process. The problem with this theory is that it requires one to believe Delawn would risk killing the girl Boney clearly loved, on the chance he could persuade Boney that while he was wasted he told Delawn to do it. Delawn would have had to guess that even if Boney believed him, he would be so grief-stricken and remorseful that he was liable to do anything—like kill Delawn, or pay some kid to do it for him.

There is one plausible scenario, however, whereby Delawn might have slit Patrice's throat without being told to do so. Let's say Delawn follows her to the apartment, and while he's outside listening to "lunch" being served, it occurs to him that if everybody else is getting a piece, why shouldn't he? So he waits for

Loverboy to leave, then he knocks on the door and tells Patrice it's his turn. Only she doesn't see it that way, and maybe she even threatens to tell Boney that his goon tried to screw her. So Delawn rapes and kills her, or maybe the other way around, then makes up the story about how he was just following instructions. He figures Patrice is dead anyway, and this way maybe he can squeeze some cash out of Boney. He's right about that, but wrong in thinking he'll ever get a chance to spend it.

DNA tests are presently being conducted to see if it was Delawn's semen that was found inside Patrice. If so, that would suggest (but not prove) that Delawn lied to Boney. But even if Boney had nothing to do with Patrice's death, he was still responsible for siccing L.T. on Delawn and then on me, and that plus pointing a loaded gun at my head in the park should be enough to assuage any lingering doubts or guilt about his fate. And it is, until Susan interrupts my ruminations with an even more outrageous statement.

"Boney didn't ask Delawn to kill Patrice," Susan says. "And I don't think he asked L.T. to kill anyone either."

"The fuck he didn't!" I neither mean nor need to shout, but this historical revisionism thing is getting way out of hand.

"Remember what I told you about where Delawn's hundred grand came from?"

"Yeah, half in cash and half by wire transfer."

"Right," she says. "And the half that was in cash lines up perfectly with the withdrawal Boney made from his own bank."

"So?"

"So that tells us Boney was no master criminal who knows how to cover his tracks. But then how come he sent the other half from a secret numbered account in the Cayman Islands?"

"I don't know," I say. "Maybe he got smarter."

"In three hours?"

"Why does it matter?" I ask, growing increasingly uncomfortable.

"Delawn had to be getting paid by two different people,"

Susan says. "And I'm convinced that it was his other client, not Boney, who sent him to kill Patrice. The same person later sent L.T. to kill Delawn, and you."

"Wow," I say. That's a pretty big theory to grow from such a small clue."

"I've got more to back it up."

"Let's hear it," I say, not really wanting to. Part of my desire to get up and run out of Susan's house right this second is pure sexual disappointment, and embarrassment over the expenditure of nearly a grand on these dopey new threads. But mostly it's my psychological self-defenses, telling me there's nothing to be gained by going any further down this dark road that Susan suddenly wants to travel. Boney is dead, and since I played a big part (okay, *the* big part) in his demise, I'd much rather continue to believe he deserved it. But before I can get my feet to move, she's talking again.

"It's always bugged me that we couldn't find any of Boney's vehicles on the surveillance video at The Grove," Susan says. "Delawn had to park somewhere, and every entrance to the garage and the surface lots has at least one camera on it."

"Maybe he borrowed a car from somebody else, or rented one."

"We ran checks on every license plate that entered, from ten minutes before Patrice arrived until twenty minutes after. I talked to all the registered owners by phone, and if there was anything even a little bit suspicious, I went out to interview them in person. I'm convinced that Delawn wasn't in any of those cars."

"So he got lucky and found a parking space on the street," I say. "We know he was there, three people saw him."

"Yeah," she says. "But one of the reasons I prefer security cameras is that people's memories don't come with time code."

"What does that mean?"

"By the time we talked to the witnesses, it was almost a week after Patrice disappeared. We already knew about the phony call from Boney's house to the modeling agency, when Peaches or some other member of Boney's entourage claimed to be Patrice confirming her meet time. So we assumed that Boney had her followed. Since Patrice arrived at The Grove at 1:17, we asked everybody if they saw any unusual activity from about 1:30 on. The guy Delawn ran into on the sidewalk remembered him and said it was around that time, and it all made sense. But it turns out Delawn didn't have to follow Patrice, because he already knew where she was going."

"Is he on the tapes earlier?" I ask, already knowing the answer.

"12:40 PM," Susan says. "He drove the Navigator, and he parked in the same structure Patrice did thirty-seven minutes later."

"It still could have been Boney who sent him," I say. "Maybe he already knew about the apartment. He could have had her followed some other time." The desperation in my voice is obvious even to me, so I decide to stop talking and think. But thinking doesn't make it any better. As Susan said, it makes no sense that the same person would pay Delawn $50,000 by the most clandestine, sophisticated method possible, and $50,000 by the most obvious. It's also hard to explain why Boney would willingly confess to me his supposed role in Patrice's death, and then suddenly go berserk when I suggested he had something to do with the killing of Delawn—unless he happened to be telling the truth. If he was, then I have an innocent man's blood on my hands, and still absolutely no idea of who the real bad guy is.

"So what do we do now?" I finally bring myself to ask.

"We can't do shit."

"Why not?"

"I called my captain a couple hours ago, right after I saw Delawn on the surveillance tape at The Grove. He ordered me to keep my mouth shut and do nothing further on the investigation unless I clear it with him first."

"You think he's worried about how the community will

react?" I'm assuming Susan will know that in this context and many others in L.A., "the community" means "the blacks."

"Probably," she says. "Aren't you?"

Susan and I finally sleep together, and while that's definitely a euphemism, in this case it's not for anything fun. It's for two fully clothed people lying on top of a bed, each of us wordlessly wrestling with our individual demons as the hours creep by. We touch from time to time and make a few half-baked attempts to recreate our magic moment at the police station. But it's clear that however much we could both use the distraction, neither one of us is anywhere near up to it. Susan rises at dawn to shower behind the closed bathroom door, and when it's my turn I do the same.

We return to the kitchen table to drink coffee and discuss our plans for the day.

"I'm driving you to your office, and you have to stay there until I come pick you up," she says.

"What if I get hungry?"

"Have something delivered."

"What if I get tired?"

Susan holds up her coffee cup.

"Look, I appreciate the concern," I say. "But no one needs to kill me anymore."

"Why do you say that?"

"Because the news has been wall-to-wall Boney for the last three days. Everyone thinks he did it."

"Everyone except the guy who really did," Susan says. "I'm gonna work on Cardenas to reopen the investigation, and in the meantime I'm not letting you take any chances."

On the drive across town we surf the radio morning shows, and hear no fewer than three commercials on three different stations for the *Mogul* special that will air tomorrow night. Since the big climax is the gunning down of Boney and I'm now fairly certain he was a victim rather than a villain, the lurid drama in the announcer's voice leaves me feeling even more disgusted than usual with myself and my career path. Trevor and the network have clearly pulled out all the stops, and the word around the office is that he's predicting "bigger than Super Bowl" ratings. He's probably right—no matter how hard they try, football players rarely succeed in killing each other.

There isn't much for me to do at work—I already faced the cameras for nearly three hours the day before yesterday, while Trevor himself fired questions at me about what I was thinking and feeling at various points over the past several weeks. This sort of interview is the backbone of Reality TV—although we faithfully record every move and utterance of the participants, few of them say anything revealing until prompted by an unseen questioner. Those coaxed confessions fill at least 50 percent of the average episode, which is why the contestants must all be at least interesting to look at, and natural exhibitionists. Since I'm not really either of those things, the *Mogul* segment producers have their work cut out for them—and good luck to you, boys and girls.

I pass some time catching up with the newspapers and magazines, which contain enough misinformation to justify invading Iraq all over again. Many of the errors serve to make me look considerably more heroic than I am—one tabloid claims I told Boney to "Go ahead and shoot me, you little bastard," and another that I wrestled the gun away from Boney and plugged him myself. Every one of these shlocky fictions makes me feel even shittier about myself—it's not enough that I got the poor man killed; now I've somehow become Dirty Harry.

When I've received enough reminders that TV has no monopoly on making stuff up, I check in with Susan. She's in a foul mood.

"Fucking Cardenas is avoiding me," she says.

"Maybe he's just busy."

"I peeked in his office window. He's surfing porn sites."

"Ask him to email me some links," I say. "I need a distraction."

"You see where this is going, don't you? They're gonna keep stonewalling me forever."

"So we'll solve the case without their help."

"I can't do that, Ted. If I violate a direct order I get fired, and my job isn't like yours. I can't just go work for the police department across the street."

"Then maybe we oughta forget about it."

"You mean let somebody get away with three murders?" she says. "I'm counting Boney's in there too."

"I don't know what to tell you," I say, and that's the truth.

But I do know how to chase a story. And after we hang up, I decide that's exactly what I'm going to do. After all, isn't this the kind of opportunity that investigative reporters live for—a total exclusive on an explosive subject? If the cops are too nervous to pursue it, all the better—I won't have to compete with or avoid them. Of course I'll have to fib a little to Susan, but it's for a good cause—it's obviously killing us both to let Boney take the blame and the real culprit get off scot-free. As for putting myself at further risk, I rationalize my way around that one by doing a 180° and deciding that Susan is right—I'm already in danger, so isn't the logical move to go out and surprise the enemy before he surprises me? Never mind, it was a rhetorical question.

The best place—in fact the only place—I can think of starting is with L.T. Susan and her colleagues already tried and failed to find a connection between him and Boney, but if I widen the search to include all potential patrons of the homicidal arts, maybe something will turn up. L.T. is still in jail and keeping his own counsel, so my plan is to take another shot at his family and friends. The trouble is, I'm about the last guy on the face of the earth with a prayer of getting close to them. Aside from being a member of a race that is not particularly welcome in L.T.'s neighborhood (according to Yahoo, his mother's home is approximately a quarter of a mile from the intersection of

Florence and Normandie, where a white trucker was yanked from his rig and beaten by a black mob at the start of the 1992 Rodney King riots), my face is rather well-known at the moment, thanks to the saturation news coverage of Boney's death. The story is naturally of special interest to "the community," and the people who answer the phones at our office and at the network report that a high percentage of the feedback I've received from the public has been along the lines of "Tell that muthafucka he be dead."

But if I can't safely approach L.T.'s peeps, I bet I know a guy who can. Since my Subaru is at Susan's, the first thing I need is transportation. Mfume generously hands over the keys to his car—a sleek Jaguar convertible—and that bolsters my impression of him as both a great guy and a lucky son of a bitch. Between my new outfit and my new wheels, I get plenty of looks from the professional wives and girlfriends on Rodeo Drive, which is not strictly on the way to my destination but close enough to justify such a bracing detour. From there I speed over the hill to Burbank, where the *Mogul* conference room scenes are taped. There is nothing presently going on in the studio, but Trevor has ordered all production personnel to remain on twenty-four-hour standby in case any last-minute changes become necessary before tomorrow night's big show. This suits my needs perfectly, because the hair, makeup, and wardrobe people are by now sick to death of watching soaps and gossiping about each other. They therefore welcome and do not question my request that they employ their considerable talents to transform yours truly into a certain well-known African American.

We're not talking about Al Jolson daubing on a little greasepaint, or Gene Wilder applying an unconvincing layer of shoe polish. We're talking about the very best, state-of-the-art modern makeup technology, the kind that turned skinny little Eddie Murphy into a thoroughly believable 350 lb. tub of lard in *The Nutty Professor*, and Robin Williams into that lovable old battleaxe Mrs. Doubtfire. They start by giving me a prosthetic nose more than twice the width of my own, and then add some jowls so prodigious that if you sat me alongside Winston Churchill, he'd look like a crackhead. I want to tell them they're overdoing it, but I'm under strict orders not to move any facial muscles until the glue dries. By the time it does and they've applied plenty of dark brown makeup and bristly white hairs, I see why I was wrong to doubt them. These drama queens are worth twice whatever Trevor pays them, because even though I know I'm staring at myself in the mirror, I could swear that the guy who's staring back is the legendary boxing promoter Don King.

I asked to look like the permanently plugged-in Mr. King instead of some generic brother because I learned years ago that it's almost as good to resemble someone famous as it is to actually *be* famous. I used to know a sitcom writer who was a dead ringer for the ultra-hip writer-director Quentin Tarantino. In the mid-nineties, when Tarantino's face first became well-known, my writer friend experienced a sudden surge in his own popularity—as evidenced by getting prime tables and snappy service in the hottest restaurants, and blowjobs from the hottest total strangers—and he didn't like it. Because he was a proud fellow (and who wouldn't be after a decade of writing jokes for the likes of Bronson Pinchot?), he couldn't accept the notion of receiving such benefits simply for looking like someone else. So whenever a maitre d' or a starlet would smile at him, he would immediately snap "No, I am not Quentin Tarantino." But to his great surprise and dismay, he continued to be shown just as much deference as when people thought he was. The whole experience was so exasperating for the poor chap that he soon got married and moved to old-money Pasadena, where everyone pretends to disdain show people.

I may have attracted some attention on Rodeo Drive, but it's nothing compared to what Dapper Don gets on East 70th Street. The moment I glide Mfume's Jag to the curb in front of L.T.'s address, a crowd gathers around it.

"Don muthafuckin' King!" announces one of the first grinning arrivals, a gentleman wearing overalls sans shirt.

"No sir," I reply in my best impresario-with-a-rap-sheet impression as I step out of the car. "But I'm told we do bear a certain resemblance."

"You need any ring girls?" asks a pretty young thing who I hope is of legal age, especially when she lifts her shirt and exposes a pair of perfectly round bare breasts. "Check this shit."

"Righteous," I remark, quickly averting my eyes. "But I am actually lookin' for a Miss Leonora Hill."

"That's my mama!" shouts a boy of around Hallie's age. "An' that's my house."

"Is that right?" I ask. "What's your name?"

"Orenthal James."

"You must be one special young man," I say, offering little O.J. my fist for a bump. "Is your mama at home?"

"Yeah. She cain't go nowhere 'cause the muthafuckin' po-lice won't give her car back."

"What you want wit 'Nora?" demands a suspicious-looking woman in a muu muu that is stretched over buttocks the size of a regulation backboard.

"We need to talk some business," I say.

"Business?" scoffs the woman. "Only business that ol' ho be in is cheatin' on the welfare."

Guffaws and catcalls ripple through the assembled onlookers. I scan the faces and pick out the most responsible-looking young man.

"Son, how'd you like to make yourself a hundred dollars?" I ask him.

"D-d-doin' what?" he stutters.

"Lookin' after my ride." I peel a fifty off the roll in my pocket (the inner bills being mostly ones) and hand it to him. "Half now, and half if I get back and it's still here."

The young man reaches behind his back and whips out the ubiquitous 9mm automatic. I'm about to surrender my wad and hope he doesn't count it, but before I can he spins to face the crowd.

"All you m-m-muthafuckas j-j-jump back!" he shouts, and apparently I've chosen my chief of security well because everyone else promptly scatters. He takes a plastic CD case from his pants pocket and turns to me again. "Can I l-l-listen to my m-m-music?" He points at the sound system in the Jag's burled walnut dash. It's hard to say no to a kid who's both polite and packing heat.

"Sho 'nuff," I say, tossing him the key. "But don't be drivin' off now, ya hear?"

He nods silently and gets in the passenger seat. O.J. escorts me to the front door of the bungalow and yells through the screen.

"Mama! A man wanna talk to you!"

"Better not be another one a them muthafuckas from the TV," a voice replies from inside. A moment later the speaker appears, a dark-skinned, middle-aged woman who still possesses a nice enough figure but nevertheless shouldn't be wearing a shortie nightgown in the middle of the day.

"Say, what Don King be doin' on my doorstep?" she says with a smile.

"The name is Jamaal Jihad," I reply. "Are you Leonora Hill?"

"I don' know yet. What you want?"

"Would you by any chance be related to an old fella by the name of Maurice Hill, lives down in Jackson, Mississippi?"

"How should I know?" she says. "I cain't even remember all the niggas be livin' in my house."

"'Ight then, I won't bother you no more. Just sign this here paper and I'll be on my way." I produce a one-page document and a pen from my breast pocket.

"I ain't signin' shit," Leonora informs me.

"C'mon now, sister. If you don't want Uncle Mo's money, don't you think we oughta give it to somebody who does?"

Leonora ushers me into her parlor without further ado, and

hollers at the half-dozen or so people who are gathered there watching *The Little Mermaid.*

"Turn that shit down and get yo asses off the couch," she snaps. "We got company. An' no, he ain't Don King."

"We be here first," grumbles a plump young woman who is aggressively multitasking—in addition to staring raptly at the TV, she smokes a cigarette and feeds Cheetos to the infant on her lap.

"Don' you be talkin' back at me, Tifney!" Leonora raises her hand to wallop the chunkster, but I step between them.

"It's cool, baby," I say. "I'll just stand here and float like a butterfly." I attempt to simulate the Ali shuffle, which no one quite knows what to make of.

"Gimme a minute to get my clothes on," Leonora says to me, then wags a warning finger at the others. "Y'all be sweet ta our guest, else I gonna come back an' fuck you up good." She exits and I waste no time getting to work.

"So, y'all be Leonora's kin?" I say to the room at large.

"Yeah," says O.J., but the only other response I get is an indistinct mumble from a muscular twenty-something guy with Lakers pennants attached to both armrests of his wheelchair. I notice a framed family photo on the mantle and cross the room to pick it up.

"Get out the way, fool!" Tifney says, incensed that I have momentarily blocked her view of the undersea adventures on the screen.

"My my, what a fine lookin' bunch," I say, studying the picture of the whole clan in their Sunday best. "I see you, and you, and you." I nod at each of the family members in turn. "And you, girl" I say to Tifney. "You look so fine in that purple dress I don't know why you don't wear it every day."

"'Cause it don' fit no mo', asshoe."

"I see. Now who's this young stud?" I ask, turning the picture around to show them who I'm pointing at.

"That's L.T.," says O.J. "He in jail."

Tifney flicks her burning cigarette at O.J., missing his face by millimeters.

"Shut up, nigga," she says. "Didn't Mama tell you not to talk 'bout L.T. to strangers?"

"He ain't no stranger," O.J. protests.

"That's right, I'm a friend of your mama," I say. "So how come the man went and busted your brother?"

"They say he try to cap some honky," replies the guy in the wheelchair. "Muthafucka shot L.T. wit a ray gun."

"Dat's the one oughts be in jail," rasps a toothless old woman I hadn't even noticed on the couch, hiding in Tifney's giant shadow.

"Sure sounds that way to me," I say. "But you know them crafty honkies."

"Everythin' chill out there?" Leonora shouts from the other room.

"We chillin' just fine!" I shout back. "Take your time, Mama."

"How long you know our Mama?" Tifney asks, squinting her porcine eyes at me.

"Golly, I can't hardly even remember," I say and then swiftly turn back to wheelchair man, who seems like my best bet. "You got any idea why L.T.'d wanna cap some honky muthafucka?"

"Un-uh," he says, looking down to avoid my gaze. Tifney has evidently heard enough, because she thrusts her baby at the old lady and makes the mighty effort necessary to propel herself to her feet.

"Where you goin', girl?" I say. Tifney ignores me and exits in the same direction Leonora did. I figure I have one more shot.

"Let me ask y'all this," I say. "Did L.T. ever talk about meeting somebody famous, like a player in the NBA or a rapper, something like that?" In my rapid-fire desperation I've clearly abandoned all subtlety, because they look at each other and then at me with naked suspicion.

"Man, is you the po-lice?" O.J. asks.

“The po-lice?” I chuckle. “Lordy, no.” Common sense would dictate that I make a break for it right now, but I already gave common sense the day off. “Guess I was just born with a natural sense of curiosity.”

“You ’bout to die wit it too,” says Leonora from the door to the hallway. She has changed into the same peach-colored pantsuit she wore for the family portrait, tastefully accessorized with a pearl brooch and a double-barreled shotgun.

“Whoa now!” I say, raising my hands in surrender. “There must be some kinda crazy misunderstandin’.” Leonora takes a step forward but then stops, her eyes focusing on something behind me.

“What the hell kinda nigga are you?” she says, and swivels her gaze from one side of me to the other. I now realize that her angry glare is actually directed at my wrists, which I am holding alongside my head. In hindsight it’s unfortunate I was in such a hurry to leave the studio in Burbank, because between my shirt cuffs and my hand makeup is a good two inches of exposed, pinkish honky.

“The kind that best be goin’!” I reply, bolting for the door.

chapter twenty-five

It's a pretty good sign that I'm able to reach the threshold in one piece. Less encouraging is the unmistakable sound of a shell being pumped into the shotgun barrel, followed by a cacophony of shouting and clambering. I leap from the porch to the walkway in a single bound and dash for the convertible. The kid I paid to keep an eye on it is still in the passenger seat, rocking his upper body in time with the bass beat that booms from the speakers.

"Look out!" I yell at the kid, and he ducks just in time to avoid being kicked in the head as I hurdle over him and into the driver's seat.

"Get lost!" I tell him.

"Where be my f-f-fifty dollars?"

The response is a sharp report that gives the hood of Mfume's car an instant case of acne and turns his windshield into a collection of spider webs. I throw it in gear and floor it, forcing several good citizens of East 70th Street to scurry out of the way. I think I hear another blast behind me as I power-slide the Jag around the nearest corner, but it's hard to say because the music is blaring so loudly.

"W-w-w'as goin' down?" my passenger shouts, reaching for his own gun. I guess I must have had just about enough of that shit, because in a single move I snatch it away from him and toss it out the window.

"Hey, m-m-muthafucka!"

"Shut up and turn that noise off," I order him in my normal voice.

"It ain't n-n-noise," he says, wounded. "It's me and B-B-Boney's song."

Did he just say *Boney*? Indeed he did, and if I hadn't been driving eighty miles an hour, trying to see through a shattered windshield, and dodging buckshot, surely I would have already recognized the voice booming from the CD.

You bes' lissen good, 'cause I won' say it twice,
His name be Lil' Killa, an' murder be his vice.

Right on the heels of Boney's smooth baritone comes a warbly, off-key soprano:

Yeah I be Lil' Killa, killin' make me laugh,
Ya niggas fuck wit me, I bust a cap right in yo' ass.

I pull the Jag to a screeching stop at the curb and turn to stare at the kid in the passenger seat, who is hoping to someday be known to the world as Lil' Killa. I didn't recognize him because I never saw any of the videotapes from the recording session at Boney's home studio, which took place in front of several *Mogul* cameras shortly before Delawn was killed. Jessica Levine supervised that shoot while I waited for Boney with the rest of the cast and crew at City Walk, and it didn't dawn on me that there was anything important to be found on the tapes.

Lil' Killa pushes the eject button on the Jag's sound system and reclaims his CD.

"You owe me f-f-fifty dollars, an' a hundred for my g-g-gat," he says.

"How long have you known L.T.?" I ask him.

"Fo'ever, I guess," he says. "He live r-r-right nex' d-d-door."

Further discussion with Lil' Killa—which is facilitated by the rest of my cash, doled out in ten dollar increments—reveals that his neighbor and lifelong best friend L.T. is also his "manager." L.T. recently proved his worth by convincing Boney, a major muthafuckin' star, to lay down a track with Lil' Killa, a young artist whose vast potential had somehow been previously overlooked by all of the record labels. Lil' Killa claims to have no idea how L.T. pulled off such a coup, and insists that when L.T. was arrested for killing Boney's bodyguard, he didn't consider the possibility that one development had anything to do with the other. I'll take his word for it, but since I'm a more suspicious sort, I can't help but wonder if perhaps L.T.'s shooting of Delawn—and his subsequent attempt to silence me—were done in trade for Lil' Killa getting his big break. If so, that means that whoever arranged the recording session is likely the person behind all of the recent mayhem.

I need to think, and I can't while Lil' Killa tries to convince me that he's going to be an even bigger star than a bunch of other guys I've never heard of. So I drop him off at a bus stop and drive in the general direction of white people. I remember that on the day Delawn was shot, there was a last-minute schedule change and instead of doing radio promos with the *Mogul* contestants, Boney laid down the duet with Lil' Killa. I wasn't there, but I distinctly remember Jessica telling me it was Lovey Mack who announced the change of plan and who kept insisting that Boney couldn't leave for City Walk until the song was in the can. I try to reach Jessica on her cell phone, but as soon as I identify myself she hangs up and won't answer when I call back. I guess she's still peeved about having been fired, even though it was Trevor who decided to give her the axe, and he only did so because she tried to get *me* fired. I could tell by the loud background noise that Jessica wasn't home when I called her, so there's no point in trying to find her there. Instead I swing by my apartment to shower away the remnants of Jamal Jihad, and then head for the office, on the chance that something on the raw videotapes from the Lil' Killa recording session might prove enlightening.

Trevor and all the *Mogul* producers are preoccupied with putting the finishing touches on tomorrow night's show, so I have a good chance of being able to work undetected. I tell Mfume that I got into a little fender bender with his car, and that I'll pay whatever it costs to make it good as new. With me out of the picture Mfume is second only to Trevor in the chain of command, and he's under so much pressure that he barely hears me. The first videotape editor I find who isn't busy is Dave IV. (The royal suffix is necessary because there are no fewer than eleven editors at Trevor Banes Productions with the given name of Dave.) I send him to find what I'm looking for, which turns out to be ten hours of tape from four cameras. Even though we fast-forward through much of it, the process of scanning the footage is painful. Most of the screen time is taken up by Lil' Killa's attempts to get his song lyrics out, and I quickly understand why Jessica thought he was retarded. It's too bad I'm not trying to build a sequence for one of those old Dick Clark blooper shows, because in addition to Lil' Killa's repeated fuck-ups there are dozens of great reaction shots of Boney and the contestants wincing and biting their tongues. When it comes time for Boney to deliver his lines, the comparison makes him sound like Placido Domingo. Any doubt I may have had about the connection between the recording session and Delawn's death is erased, because even a middle-aged white guy who hasn't bought a CD since the Eagles broke up the first time is qualified to say that Lil' Killa is wack.

Unfortunately there isn't a single frame of Lovey Mack on any of the tapes, and I don't know why I thought there would be. Since Lovey is on probation and has supposedly severed all ties to MF Music (except of course those that pass through the Cayman Islands), he has been careful not to show his face on camera. Before every one of our shoots he made sure the producers reminded the videographers not to let their lenses stray in his direction, and they have dutifully complied. (The only exception is Deb, and she was at City Walk, not Boney's house, during the recording session.) I keep hoping, though, and Dave IV is mighty cranky by the time I finally concede the tapes are worthless and throw in the towel.

I decide it will be better if I tell Susan in person about my adventure in South Central, so I call and ask her to meet me for dinner at Chez Jay in Santa Monica. On my way out of the office, though, something piques my curiosity. Half a dozen editors and segment producers are crammed into Dave IV's edit bay, a tiny closet that's meant to hold two people max. As a result they're spilling out of the doorway, and the ones in the rear are craning their necks to get a view of the monitor inside. From my professional experience, I know this level of interest can only mean one thing—they're looking at somebody's privates.

I'm kind of surprised, since Dave IV is rewinding the tapes I just viewed, and I didn't notice any T or A on them. But when I wedge my way in to have a look, I see that my surmise is correct. Dave IV has come across the Holy Grail of outtakes—a full Sharon Stone, so dubbed in honor of the shining moment of Ms. Stone's acting career, when she flashed her naked beaver at a roomful of cops in *Basic Instinct*. With the thousands of hours of videotape we shoot to make each episode of *The Mogul*, semi-Sharons are quite common, but the real deal is rare because it requires an attentive camera operator, a short dress, and an absence of underwear. Our contestant LaFonda was thoughtful enough to do her part on the day of the recording session, and one of our alert documentarians zoomed in to get the goods while Boney and Lil' Killa took a break.

The assembled group is having a heated argument as to whether LaFonda's pubes should be classified as "LAX"—a narrow strip of landing lights leading to the labia—or "Phil Jackson"—a more horizontally-oriented tuft resembling the soul patch worn by the famous basketball coach. To bolster his argument in favor of the latter, Dave IV releases the freeze frame of LaFonda's crotch and lets the tape play while she crosses and re-crosses her legs.

"I've got three words for you losers," Dave IV says. "Phil fucking Jackson." But those with their money on LAX aren't quite ready to concede defeat, and the trash talking gets so loud that I almost don't hear the sound that comes from the tape.

"We gotta talk, dog." The voice is unmistakably Boney's.

"Quiet!" I bark, interrupting the pubic debate.

"'ight, les' go in the other room," another voice on the tape says, and again there can be no doubt—it's Lovey.

"Freeze that and everybody out," I command. As the staff members leave the edit bay they all look at me like I'm the biggest asshole in the world, but so what—I may have struck gold. It seems that one of the camera operators kept rolling when he wasn't supposed to, because he was getting excellent close-ups of LaFonda's genitalia. Since Boney was wearing a wireless mike and all the cameras record the sound from the master sound mixer whenever they're rolling, we might be able to hear a private conversation he had with Lovey. The key factor will be how long the camera operator kept taping, which will in turn be determined by if and when LaFonda decided to quit airing out the meat curtains.

"Roll it," I tell Dave IV.

Because the picture and sound are unrelated to each other and I have no interest in LaFonda's dusky charms, I close my eyes. First I hear some rustling and a burst of radio static, and I fear that Boney and Lovey's conversation took place beyond the range of the wireless receiver. But then the static fades and their voices come through loud and clear.

"Wassup, dog?" says Lovey.

"I's all done with this shit," Boney replies. "Over an' out."

"Be chill, now. A couple more takes and we got it."

"Got what?" Boney scoffs. "Ain't nobody gonna pay ta hear that lil' nigga whine."

"That ain't our problem. All we gotta do is lay it down the best we can, then hand it over to the man."

"What the fuck fo'? He cain't sell it no better'n you can."

"Those muthafuckas make bank in ways I don' even try ta unnerstan'," Lovey says. "Half the time all they be doin' is tradin' favors with one another so's they can get somethin' else they want later on."

"So why the fuck we need 'em?"

"Same reason we need bitches, boy. We just do."

"Muthafuck," Boney says, and there's a loud smack that must be him punching his own hand. "One a these days I gonna write me a song called 'Fuckin Liars.'"

I swear that's what it sounds like, just as it did when the identical phrase served as Delawn's final words. Except now that I hear them in a fuller context, I realize that on both occasions I misunderstood. The two dead men were each expressing in their own dialect a sentiment shared by me and millions of other decent, hardworking Americans: fucking *lawyers*.

Lest we've forgotten, MF Music's lawyer is one Richard Slatkin. I know that he was acquainted with Patrice Williams, since the one and only time I saw her alive was at his house. There are a few other facts to bear in mind as well. Sara recently surprised me by telling me that she and Richard were having serious marital problems. Richard's first marriage ended when he became enamored of a younger, sexier woman (who at the time was inconveniently married to me). Since history has a way of repeating itself—and that goes double for philanderers—it's not hard to imagine how Patrice could have become Richard's new Sara. But for me the most compelling "coincidence" remains Sara's visit to the Beverly Hills Hotel and Delawn's subsequent death. Susan's main argument against there being any connection between the two was that attorneys are too smart and too selfish to stick their necks out for the people who pay them. That line of reasoning doesn't apply, though, when lawyer and client are one and the same person.

Maybe I really am a racist, because before I heard Boney and Lovey talking on that tape I had been picturing Patrice's mystery lover as a cross between Kobe Bryant and Bill Cosby. That's not to say that I believe either of those gentlemen to be capable of hiring a hit man to cover up his transgressions; I was just filling in the blank spot with famous black faces. But in retrospect it didn't have to be anybody famous or black, just somebody who knew Delawn—which of course Richard did from the many times Delawn drove Boney to his home and office. Another clue hiding in plain sight was the photo of Patrice on the cover of *Booty*. The magazine's editors recognized that she had something men of all races and creeds would crawl through broken glass to get a piece of, and that's why they posed her with one black hand and one white one covering her breasts. Patrice certainly got my attention, and I'm sure she had a similar effect on Richard. After all, he and I threw our lives away for the same beautiful, faithless woman once before.

If Richard was indeed having an affair with Patrice, he was definitely playing with fire. Along with the personal and financial costs of another divorce, he was risking even worse forms of retribution at the hands of Boney. Let's say that after getting a look at how Richard's wife was living, Patrice decided that she wasn't receiving nearly enough love—love being defined as lavish gifts, plum movie roles, and cold, hard cash. If and when she expressed her disappointment to Richard, his first response would have been to try to appease her. If that didn't work, he'd have broken it off. But what if Patrice had felt used and abused, and had threatened to share her sorrows with Sara, or Boney, or the *National Enquirer*? Paying fifty grand to Delawn to make the problem go away permanently would no doubt seem like a bargain. And when Richard later became nervous that Delawn might talk—after Sara told him about running into Susan at the hotel, he must have figured out that I was helping her investigate Patrice's death—Richard would have decided that the killer also had to be killed. The only things he needed to make it happen were a gun and somebody to fire it, and when you have hundreds of fame-hungry gangstas seeking your services, neither one is hard to come by.

Susan's been waiting at the restaurant for half an hour when I arrive, but any irritation she feels at my tardiness pales in comparison to what she experiences as I start to tell her about my day. When I disclose that while I was supposedly taking a nap on Trevor's sofa, I was actually paying a visit to East 70th Street disguised as Don King, she looks like she might draw her piece and plug me herself. But I tell her to conserve her energy because she's going to need it, and she listens to the rest of my tale without interrupting.

"So?" I ask her when I'm done. "What do you think?"

"I can't decide whether you deserve a bravo or a beating."

We table the question while she calls Captain Cardenas at home. He immediately begins to read her the riot act, but when she states flat-out that she knows who is behind the killings of Patrice and Delawn—and it's not Boney—he stops yelling and tells her to stand by for further instructions. While we're waiting for him to phone back, I point out to Susan that she's somewhat overstated the strength of our case. The evidence pointing to Richard is intriguing, maybe even damning, but it's a long ways from proving him guilty beyond a reasonable doubt. Susan replies that she is well aware of that, but after sixteen years on the force, she knows when Lady Justice needs a little kick in the ass to get her moving.

Cardenas calls and orders Susan to bring me and meet him ASAP at Cedars-Sinai Medical Center, where the rich and famous go to give birth, postpone death, and have gerbils coaxed out of their colons (or so they say). Susan has no idea as to why the captain would choose this odd location and he doesn't volunteer an explanation, either on the phone or when we join him in the hospital lobby just after midnight. He just scowls and indicates with a jerk of his head that we are to follow him into the elevator. We exit on the top floor, which looks more like a luxury hotel than a medical facility. Cardenas leads us to the end of the corridor, where a uniformed LAPD officer stands guard outside a closed door.

"Captain Cardenas, Detective DeRosa, and this other shit-head," is how Cardenas announces us.

"They're expecting you," the uniform replies, opening the door and standing aside.

We enter a large, elegantly decorated two-room suite, where maybe ten people are engaged in various activities. The center of this small but busy universe is the bed, where a slender middle-aged man lies on his side facing us. His generic hospital gown, sickly pale skin tone, and contorted features cause me not to recognize the patient until the Filipina nurse standing behind him speaks.

"Excuse me Mr. Mayor, you need to stop squeezing your cheeks."

"I'm not squeezing, damn you!" sputters the Honorable Roberto P. Torremolinos. "When do I get another pain pill?"

"Two and a half hours," replies the nurse.

"Oh, fuck me," moans the mayor of El Pueblo de Nuestra Senora la Reina de Los Angeles, aka L.A. "It feels like I'm shitting a sea urchin."

Another familiar face steps forward to greet us.

"Captain, Detective," the man nods at my companions, and then to me says, "Hi, I'm Pete Lamonica."

"Ted Collins," I say, shaking the hand of the most famous and highly regarded law enforcement officer in the world. Becoming chief of a big-city police department is the pinnacle of achievement for a cop, and a height very few ever reach. Peter Lamonica has done it three times, in Philadelphia, Chicago, and now Los Angeles. And although it's hard to believe that one average-looking, late-middle-aged man who refuses to carry or fire a gun could make a significant dent in urban crime, Chief Lamonica somehow keeps pulling it off. Burglaries, rapes, murders—they're all way down within the city limits (or at least they were until I helped ignite the recent killing spree). So are officer-involved shootings, high-speed chases, and complaints of police brutality. In fact if

Lamonica doesn't get another gig and blow town pretty soon, the Channel 6 reporters may have to start looking for some actual news.

"Good to meet you," he says. "Can I call you Ted?"

"Please."

"Great. Call me Pete."

"You can all continue to call me Mr. Mayor," says Torremolinos. "And you can tell me who fucked everything up this time." I see Cardenas flinch like a dog that can already feel the boot in its ribcage, but Susan comes to his rescue.

"That would be me, sir," she says. "Susan DeRosa, Detective Sergeant Valley Division homicide."

"For now," grunts Torremolinos.

"Mr. Mayor, I'm a little behind on the facts," says Chief Lamonica. "Would you mind if Detective DeRosa gives us a quick review?"

"Allow me," the mayor says. "Your people turned another pile of shit into Jesus, and now I get to play Pontius Pilate."

"I think this is a conversation best had in private," Lamonica says. "Would everyone else please clear the room?" Even though he barely raises his voice to make the request, an immediate and swift exodus begins. I guess that's what they call leadership. Other than Susan, Cardenas, and me, only the nurse on the far side of the bed remains behind.

"I have to put antibiotic on the stitches," she says, referring to the mayor. "And this bad boy won't open up."

"I'll handle that," Lamonica says, taking the tube of ointment from the nurse. "I was a medic in Vietnam."

"Good luck," she says, and exits. As the chief of police takes the nurse's place at the mayor's backside, His Honor tries to whip his head around.

"What the hell are you doing?" Torremolinos says, but the sudden movement produces a jolt of pain that makes him scream. "Yiiiiii!"

"Just relax," says Lamonica, giving the mayor a soothing

pat on the hip and pulling on a rubber glove. "Detective, would you bring us up to date please?"

Susan does her best to deliver a complete yet succinct summary, also balancing the need for occasional eye contact with the chief against the hazards of making same with the mayor. Lamonica performs his medicinal chore by feel, and must have a genuine healing touch because Torremolinos's grimace slowly begins to soften. If it were up to me, I'd award the Medal of Valor on the spot to both Detective DeRosa and Chief Lamonica. But alas it's not.

"Just fucking great," the mayor snarls when Susan finishes her report. "You better get your hand outta my ass, because Jesse Jackson and Al Sharpton are gonna be climbing up there any minute."

"Sir, if I may," says Susan. "None of this changes the fact that Raymond Bonaparte pointed a loaded weapon at Mr. Collins. Obviously, we wish we'd known—"

"Save all that crap for the press," Torremolinos says, cutting her off. "I'll be sure and point you out to 'em."

"How do you suggest we proceed from here, Captain?" Lamonica asks. Cardenas looks startled, apparently believing that his wish had come true and he had become invisible.

"Well, we need to consider all the issues carefully," the captain says. "Because I feel there are issues here that require careful consideration."

"I see," says Lamonica. "Detective, what do you think?"

"We should seek a warrant to take a blood sample from Richard Slatkin," Susan says. "We know the semen stain on the underwear we found at the murder scene doesn't match either Boney or Delawn's DNA. Hopefully it matches Slatkin's."

"Say it does, then what?"

"Follow the money," Susan replies. "If we persuade the FBI to use the Patriot Act and we know what we're looking for, we might be able to crack the bank account in the Caymans."

"Maybe," Lamonica nods. "Any other ideas?"

"Yes sir. I think we should ask Lovey Mack to help us flip the shooter, L.T. Jones."

"Mr. Mack hasn't been of much assistance in the past," says the chief.

"No he hasn't," Susan admits. "But maybe he'll be upset enough about losing his biggest star that he'll want to get revenge on the man who's responsible."

"Upset?" snorts Mayor Torremolinos. "The guy's fucking ecstatic. The best career move a rapper can make is to get himself killed." He then notices that Chief Lamonica has left his bedside and is washing his hands in a nearby sink. "Hey Chief, where are you going? That was actually helping."

"You need to rest now, Mr. Mayor," says the chief. "And I need to have a word with my good friend Ted."

chapter twenty-six

THE CHIEF'S GOOD friend is caught off guard by this development, but when he holds the door for me I really have no choice but to join him in the hallway.

"Carlos, will you tell hospital security we're going topside for a few minutes?" he says to the uniformed cop guarding the door.

"Yes, sir," the cop answers, and uses a two-way radio to relay the information. Lamonica and I walk up a flight of stairs, through a fire door, and now we're out on the roof of Cedars-Sinai. It's a clear night by Southern California standards, meaning that if you really try you can sort of make out the moon and the Hollywood sign. The hospital is one of the taller buildings in this part of town, and the city spreads out below us in every hazy direction. The chief begins strolling slowly around the roof's perimeter and I keep pace, staying on his inside shoulder just in case he lured me up here to push me off.

"Nice view," I observe.

"Yeah, especially compared to the mayor's ass," he says. "You're a very resourceful guy, Ted. You'd make a good cop."

"Thanks," I reply. "But I recommend you check my record before you pin a badge on me."

"I already did. Apparently you used to have some, shall we say, reality avoidance issues."

"And now I'm in Reality TV. Talk about the punishment fitting the crime."

"That's more or less what I want to talk about," he says. "But first let me ask, have you ever been to Canada?"

"Quite a few times. I lived in Montreal for a year right after college."

"So you must know they don't have anywhere near the violent crime per capita that we do."

"Uh-huh," I acknowledge. "Although they do frequently bore each other to death."

"The hosers may be a little dull," he chuckles. "But I don't think that's why it's so much safer up there. It's not because there's any gun shortage, either. They've got more hunting rifles than hockey sticks."

"So how come they're so peaceful and we're such a bunch of trigger-happy soreheads?"

"In a word? Slavery."

"Isn't there some new law against that?"

"A hundred forty years is nothing when you're really pissed off," Lamonica says. "And we found plenty of other ways to keep 'em down in the meantime."

"True enough."

"You want to know the secret to my success?"

"Sure," I reply, right away envisioning the magazine article I'm going to write and sell for ten grand, minimum.

"Okay, but this is all off the record." At least I didn't have a chance to start spending it. He continues, "My most important rule is, don't waste time on how things oughta be. Like those idiots on talk radio, who spend all day screaming that the blacks should just get over it. They're *not* over it, and they don't give a shit if anybody else thinks they oughta be. So if I want to be effective in my job, I have to deal with 'em as they are." I can't decide if this point is impenetrably subtle or thunderingly obvious, but you can't argue with the man's results. And there's more:

"African Americans make up 10 percent of our population, and I spend 90 percent of my time dealing with them. The assistant chiefs and the division heads take care of everything else."

"I think you're being a little too modest," I tell him.

"No," he says, stopping abruptly and turning to face me. "I'm not."

"Okay," I say, buckling under the brute force of the chief's personality.

"We've made a lot of progress in the last couple of years, Ted. I'm sure you know that."

"Yes sir, you've done an incredible job."

"I asked you to call me Pete, remember?"

"Right. Sorry . . . Pete."

"This department is on its way to becoming something L.A. can be proud of. It can also serve as an example to places all across the country. If the city that made Rodney King a household name can heal itself this quickly, then anybody can do it." It's too bad the chief's not running for something, because he'd definitely get my vote.

"So the question I need to ask you, Ted," he says, "Is do you really want to ruin everything we've done, just to get back at the guy who stole your wife?"

"Whoa," I say, mentally snatching my ballot back from the box. "This has nothing to do with Richard Slatkin stealing my wife. I didn't even know he was involved until a few hours ago."

"But I'll bet it didn't exactly crush you when you figured it out."

"Chief . . . Pete. Let's back up. I realize that some people might react badly when they find out that Boney was unfairly targeted—"

"They'll burn this fucker down," he proclaims in his sharpest tone yet, sweeping his arm across the horizon. "I'd need a hundred thousand cops to stop 'em, and I barely have ten."

"So you want to let a guy get away with two cold-blooded killings, plus causing another?"

"I want to keep the peace," he says. "That's my job. If I thought Richard Slatkin was a threat to anybody else, including you, I'd arrest him in a heartbeat, even though I seriously doubt we could get a conviction."

"Why not?"

"Even if the evidence lines up exactly the way DeRosa's hoping, it's all circumstantial, with the possible exception of the shooter's testimony. The defense will attack whatever a career criminal has to say as unreliable and motivated by whatever deal we had to make to get him to talk, and if I was on the jury, I'd agree."

"Can't you at least do a little digging, to see if we're on the right track?"

"We could, but it's impossible to keep something like that from leaking. And once the media got hold of it, the pressure to pursue the case would be overwhelming. So we'd wind up with the worst of all worlds—the black community would go crazy when they first heard Boney was innocent, and even crazier when Slatkin got acquitted. Thousands, no *millions* of ordinary people would wind up paying for those crimes, but I guarantee you that Slatkin wouldn't be one of them."

After about half a minute, I'm finally able to break free of Pete Lamonica's laser-beam gaze and cross to the railing at the edge of the roof. I look down eight stories into the turbine of some giant piece of cooling equipment, an action that would ordinarily give me intense vertigo but under the present circumstances has no effect whatsoever.

"What about the others who know?" I ask without turning to look at him.

"I can control my people and the mayor," he says. "The only one I can't control, Ted, is you."

I receive another invitation to sleep at Susan's, and while I don't really want to be alone, I know that I will be no matter where I go. As Chief Lamonica has so eloquently explained, the decision and the responsibility for its consequences (i.e. urban insurrection, senseless violence, permanent tears in the social fabric) are all mine. So I tell Susan I'm going to spend the night at my apartment, and assure her that if any more hit men drop by, I'll brain 'em with a frying pan. I'm not sure I actually own one, but it doesn't matter—LAPD has announced that both murder investigations are officially closed, so Richard would be a fool to risk sending another thug after me. And whatever else he may be, the man is certainly no fool.

The Skipper must be suffering from insomnia because he's still in his recliner when I fall into the rack just shy of 2:00 AM, and his plasma TV lights up my entire bedroom as it displays *Groundhog Day* in crystal-clear HD. In deference to the neighbors, the Skipper has his surround sound turned off and is wearing headphones, but *Groundhog* is probably my favorite movie and I know all the lines without having to hear them. I leave my curtains open and prop myself up at an angle to enjoy the show, and right about the time Bill Murray learns to love the present and will thus be permitted to bone Andie McDowell, I fall into a deep, dreamless sleep.

It would be way cool if Sonny & Cher's "I've Got You Babe" was playing on my clock radio when it turns itself on at 10:30, but instead I am awakened by Shaggy insisting "It Wasn't Me." (That's probably what Bill was telling Andie by Thanksgiving, anyhow.) I shower, shave, and call Susan to let her know I'm still alive. She asks me if I've made any decisions, and I tell her that right now I'm stuck on Starbucks vs. The Coffee Bean. I ultimately choose the latter and start to head to the office, but then I ask myself why. There's nothing for me to do there, and no one for me even to talk to since all hands will be fully occupied with finishing tonight's show. I should instead take the day off and do something with Hallie, although that would mean dealing with Sara and possibly Richard, and I'm not sure I'm up to it. I try to imagine such an encounter, and I must be doing an excellent job of it because my phone rings and according to the caller ID, it's Richard.

"Hello," I answer, trying my best to sound normal.

"Ted, Richard Slatkin," he says. "Are you very busy today?"

"Why do you ask?"

"Sara ran off to Palm Springs with one of her girlfriends, and Hallie has no school all week. She's kind of bored just hanging around the house, so I thought maybe you two could spend some time together."

It's hardly a surprise that with Sara out of town, Richard would want to get rid of Hallie. Even though his staff handles all the actual parenting duties, it's been clear to me from day one that he considers my daughter's presence in his life as an inconvenience at best. What's worse is that Hallie knows it too. But every time either one of us has tried to say anything about it to Sara, she's immediately turned everything around and made the conversation about my well-documented shortcomings.

"Sure," I tell the shithead. "When can I pick her up?"

"Anytime you want," Richard replies. "I'll call the housekeeper and tell her you're coming."

As I change course for Bel-Air, I can't help but feel conflicted. Of course I welcome any opportunity to take Hallie away from the Slatkin house of horrors. But I know I'll eventually have to bring her back, and under the circumstances that's a very tough pill to swallow. The worst part is being in the dark. If only I had some confirmation that my suspicions about Richard are correct, then at least I could operate from a position of certainty and therefore—theoretically at least—strength. Maybe I could even use the information as leverage against him, although I would have to weigh the potential advantages against the likely parade of hitmen. In any case, if I do a little sleuthing on my own and keep whatever I learn to myself, there shouldn't be much risk of accidentally starting a race war.

I decide that one way or another, this story is going to end where it began—with a close-up on Patrice Williams's panties. If I can surreptitiously obtain a sample of Richard's DNA—which can be extracted from a strand of his hair, or a drop of his saliva—

and Susan can have it tested against the semen stain on the underwear found under the bed in the love shack, then I'll be satisfied. If there's no match, I'll accept that I was wrong and resumé viewing Richard as a garden-variety rat bastard, rather than of the sociopathic strain. If the DNA does match, I'll have a few more decisions to make—but no need to worry about those yet.

I call Deb and ask if she can watch Hallie for a few hours, and she agrees to without even asking for an explanation. She must have finally gotten licky—I mean lucky. Next I stop at a Von's supermarket to buy rubber gloves and Ziplock freezer bags, and then at Bed, Bath & Beyond for a toothbrush. A sales clerk advises me that if money is no object I should go with the Sonicare, which costs three times as much as all the other electric toothbrushes but is worth it for the way it magically removes plaque even between the teeth. I decide to purchase only a replacement head, which the clerk patiently tries to explain will be useless without the base and charger, until the woman behind me in line gets exasperated and tells the clerk to just let the dumbass find out for himself.

When I arrive to pick up Hallie, she's waiting by the front door with her suitcase. She runs and jumps into my arms, and I feel so guilty about bailing on her that I almost abandon my whole plan, at least for today. But when I ask Hallie how she'd feel about playing with Aunt Deb she seems genuinely enthusiastic, especially when I mention that Deb has promised to do anything she wants. Without hesitation, she announces her choice: Hallie and the stridently unglamorous Deb will be getting extreme makeovers.

Once I've left Hallie and two hundred of my hard-earned dollars in Santa Monica, I speed back to Bel-Air and press the Call button on the intercom at the gate.

"Slatkeen residence," Anna the housekeeper answers.

"Hi, it's Ted Collins again. Hallie forgot to bring her favorite doll and she's having a fit."

Anna buzzes me into the motor court but insists that I wait outside while she goes to Hallie's room and retrieves the doll. But after the second time I tell her that her long trudge through the house has yielded the wrong Jessica Simpson, she sighs in exasperation and lets me accompany her on trip number three. Anna stays right by my side as we climb the stairs and turn toward Hallie's room, which means I must reach into my pocket and find the Send button on my cell phone by feel. Seconds after I press it, bells begin to chirp throughout the house. Anna hesitates, unable to decide which of the conflicting rules that have been drilled into her should take precedence in this situation. I make it easy on her by forging straight ahead into Hallie's room.

"I be right back," Anna says to me. "You wait, yes?" She scurries off to answer the phone. As soon as Anna is out of sight, I dart down the hallway to the double doors at the far end, which lead to the master suite. To make sure I'm alone I first check the bedroom, den, gym, and both "his" and "her" walk-in closets, finding them all unoccupied. The Lord and Lady of the manor each have their own vast bathrooms as well, which makes it easy for me to head straight for the prize.

I'm pleased to see that my ability to predict human behavior—or at least the behavior of highly predictable humans—remains keen: A Sonicare electric toothbrush rests in its cradle beside the sink. I slip on my rubber gloves, unscrew the head and seal it inside a Ziplock bag, then replace the part I've taken with the one I just bought. Next I locate Richard's hairbrush and transfer a good-size clump of dark-brown locks from its bristles into another bag. When I'm putting the brush back in the top drawer, I notice a rotary nose hair trimmer. There would be something kind of poetic about using Richard's wussiness to take him down—real men like me grab their protruding strands between two fingers and yank. I take out another bag.

"What are you doing?" a familiar voice says behind me.

Startled, I drop the trimmer and whirl around to see Sara standing in the doorway.

"I . . . got something stuck in my teeth and I was looking for floss." My explanation has too many obvious shortcomings to merit a response, and I get none. Sara just stands there in her bathrobe with her arms crossed, looking more haggard than I've ever seen.

"I thought you went to Palm Springs," I add lamely.

"I'm not going anywhere," Sara says. "I just needed a little break from Hallie."

"No problem, take all the time you need." I head for the door but Sara doesn't move out of the way. I'm forced to stop a few feet away from her and there's a long, heavy silence while she waits for me to tell her what I'm really up to, and I try to come up with some better bullshit. It's certain that if I don't she will report me to Richard, and God only knows what he'll do in response. Nothing remotely credible is coming to mind, though, so I stall for more time.

"Is there someplace we can sit and talk for a minute?" I ask.

Sara nods listlessly and I follow her to the adjacent den, which is filled with bookshelves, comfortable furniture, and a marble fireplace. As we take places on opposite ends of the couch, Anna the housekeeper comes running in.

"Ay!" Anna says upon seeing me, clasping her forehead in her hand. "I sorry, Missus, he no supposed to—"

"It's all right, Anna," Sara cuts her off. "Close the double doors on your way out." Anna looks very doubtful, but orders are orders and so she exits.

"Are you okay?" I ask Sara when we're alone. "You look kinda… scary."

"Thanks," she says. "I'm trying to get off Paxil, and I haven't been able to sleep."

"I see."

"So what do you want to talk about, Ted?"

"First of all, I need to know something," I say. "That day you surprised me at the Beverly Hills Hotel, did you figure out who the woman was I was talking to?"

"Why do you ask?" Sara replies, poker-facing it.

"When you told Richard about it, how did he react?"

"I didn't say I told Richard. Don't try to put words in my mouth."

"Okay," I say. "Do you know if your husband has a bank account in the Cayman Islands?"

"No."

"No, he doesn't, or no, you don't know?"

"No, it's none of your damned business."

"Hallie says he goes there all the time," I bluff.

"It's his favorite place to scuba dive," she says. "Is there some law against that?"

"No," I tell her. "But there are a few other laws Richard should be aware of."

"Such as?"

This is the moment of truth—if I tell Sara what I suspect and why, I probably won't be able to control what happens afterward. But if I don't say anything, my daughter will continue to live with a man who might be a murderer. To me, that's an even scarier prospect than seeing L.A. on fire.

"Such as the law against having people killed," I say.

Sara stares at me blankly for a beat, then her face softens and she begins to laugh.

"That's funny?" I ask her.

"Sort of," she says. "You've finally gone nuts."

"I don't think so, Sara."

"Oh yeah, definitely. You had me fooled for a while, getting a job and quitting the booze and blow. But the jealousy and envy never went away, did they?"

"Trust me, I don't envy Richard."

"Of course not," she mocks me. "What does he have that a big success like you could possibly want?"

I resist the temptation to respond in kind, and instead set out to give Sara a full, detailed account of everything's that happened since the day I first saw Patrice and Boney behind the pool house. I put special emphasis on the things that most clearly implicate Richard—the wire transfer, Delawn's dying declaration, and the taped conversation between Boney and Lovey. I finish by telling her why I'm here today, and showing her my evidence bags containing Richard's hair and saliva samples. The whole thing takes maybe half an hour, and I'm hoping that my patient, methodical approach will at least convince her I'm not deranged. It doesn't.

"That's it?" she says when at last I'm done.

"Yeah, pretty much."

"Well you should have saved your breath, because you haven't convinced me of anything except that you're crazy."

"Not to mention dangerous," someone says from the doorway behind us, causing Sara and I both to startle. We turn to see Richard step into the room.

chapter twenty-seven

I SPRING TO MY feet, ready to defend myself by any means necessary. But Richard is his usual smug self and doesn't come any closer.

"How long have you been out there?" Sara asks him as she rises off the couch.

"About fifteen minutes," Richard says. "Anna didn't like how Ted snuck in here, so she called me."

"Did you hear what he's been saying?" Sara asks.

"Yeah, the sound carries right through there." Richard indicates the fireplace, which also opens to the bedroom on the other side and allows a fire to be enjoyed from either room. "I should have said something sooner, but I was riveted by Ted's little fairy tale."

"The police know I'm here," I lie.

"Glad to hear it," Richard says. "That should make it easy to have you arrested for trespassing."

"How about if I turn myself in," I offer. "At the same time I hand over your DNA." I hold up my plastic bags. Richard scoffs.

"Anybody who's ever seen a cop show knows you can't use evidence that was obtained illegally."

"Maybe they'll get a search warrant and collect some new samples," I say.

"Highly unlikely," Richard replies. "And even if they do, I can assure you that I have absolutely nothing to worry about."

"See, Ted," Sara hisses. "I told you you were insane." I ignore her and keep my gaze on Richard.

"So you're saying that your DNA isn't going to match any of the evidence?" I ask him. "The stains on Patrice's underwear, or the semen that was found inside of her after she was killed?" Richard doesn't answer me right away. "I'm sorry, is that a difficult question?"

"It's an irrelevant question," he says, but he's finding it harder and harder to sound blasé.

"Irrelevant because you weren't having an affair with Patrice Williams?"

"Irrelevant because it doesn't matter if I was."

"Really?" I cock an eyebrow and turn to Sara. "Is that how you feel about it?"

"How my wife feels is none of your concern," Richard snaps, but it's clear from the way Sara is looking at him that the genie is out of the bottle.

"Were you sleeping with her?" she asks him quietly.

"Do you really think it's proper to discuss the private details of our marriage in front of your ex-husband?" Richard says, with a note of condescension that I could have advised him against using.

"I'm not asking for a discussion," Sara says. "Just a simple yes or no."

"It's not a simple situation," he says, the last vestiges of his cool evaporating before our very eyes. "This son of a bitch is accusing me of murder."

"Several, actually," I interject.

"I'm not telling him anything that he might be able to twist around to make me look guilty," Richard says.

"Okay, let's have a show of hands," I suggest. "Who still doesn't think that Richard was fucking Patrice Williams?" I make a show of trying to count the raised hands, of which there are none. "Sorry, Richie. It looks like you haven't even fooled yourself."

"You can say whatever you want, wise ass," he sneers. "I didn't have anyone killed."

"You know, I really think you did."

"Then you'd better be able to prove it, because if you can't I'm going to sue you for everything you haven't got."

Richard and I have a long stare-down, during which I reflect that I've probably already done as much damage as I can. Proving that Richard was sexually intimate with Patrice might cost him his marriage, but it won't be enough to convict him of murder. I'm thinking it's about time for me to go when Sara surprises us both by speaking up.

"What about the bank account in the Caymans?" she says, and I see the tendons in Richard's neck tighten involuntarily.

"What about it?" I ask her.

"If you found out who it belonged to, would that help solve these killings?"

"Definitely," I say.

"But once again irrelevant," Richard counters. "The reason people keep money in the Caymans is to take advantage of their banking secrecy laws. There's no way to trace who owns an account there."

"What if you know their account number and password?" Sara asks him. "What if one night they got drunk and forgot to close their safe, and somebody who thought they had a right to know what was in it anyway took everything out and photocopied it?"

"You fuck—" Richard starts to shout at her, then catches himself and takes a deep breath. "Okay, why don't we all calm down and see if we can work this out," he says in his most lawyerly manner. Richard sits in an armchair facing Sara and me, and we both lower ourselves back onto the sofa.

"Obviously I never meant for things to get so out of hand," Richard says. "It started as a simple flirtation, then a one-time weekend fling in Vegas." Sara breathes in sharply and covers her mouth as though she might vomit, but Richard ignores her and keeps going.

"Unfortunately, I allowed myself to see her a few more times here in town, and somewhere along the way Patrice got rather attached."

"Well, who could blame her," I can't resist saying. "Once she got a taste of Slatkin the Sex God."

"She started demanding that I leave you and marry her," he says to Sara. "When I told her that was never going to happen, she became hysterical and abusive. She made all kinds of wild threats, and I was mostly afraid she was going to hurt you or Hallie."

"That's a fucking load," I say. "You were mostly afraid Boney was going to hurt you."

"I won't deny that was a consideration," Richard says evenly. "In any event, it was clear that Patrice posed a real and growing danger to the great life we've built together."

"So you…" Sara whimpers.

"Had her killed," Richard finishes for her. In hindsight, I really should have thought to bring along a tape recorder.

Sara starts sobbing uncontrollably, and Richard tries to hand her a box of Kleenex from the side table by his chair. She won't take it from him, so I do and place it on the couch between us.

"As regrettable as it was, that would have at least been the end of it," Richard says. "If Ted here hadn't abused our hospitality and trust in order to advance his own career."

"Yeah, I'm a bad, bad man."

"You saw Boney with Patrice here at my home, didn't you?" Richard says, his voice rising. "And when she disappeared, you tricked me into letting Boney do *The Mogul* so you could spy on him."

"I guess that makes us even—I tell a couple of white lies, you cheat on your wife and then start killing everybody."

"Boney and Delawn would both be alive today if you hadn't stuck your nose where it doesn't belong."

"We could say the same thing about your pee-pee."

Sara gets up and hurries out of the room. For several minutes Richard and I regard each other in silence, interrupted only by the distant sound of Sara retching.

"So," Richard finally says "the question is what do we all do now." He waits for me to offer a suggestion, but I opt to let him twist in the wind. "We can't bring dead people back," he says.

"No. But we could send you to join them," I say, and I can tell by the way Richard's face flushes he doesn't much like the sound of that.

"What would that accomplish, besides publicly humiliating Sara and allowing the heirs of three inconsequential negroes to take every penny she and I have?"

"Richard, I'm shocked. I thought you were a Democrat."

"Fuck off."

"There's one other matter we haven't touched on," I say. "Maybe I'm being overly sensitive, but I'm kind of hurt that you sent L.T. to kill me."

"I didn't. He acted on his own when he saw you and Delawn on TV."

"Somehow I find that unlikely."

"It's the truth, and I don't really care if you believe it."

"You know, if I were in your position, I think I might try to adopt a more conciliatory tone."

"That's because you don't know shit about my position," he sneers. "Do you think I'd ever be dumb enough to put my balls in your hands?" I always thought Richard's eyes were cold, but now they're approaching absolute zero.

"Like I said, the police know I'm here," I remind him. Where could he have a gun hidden? If I jump on him quickly enough, shouldn't I be able to stop him from getting to it? I mean the guy does yoga and Pilates, he's practically a woman.

"I have no intention or need to hurt you," he says. "You're not a threat to me."

"Oh, I'm not?" What the fuck does the bastard have to be so smug about? Is he so shrewd that he knows how much pressure

Chief Lamonica is putting on me to keep quiet? And even if he does, how can be sure I'll cooperate? *I'm* not even sure I will.

"Right after Sara and I got married, I took her with me on one of my dive trips to the Caymans," Richard says. "One day before I went out on the boat, I filled her purse with cash and told her to go see a guy I know at one of the more discreet banks. I'm told he took excellent care of her." It takes me a moment to see where he's going.

"So you're saying the money you wired to Delawn came from Sara's account?"

"I didn't wire anything to anybody," he says with mock innocence. "I don't even have an account in the Caymans."

"Forget about it," I tell him. "No one's going to believe that Sara took out a hit on Patrice."

"Why not? She's a very jealous woman. She was also acquainted with Delawn Purvis. Whenever he brought Boney over here, he'd wander out back and try to catch Sara sunbathing. I think he had a thing for white chicks."

"Amazing," I say, meaning it. "Every time I think I've seen the lowest form of human life, you come along and prove I haven't."

"We all do what we have to do."

In my peripheral vision I see Sara appear in the doorway. She's behind Richard, and I don't move my eyes or do anything else to let him know she's returned—it's better to let her hear this shit for herself.

"So you're prepared to let your wife take the fall for the crimes you committed," I say to Richard.

"That's not really the point, Ted" he replies condescendingly. "The point is that you have to make a decision about what you're going to do first, and unless you're absolutely certain that I won't sacrifice Sara to save myself, then you either have to be willing to send the mother of your only child to prison—or God forbid the gas chamber—or you have to keep your mouth shut."

"What if I don't say anything but the police come after you anyway?"

"I seriously doubt they will. It would be very unwise politically. But just to be on the safe side, I propose that we replace those DNA samples you stole from my bathroom with your own hair and saliva. When they fail to produce a match, that should be the end of it."

I'm only half listening to him now, because I'm afraid that both Richard and Chief Lamonica are right—as grotesquely unfair as it seems, the way to do the greatest good for the greatest number is simply to let him get away with it. Sara is also correct—I am still jealous and looking for revenge, and that's why I'm really here. And no matter how strong and well-justified those feelings might be, I can't ignore the impact they'll have on others, or else I'm no better than Richard. So the only thing left to do is stand up and walk out. But before I can he has something more to say.

"I know this must be very hard to accept," Richard tells me. "And I'm sorry that punk gave you such a scare. I'd like to make it up to you."

"How?"

"First off with some money, say fifty thousand. And then with something I know you value much more. I can see to it that you get full physical and legal custody of Hallie."

Out of the corner of my eye, I see Sara flinch.

"Isn't that up to the court and her parents to decide?" I ask.

"Trust me, I can make it happen," Richard says. "And it'll be a pleasure. If I never see another fucking Barbie again, it'll be too soon."

The one thing that is sure to bring even the most bitterly estranged couple together is an attack on a child of theirs by an outsider. So it's really no surprise that Sara and I both lunge at Richard after he makes such a nasty and unnecessary comment. What *is* a little surprising, though, is that Sara is holding a fireplace poker, and she brings the hooked end down with such force on the side of Richard's head that blood instantly shoots out of his mouth and nose.

"Auughh," he burbles, slumping over in his chair. I find myself momentarily paralyzed, and all I can do is watch as Sara jerks back on the handle, retrieving the poker and a baseball-sized chunk of Richard's cranium that's stuck to it. I'm pretty sure he's already well on the way to being dead, or at least that's how I rationalize my failure to stop Sara from administering three more emphatic blows.

Here's the plan Sara and I work out (actually I do all the work—she just nods in numb agreement): I'm going to get in my car and leave, without calling the police. When they contact me later about Richard's death, I'll give them a full account of the conversation I had with him and Sara, right up to the point where he admitted he used Sara's bank account in the Caymans to pay Delawn. Then I'll say that I departed, leaving husband and wife to cope with their marital crisis in private. The reason for this scheme is that I want to give Sara and her lawyers an opportunity to spin the killing any way they want, but I'm not willing to tell any whoppers myself under oath (i.e. "He felt so ashamed he beat himself to death before we could stop him.") By saying I wasn't there, I'm giving Sara an open field and letting her run the ball any direction she wants. I suppose she could try to screw me—for instance by saying *I* killed Richard —but I'm confident that she won't and that no one would believe her if she did. All of the evidence points the other way.

The only major downside to my plan is that I have to lie to Susan. Even if I was certain she would keep the secret, it's not fair to put her in that position. Cops have a sworn duty to uphold the law, and to let judges and juries decide how much weight to give to any extenuating circumstances. I on the other hand feel no such obligation to the formalities of jurisprudence —if ever a man deserved to have his skull summarily staved in, it was Richard Slatkin.

My first call is to Deb, who reports that she and Hallie are at a day spa on Montana Avenue, and that a seaweed wrap isn't really as stupid and smelly as it sounds. I go to meet them, and along the way I phone Susan to give her the truncated version of the events at the Slatkin house. She is initially excited to have her investigative instincts confirmed, so much so that she doesn't even remember to yell at me for going solo on yet another dangerous escapade. But then she just as quickly falls into a funk, because she fears Chief Lamonica still won't want to bring Richard to justice. I wish I could tell her that justice has already been meted out with a fireplace tool, and that while the more vocal members of the black community may still raise hell about Boney, the fact that the real killer has himself been killed should serve to mollify the masses. I made a commitment to Sara, though, and therefore I can't say anything yet about Richard's fate.

I feel much less anxious once I arrive at the spa and reunite with Hallie. It's essential that I be the one to tell her that her stepfather is dead and her mother has to explain what happened to the police, so I'm keeping her close by until it's time to have that terrible conversation. But I also need to talk to Trevor, so I ask Deb to come with us to the office and keep Hallie entertained while I do.

It's a few minutes after 4:00 PM when I walk past the sputtering Tanya and into Trevor's office. *The Mogul* two-hour special starts at 8:00 PM, which is less than an hour from now on the East Coast. The final edited version was delivered to the network at midday, and the exhausted staff has long since gone home to sleep. Trevor seems as energetic as ever, though, standing at attention behind his desk and telling whoever is on the other end of the phone line that he had better deliver one million additional Shockers by next week, or there's a gentleman in Taiwan who will.

"I have to talk to you," I say, interrupting him. Trevor stares at me for a beat, no doubt thinking of all sorts of ways he could clarify our relationship for me. But instead he speaks into his headset.

"I'll ring you back shortly," he says. "*Joi-kin.*"

My reason for bursting in on Trevor like this is simple—I don't want him to be able to claim later that I withheld information pertaining to the Boney story until after the episode aired. And since it will soon become a matter of record that Richard confessed his misdeeds to me around 1:30 PM, I have no good excuse for not alerting Trevor. As a practical matter there isn't anything he can do about it, anyway—the show is in the can, and the new ending that reveals Who Really Dunnit will appear in the newspapers and on the TV newscasts tomorrow.

Or so I assumed, because once again I've underestimated Trevor. When I finish recounting the incident (once again omitting Richard's death), he marches swiftly to the door and fires a command at Tanya.

"Get me Roger Dominus and Stanley Green immediately," he says, then returns to his desk.

"What's going on?" I ask.

"You are."

"Beg your pardon?"

"There isn't time for anything else, and I be damned if I'll let someone else have my story."

"Mr. Dominus on one and Mr. Green on two," Tanya announces over the intercom. Trevor presses a button on his speakerphone.

"Roger, where is your helicopter presently?"

"Santa Monica FBO," Dominus says over the speaker. "Why?"

"Meet me there at once," Trevor says. I haven't time to explain, but it's absolutely critical."

"Okay, relax. Where are we going?"

"Burbank."

"Wait," I blurt out, but Roger probably doesn't hear me because Trevor has already switched to his other line.

"Stanley, we have an urgent situation," Trevor says.

"It better not be about tonight's show," replies Stanley Green, the thuggish chairman of the network that airs Trevor's two biggest hits, *The Mogul* and *Castaway*.

"I'm afraid so," Trevor says. "But the good news is, you're about to have an exclusive on the most sensational story of our lifetimes."

"I thought I already had that."

"It's gotten much better. What I need is another half hour at the end of the broadcast."

"What did you say?" Green snorts.

"Roger will be going live from the boardroom set in Burbank with Ted Collins, my co-executive producer."

"I don't care if it's Roger and the co-executive messiah. I can't give you any more airtime, Trevor."

"You simply must," Trevor says.

"What do you mean, I 'simply must'?" Green bristles, doing a pretty fair impression of Trevor's South African accent.

"You must or I will immediately cease production on all of the shows I'm making for you, and never do another," Trevor says crisply. "I'll call you from the air to discuss the details." He hangs up without giving Green a chance to respond and hustles me out the door.

I refuse to go anywhere without Hallie and Deb, so we all cram ourselves cheek-by-jowl into the cabin of Roger's Jet Ranger for the short flight from Santa Monica to Burbank. We pass just north of Cedars-Sinai, and as I look down on its roof I can't help but hear the words Chief Lamonica spoke to me there less than twenty-four hours ago. They'd better hurry up and announce Richard's death, because without it the news of Boney's innocence will no doubt have exactly the incendiary effect Lamonica predicted. It's strange that I haven't heard from the police already and I want to call Sara to ask her why, but I can't with Hallie on my lap and both of us shoehorned between Trevor and Roger in the rear of the chopper.

When we arrive at the studio, Roger and I are both whisked directly into makeup. While we're in the chairs, the East Coast feed begins with Roger on tape, promising a *Mogul* like no one has ever seen before. Stanley Green then arrives to duke it out with Trevor in person, and everyone can hear them in the hallway shouting at each other. According to Green, the cost of preempting an episode of *Trauma Center*, the long-running hospital drama that is scheduled to air after the *Mogul* special, will be upwards of $3 million dollars. And that doesn't include the damage it will do the network's relationship with the studio that produces *Trauma Center*, which is already under severe strain due to all of the previous incursions of Reality into prime-time (until recently the studios' exclusive domain). When push comes to shove, however, Trevor takes the same brusque stance he did on the phone: It's my way or the highway.

Perhaps to save a bit of face, Green demands to know what the big fucking deal is that necessitates a new ending. And I must admit I am impressed and amazed when Trevor refuses to tell him. I guess I shouldn't be—Trevor was very clear that in order to avoid any leaks, I am only to talk to Roger and him about the story until we go on the air live. But freezing out the head of the network, especially while simultaneously extorting millions of dollars worth of airtime from him, takes some real balls. I guess since Trevor's been dealt an unbeatable hand, he's decided to shove every chip he has into the middle of the table.

Halfway through the taped portion of the show, I'm finally able to sneak outside and dial Sara's cell phone. My call goes straight to voice mail so I try her home number, and to my surprise she answers on the first ring.

"What's going on?" I ask her.

"Nothing much," she says. "Richard's still dead."

"You mean they haven't removed the body yet?"

"I haven't called anyone."

"My God, Sara. What are you doing?"

"Sitting here watching your show. It's not bad." There's a distant quality to her voice that suggests she's misplaced some or all of her marbles.

"Sara, listen to me," I say. "The longer you go without calling the police, the worse it's going to look."

"I just need a little more time to think."

"Do you remember what we decided to say?" I ask her.

"I think so. When you left Richard was still alive and we were arguing."

"Okay, that's good. But I'm going on live TV in less than an hour to tell the world he's a multiple murderer. So the police will be coming anyway, and it'll be a lot better if you call them first."

"I promise I'll get to it as soon as I can," she says, as though she were talking about organizing the kitchen junk drawer.

When I come back inside the studio and approach the boardroom set, the stage manager shushes me. Roger is seated at his customary place at the center of the big table, about to do a live promo during a commercial break. The red light goes on, someone cues Roger, and he begins reading off the teleprompter.

"This is Roger Dominus. If you've been following the story of Boney in the newspapers or on TV, you probably think you know how it ends. Well trust me, you don't. In one hour, I'll be back here live to reveal stunning new details that haven't yet been reported anywhere. So don't go away, or else you'll miss the most unbelievable but true story you'll ever hear."

The red light blinks off and Trevor applauds.

"Well done, Roger. You could have been a network anchorman."

"It doesn't pay enough," Roger jokes, which is no doubt hilarious to all the wage slaves on the crew.

Trevor spots me and comes over to have a private word.

"How are you feeling, Ted?"

"Fine."

"I don't need to tell you that Roger isn't exactly God's gift to live television," he confides. "You're going to have to carry a good deal of the conversation without him."

"You want me to ask myself questions?"

"Let's hope it doesn't come to that," Trevor says. "In any case, the plain facts are so sensational that you can't really screw them up."

"Thanks for the vote of confidence," I say. Trevor claps me on the back, his way of saying of "You're welcome," then returns to Roger's side.

I make my way to the green room, where Hallie and Deb are ignoring *The Mogul* in favor of a no-prisoners game of hot hands.

"How are you doing, sweetie?" I say.

"I'm bored," Hallie says. "When are you going to be on TV, Daddy?"

"In a little while," I tell her. "But I think you and Aunt Deb should go on home. It's past your bedtime." Since I haven't yet told Hallie anything about Richard, I can't very well let her hear me accusing him of murder on TV. So I either have to make sure she isn't watching or I have to break the news to her ahead of time, meaning now. But then she'll probably want to call her mom, and I'd rather that Sara stay focused on reporting Richard's death. Besides, I dread trying to explain all this sordidness to Hallie in a way she can understand. I know I'll have to do it soon, but I tell myself it'll be easier once the pressure of being on live nationwide TV is behind me.

I briefly explain my dilemma to Trevor and as usual he has a ready solution—while I'm on the air, Hallie and Deb will be *in* the air, receiving their very own private scenic tour of L.A. by night. I see them off at the helipad, then join Trevor and Roger in the latter's dressing room to make final preparations. The plan is as basic as it gets—I'm going to tell the story of Richard's crimes and how I discovered them, with Roger throwing in just enough questions and reactions to remind everyone that even though I'm doing all the talking, he is still The Mogul. We script a dozen or so of these interjections and number them, so that, for example, when Trevor holds up three fingers, Roger can consult his handwritten notes and say, "That's amazing."

I tell them I need a few minutes alone before show time, and close myself in another room to call Susan and give her a heads-up.

"Are you nervous?" she asks.

"Maybe," I say. "A little while ago I tried to pass gas, and it got turned back at the border."

"You'll probably loosen up once you get going."

"Yeah. This isn't a perfect segue, but are we ever going to have sex?"

"I don't know," Susan says. "Should we?"

"Will you still like me afterwards?"

"Not being familiar with your technique, that's hard to say."

"I'm decent on the fundamentals," I tell her. "Always try to make contact, don't swing at the first pitch, never chase anything in the dirt. Anyway, what I'm mostly worried about is my baggage."

"How so?"

"Hallie's going to be around more."

"That's great, it's what you wanted in the first place."

"I mean a lot more. I may have her living with me full time for a while."

"Ted, do you know why I let myself get close to you? I'll give you a hint, it's not because you're so smart, or funny, or sexy."

"But… I am all those things, right?"

"It's because you're a good guy, and the best part of you is how you treat your daughter. You always do what's right for her, even when it means you have to eat a little shit. Or a lot. So I'll never see Hallie as baggage." I let this sit for a moment.

"I think we should have sex," I eventually say.

"You know the address."

Five minutes before we go live, I take my place on the set across from Roger. From the way he's twitching and sweating, you'd think *he* was the one who has to keep America spellbound for half an hour, while I contribute only the occasional "Wow," and "So then what happened?" While the crew does their sound and lighting checks, Trevor remains by Roger's side, telling him what a natural he is and how there's absolutely nothing to worry about. These blandishments don't seem to be having the desired effect, however, and Trevor finally resorts to asking Roger to write down on a piece of paper how much extra money he thinks each of them will make from tonight's extended broadcast. Roger does so, and Trevor then takes the pen from him, makes a big "X" through the figure, and writes his own above it. Based on Roger's ear-to-ear grin, it appears that Trevor's number is considerably bigger.

I guess I've been burning the candle at both ends a little too long, because the sight of those two fuckheads chuckling over their latest windfall causes the flames to converge in the middle and blow up like a grease fire. I wonder how jolly they'd be if I just tore off my mike and trotted out the door? God knows I want to—any little ego boost I might get from my moment in the spotlight will pale next to the pain of exposing Hallie to such an ugly scandal, not to mention the guilt over my failure to heed Chief Lamonica's warning. Lest I forget the latter, every time I put my hand in my pocket I feel the sharp edge of the business card Lamonica gave me, with his private cell phone number handwritten on the back. I've had plenty of desire and opportunities to throw it away, but somehow I can't. If the public revelation of the truth about Boney's death does lead to further violence, I'll have still more victims jostling for space on my overcrowded conscience.

If I bailed right now, on the other hand, Roger and Trevor would be mighty screwed. The thought of the former having to ad-lib on nationwide TV for thirty minutes, and the latter having to explain himself to an enraged Stanley Green, is enough to take me all the way from anger to amusement. How sweet would it be to stick it to those guys? And when will I ever get a better chance? Of course, they would probably make every effort to return the favor. And I wouldn't really be stopping the story from getting out—at best I'd be slowing it down a little. Is such a brief victory really worth incurring the wrath of two of the most powerful and vindictive men alive? Their standard response to even minor slights is to annihilate whoever displeases them. I can't imagine what the punishment would be for embarrassing them publicly, and doing serious damage to their business interests. A lawsuit? A couple of broken legs? I wonder if Trevor has enough political juice to have me declared an enemy combatant and shipped off to Gitmo. In any case, it's too late.

"Ten seconds to air," the stage manager announces. "Standby."

Before he leaves the set, Trevor gives Roger one final slap on the back, and then decides I might need some last-minute encouragement as well.

"Remember Ted, less is more," Trevor says. "You writers tend to get terribly windy."

The stage manager cues Roger and he begins reading the intro off the teleprompter. I'm not really listening, though, because my mind has suddenly left the building and the earth itself to search for little Hallie somewhere up there in the big dark sky. Dimly I hear Roger saying my name, and by the silence that follows I realize he's waiting for me to answer.

"Hm?" I say, bringing my attention back to The Mogul. His first response is to give me The Look, right there on live TV.

"I said," Roger replies with a nasty edge to his voice, "Please tell us who is truly responsible for the murders of

Patrice Williams and Delawn Purvis." I take a few moments to consider the question, then respond with one of my own.

"You mean Boney didn't do it?"

"What the fuck?" Roger blurts, a big no-no per the FCC, and looks desperately off-camera to Trevor.

"Sorry," I tell Roger, then smile directly into the camera. "But I'm outta here."

three months later

I TURN FORTY IN a few days, and Susan is trying to ease the pain by taking me on a romantic weekend getaway to Big Sur. I tried to convince her to save her money, since we couldn't possibly have any more romance than we do in an average weekend at her place without suffering third-degree burns. She wouldn't take no for an answer, though, so I've stocked my shaving kit with all manner of salves, balms, and (as a last resort) batteries.

Susan and I fornicate at such a furious clip for several reasons, the most obvious being that it's great. I mean really, *really* great, Tony the Tiger GRRRRRREAT!! Not to take anything away from the women I've been with before, but it turns out they were all frigid sea hags. Yes, including Sara. *Especially* Sara. Of the many gifts Susan has given me, the greatest is freedom from the spell of Sara's body. It turns out that's all it ever was—a beautiful body saddled with a decidedly unbeautiful mind, and as soon as I began making love to Susan, I understood that once and for all. I know I should have been able to get there much sooner and on my own, but in this area I seem to be an exceptionally slow learner. Years ago, I used to listen to Deb's extended feminist tirades about how all heterosexual intercourse is rape, and then when she was done I'd ask her if she was possibly in the mood for a purely consensual BJ.

The other reason Susan and I squeeze a lot of the juicy into every opportunity is that we don't get nearly enough of them.

Hallie lives with me now, and only spends every other weekend with her mom. This extreme reversal of the custody schedule was Sara's idea—I wouldn't have been quite so greedy, but Sara felt she couldn't be a good mother until she recovered from her personal tragedy. Since much of said recovery takes place in such therapeutic settings as Paris, Milan, and Maui, Sara doesn't always make it back in time for her semi-weekly parenting duties. We somehow manage without her.

But that means I have to manage without a bedmate as well. I occasionally ask Hallie if she'd like to have Susan join us for dinner, and she usually says yes. We meet in restaurants and afterward go our separate ways, though, because I don't want Hallie to feel like anyone or anything is encroaching on her turf. She's already experienced more than enough of that thanks to her mother's ill-advised second marriage, and I have promised myself that no matter what the cost to me, I will never let Hallie doubt her place as the undisputed heavyweight champion of my heart. Susan says she understands and I believe her, but I also know that she won't wait forever, and shouldn't. Maybe that's another reason we're so good together in bed—we both suspect that every time could be our last.

Once in a while we hook up for a nooner, but that's getting tougher and tougher due to Susan's work schedule. On the direct and highly unusual orders of Chief Pete Lamonica, Detective DeRosa recently became Captain DeRosa, and she takes her new responsibilities quite seriously. The top brass are reportedly very pleased by the energy and innovation that Susan has brought to the Homicide Division, though of course there are always some people who don't like change. Her former boss Captain Cardenas, now at the helm of the distinctly less glamorous Traffic Division, is suspected of being the person responsible for the proliferation of pussy-eating rumors on the walls of the Valley Bureau men's room. Given Susan's permission and a box of Sharpies, I would happily cover the stalls with detailed rebuttals.

It's not like I don't have the time. Although I want to spend every minute with Hallie, they apparently have some arcane law that requires children to attend school. So from 8:00 AM until 2:50 PM every weekday, I'm on my own. A schedule like that should be a writer's dream, but to say that so far I haven't accomplished shit would be unfair to shit. Maybe the reason I've been so lazy is because the only story I want to write is the only one I can't—the tale of the doomed love triangle of Richard, Patrice, and Boney. I have received dozens of lucrative offers for books, articles, and of course Reality shows—but even if I were legally able to accept any of them, I wouldn't. Telling the whole truth is out of the question and so is lying, leaving me with only one deeply unsatisfying option—silence.

With the help of Pete Lamonica and several of his high-powered lawyer friends, I've managed to muzzle Trevor and Roger as well. Since they are the only ones who actually heard my story about Richard's confession, and I have steadfastly denied telling them any such things, they would be inviting a multi-million dollar defamation suit from Sara if they whisper a word of it to anyone. They could successfully defend themselves from such an action if they could establish that what I told them was true, but that could prove difficult. Immediately after I walked off the *Mogul* set I called Chief Lamonica, and he was able to catch the first LAPD unit responding to Sara's 911 call just as it reached her house. Lamonica ordered his officers to stand down until he arrived, and when he did he was accompanied by his good friend the L.A. County Coroner. They went in alone, examined the body and the area around it, and found both to be consistent with Sara's tearful description of how her dear husband had slipped in the shower.

Richard Slatkin was cremated the next day and his ashes scattered at sea along with those of a chair, a closet full of clothing, and anything else that could provide scientific proof that the man ever trod the earth. His housekeeper Anna was rewarded for her years of loyal service with a spacious home in the hills overlooking her native San Salvador, where she is happily housing her entire extended family and sees no reason why she should ever again visit the violent, treacherous *Estados Unidos*. Richard's memorial service had a surprisingly small turnout, given his prominence in the entertainment community. One former client did travel all the way across the country to attend, however, and when he took the podium fondly recalled that many years ago, the deceased had gotten him his very last acting job. Therefore Richard can also be said to have played an indirect role in the deaths of Nicole Simpson and Ronald Goldman, for it was on the set of the ill-fated TV pilot *Frogmen* that Richard's longtime friend and client O.J. learned how to handle a knife. I heard about all this second hand, however—I chose to skip the service and pay my respects privately by standing at the ocean's edge in Malibu and taking a nice long piss.

It also fell to the attorneys to hash out the financial issues. Trevor flatly refused to share with me any of his profits from the sale of the Shockers (which reportedly totaled more than $20 million, despite the episode's oddly abrupt ending). Trevor made it known that he would fight me on that front until one or both of us was dead, and I believed him. Anyway, I didn't really want money that was directly associated with such an ugly series of events. I needed to eat and provide a decent home for Hallie, though, so I accepted a year of severance pay and medical coverage in exchange for a full release of any and all legal claims I might make, plus my promise never to divulge even the most innocuous details of my employment at Trevor Banes Productions. I'm sure it galled Trevor to shell out such a lavish sum—about as much as he makes while squatting for his morning military-style dump—so his lawyers must have worked hard to convince him that the rewards of stomping me to death weren't worth the risk to his shoes.

In any case, I'm happy enough with the result. Thanks to Trevor's parting gift, I was able to say goodbye to my squalid apartment and rent a small, sunny bungalow for Hallie and me on the south side of Santa Monica, near the community college. I mosey over to SMC every day to swim laps at the fabulous aquatic center and smile at the fabulous girls, and I'm hopeful that someday one of them might forget to scowl back. I also frequent the college library and the neighborhood coffee houses, where the java jockeys all know my name and tolerate my indolence. I know this shiftless lifestyle can't go on forever, and I guess I wouldn't want it to. But for now it feels perfectly fine to pass the time catching up on my reading, honing my crossword skills, and making sure I'm at least half an hour early for what is now my absolute favorite event of the day: carpool.

I am always first in line, which clearly annoys several nannies who covet the pole position so that they can flirt with Alfonso, the ruggedly handsome crossing guard, while waiting for the school bell. But Hallie's face always lights up when she comes out of her classroom and sees my car at the head of the queue, so the amorous señoritas will just have to continue eating my dust. Today Hallie seems extra excited to be sprung from the salt mine, breaking from the orderly line of students and running to my car. This earns her a sharp reprimand from the assistant principal, which both Hallie and I ignore. I want to hit In-N-Out Burger for fries and a shake, but Hallie isn't hungry and demands that we go straight home. Some people would say that I shouldn't let her order me around like this, because it will set the bar too high for any man who ever tries to live with her later. And to them I reply, "Exactly!"

Okay, not really. Like my lack of gainful employment, my overindulgence and Krazy Glue-style bonding with Hallie are only temporary. We've both earned a little pampering, and I'll know when it's time to start easing us back into reality—as in life, not TV. You couldn't ease me back into that other kind with a Kalashnikov.

For dinner I want Mexican and Hallie wants sushi, so guess where we go? A while back we discovered a Japanese place in Venice where the fish is fresh and you don't have to be a cofounder of Google to cover the tab, so we chow down there pretty regularly. I head for our usual corner of the sushi bar, but Hallie's curiosity is suddenly drawn by the entrance to a dark side room.

"What's in here?" she asks, wandering through the doorway.

"Nothing, sweetie," I say, following her. "It's just—"

"SURPRISE!!"

I guess I've had too many of the unpleasant variety, because as the overhead lights flare on, my instinctive reaction is to leap in front of Hallie and into a fangs-bared fighting crouch—much to the amusement of Susan, Deb, and around thirty other people who grin back at me.

"Don't bite me, it was her idea!" Deb says, pointing at Susan.

"No, it was *my* idea!" Hallie insists. "Susan just helped."

"It's true," Susan confirms. "You're gonna have to beat up Hallie." Instead I pick up the guilty party and give her a scolding look.

"You're in a lot of trouble, young lady," I tell Hallie as I look around the room at all the faces beneath the "HAPPY BIRTHDAY" banners and party hats. "There're people here I've been avoiding for years."

"No kidding," says gravel-voiced Virginia Martin, who was briefly my editor at the *LA Times* and who I never expected to see again, especially under circumstances such as these. "You and I have some unfinished business."

"If it's about that pet name I had for you, maybe we can discuss it in private," I say, referring to my impromptu resignation speech in which I loudly and repeatedly referred to Virginia as a smelly c-word.

"Please, my husband thinks that's a term of endearment," Virginia growls. "I'm talking about the story you owe me."

I can't for the life of me remember what story she's talking about, and I have no time to ask because I am quickly surrounded by other party guests, many of whom I am astounded to see at any event in which I am the guest of honor, save perhaps a lynching. Here is Bill Velasquez, one of several friends I took swings at over the years after falsely accusing them of snorting my last line of blow. And over there is Cynthia Stevens, a kind and very talented photographer whose efforts to help me clean up I acknowledged by borrowing and then pawning her camera gear. All of these transgressions seem to have been forgotten, however, or at least reclassified from reprehensible to risible. I guess if you want to keep being thought of as a rat bastard, you just can't rest on your laurels.

That old scalawag Tom O'Brien apparently thought the party began at six Eastern Time, and began drinking accordingly. He is in the middle of slurring his way through a pitch for me to join him as a producer of a can't-miss new program titled *Who's The Ho?* (in which male contestants spend an hour in a motel room with two women, then try to guess which is the professional prostitute and which the aspiring actress) when my phone rings and I see that it's Sara calling.

"I can't talk now," I tell her. "I just found out I have friends."

"Yeah, Hallie was so excited about planning your party," Sara says. "Happy birthday, Ted."

"Thanks."

"Listen, about this weekend," she goes on before I can stop her. "I know I'm supposed to take Hallie, but I just got a call from the Wellness Institute and they had a cancellation."

"How much more wellness do you need?" I snap, accustomed to this sort of thing but nonetheless exasperated. Susan and I are supposed to leave for Big Sur on Friday.

"Who's that, Daddy?" Hallie asks, poking me on the arm.

"It's your mom. You want to talk to her?"

"Is she calling to bail again?"

"Well…" I begin, but I can't follow up with any serviceable spin fast enough to fool Hallie. She takes the phone from me.

"Have a good time, Mom," she says pleasantly. "I don't

need any more t-shirts." Hallie ends the call and hands the phone back to me. "So what do you want to do this weekend?"

"Uh, actually . . ." I stammer, before I notice Susan standing behind Hallie, urgently shaking her head.

"Hallie, can I talk to your daddy for a minute?" Susan asks.

"Sure," Hallie says. "I'm gonna get some more spicy sea eel."

Hallie heads for the sushi-san and Susan steers me to the quietest corner of the room.

"Don't tell Hallie we were planning to go away," Susan says. "It might make her feel guilty."

"I can't believe that Sara is pulling this crap again," I fume. I feel it's important to show—and maybe even exaggerate—how annoyed I am by the demise of our mini-vacation. "For three years I couldn't get any time with Hallie, now I can't get any time without her."

"Don't worry, we'll just reschedule," Susan says, but I can tell she doesn't necessarily believe that any more than I do. I'm only able to meet her eyes for a moment, and then my old pal Guilt compels me to look away. Across the room, Tom O'Brien is entertaining a group of guests with an account of one of his drunken escapades. Tom's an embarrassment but he's not the slightest bit embarrassed about it, and that suddenly seems like a pretty good way to be. It's my birthday, I can do whatever I want, and what I want is a big fucking drink.

I scan the room for a waiter, but before I find one I see Hallie and Deb having some sort of intense conversation. I'm tempted to go eavesdrop, but before I can they end their discussion with a high-five, and then come straight over to me.

"Aunt Deb and I are going to have a girls-only weekend," Hallie announces.

"You are?" I say, totally off guard.

"Yeah," Deb says. "We're gonna spend most of it wrapped in seaweed." I stare at Deb for a moment, unable to decide whether I should be grateful or pissed. She knows that Susan and I had a getaway planned, and she's trying to do me a favor by not letting Sara ruin it. But she had no business taking it upon herself to tell my daughter that Susan and I sometimes spend the night together. As far as Hallie knows, we're Just Good Buds.

"Why don't you and Susan go away somewhere romantic?" Hallie asks.

"Excuse me?"

"You know, like San Francisco or Santa Barbara," my seven-year-old travel agent suggests. "You're kind of a lame boyfriend."

Hallie and Deb go off to plan their spa weekend, and after watching them for a moment, I return to Susan's side. She's chatting with some people and about to take a bite of a California roll, but I snatch it away from her lips and plant my own there instead. When I finally let her come up for air many seconds later, Susan's cheeks are the color of the Rising Sun.

"That was bordering on illegal," she says.

"So arrest me," I reply. And a few hours later, she does.